THE COLLECTED PLAYS
OF
TERENCE RATTIGAN

CONTENTS

v

PREFACE

IT will save a good deal of falsely modest circumlocution if I state at once that the five plays in this volume have all had very long runs. Two of them, *French Without Tears* and *While the Sun Shines*, both played for over a thousand performances, and I have it on the authority of the late Mr. John Parker, the omniscient editor of *Who's Who in the Theatre*, that, on those grounds, I can lay claim to a sort of world's record, in that I am apparently the only playwright, until now, who has written two plays so blessed with longevity. *Flare Path* ran for eighteen months, *The Winslow Boy* for fifteen, and *Love in Idleness*, after a season in London limited first to three months and then extended to six, survived nearly two years on Broadway.

I have a highly superstitious nature and in reciting these, to me, agreeable figures, it is not, let me assure the reader, hubris that has led me so to invite the all-too-possible Nemesis of five quick successive future flops. In fact, I have composed that complacent-seeming opening paragraph with my fingers firmly crossed. But facts are facts and it would be highly dishonest of me, just because I am now enjoying the honour at last of a collected edition, and indeed of writing a real preface to it just like a real dramatist, to attempt either to deny or to conceal the most relevant fact of all—that I am—or rather have been until now—avaunt Nemesis—a popular playwright.

This fact has not, I admit, caused me anything but the most acute, if slightly mystified, pleasure until now, when, in attempting to repay my publishers' compliment by taking myself seriously as a dramatic author, I find myself at some disadvantage. I envy now those dramatists, and there are not a few, who, in their prefaces, are able confidently to commend their plays to the discriminating reader on the bare grounds that undiscriminating audiences have firmly rejected them. Students of my friend Stephen Potter's Lifemanship Manuals will know what I mean when I say that in the matter of writing prefaces to plays a dramatist is instantly 'one up' from the moment he is able to state that 'his play pleased not the million', a quotation which must of necessity bear two strong inferences to the reader; if, on the one hand, he is able to admire the play he can plainly count himself as one in a million; but if, on the other, he is not, he stamps himself at once as a boor, who, like the rest of the scorned 'general', cannot tell caviare from suet pudding.

These five plays, however, as I have already had the honesty to confess, did please the million, and I find myself thus inevitably 'one down'. I am not able, as is my 'one-up' rival, to attack the state of the modern theatre, to deplore the commercialism of Shaftesbury Avenue (all these plays were performed either in Shaftesbury Avenue or within a hundred yards of it), to revile the short-sightedness of West End managers (all my managers have had offices in the West End, and none of them, with regard to my own plays, has seemed noticeably myopic), to pay tribute to the courage and enterprise of small repertory theatres outside London. (I would willingly do so, were I not deterred by the memory of one earnest young repertory manager who once said to me, in all good faith: 'What's so nice about doing your plays in my theatre is that their profits pay for the good ones.') While, of course, the claims of gratitude, no less than of ordinary self-preservation, prevent me from flattering my dear but as yet untried friend, the reader, at the expense of my old and trusted ally, the audience.

Yet, to me at least, the impartiality of my hypothetical rival, the unpopular dramatist, in prefatorially attacking the West End theatre, is also rather suspect. Lady Bracknell's reproof to her nephew seems apposite in this context: 'Never speak disrespectfully of Society, Algernon. Only people who can't get into it do that.' I don't want to be as snobbish as Lady Bracknell nor to patronize my highbrow rival from the pinnacle of my lowbrow success, but I sometimes mildly wonder, when reading his vituperations against Shaftesbury Avenue, whether a nice solid two-year run for one of his plays at, say, the Globe Theatre, would not have slightly mellowed his views.

But this is perhaps unfair. My rival's point would no doubt be that the mere fact that a West End audience may occasionally support a masterpiece will not prevent them from supporting a lot of rubbish as well; and that a system that allows such over-free enterprise must be wrong. So perhaps a fairer test would be to imagine him enjoying five solid successes in a row, three of them running concurrently at adjoining theatres in Shaftesbury Avenue, a privilege I briefly enjoyed with three of the plays in this volume, and then see with what sincerity he will continue to inveigh against the moribund state of the West End theatre.

Nevertheless, despite my own highly prejudiced complacency about the health of that institution, I am forced to grant the validity of my rival's point regarding the disconcerting contrariety of audiences' taste in theatrical entertainment. Not even I, their most fervent partisan, could possibly deny that they often do support rubbish. Perhaps, even, very often. The mistake so continually made, though, is to suppose that they always do, and always have done. For, in truth, has the record of their taste over the centuries really been so abysmal? They have certainly preferred *The Merchant of Venice* to *Measure for Measure*, which I think is misguided of them, but they have also preferred *Hamlet* to *Timon of Athens*, in which judgement I think they are entirely correct. They have preferred *The School for Scandal* to *The Rivals*, and here again I believe them to be wrong; but they have shown discrimination in choosing that masterpiece of triviality *The Importance of Being Earnest*, which was rather sneezed at by the critics of the time, in preference to the other, more portentous plays of Wilde. With Shavian drama they have generally plumped for the early and middle period plays; their especial favourites, I imagine, having been —I can be contradicted no doubt by the statistician—*Candida, Arms and the Man, Man and Superman, Pygmalion, The Devil's Disciple*, and *St. Joan*. Apart from woefully ignoring, in my view, one near-masterpiece, *Heartbreak House*, and one great work of philosophical literature, *Back to Methuselah*, has their choice, in fact, been so despicable? It would be easy to find many other instances of their taste and perspicacity over the years if it were not that in defending a West End audience, one is continually confronted by the unanswerable and disturbing fact that, as well as flocking to *Hamlet* they also flock, and possibly in even greater numbers, to *Voici Les Nues de Soho*.

The essential point, of course, about the West End audience, or indeed about any audience, for I have never yet found any great difference, except in minor detail, between the audiences of London, Paris, Rome, New York, or the larger British cities —I cannot, I admit, speak for other audiences—is that no power on earth can coerce them or persuade them, or educate them to go to see what *they* don't want to see; and that, equally, they cannot be coerced or persuaded or educated from seeing what *you* don't want them to see. They will pack the Old Vic and a John Gielgud season certainly, but that is because they want to, not because you think they should. At the same time they will be queuing to see a moronic thriller or an infantile farce, or arriving in bus-loads to stare happily at bored naked ladies in licensed statuesque poses. Audiences, in short, are unreliable, wilful, incorrigible, obstinate, complacent, and hopelessly contradictory in their choice of entertainment, and I can well see why it is that, to many writers on the theatre, such qualities must seem utterly infuriating. That they don't to me is perhaps just a lucky accident.

Or is it? That is what I must now, I suppose, attempt to examine, with special reference to the five plays in this volume. Was I, when writing them, as some of my critics appear to think, just one of those lucky gamblers in a casino who throw a chip on to zero and see it come up five times running? Or do these five plays possess some quality in common that has spectacularly appealed to this strange and unpredictable monster?

As a dramatic author I have acquired a deep distrust for coincidence, and five zeros in succession stretches credulity too far. Besides, since 1946 when *The Winslow Boy* was produced, the roulette wheel, if such there be, would have stopped at zero four times in five more throws. I think then I have made a case for discarding the lucky gambler theory.

We have seen that an audience can be as attracted by the

moronic as by the sublime. Now there is certainly no world
masterpiece among these five plays; but neither is any of them,
I venture to submit with only a slight fear of correction, the
work of a moron. *French Without Tears* shows traces, I grant, of
the style of humour known as 'undergraduate', but doubtless
the reason for that is that I was an undergraduate when I
wrote it. Nor do I think that I was by any means a moronic
undergraduate. In fact, in those days I considered myself an
intellectual, on the admittedly slender grounds of a scholar's
gown, a passionate worship of Shakespeare, and a reputation
for the kind of dialectic that is exercised after a fair amount of
mulled claret in a friend's room. What is more, although I
nurtured a secret longing one day to see the name T. M.
RATTIGAN blazing in Shaftesbury Avenue, I would myself
vehemently inveigh against the appalling taste of West End
audiences—too self-evident even to be cause for argument—
and proclaim that the sort of plays I was going to write would
certainly stand no chance in the world of pleasing such people.
And yet they *have* pleased such people, my name does inter-
mittently illuminate Shaftesbury Avenue, although T. M. has
long since given way to the more imposing, more adult
Terence, and I am still left with the question, why?

To answer it, perhaps, I should enlist the help of the
dramatic critics. They have, after all, been writing about my
work with a fair degree of attention for the last twenty years
and though admittedly their views of its literary merit have
greatly varied and even fluctuated a little, a consensus of their
expert opinions regarding its purely theatrical quality, its
element of audience appeal, should surely provide the clue to
the riddle I am trying to solve.

Now at this point I have to make a confession very damaging
to my *amour propre* and one which entirely explodes the pose
which I have often assiduously tried to assume, that of the
urbane, even-tempered, world-hardened cynic, utterly indif-
ferent alike to praise or to blame. One pictures such an author
either not reading his notices at all, or, at most, glancing curtly
through them, an amused, slightly bored smile playing over his
lips, and then casting them quickly into the waste-paper basket

with a half-yawn and a contemptuous shrug. I feel quite sure
that my friends Noël Coward, J. B. Priestley, and Peter
Ustinov do indeed present just such a picture on the morning
after one of their first nights: I can even see now the elegant
dressing-gown of the first as he gently flicks over the pages of
the *Daily Telegraph* in impassive search of W. A. Darlington—
a search so impassive that it is abandoned halfway for the
leader page; I can equally smell the pipe-smoke of the second
as he glances at the cricket scores in *The Times* on his leisurely
progress towards Anthony Cookman; and I can quite clearly
hear the gently mocking voice of the third as he blandly
reads out to a friend passages of Alan Dent's notice in a
broad Scottish accent entirely indistinguishable from the
original's.

Alas, the picture that I present on such an occasion is shame-
fully different. Bedraggled, hungover, voiceless from chain
smoking, still in the clothes I had worn at the theatre, for after
all it is still only five-thirty in the morning, the newspapers
having been bought at their respective headquarters an hour
or so before, I would be seen stretched out on the floor of my
own, or somebody else's, sitting-room, reading over and over
again, with wild anxious, red-rimmed, staring eyes, the brief
paragraph in the *Daily Mirror* that states that last night
Mademoiselle Mignon Migraine, the French film actress, lost
her pearl necklace in the foyer of a theatre while attending a
play of Mr. Rattigan's that was (or was not) the sort of thing
we have now come to expect of him. The major critics have
long since been torn bodily from their parent newspapers, and
are spread out fanwise on the carpet before me—an unneces-
sary process, for their comments are by now pretty well learnt
by heart. Hysterical cries of 'Damn Darlington!' or 'Bless
Cookman!' or 'Is Dent quite mad?' have recently rent the
early morning air. Now I am holding my head in an attitude
of feverish concentration, trying desperately to puzzle out
exactly what sort of thing the *Daily Mirror* does in fact expect
from me, a good play, a bad play, or just a middling play?

In short I take my notices seriously. Let me hasten to add
that I don't for a moment admit that I have ever been guided

by them in my subsequent work, or influenced by them in my own judgement of it. I just take them seriously.

The equally shameful admission follows therefore that I keep them, pasted meticulously by my meticulous secretary, into tome after tome, duly labelled by her and placed within easy reach of me. In fact, if anyone were to ask me what the critic of the *Lowestoft Echo* had thought of the production of *The Winslow Boy* by a local boys' school six years ago, a rather unlikely contingency I suppose, I should nevertheless be instantly able to tell him.

In saying, therefore, that I must now enlist the critics' help in trying to solve the problem of these plays' popularity, it would plainly be idle for me to attempt to use some such temptingly nonchalant phrase as: 'I cannot, at the moment, recall exactly', or 'Speaking from memory, I venture to think—', or the more bold: 'A friend of mine who makes it a hobby to collect theatrical notices tells me—'. No. The truth is now out, and I must be honest. I *can* recall exactly. I am *not* speaking from memory. The friend with the eccentric hobby is myself.

So to these all too accessible records. *French Without Tears* which slipped timidly unheralded into London in November 1936 had the luck to follow four or five portentously heralded flops. It was received with great good humour by the Press, who were no doubt tired of slamming away at all the season's major offerings and were in search of something, however trivial and unimportant, to praise. Kay Hammond, whose enchanting performance in this comedy I am sure is a lively memory to all who saw it, claims that I stared up at her from the pile of notices, for it was on the floor of *her* sitting-room that I was stretched out that early autumn dawn, and whispered in blank and awestruck amazement: 'But I don't believe it. Even *The Times* likes it.'

Still, good humour is not acclaim, and there was very little in those reviews which made me or anyone else think that I was going to continue writing successful plays. In fact, as the years rolled by and the *French Without Tears* sign became an accepted landmark in Piccadilly Circus, I grew resentful of the 'lucky fluke' or 'one-play Rattigan' attitude which theatrical columnists had by then almost unanimously adopted. Quite wrongly resentful, because I could not possibly expect others to know of the high theatrical ambitions that burned in me nor of my intense longing to be taken seriously as a professional playwright.

That longing had to remain unfulfilled for six long years until, in the intervals of whirling about over the South Atlantic in uneventful search of seemingly non-existent submarines, I wrote *Flare Path*, and later found myself on leave in London to attend its first night at the Apollo Theatre. Looking back now I seem to remember spending most of that evening standing rigidly to attention, while Air Marshal after Air Marshal approached the humble Flying Officer to tell him how his play should really have been written. The Press, however, was distinctly more amiable than the Air Marshals, and at long last I found myself commended, if not exactly as a professional playwright, at least as a promising apprentice who had definitely begun to learn the rudiments of his job.

I was mightily pleased by this at the time, but on browsing through the records now I still can find very little that might help me solve my immediate problem. In the reviews of *While the Sun Shines* I can find even less. Not that they were unkind. On the whole I was let down very lightly for my retrogression from semi-tragedy back to light comedy. But the major critics, with one notable exception, did not find the piece worthy of their serious consideration. The exception was the late James Agate, the then critic of *The Sunday Times* who, in his highly flattering notice, made mention of Shaw's comments on Oscar Wilde, and found in the comedy certain qualities of dramatic skill and craftsmanship, instances of which I might well now quote as helpful in the present context had not the same critic previously dismissed *French Without Tears* in five lines as: 'Nothing. It has no wit, no plot, no characterization, nothing. Fifty Marie Tempests and fifty Charles Hawtreys could make nothing of it, for it is nothing.' Now one cannot grow from nothing into Oscar Wilde between one light comedy and another, especially, if the second is quite consciously modelled

on the first, as was *While the Sun Shines* in mood, manner, and
style on *French Without Tears*. Unhappily therefore I must
refrain from quoting from a judgement which by the very
violence of its fluctuation must be suspect no less to my readers
than to myself.

Up to now, then, the only clues to our problem that the
search has provided are that the critics seemed, until this time,
fairly well agreed that I possessed a certain elementary sense
of construction and a flair for the sort of glib and facile comic
naturalism in which it almost appears that the actors are
making up their own lines as they go along. Among the notices
for *French Without Tears* and *While the Sun Shines* such phrases
abound as 'high-spirited charade', 'youthful romp', 'high
jinks', etc. This obstinate refusal to refer to either of these two
pieces by the designation with which their author had dignified
them, became even more marked when *Love in Idleness* appeared
at the Lyric Theatre in 1944. This comedy was graced, and, I
am sure too, greatly enhanced by the two exquisite performances of the world-famous Lunts; who nevertheless, and with
the generosity typical of them, were even more indignant than
I to read, amid the wildly enthusiastic acclaim for their own
magic, the general critical consensus that the piece they had
chosen to perform might just as well have been the telephone
book for all the difference it would have made to the delights
of the evening. When this judgement was repeated in America
with still more vigour and self-certainty, they were even goaded,
I believe, seriously to challenge one of their most fervent
critical partisans to sit through a two-and-a-half-hour recital
by them of the Manhattan directory and were not surprised
when the challenge was cravenly rejected.

Despite their warm championship of the play's merits,
however, critical opinion of myself as a writer of comedy had
now hardened into a virtual certainty that I was in fact no
such animal. I was a wily compiler of stock comic situations
and familiar comic characters, a fluent and by now experienced
provider of opportunities for expert comedians to be expertly
comic, and an unscrupulous exploiter of the notorious penchant
of an English (or American) audience to laugh at almost any-

B

thing provided they don't have to think. The rather phenome-
nal success in England of the three 'charades' was explained
away as the result of the popularity and skill of the performers
I had in each instance engaged to be funny in them. Rex
Harrison, Kay Hammond, Roland Culver, Robert Flemyng,
Ronald Squire, Michael Wilding, Jane Baxter, and now the
Lunts—how, the critics seemed to ask each other, could any
so-called author fail to gather laughs from easy-going audiences
with such comedians to conceal with their brilliant inventive-
ness the poverty of the original script?

It was in this critical atmosphere that I wrote *The Winslow
Boy*. I have claimed above that I have never allowed myself to
be guided in my subsequent work by anything the critics may
have had to say in disparagement or praise about my previous
endeavours, and in examining my motives for turning, at this
stage in my career, from light to serious comedy, I can acquit
myself of any attempt to try and 'give them what they want'.
(I mean, of course, the critics. Audiences, apparently, had
already got it.) True, I totally disapproved—and still do disapprove—of the widely held notions that writing seriously for
the theatre inevitably means writing serious plays, that serious
plays are more difficult to write than comedies—in my case
the reverse has been true—and that it is necessarily worthier to
make an audience weep than to make it laugh. Nor did I, even
in my most self-doubting moments, accept the critics' assess-
ment of my comedies as 'romps and charades' and, although I
was the first to admit that I had always been blessed in my
choice of casts, I was, naturally enough, never tempted to
ascribe to the brilliance of their acting the laughter that the
plays aroused in an audience, for they had already aroused
much the same laughter in me during the privacy of composi-
tion. In fact I never wavered in my own conviction that the
three comedies had been critically misjudged; that, far from
being aimless and vapid displays of juvenile high spirits, they
were put together with the utmost care and craftsmanship;
that the absence of epigrams, literary phrasing, and verbal
wit was deliberate, and was not only not a vice but was in fact
a virtue, representing on my part a notable triumph over the

temptation to the adolescent in me to 'show off'; finally that, despite the jeers of the serious-minded, the comedies had an element of the pioneering and the experimental in them that had been entirely overlooked, and that did in fact allow me to claim to have contributed something, however small, to the development of the contemporary theatre.

The temptation, then, for me at this stage, was far more to continue with light comedy than to abandon it in apparent critical defeat. The reason I did abandon it temporarily, for I was to return to it at intervals over the next few years, was not at all because I thought the time had come for me to make an advance, but simply because I had conceived an idea for a play which could not be expressed in any other mood but that of serious comedy. That idea, as is now fairly well known, though at the time the information had to be rigorously concealed, had sprung from the facts of the Archer-Shee case and had so fascinated and moved me that unlike many ideas that will peacefully wait in the store-room of the mind until their time for emergence has come, it demanded instant expression.

So *The Winslow Boy* was written, and the task, though not easy, proved on the whole a good deal less arduous than that of writing light comedy. It was produced at the Lyric Theatre in 1946 and, to my surprise, provided something of a critical sensation. It was generally felt to be very strange that a notoriously insincere farceur could so readily turn his hand to matters of fairly serious theatrical moment, and I found myself on the one hand warmly commended for my courage, and on the other sternly reprimanded for having hidden for so long my light under a bushel. I was myself conscious neither of the virtue nor of the vice, but for all that basked happily, if with a few pangs of conscience, in the sun of the critics' praise.

The chief quality the critics found in *The Winslow Boy* and which may represent the answer to the question I asked so long ago that it has now probably been forgotten—in case it has, it was what single quality have these five plays in common that has made them appeal to an audience?—was that strange, almost mystical element in the craft of playwriting known as 'sense of theatre'. True, they had not ascribed this quality to any of the four other plays in this volume, with the possible exception of *Flare Path*, nor, in retrospect, were they prepared to concede it now, but I myself am strong in the conviction that it does in fact represent that common denominator for which we have been searching. I *have* a sense of theatre. I am not at all sure what it is, I admit, but I do know that I have it now, that I had it at the age of eleven when I made my first, most unimpressive, attempt at writing a play, and that, if I should ever lose it I should also lose any hope I may have of achieving my ambition—and please do not jibe at it, for it is harmless—to write, before I die, one great play.

By this I must on no account be interpreted as seeking to imply that a sense of theatre is a quality that, in itself and by itself, is particularly commendable. To achieve greatness many, many other, far more laudable, qualities must, of course, be added. But I do insist that sense of theatre is one faculty that all great dramatists have possessed in common and that without it, though remaining no doubt great poets or great philosophers or great novelists, they would never have been great dramatists.

Now although it may be hard to say exactly what sense of theatre is, it is comparatively easy to say what it is not. It has nothing, for instance, to do with those problems of construction, technique, and craftsmanship which may be learnt, as I learnt them myself, by an assiduous study of the acknowledged models. Anyone may acquire the knack of writing an actable play. The fact that so few aspirants do, in effect, take the trouble to do so does not alter the truth of the assertion. It is, unhappily, a general belief that the technical difficulties of playwriting are so great that those young dramatists who have 'something to say' and the gift of words in which to say it, may readily be forgiven for not trying to surmount them. I am less forbearing. I believe sloppy construction, untidy technique, and lack of craftsmanship to be grave faults, the more grave in that they may, with nothing more than industrious application, be so easily avoided. I am perfectly prepared to concede that rules are made to be broken, but I think that at least they should be learnt first. Otherwise what fun can there be in breaking them?

Still these rules, learnt, applied, and broken as they may have been by all the masters from Sophocles to T. S. Eliot, have, as I have said, nothing to do with sense of theatre. What else is it not? Perhaps, by multiplying negatives we may yet arrive at a positive. It is not, I venture to think, anything to do with eloquence, the poetic gift, or the powers of rhetoric. Such qualities are, I grant, most warmly to be encouraged and commended. The revolution in the contemporary theatre begun a few years ago by T. S. Eliot and Christopher Fry, and maintained and developed by such dramatists as James Forsyth, Ronald Duncan, Peter Ustinov, and the late and much-missed James Bridie, is, I sincerely believe, a movement to be whole-heartedly welcomed, for it has rescued the theatre from the thraldom of middle-class vernacular in which it has been held, with rare intervals, since Tom Robertson, and has given it once more, a voice. But the movement will not survive unless its future exponents possess as strong a sense of theatre as the authors I have mentioned.

'The thraldom of middle-class vernacular.' Such a phrase, from myself, must seem patently insincere. The merest glance at any of the five plays in this volume will show how very little I appear to resent such servitude. And yet the tribute to the poetic school is from the heart. I believe, with Tchekov's Trigorin, that everybody must write as he pleases and as best he may. I 'please to write' in the naturalistic convention and the 'best I may' would quickly become the worst if I denied myself my gift for telling a story and delineating character in the terms of everyday speech. But surely a lover of Shakespeare may be believed when he says that he welcomes poetry in the theatre?

One last negative and I think that then, a positive may begin dimly to emerge. Sense of theatre does not lie in the explicit. An analysis of those moments in the great plays at which we have all caught our breaths would surely lead to the conclusion that they are nearly always those moments when the least is being said, and the most suggested. 'As kill a King? . . . Ay

Lady 'twas my word.' 'She'll come no more. Never, never, never, never, never.' 'Finish, good lady, the bright day is done and we are for the dark.' 'Cover her face: Mine eyes dazzle: she died young.' 'Mother, give me the sun.' One can multiply instances, but surely the point is here.

Has not sense of theatre then something to do with the ability to thrill an audience by the mere power of suggestion, to move it by words unspoken, rather than spoken, to gain tears by a simple adverb repeated five times or in terms of comedy to arouse laughter by a glance or a nod? Surely, in comedy as in tragedy, it is the implicit rather than the explicit that gives life to a scene and, by demanding the collaboration of an audience, holds it, contented, flattered, alert and responsive.

The power of implication in drama admits no argument. About comedy my view can plainly be challenged by the supporters of the Congreve-Wilde 'gilded phrase' school. It is too large a question to enter into now. Let me merely state that I have always firmly believed that the weapons of understatement and suggestion are even more effective in comedy than in tragedy, and I have with diligence, discipline, and self-restraint always practised that belief. In so far as this theory of comedy ran counter to the accepted critical opinion I can therefore justify the claim I have made above that the three comedies in this book had in them a small element of pioneering and experiment.

To return to the wider subject. I am sure that this instinct for the use of dramatic implication is in fact a part of the mystique of playwriting, and, in my view, by far the most important part; for it is the very quality that can transform a mere sense of theatre into a sense of drama. I am equally sure that it is, in fact, an instinct, unhappily not to be learnt, but only inherited, in that it implies in its possessor a kind of deformity of the creative mind, a controlled schizophrenia which will allow a dramatist to act as an audience to his own play while in the very process of writing it. It is this eccentric faculty, and only this, that will enable him to master those most vital problems of the whole craft of playwriting—what *not* to have your actors say, and how best to have them *not* say it.

I hope that in the preface to the next volume I may have the opportunity of examining further this topic of sense of theatre, and its relationship with the loftier sense of drama. For the time being, and with special reference to the three comedies in this volume. I should like to take leave of the question and of the reader with an anecdote of my early days as a professional writer.

A film producer of Central European origin, and with little command of the English tongue, who had commissioned me to 'inject' some comedy into a script, ordered me peremptorily to his office one day and pointed with furiously shaking finger to a line in a scene which I had written for him. 'How,' he demanded, 'can this be funny?'

The line he had pointed to consisted of the single word 'Yes'. He was paying for clever and witty lines, and considered himself cheated. Even he, he felt, could have composed this one, and thereby have saved the expense which, though not much, was anyway something.

I could not explain to him why the word 'Yes' in that particular context was funny. I doubt, anyway, if I could have explained it to myself. I could only assure him with youthful and fervent conviction that not only was it utterly hilarious, but that it would get a far better laugh than any of the prettily phrased epigrams that I had laboriously turned for him, and that in fact it had been a hundred times more difficult to write. Reluctantly he relented and allowed my cherished monosyllable to stay.

I think he was glad he did. I can hear the laugh now. It was, happily, by far the biggest in the film.

I trust this little story will provide a suitable moral for the reader who, should he share the film producer's suspicions regarding some of the lines on the ensuing pages, must accept my assurance that if they do not read well they certainly acted better.

TERENCE RATTIGAN

FRENCH WITHOUT TEARS

FOR
V.R.

Characters:

KENNETH LAKE
BRIAN CURTIS
HON. ALAN HOWARD
MARIANNE
MONSIEUR MAINGOT
LT.-CMDR. ROGERS
DIANA LAKE
KIT NEILAN
JACQUELINE MAINGOT
LORD HEYBROOK

The action passes in the living-room at 'Miramar', a villa
in a small seaside town on the west coast of France.

French Without Tears was first produced at the Criterion Theatre, London, on November 6th, 1936, with the following cast:

KENNETH LAKE	...	*Trevor Howard*
BRIAN CURTIS	...	*Guy Middleton*
HON. ALAN HOWARD ...	...	*Rex Harrison*
MARIANNE	...	*Yvonne Andre*
MONSIEUR MAINGOT ...	...	*Percy Walsh*
LT.-CMDR. ROGERS ...	...	*Roland Culver*
DIANA LAKE	...	*Kay Hammond*
KIT NEILAN	...	*Robert Flemyng*
JACQUELINE MAINGOT	...	*Jessica Tandy*
LORD HEYBROOK ...	...	*William Dear*

Directed by HAROLD FRENCH

ACT I

SCENE: *The living-room at 'Miramar', a villa in a small seaside town on the west coast of France.*
TIME: *July 1st, about 9 a.m.*

The room is rather bare of furniture. There is a large, plain table in the centre, surrounded by eight kitchen chairs. There are two dilapidated armchairs against the back wall. The wallpaper is grey and dirty-looking.

On the L., two french windows open out on to a small garden. They are open at the moment, and the sun is streaming through. There is a door back R. leading into the hall, and another down-stage R. leading into the kitchen.

The table is laid for breakfast, with an enormous coffee-pot in the middle and a quantity of rolls.

As the curtain rises KENNETH *is discovered sitting at the table. He is about twenty, good-looking in a rather vacuous way. At the moment he is engaged in writing in a notebook with one hand, while with the other he is nibbling a roll. A dictionary lies open before him.*

There is the sound of someone heavily descending the stairs. The door at the back opens and BRIAN *comes in. He is older than* KENNETH, *about twenty-three or twenty-four, large, thick-set, and red-faced. He wears an incredibly dirty pair of grey flannel trousers, a battered brown tweed coat, and a white sweater.*

BRIAN. Morning, Babe.
    KENNETH *doesn't look up.* BRIAN *goes to the table, picks up a letter, and opens it.*
KENNETH. (*Looking musingly ahead.*) She has ideas above her station.
BRIAN. What's that?
KENNETH. How would you say that in French?
BRIAN. What?
KENNETH. She has ideas above her station.

BRIAN. She has ideas above her station. She has ideas . . .
He stuffs his letter in his pocket and goes to kitchen door calling.
Marianne!

VOICE. (*From the kitchen.*) Oui, Monsieur?

BRIAN. (*With an appalling accent.*) Deux œufs, s'il vous plaît.

VOICE. (*Off.*) Bien, Monsieur.

BRIAN. Avec un petit peu de jambon.

VOICE. (*Off.*) Oui, Monsieur. Des œufs brouillés, n'est-ce pas?

BRIAN. Brouillés? Ah, oui, brouillés. (*He closes the door.*) I'm
getting pretty hot at this stuff, don't you think? You know,
nowadays it's quite an effort for me to go back to English.

KENNETH. If you're so hot, you'd better tell me how to say she
has ideas above her station.

BRIAN. Oh, yes, I forgot. It's fairly easy, old boy. Elle a des
idées au-dessus de sa gare.

KENNETH. You can't do it like that. You can't say au-dessus de
sa gare. It isn't that sort of station.

BRIAN. (*Pouring himself out a cup of coffee.*) Well, don't *ask* me.

KENNETH. I thought you were so hot at French.

BRIAN. Well, as a matter of fact, that wasn't strictly the truth.
Now if a Frenchman asked me where the pen of his aunt
was, the chances are I could give him a pretty snappy come-
back and tell him it was in the pocket of the gardener.

KENNETH. Yes, but that doesn't help me much.

BRIAN. Sorry, old boy.

KENNETH. I suppose I'd better just do it literally. Maingot'll
throw a fit.

BRIAN. That doesn't bother you, does it?

KENNETH. You're not going into the diplomatic. He doesn't
really get worked up about you.

BRIAN. Well, I don't know about that. The whole of his beard
came off yesterday when I was having my lesson.

KENNETH. No, but he doesn't really mind. It's absolute physical
agony to him when I do something wrong. He knows as well
as I do that I haven't got one chance in a thousand of
getting in.

BRIAN. (*Cheerfully.*) Don't say that, old boy. You're breaking
my heart.

KENNETH. (*Gloomily.*) Yes, but it's true. (*He starts to write again.*)

BRIAN. As a matter of fact, Alan told me you had a pretty good chance.

KENNETH. (*Looking up, pleased.*) Did he really?

BRIAN *nods.*

BRIAN. He ought to know, oughtn't he? Isn't he Maingot's red-hot tip for the diplomatic stakes?

KENNETH. If he was keener about getting in he'd walk it. He will anyway, I should think.

BRIAN. I think I'll make a book on the result this year. I'll lay evens on Alan—a class colt with a nice free action; will win if he can get the distance.

KENNETH. What about me?

BRIAN. I'll lay you threes about yourself.

KENNETH. Threes? More like twenties.

BRIAN. Oh, I don't know. Nice-looking colt—good stayer. Bit of a dog from the starting-gate, perhaps. Say seven to two, then.

Enter ALAN *through the door at the back. He is about twenty-three, dark and saturnine. He wears carefully creased grey flannel trousers and a German 'sport jacket'.*

Morning, Alan. We were just talking about you.

ALAN. Good morning, Brian. Good morning, Babe. (*He looks at his place at the head of the table.*) Not one blood-stained letter. What were you saying about me?

BRIAN. I'm making a book on the diplomatic stakes. I'm laying evens about you.

ALAN. (*Sitting down.*) That's not very generous.

BRIAN. Hell, you're the favourite

ALAN. What about the startling rumours that the favourite may be scratched.

KENNETH. (*Looking up quickly.*) Why, have they accepted your novel?

ALAN. Do I look as if they'd accepted my novel?

BRIAN. I don't know how you do look when they accept your novels.

ALAN. I hope, my dear Brian, that one day you'll have a chance of finding out.

KENNETH. Well, what's this talk about your scratching?

ALAN. Perhaps just to give you a better chance, ducky.

BRIAN. You're not serious about it though, old boy?

ALAN. Probably not.

KENNETH. But you must be mad, Alan. I mean even if you do want to write you could still do it in the diplomatic. Honestly, it seems quite crazy—

ALAN. You're giving a tolerably good imitation of my father.

BRIAN. What does His Excellency have to say about the idea, by the way?

ALAN. His Excellency says that he doesn't mind me choosing my own career a bit, provided always it's the one he's chosen for me.

BRIAN. Broad-minded, eh?

ALAN. That's right. Always sees two sides to every question— his own, which is the right one; and anyone else's, which is the wrong one.

KENNETH. But seriously, Alan, you can't really be thinking—

ALAN. Oh, stop it, child, for God's sake. I didn't say I was going to scratch.

KENNETH. You said you were thinking of it.

ALAN. Well, you know that. I'm always thinking of it. I very rarely think of anything else. But I won't do it, so don't worry your dear little head about it.

He taps KENNETH *on the head with a brioche.* KENNETH *sulkily returns to his work.*

Enter MARIANNE, *the maid, with a plate of scrambled eggs and bacon, placing them in front of* BRIAN.

BRIAN. Ah, mes œufs, as I live.

MARIANNE. (*To* ALAN.) Monsieur le Commandant, va-t-il aussi prendre des œufs avec son déjeuner, Monsieur?

BRIAN. Oh, well—er—(*To* ALAN.) She's talking to you, old boy.

ALAN. Je ne sais rien des habitudes de Monsieur le Commandant, Marianne.

MARIANNE. Bien, Monsieur. Alors voulez-vous lui demander s'il les veut, Monsieur, lorsqu'il descend?

ALAN. Bien.

Exit MARIANNE.

BRIAN. What did she want?

ALAN. She wanted to know if the Commander took eggs with his breakfast.

BRIAN. I meant to ask you. Did you see him when he arrived last night?

ALAN. Yes, I went to the station with Maingot to meet him.

BRIAN. What's he like?

ALAN. Very naval commander.

BRIAN. Yes, old boy, but what's that?

ALAN. You know. Carries with him the salty tang of the sea wherever he goes.

BRIAN. Pity he's carried it here. Paucot-sur-mer could do without any more salty tang than it's got already. Has he a rolling gait?

ALAN. He was sober when he arrived.

BRIAN. No, old boy, drunk or sober, all sailors have a rolling gait.

MONSIEUR MAINGOT *comes in hurriedly through the door at the back. He is about sixty, with a ferocious face and a white beard.*

MAINGOT. Bonjour—Bonjour—Bonjour!

All three rise. He shakes hands with each in turn, then sits down at the head of the table R. at the opposite end to the three boys.

Mon Dieu, que je suis en retard ce matin! (*He opens a letter.*)

BRIAN. (*Speaking in a whisper to Alan.*) What's he like, though, really?

ALAN. (*Also in a whisper.*) Pretty hellish, I thought.

BRIAN. Po-faced, I suppose?

MAINGOT. (*Roaring into his letter.*) Français! Voulez-vous parlez français, Messieurs, s'il vous plaît.

Pause.

(*Looking up from his letter.*) Qu'est-ce que c'est que ça, po-faced?

ALAN. Nous disions que Monsieur le Commandant avait une figure de vase de nuit, Monsieur.

MAINGOT. Ah! Mais c'est pas vrai.

ALAN. Nous exaggérons un peu.

C

MAINGOT. Je crois bien.

He returns to his letters.

> KENNETH *surreptitiously pushes his notebook towards* ALAN, *pointing at a certain sentence.* ALAN *reads it and shakes his head violently.* KENNETH *looks pleadingly at him.* ALAN *considers and is about to speak when* MAINGOT *looks up.*

Dîtes-moi, est-ce-que vous connaissez un Lord Heybrook? (*Looking at letter.*)

ALAN. Non, Monsieur.

MAINGOT. Il voudrait venir le quinze Juillet.

ALAN. (*To* BRIAN.) Do you know him?

BRIAN. Lord Heybrook? No, old boy. (*Confidentially.*) As a matter of fact, I knew a peer once, but he died. What about Lord Heybrook, anyway?

ALAN. He's coming here on the fifteenth.

MAINGOT. (*Roaring.*) Français, Messieurs—français!

Pause.

> MAINGOT *takes up the* Matin *and begins to read.* KENNETH *again pushes his notebook towards* ALAN, *and* ALAN *again is about to speak.*

(*Roaring.*) Ah! Ce Hitler! (*Throwing paper on floor.*) Quel phenomène!

> ALAN *closes his mouth and* KENNETH *pulls his notebook back quickly.*

(*To* BRIAN.) Aha, Monsieur Curtis, vous étiez saôul au Casino hier soir, n'est-ce pas?

BRIAN. (*Puzzled.*) Saôul?

ALAN. Drunk.

BRIAN. Oh, non, Monsieur. Pas ça. Un peu huilé, peut-être.

> COMMANDER ROGERS *comes in. He is about thirty-five, dark, small, very neat, rather solemn. All get up.*

MAINGOT. Ah, Bonjour, Monsieur le Commandant, et comment allez-vous? J'espère que vous avez bien dormi?

Ah, pardon! (*Introducing the others.*) Monsieur Curtis—Monsieur le Commandant Rogers. Monsieur Lake—Monsieur le Commandant Rogers. Monsieur Howard—vous connaissez déjà.

> BRIAN *and* KENNETH *shake hands.*

ALAN. Bonjour! (*To* ROGERS.)

ROGERS. Yes, we met last night. (*Indicating a chair.*) Shall I sit here?

ALAN. That's Kit Neilan's place, as a matter of fact. I think this is your place. (*He shows a place next to* MAINGOT.)

MAINGOT. (*Rising.*) Ah! Pardon, Monsieur le Commandant. Voilà votre place. Asseyez-vous donc et soyez à votre aise.

ROGERS. Thanks. (*He sits.*)

ALAN. I've been told to ask you if you like eggs with your breakfast.

MAINGOT. Oui, Monsieur. Mais voulez-vous parlez français, s'il vous plaît.

ROGERS. (*Smiling apologetically.*) I'm afraid I don't speak your lingo at all, you know.

MAINGOT. Lingo? Ah, oui, langue. C'est ça. Mais il faut essayer. You—must—try.

ROGERS. (*Turning to* MAINGOT, *then to* ALAN.) Oui—Non.

ALAN. What?

MAINGOT. Pardon?

ROGERS. Oui, je ne—want any eggs.

ALAN. Right, I'll tell Marianne. (*He gets up and goes into the kitchen.*)

MAINGOT. (*To* ROGERS.) Il faut dire: Je ne veux pas des œufs pour mon petit déjeuner.

ROGERS *smiles vaguely.* MAINGOT *laughs.*

Ça viendra, ça viendra.

Re-enter ALAN.

BRIAN. I say, sir, did you have a good crossing?

ROGERS. Pretty bad, as a matter of fact. Still, that didn't worry me.

BRIAN. You're a good sailor?

ALAN *laughs.*

Oh, of course you would be. I mean you are, aren't you?

MAINGOT *gets up.*

MAINGOT. Eh, bien. Par qui vais-je commencer?

KENNETH. Moi, Monsieur.

MAINGOT. *Par* Moi. (*Rising.*) Alors, allons dans le jardin. (*Bowing.*) Messieurs!

He goes out into garden, followed by KENNETH.

ALAN. Poor Babe! He's going to be slaughtered.

ROGERS. Really. Why?

ALAN. (*Shaking his head sadly.*) Elle a des idées au-dessus de sa gare.

ROGERS. What does that mean?

ALAN. It doesn't mean she has ideas above her station.

ROGERS. The Professor is pretty strict, I suppose.

ALAN. Where work is concerned, he's a sadist.

ROGERS. I'm glad to hear it. I want to learn as much French as I can, and I'm starting from scratch, you know.

BRIAN. Are you learning it for any special reason, sir?

ROGERS. Yes. Interpretership exam. in seven months' time.

ALAN. If you stay here for seven months you'll either be dead or a Frenchman.

ROGERS. How long have you been here?

ALAN. On and off for a year, but then, I have a way of preserving my nationality. I wear a special charm. (*He indicates his German coat.*)

ROGERS. Are you very pro-German, then?

BRIAN. He only wears that coat to annoy Maingot.

ROGERS. Oh, I see. What do you wear in Germany?

ALAN. A beret usually. Sabots are too uncomfortable.

ROGERS *laughs politely. There is a pause, broken suddenly by a roar coming from the garden.*

MAINGOT. (*Off.*) Aha, ça c'est formidable! Qu'est ce que vous me fichez là donc? 'Elle a des idées au-dessus de sa gare'. Idiot! Idiot! Idiot!

The noise subsides. ALAN *shakes his head.*

ALAN. Poor Babe. But he had it coming to him.

BRIAN. The Babe was having the horrors this morning before you came down. He said he hadn't one chance in a thousand of getting in.

ALAN. He hasn't.

ROGERS. Of getting in what?

ALAN. The diplomatic.

ROGERS. Oh, I suppose you're all budding diplomats?

BRIAN. All except me. I'm learning French for—er—commercial reasons.

ALAN. He's learnt a lot already. He can say 'How much?' in French, and you know how valuable that phrase is in the world of—er—commerce.

BRIAN. (*Laughing heartily.*) Yes, old boy, and that's not all. I can say, 'Five francs? Do you think I'm made of money?'

ALAN. (*Laughing too.*) 'Cinq francs? Crois-tu que je sois construit d'argent?'

They both suddenly become aware that ROGERS *isn't laughing. They stop and there is rather an awkward pause.* ALAN *and* BRIAN *exchange a brief glance.* BRIAN *silently frames the word 'Po-faced' in his mouth.*

ROGERS. (*With a wooden face.*) Who else is staying here at the moment?

ALAN. There's only Kit Neilan, I think, that you haven't met.

ROGERS. Oh! Is he going into the diplomatic, too?

ALAN. Yes. (*To* BRIAN.) By the way, Brian, what odds did you lay against Kit in your book?

BRIAN. I didn't, but I should think five to two against would about meet the case.

ALAN. I don't know. The odds must have lengthened considerably these last few weeks.

BRIAN. Why? Oh, you mean Diana. I say, old boy, I hadn't thought of that. You don't think there's a chance of a well-fancied colt being withdrawn before the big contest?

ALAN. No. She won't marry him. That is, not until she's exhausted other possibilities.

ROGERS. Er—who is this girl?

BRIAN. Diana? She's Babe's—Kenneth Lake's sister. She's staying here.

ROGERS. Oh! Is she learning French, too?

BRIAN. No. She just stops us from learning it. No, she's staying here because her people live in India and she's got nowhere else to go.

ROGERS. Pretty dull for her here, I should think.

ALAN. That girl wouldn't find it dull on a desert island.

BRIAN. Unless it *was* deserted.

ALAN. True. But one feels somehow it wouldn't be deserted long if she were on it.

ROGERS. What do you mean by that?

ALAN. I've no idea. She's a nice girl. You'll love her.

BRIAN *hides a smile.*

At least, it won't be her fault if you don't.

ROGERS. (*Politely.*) I don't quite follow you, I'm afraid.

ALAN. I'm sorry, sir. I was forgetting you're of an age to take care of yourself.

ROGERS. (*Testily.*) There's no need to call me 'sir', you know.

ALAN *raises his eyebrows.*

What you're implying is that this girl is—er—rather fast.

ALAN. I'm not implying it. I'm saying it. That girl is the fastest worker you're ever likely to see.

ROGERS. Oh! (*He goes back to his food.*)

BRIAN. (*Conciliatorily.*) What he means is that she's just naturally full of joie de vivre and all that. She's all right really. She just likes company.

ALAN. (*Under his breath.*) A battalion, you mean.

ROGERS. You sound embittered.

ALAN. Embittered? Oh, no. Oh, dear me, no. (*He breaks a roll open rather violently.*) Both Brian and I, for reasons that I won't go into now, are immune. Only I thought it just as well to let you know before you met her that Diana Lake, though a dear girl in many ways, is a little unreliable in her emotional life.

ROGERS. You mean she isn't in love with this chap Kit What's-his-name, who wants to marry her?

ALAN. The only reason I have for supposing she isn't is that she says that she is. But that's good enough for me.

Pause. BRIAN *gets up.*

BRIAN. Well, Maingot's simple French Phrases are calling me.

ROGERS. (*Evidently glad to change the subject.*) Maingot's Phrase-book. He's given me that to do, too.

BRIAN. Good. Then very soon now you will be able to walk into a chemist's and say in faultless French, 'Please, sir, I wish a toothpaste with a slightly stronger scent.'

ROGERS. Oh, really.

ALAN. Then think how nice it'll be if you're in a railway carriage, and you're able to inform a fellow traveller that the guard has just waved a red flag to signify that the locomotive has run off the line.

ROGERS. Sounds a bit out of date, I must say.

BRIAN. Maingot's grandfather wrote it, I believe.

The telephone rings. BRIAN *turns round.*

Do you know, I have a nasty feeling that's Chi-Chi.

ROGERS. Who's Chi-Chi?

BRIAN. That's not her real name.

MAINGOT'S *voice is heard from the garden.*

MAINGOT. (*Off.*) Monsieur Howard.

ALAN. (*Getting up, calling.*) Oui, Monsieur?

MAINGOT. (*Off.*) Voulez-vous répondre au téléphone, je vous en prie?

ALAN. Bien, Monsieur. (*He goes to telephone and takes off the receiver.*) Hullo . . . Bien. (*He holds out the receiver to* BRIAN.)

BRIAN. Me? Hell! (*He takes the receiver.*) Hullo . . . Ah hullo, Chi-Chi, comment ça va? Comment-allez-vous? . . . Quoi? . . . Quoi? . . . Wait a moment, Chi-Chi. (*Lowers receiver.*) (*To* ALAN.)

Take it for me, old boy. I can't hear a word the girl's saying.

ALAN *comes and takes it.*

ALAN. Hullo, Oui, il ne comprend pas . . . Bien. Je le lui demanderai.

(*To* BRIAN.) Can you see her tonight at the Casino? She wants you to meet her sister.

BRIAN. Ask her if it's the same one I met on Tuesday.

ALAN. (*In 'phone.*) Il voudrait savoir s'il a déjà rencontré votre sœur. . . . Bon. (*To* BRIAN.) She says it's a different one.

BRIAN. Tell her it's O.K. I'll be there.

ALAN. (*In 'phone.*) Il dit qu'il sera enchanté. . . . Oui . . . au revoir. (*He rings off.*)

BRIAN. I told that damn woman not to ring up here.

(MAINGOT *enters from window.*)

MAINGOT. Alors. Qui est ce qui vient de téléphoner?

BRIAN. (*Apologetically.*) C'était quelqu'un pour moi, Monsieur.

MAINGOT. Pour vous?

BRIAN. Oui, une fille que je connais dans la ville.

MAINGOT. Une fille. (*He bursts into a stentorian roar of laughter and goes back into the garden.*) Une fille qu'il connait! Ho! Ho!

BRIAN. Now what's bitten him?

ALAN. A fille doesn't mean a girl, Brian.

BRIAN. It says so in my dictionary. What does it mean, then?

ALAN. A tart.

BRIAN. Oh! (*He considers a second.*) Well, I hate to have to say it, old boy, but having a strict regard for the truth that's a fairly neat little description of Chi-Chi. See you two at lunch time.

He goes out.

ALAN. There in a nutshell you have the reason for Brian's immunity to the charms of Diana Lake.

ROGERS. (*Icily.*) Really?

ALAN. (*Easily.*) Yes. (*Pause. He takes a cigarette.*) This place is going to be rather a change for you after your boat, isn't it?

ROGERS. (*Stung.*) You mean my ship, don't you?

ALAN. Oh, is there a difference?

ROGERS. There is.

ALAN. Of course. It's a grave social error to say boat for ship, isn't it? Like mentioning a lady's name before the royal toast or talking about Harrow College.

ROGERS. Yes, that would be very wrong.

DIANA LAKE *comes in from the garden. She is in a bathing wrap which she wears open, disclosing a bathing dress underneath. She is about twenty, very lovely.*

DIANA. Good morning. (*She stops at the sight of* ROGERS, *and decorously pulls her wrap more closely about her.*)

ROGERS *and* ALAN *get up.*

ALAN. Good morning, Diana. I don't think you've met Commander Rogers.

DIANA *comes forward and shakes hands.*

DIANA. How do you do?

ROGERS. How do you do?

DIANA. (*To* ROGERS.) I didn't know you'd—you must have arrived last night, I suppose?

ALAN. Don't you remember? You asked me what train he was coming by.

DIANA *comes round the table; kisses him on the top of his head.*

DIANA. Do sit down, Commander Rogers. (*He sits.*) How are you this morning, Alan?

ALAN. (*Feeling her bathing dress.*) I'll bet you didn't go in the water.

DIANA. Yes, I did.

ALAN. Right in?

DIANA. Yes, right in. Ask Kit.

ALAN. (*Really surprised.*) Kit? You don't mean to say that you got Kit to go bathing with you?

DIANA. Yes, I did. He's fetching my towel. I left it behind.

ALAN. God! you women.

DIANA. What?

ALAN. Without the slightest qualm and just to gratify a passing whim, you force a high-souled young man to shatter one of his most sacred principles.

ROGERS. What principle is that, if I might ask?

DIANA. (*Emphatically.*) Never, under any circumstances, to do anything hearty.

ROGERS. (*Challengingly.*) Personally, I rather like an early morning dip.

ALAN. (*As if the words burnt his mouth.*) An—early—morning—dip?

ROGERS. Certainly. That's hearty, I suppose.

ALAN. Well—

DIANA. I quite agree with you, Commander Rogers. I don't think there's anything nicer than a swim before breakfast. Ashtray? (*Hands it to* ROGERS.)

ALAN. You'd like anything that gave you a chance to come down to breakfast in a bathing dress.

DIANA. Does it shock you, Alan?

ALAN. Unutterably.

DIANA. I'll go and dress then.

ALAN. No. There's no point in that. You've made one successful entrance. Don't spoil it by making another.

ROGERS. I don't think I quite understand you.

ALAN. Diana does, don't you, angel?

DIANA. (*Sweetly.*) Has another publisher refused your novel, Alan?

ALAN, *momentarily disconcerted, can find nothing to say. Pause.*

Enter KIT *through the french window. He is about twenty-two, fair and good-looking. He wears a dressing-gown over his bathing dress, and carries two towels over his arm.*

KIT. (*Sullenly.*) Morning.

ALAN. (*In gentle reproof.*) Well, well, well.

KIT. (*Shamefacedly.*) Well, why not?

ALAN *shakes his head sadly.*

ALAN. I don't think you've met Commander Rogers.

KIT. (*Shaking hands.*) How do you do? I heard you were coming. (*He begins to dry his hair on a towel, throwing the other one to* DIANA.)

ALAN. Did Diana go in the water?

KIT. No.

DIANA. Kit, you dirty liar.

KIT. I've done enough for you already this morning. I'm not going to perjure myself as well. (*He sits down gloomily and pours himself out a cup of coffee.*) I had hoped you wouldn't be here, Alan, to witness my shame.

ALAN. You of all people an early morning dipper.

KIT. (*Shuddering.*) Don't put it like that. You make it sound worse than it is. Say a nine o'clock bather. Oh, hell, this coffee's cold. Marianne!

ALAN. Mere toying with words can't hide the truth. Do you know I think that girl could make you go for a bicycle tour in the Pyrenees if she set her mind to it.

KIT. She could you know, Alan, that's the awful thing.

Slight pause.

ROGERS. I once went for a bicycle tour in the Pyrenees.

ALAN. Really?

KIT *splutters into his coffee simultaneously.*

JACQUELINE *comes out of the kitchen. She is about twenty-five or twenty-six, not unattractive, but nothing in looks to compare with* DIANA. *She wears an apron and has a handkerchief tied over her hair.*

JACQUELINE. Marianne's upstairs. Do you want anything? (*She speaks with only the barest trace of accent.*)

KIT. Hello, Jack.

ALAN. Good morning, darling.

JACQUELINE. (*Going to* ROGERS.) How do you do, Commander Rogers. I'm so glad you could come to us.

ROGERS. (*Shaking hands.*) Er——how do you do?

JACQUELINE. I hope you've found everything you want.

ROGERS. Yes, thank you.

JACQUELINE. Did Marianne ask you if you wanted eggs for breakfast?

ROGERS. I don't want any, thanks.

JACQUELINE. I see. Well, don't worry about asking for anything you need. By the way, do you drink beer at meals or do you prefer wine?

ROGERS. (*Sitting.*) Beer, please. Nothing like a can of beer.

ALAN. No, I suppose there isn't.

JACQUELINE. (*To* KIT.) What were you shouting about, by the way?

KIT. Jack, darling, the coffee's cold.

JACQUELINE. Of course it's cold. You're half an hour late for breakfast.

KIT. Yes, but . . .

JACQUELINE. You can't have any more because Marianne's doing the rooms.

KIT. I thought perhaps, Jack, darling, knowing how much you love me, you might be an angel and do something about it.

JACQUELINE. Certainly not. It's against all the rules of the house. Besides, you'd better go and get dressed. I'm giving you a lesson in five minutes.

KIT. In the near future, when I am Minister of Foreign Affairs, this incident will play a large part in my decision to declare war on France.

JACQUELINE *pushes him back into his chair and grabs the coffee-pot.*

JACQUELINE. Ooh! This is the last time I'm going to do this for you.

She goes back into the kitchen.

KIT. (*To* DIANA.) You see what a superb diplomat I should make.

ALAN. Rather the Palmerston tradition, wasn't it?

ROGERS. Was that Maingot's daughter.

KIT. Yes. Her name's Jacqueline.

ROGERS. Jacqueline? (*Brightly.*) I see. That's why you call her Jack.

KIT. (*Looking at him distastefully.*) Yes, that's why we call her Jack.

ROGERS. She speaks English very well.

KIT. She's been in England half her life. I believe she's going to be an English school-marm. You'll like her. She's amusing. (*He continues to dry himself.*) Hell! I still feel wet.

He glares at DIANA *who comes behind his chair and dries his hair with her own towel.*

DIANA. You've got such lovely hair, darling. That's why it takes so long to dry.

KIT. (*To* ALAN.) You know, Alan, this is a nice girl.

ALAN. (*Tilting his chair back and gazing at* DIANA.) Yes, she's nice. She's good, too.

ROGERS *gets up.*

ROGERS. Well, I must go upstairs. I want to get my room shipshape.

ALAN. And above board?

ROGERS. (*Turning savagely on* ALAN.) Yes, and above board. Any objection?

ALAN. (*Airily.*) No, no objection at all. Make it as above board as you like.

ROGERS. (*Bowing stiffly.*) Thank you. I'm most grateful.

Exit ROGERS.

ALAN. (*Pensively.*) Do you know, I don't think he likes me.

KIT. Who does? I'm the only one who can stand you and then only in small doses.

DIANA. Kenneth adores you, anyway. He's quite silly the way he tries to imitate you.

ALAN. Your brother shows remarkable acumen sometimes.

DIANA. And then, of course, I adore you too. You know that.

KIT *swings his chair round and pulls her roughly down on to his knee.*

KIT. Hey! I'm not going to have you adoring anybody except me. Do you understand? (*He kisses her.*)

DIANA. Darling, you're not jealous of Alan, are you?

KIT. I'm jealous of anyone you even look at.

DIANA. All right, then in future I won't look at anyone except you.

KIT. That's a promise?

DIANA. That's a promise.

ALAN, *still leaning back in his chair, whistles a tune softly.*

(*Feeling* KIT's *hands.*) Darling, you *are* cold.

KIT. Yes, I know. I think I'll go and dress and not wait for the coffee. (*He gets up.*) You've probably given me pneumonia. But I don't mind. You could tear me up in little pieces and trample on them, and I'd still love you.

DIANA. Sweet little thing. Take these things upstairs, darling, will you? (*Gives him towels.*)

KIT *goes out.*

ALAN. That's no reason why you should, you know.

DIANA. Should what?

ALAN. Tear him up in little pieces and trample on them.

DIANA *crosses over to the window where she stands, looking out.*

So you're not going to look at anyone except Kit.

DIANA *doesn't answer.* ALAN *gets up and walks over to the window. He puts his arm round her waist and his cheek against her.*

(*After a pause.*) This doesn't mean I'm falling for you.

DIANA. (*Gently.*) Doesn't it, Alan?

ALAN. No, it doesn't.

He walks over to the armchair and sits.

DIANA. I *am* disappointed.

ALAN. What do you think of the Commander?

DIANA. I think he's quite nice.

ALAN. Yes. (*Gently.*) Yes. I want to tell you, it's no good starting anything with him.

DIANA. Don't be silly, Alan.

ALAN. It really isn't any good, darling, because you see I've warned him against you.

DIANA. You warned him? (*Coming to* ALAN.) What did you say?

ALAN. I told him what you are.

DIANA. (*Quietly.*) What's that?

ALAN. Don't you know?

DIANA. Alan, much as I like you there *are* times when I could cheerfully strangle you.

ALAN. Is this one of them, darling?

DIANA. Yes, ducky, it is.

ALAN. Good, that's just what I hoped.

DIANA. This is rather a new rôle for you, isn't it, playing wet nurse to the Navy?

ALAN. You don't think it suits me?

DIANA. No, darling, I'm afraid I don't. What are you doing it for?

ALAN. It's not because I'm fond of the Commander. As a matter of fact it would rather amuse me to see you play hell with the Commander. But I do like Kit, that's why. So no hanky-panky with the Navy or . . .

DIANA. Or what?

ALAN. Or I shall have to be rather beastly to you, darling, and you know you wouldn't like that.

DIANA. You don't understand me at all, Alan.

ALAN. I understand every little bit of you, Diana, through and through. That's why we get along so well together.

DIANA. (*Tearfully.*) I ought to *hate* you.

ALAN. Well, go on trying, darling, and you may succeed. (*He kisses her on the back of the neck.*) I've got to go and finish some stuff for Maingot. See you at lunch time. (*He goes to the door.*)

DIANA. Alan?

ALAN. (*Turning at door.*) Yes?

DIANA. What do you mean by hanky-panky?

ALAN. *I* should tell *you*.

He goes out.

DIANA *kicks petulantly at the window. She goes to the table, opens her handbag, takes out a small mirror and looks at herself.*

Enter JACQUELINE *from the kitchen with the coffee-pot.*

DIANA. Oh, thank you so much.

JACQUELINE. Where's Kit?

DIANA. He's gone up to dress. He felt cold.

JACQUELINE. Isn't that like him. Well, you can tell him that I'm not going to make him any more coffee however loud he screams.

DIANA. Yes, I'll tell him, and I think you're quite right.

Enter ROGERS *through the door at the back.*

ROGERS. (*Nervously.*) Oh, hullo.

JACQUELINE *goes out into the kitchen.*

DIANA. (*Brightly.*) Hullo, Commander Rogers.

ROGERS *goes over to the bookcase at the back.*

Looking for something?

ROGERS. Yes, Maingot's Phrase Book, as a matter of fact. (*He bends down and pulls a book out.*) Here it is, I think. (*He looks at the title.*) No, it isn't.

DIANA. Let me help you. I think I know where it is.

ROGERS. Oh, that's very good of you.

DIANA *bends down at the bookcase and pulls a book out.*

DIANA. Here. (*She hands it to him.*)

ROGERS. Oh, thanks most awfully.

DIANA. (*Going back to the table.*) Well, what are your first impressions of Monsieur Maingot's establishment?

ROGERS. Oh, I—er—think it ought to be very cheery here.

DIANA. I'm sure you'll love it.

ROGERS. Yes, I'm sure I will.

DIANA. The boys are so nice, don't you think?

ROGERS. Er—yes, I think they are—some of them. (*He makes a tentative move towards the door.*)

DIANA. (*Quickly.*) I suppose you find Alan a bit startling, don't you?

ROGERS. Alan?

DIANA. The one with the German coat.

ROGERS. Oh, yes. Yes, he is a bit startling. Well, I ought to be getting along.

DIANA. Why? You've got your room pretty well shipshape by now, haven't you?

ROGERS. Oh, thanks, yes, I have.

DIANA. Well, don't go for a bit. Stay and talk to me while I have my coffee. Have you got a cigarette?

ROGERS. (*Coming to her.*) Yes, I have. (*Offers her one.*)

DIANA. (*Takes one.*) Thanks. I was saying about Alan——

ROGERS. Match?

DIANA. Thanks. (*He lights it.*) What was I saying?

ROGERS. About Alan.

DIANA. Oh, yes, about Alan—he's really very nice but you mustn't take everything he says seriously.

ROGERS. Oh. Oh, I see. No, I won't.

DIANA. He's just the tiniest bit—you know (*she taps her forehead significantly*) unbalanced.

ROGERS. Oh, really.

DIANA. I thought it as well to warn you.

ROGERS. Yes. Thank you very much.

DIANA. Otherwise it might lead to trouble.

ROGERS. Yes, it might.

Pause.

DIANA. Poor Alan. I'm afraid he's got it very badly.

ROGERS. Er—got what?

DIANA. Well—(*She leans back and blows a puff of smoke into the air.*) Of course I oughtn't to say it. (*Pause. She throws him a quick glance to see if he has caught her meaning. Evidently he hasn't.*)

ROGERS. Oh.

DIANA. I'm awfully sorry for him of course.

ROGERS. (*Puzzled, but polite.*) Of course.

DIANA. It's so funny, because from the way he behaves to me and the things he says about me, you'd think he hated me, wouldn't you?

ROGERS. Yes, you would. (*Pause.*) Doesn't he?

DIANA. (*Laughing.*) No. Oh no. Far from it.

ROGERS. (*The light of understanding in his face at last.*) Oh, I see. You mean he's rather keen on you?

DIANA. I mustn't give him away. It wouldn't be fair. But if he ever talks to you about me, as he probably will, and tries to give you the impression that I'm a (*smiling*) scheming wrecker of men's lives, you needn't necessarily believe him.

ROGERS. No—no, I won't, of course. But I don't see why he should, you know.

DIANA. (*Embarrassedly.*) Well, you see, Commander Rogers, I like Alan, but I don't like him as much as perhaps he wants me to, and I suppose that makes him feel rather embittered.

ROGERS. Ah, yes. I see.

DIANA. (*Gaily.*) Well, don't let's talk any more about it, because it's not a very pleasant subject. Tell me about yourself. Tell me about the Navy. I'm always thrilled to death by anything to do with the sea.

ROGERS. Really, that's splendid.

Pause.

DIANA. It must be a wonderful life.

ROGERS. Yes, it's a pretty good life on the whole.

DIANA. Marvellously interesting, I should think.

ROGERS. Yes, pretty interesting.

DIANA. I bet you've had any amount of wildly exciting experiences.

ROGERS. Oh, well, you know, things have a way of happening in the Navy.

DIANA. Yes, I'm sure they have. (*Pause.*) You naval people never talk about yourselves, do you?

ROGERS. Well, you know, silent service and all that.

DIANA. Yes, I know, but I do hope you're not going to be too silent with me, because honestly, I am so terribly interested.

ROGERS. (*Smiling.*) I'll try not to be too silent then.

Pause.

DIANA. What are you doing this morning?

ROGERS. Nothing special. Why?

DIANA. How would you like to have a look round the town?

Enter JACQUELINE *from the kitchen.*

JACQUELINE. Hasn't Kit come down yet?

ROGERS. (*To* DIANA.) Oh, I'd love to.

DIANA. Good. I'll go and get dressed and we'll go for a little stroll.

ROGERS. But isn't it rather a bore for you?

DIANA. No, of course not. I'd love it. (*She goes to the door.*)

JACQUELINE. Diana?

DIANA. Yes?

JACQUELINE. (*Pouring out a cup of coffee.*) If you're going past Kit's room you might give him this. (*She hands her the cup.*)

DIANA. Right, I will. (*To* ROGERS.) Are you sure I'm not dragging you away from your work or anything?

JACQUELINE goes back into the kitchen.

ROGERS. Oh, no. That's quite all right. I haven't been given anything to do yet.

DIANA. Good. Well, I'll go and put some clothes on.

She turns to go. ALAN comes in and almost collides with her in the doorway.

(*Turning.*) I'll meet you down here then in about a quarter of an hour?

ROGERS. Right.

DIANA smiles at ROGERS, walks past ALAN without glancing at him and goes out.

ALAN. (*Going to the table and sitting.*) Going for a little constitutional, Commander? (*He has some books in his hands. He places them on the table in front of him and opens a notebook.*)

ROGERS. Yes. (*He turns his back.*)

ALAN. (*Taking a fountain pen from his pocket and unscrewing the top.*) You've got a nice day for it. (*Pause. He writes in his notebook and begins to sing the Lorelei. Without looking up.*) It's a lovely song, the Lorelei, don't you think?

ROGERS. It *could* be.

ALAN. True. (*He continues to write.*) It's a stupid fable anyway. I ask you, what sailor would be lured to his doom after he had been warned of his danger?

ROGERS. (*Turning quickly.*) If you think that's funny, I don't.

Enter KENNETH through the window.

KENNETH. Oh, Commander Rogers, Maingot wants to see you a moment.

Pause. ROGERS is standing facing ALAN across the table, and ALAN is still writing.

ROGERS. Right. Thank you. (*He marches out into the garden.*)

ALAN. (*After a pause.*) Well, Babe, I suppose you were murdered by the old man.

KENNETH. (*Wearily.*) More so than usual this morning.

Pause. ALAN goes on writing.

ALAN. (*Without looking up.*) Babe, I don't like your sister.

KENNETH. (*Walking round the table and looking over ALAN's shoulder at what he is writing.*) Don't you? I thought you did like her, rather a lot.

ALAN *looks up. Pause.*

Enter JACQUELINE *from the kitchen. She has taken off her apron and the handkerchief over her hair.*

JACQUELINE. Good morning, Kenneth.

KENNETH. Good morning, Mam'selle.

JACQUELINE. Had your lesson?

KENNETH. Yes. I've got to do the whole damn thing again. (*He goes to the door.*) Alan, I wish to God I had your brains.

He goes out.

ALAN *looks after him a moment, then goes back to his work.*

JACQUELINE. (*Looking at her watch.*) Kit is a monster. He's never been on time for his lesson yet. (*She goes to the window and looks out.*)

ALAN. (*Looking up from his work.*) What have you done to your hair, Jack?

JACQUELINE. (*Turning round.*) Do you like it? (*Her hair is done in the same way as* DIANA'S.)

ALAN. (*He gets up and walks over to her, holding her out at arm's length and studying her hair. Doubtfully.*) No, it's a mistake, Jack. You won't beat her by copying the way she does her hair.

JACQUELINE. He'll like it, Alan, I'm sure he will.

ALAN. He won't notice it.

JACQUELINE. He will, you see.

ALAN. I'll bet you five francs he doesn't.

JACQUELINE. All right. That's a bet.

ALAN. Go and change it while there's still time. Make it look hideous like it used to.

JACQUELINE. (*Laughing.*) No, Alan.

Pause.

ALAN. Poor Jack. I must find you someone else to fall in love with.

JACQUELINE. So long as you don't tell him that I adore him, I don't mind what you do.

ALAN. Anyone less half-witted than Kit would have seen it years ago.

JACQUELINE. Am I very obvious, Alan? I don't want to bore him.

ALAN. Go and change that hair.

JACQUELINE. Do you think if Diana were out of the way I should stand a chance?

ALAN. You're not thinking of putting her out of the way, are you?

JACQUELINE. (*Smiling.*) I'd do it painlessly, Alan.

ALAN. Why painlessly?

JACQUELINE. I'm not jealous of her really, though.

ALAN. Oh, no. Not a bit.

JACQUELINE. Honestly, Alan, I wouldn't mind if she made him happy. But she doesn't. She seems to enjoy making him miserable. And now that the Commander's here it's going to be much worse. You know what I mean, don't you?

ALAN. I have an idea.

JACQUELINE. Can't we do anything about it, Alan?

ALAN. Yes. Go and change that hair, Jack. It's the only chance.

JACQUELINE. No, I won't do anything of the sort.

Enter KIT, *dressed.*

KIT. (*Walking right up to* JACQUELINE *and taking her hands earnestly.*) Jack, I have something to tell you. (*To* ALAN.) Go away, Alan, this is confidential.

ALAN *goes back to the table and his work.*

JACQUELINE. What is it, Kit?

KIT. I haven't done that work you set me.

JACQUELINE. Oh, Kit. Why not?

KIT. Well, I took Diana to the Casino last night, and——

JACQUELINE. Kit, really——

KIT. But as a great treat I'll translate you some La Bruyère this morning. Come on. (*He pulls her towards one of the arm-chairs.*)

JACQUELINE. I set you that work specially because I thought it would interest you, and anyway you can't afford to slack off just now before your exam.

KIT. (*Hands a her book.*) Now sit down and read your nice La Bruyère and be quiet. Are you comfortable? (*Opening his own book.*) Page one hundred and eight. Listen, Alan. You can learn a lot from hearing French beautifully translated. Chapter four. (*Translating.*) Of the heart . . .

JACQUELINE. Of love.

KIT. Of love, then. (*Translating.*) There is a fragrance in pure love . . .

JACQUELINE. In pure friendship.

KIT. (*Translating.*) Friendship can exist between people of different sexes.

ALAN. You don't say.

KIT. I don't. La Bruyère does. (*Translating.*) Friendship can exist between people of different sexes, quite exempt from all grossness.

JACQUELINE. Quite free from all . . .

ALAN. Hanky-panky.

JACQUELINE. Quite free from all unworthy thoughts.

KIT. Quite exempt from all grossness. (*Looking up.*) I know what it is. It's been bothering me all the time. You've changed your hair, haven't you, Jack?

JACQUELINE. (*Giving* ALAN *a quick glance.*) Yes, Kit, I've changed my hair.

KIT. Alan, do look at Jack. She's changed her hair.

ALAN. (*Looking up.*) So she has. Well—well—well.

KIT. I knew you'd done something to yourself. (*He studies her.*) It's queer, you know. It makes you look quite . . .

JACQUELINE. (*Eagerly.*) Quite what, Kit?

KIT. I was going to say alluring.

He laughs as if he'd made a joke; JACQUELINE *laughs, too.*

JACQUELINE. You do like it, anyway, Kit?

KIT. Yes, I do. I think it's very nice.

JACQUELINE. You think I ought to keep it like this?

Before KIT *can answer,* ROGERS *has appeared from garden.*

ROGERS. Sorry, Maingot wants to take me now, so would one of you mind telling Diana—er—I mean Miss Lake, that we'll have to postpone our walk?

Pause.

ALAN. Yes, I'll tell her.

ROGERS. Thank you.

He goes back into garden.

JACQUELINE. (*Breaking a silence.*) You think I ought to keep it like this?

KIT. (*Turning slowly.*) Keep what?

JACQUELINE. My hair.

KIT. Oh, don't be such a bore about your hair, Jack. Yes, keep it like that. It'll get a laugh anyway.

He goes out quickly. Pause. JACQUELINE *closes her book with a slam and rises.*

JACQUELINE. Five francs please, Alan.

CURTAIN

ACT II

Scene 1

SCENE: *Same as Act I.*

TIME: *A fortnight later, about 2 p.m.*

Lunch is just finished. All the characters seen in Act I are still sitting at the table. MAINGOT *sits at one end,* ALAN *facing him at the other end. On* MAINGOT'S *right are* ROGERS, DIANA, *and* KIT, *in that order, facing the audience. On his left are* BRIAN, KENNETH, *and* JACQUELINE, *also in that order, with their backs to the audience.*

On the rise of the CURTAIN *conversation is general.* ALAN *is talking to* JACQUELINE, BRIAN *to* MAINGOT, *and* ROGERS *to* DIANA. *After a few seconds conversation lapses and* ROGERS' *voice can be heard.*

ROGERS. Oh, yes, Tuppy Jones. Yes, he's in Belligerent. I know him quite well. Cheery cove. (*He chuckles.*) There's an amusing story about him as a matter of fact. He got a bit tight in Portsmouth, and broke seven Belisha Beacons with an air pistol.

MAINGOT. (*Turning politely to* ROGERS.) Eh, bien, Monsieur le Commandant, voulez-vous raconter votre petite histoire en français? Please to tell your little story in French.

ROGERS. (*Confused.*) Oh, no, sir. That's a bit unfair. I don't know enough.

MAINGOT. You should have learnt enough, my Commander.

ROGERS. But, dash it, sir, I've only been here a few days.

MAINGOT. Two weeks, my Commander. After two weeks my pupils are usually enough advanced to tell me little stories in French.

ROGERS. Well, I'm afraid I can't tell this one, sir. It wasn't a story anyway.

ALAN. (*Leaning forward malevolently.*) Au contraire, Monsieur, l'histoire de Monsieur le Commandant était excessivement rigolo.

31

MAINGOT. Bien. Alors, racontez-la vous même.

ALAN. Il parâit qu'il connait un type qui s'appelle Tuppy Jones. Alors ce bonhomme, se promenant un soir par les rues de Portsmouth, et ayant un peu trop bu, a brisé, à coups de pistolet à vent, sept Belisha Beacons.

MAINGOT. (*Who has been listening attentively, his ear cupped in his hand.*) Et puis?

ALAN. C'est tout, Monsieur.

MAINGOT. C'est tout?

KIT. Vous savez que ce Tuppy Jones était d'un esprit le plus fin du monde.

MAINGOT. Je crois bien. Au même temps, je n'ai pas tout à fait compris. Qu'est-ce que ça veut dire—Belisha Beacons?

ALAN. Ah, ça c'est un peu compliqué.

BRIAN. (*Showing off his French.*) Belisha Beacons sont des objets——(*He stops.*)

ALAN. Qui se trouvent actuellement dans les rues de Londres——

KIT. Et qui sont dédiés au salut des passants.

MAINGOT. Aha. Des emblèmes religieux?

ALAN. C'est ça. Des emblèmes religieux.

MAINGOT. (*To* ROGERS.) So one finds it funny in England to break these religious emblems with a wind pistol?

ROGERS. (*Not having understood.*) Well—(MAINGOT *shrugs his shoulders sadly.*)

(*Angrily to* ALAN.) Damn you, Howard.

BRIAN. That's not fair.

ALAN. It was a very good story, I thought.

MAINGOT. (*Rising, having finished his wine.*) Bien, Messieurs, Mesdames, la session est terminée. (*He gets up.* ALL *get up after him.*)

(*Holding up his hand.*) One moment please. I speak in English for those who cannot understand. How many of you are going tonight to the Costume Ball and great battle of flowers at the Casino? Please hold up your hands.

KIT. (*To* ALAN.) Good lord! Is it July the fourteenth? I'd no idea.

All hold up their hands.

MAINGOT. All of you! Good. The festivities commence at eight o'clock; there will be no dinner 'ere. All right.

MAINGOT moves to window and stops.

One moment, please. I give my history lecture at two-thirty, that is to say in twenty minutes' time. All right.

He goes out into garden.

ROGERS and DIANA are moving towards the french windows. KIT catches them up.

KIT. (*To* DIANA.) What about a game of Japanese billiards, Diana?

DIANA. (*Indicating* ROGERS.) Bill's just asked me to play, Kit. I'll play you afterwards. Come on, Bill.

ROGERS. Sorry, Neilan.

ROGERS and DIANA go out together. KIT goes to an armchair and sits sulkily. BRIAN has pulled out a wallet and is fumbling inside it. ALAN is going out through the window when KENNETH catches him up.

KENNETH. Alan, will you help me with that essay now? You said you would.

ALAN. Oh hell! Can't you do it yourself?

KENNETH. Well, I could, but it might mean missing this dance tonight, and I'd hate that. Do help me. It's on Robespierre, and I know nothing about him.

ALAN. There's a chapter on him in Lavisse. Why don't you copy that out? The old man won't notice. He'll probably say that it isn't French, but still——

He goes out.

KENNETH. (*Shouting after him.*) Alan, be a sportsman.

ALAN. (*Off.*) Nothing I should hate more.

KENNETH. Oh, hell!

KENNETH turns sadly and goes past KIT to the door at the back.

KIT. (*Moodily.*) What Alan wants is a good kick in the pants.

KENNETH. (*At door.*) Oh, I don't know.

He goes out. BRIAN puts his wallet back in his pocket.

BRIAN. I say, old boy, I suppose you couldn't lend me fifty francs, could you?

KIT. No, I couldn't. At any rate, not until you've paid me back that hundred you owe me.

BRIAN. Ah, I see your point. (*Cheerfully.*) Well, old boy, no ill feelings. I'll have to put off Chi-Chi for tonight, that's all.

KIT. You weren't thinking of taking her to this thing at the Casino, were you?

BRIAN. Yes.

KIT. What do you think Maingot would have said if he'd seen her?

BRIAN. That would have been all right. I told him I was taking the daughter of the British Consul.

KIT. But she doesn't exactly look like the daughter of the British Consul, does she?

BRIAN. Well, after all, it's fancy dress. It's just possible the daughter of the British Consul might go dressed as Nana of the Boulevards. Still, I admit that if he'd actually met her he might have found it odd that the only English she knew was 'I love you, Big Boy'.

KIT. How do you manage to talk to her, then?

BRIAN. Oh, we get along, old boy, we get along. (*Going to window.*) You couldn't make it thirty francs, I suppose?

KIT. No, and I don't suppose Chi-Chi could either.

BRIAN. Oh, well, you may be right. I'd better pop round in the car and tell her I won't be there tonight.

KIT. Oh, listen, Brian, if you want someone to take, why don't you take Jack?

BRIAN. Isn't anyone taking her?

KIT. Yes, I'm supposed to be, but——

BRIAN. (*Surprised.*) You, old boy? What about Diana?

KIT. Oh, she's being taken by the Commander.

BRIAN. Oh.

Pause.

As a matter of fact, I don't think I'll go at all. I don't fancy myself at a battle of flowers.

KIT. Nor do I, if it comes to that.

BRIAN. Oh, I don't know. I think you'd hurl a prettier bloom than I would. Well, so long.

He goes out. KIT *sits biting his nails. The ferocious din of a sports car tuning up comes through the window.* KIT *jumps up.*

KIT. (*Shouting through the window.*) Must you make all that noise?

BRIAN. (*Off, his voice coming faintly above the din.*) Can't hear, old boy.

The noise lessens as the car moves off down the street. JACQUELINE *and* MARIANNE *come in, the latter bearing a tray.*

KIT. (*Turning.*) God knows why Brian finds it necessary to have a car that sounds like—like five dictators all talking at once.

JACQUELINE. (*Helping* MARIANNE *clear.*) It goes with his character, Kit. He'd think it was effeminate to have a car that was possible to sit in without getting cramp and that didn't deafen one.

KIT. (*Sitting again.*) I wonder what it's like to be as hearty as Brian?

JACQUELINE. Awful, I should think.

KIT. No, I should think very pleasant. Have you ever seen Brian bad-tempered?

JACQUELINE. No, but then I think he's too stupid to be bad-tempered.

KIT. It doesn't follow. Cats and dogs are bad-tempered, sometimes. No, Brian may be stupid but he's right-minded. He's solved the problem of living better than any of us.

MARIANNE *goes out with a loaded tray.*

It seems a simple solution, too. All it needs, apparently, is the occasional outlay of fifty francs. I wish I could do the same.

JACQUELINE. I expect you could if you tried.

KIT. I have tried. Often.

JACQUELINE *is folding up the table-cloth.*

Does that shock you?

JACQUELINE. Why should it?

KIT. I just wondered.

JACQUELINE. I'm a woman of the world.

KIT. (*Smiling.*) That's the last thing you are. But I'll tell you this, Jack. I like you so much that it's sometimes quite an effort to remember that you're a woman at all.

JACQUELINE. Oh.

She puts the table-cloth in a drawer of the table and shuts it with something of a slam.

I thought you liked women.

KIT. I don't think one likes women, does one? One loves them sometimes, but that's a different thing altogether. Still, I like you. That's what's so odd.

JACQUELINE. (*Brightly.*) Thank you, Kit. I like you, too.

KIT. Good. That's nice for both of us, isn't it?

He returns his gaze to the window. JACQUELINE, *in a sudden fit of temper, kicks the leg of the table.*

Clumsy!

JACQUELINE. (*Limping over to the other armchair and sitting.*) Have you found anything to wear tonight?

KIT. Supposing I didn't go, would you mind?

JACQUELINE. Well, I have been rather looking forward to to-night.

KIT. Alan could take you. He's a better dancer than I am.

JACQUELINE. (*After a pause.*) Why don't you wear that Greek dress of my brother's?

KIT. Jack, you know, I don't think I could cope with a battle of flowers. (*He turns and meets her eyes.*) Could I get into this dress of your brother's?

JACQUELINE. Yes, easily. It may be a bit tight.

ALAN *comes in through the window.*

KIT. That reminds me. I hope there'll be plenty to drink at this affair.

ALAN. (*Morosely.*) There's nothing else for it. I shall have to murder that man.

JACQUELINE. Who?

ALAN. The Commander.

KIT. Surely that's my privilege, isn't it?

ALAN. I've just been watching him play Japanese billiards with Diana. Now you would think, wouldn't you, that Japanese billiards was a fairly simple game? You either roll wooden balls into holes or you don't. That should be the end of it. But as played by the Commander it becomes a sort of naval battle. Every shot he makes is either a plunging salvo or a blasting broadside, or a direct hit amidships.

KIT. At least he has the excuse that it amuses Diana. (*He gets up.*) Will you explain to me, Alan, as an impartial observer,

how she can bear to be more than two minutes in that man's
company?

ALAN. Certainly. He's in the process of falling in love with
her.

KIT. Yes, that's obvious, but—

ALAN. When one hooks a salmon one has to spend a certain
amount of time playing it. If one doesn't, it escapes.

KIT. Is that meant to be funny?

ALAN. Of course. When the salmon is landed, all that's necessary is an occasional kick to prevent it slipping back into
the water.

KIT. (*Angrily.*) Don't be a damned fool.

ALAN. Tomorrow a certain Lord Heybrook is arriving. Diana
is naturally rather anxious to bring the Commander to the
gaff as quickly as possible, so that she can have two nice fat
fish gasping and squirming about on the bank, before she
starts to fish for what'll be the best catch of all of you, if she
can bring it off.

Pause. KIT *suddenly bursts out laughing.*

KIT. No wonder you can't get anyone to take your novel.

ALAN. (*Hurt.*) I can't quite see what my novel has got to do
with the machinations of a scalp-hunter.

JACQUELINE *rises in alarm.*

KIT. (*Walking over to* ALAN.) Listen, Alan. One more crack like
that——

JACQUELINE. (*Hurriedly, to* ALAN.) Kit's quite right. You
shouldn't say things like that.

KIT. (*Turning to her savagely.*) What do you know about it,
anyway?

JACQUELINE. Nothing, only——

KIT. Well, please go away. This is between Alan and me.

JACQUELINE. Oh, I'm sorry.

JACQUELINE *goes into garden.*

KIT. Now. Will you please understand this. I am in love with
Diana, and Diana is in love with me. Now that's not too
hard for you to grasp, is it? Because I'll repeat it again slowly
if you like.

ALAN. (*Genially.*) No, no. I've read about that sort of thing in books. The Commander, of course, is just an old friend who's known her since she was so high.

KIT. The Commander's in love with her, but you can't blame Diana for that.

ALAN. Of course I don't. It was a very smart piece of work on her part.

KIT. (*Swallowing his anger.*) She's too kind-hearted to tell him to go to hell—

ALAN. I suppose it's because she's so kind-hearted that she calls him 'darling', and plays these peculiar games with him all over the place.

Pause.

KIT. I called you an impartial observer a moment ago. Well, you're not. I believe you're in love with Diana yourself.

ALAN. My dear Kit! As a matter of fact, I admit it's quite possible I shall end by marrying her.

KIT. You'll what?

ALAN. But that'll only be—to take another sporting metaphor —like the stag who turns at bay through sheer exhaustion at being hunted.

Pause.

KIT. (*Aggressively.*) God! Alan, I've a good mind to——

ALAN. I shouldn't. It'd make us both look rather silly.

DIANA *and* ROGERS *heard off in garden.*

Besides, you know how strongly I disapprove of fighting over a woman.

DIANA *appears at window,* ROGERS *following.*

ROGERS. (*Coming in through window.*) Well, of course, there was only one thing to do. So I gave the order—all hands on deck—— (*Stops at sight of* KIT *and* ALAN).

ALAN. And did they come?

ROGERS. (*Ignoring* ALAN, *to* DIANA.) Let's go out in the garden, Diana.

DIANA. (*Languidly throwing herself into an armchair.*) It's so hot, Bill. Let's stay here.

KIT. Aren't you going to play me a game of Japanese billiards, Diana?

DIANA. You don't mind, do you, Kit? I'm quite exhausted as a matter of fact.

KIT. (*Furious.*) Oh, no. I don't mind a bit.

He goes out into the garden. Pause. ALAN *begins to hum the Lorelei.* ROGERS *walks towards window.*

ALAN. Don't leave us, Commander. If one of us has to go, let it be myself.

ROGER *stops.* ALAN *walks to door at back.*

I shall go aloft.

He goes out.

ROGERS. Silly young fool. I'd like to have him in my ship. Do him all the good in the world.

DIANA. Yes. It might knock some of the conceit out of him.

ROGERS. Y-e-s. Has he been—bothering you at all lately?

DIANA. (*With a gesture of resignation.*) Oh, well. I'm awfully sorry for him, you know.

ROGERS. I find it hard to understand you sometimes, Diana.

He sits in chair beside her. She pats his hand.

At least I think I do understand you, but if you don't mind me saying it, I think you're too kind-hearted—far too kind-hearted.

DIANA. (*With a sigh.*) Yes, I think I am.

ROGERS. For instance—I can't understand why you don't tell Kit.

DIANA. (*Rising.*) Oh, Bill, please——

ROGERS. I'm sorry to keep on at you about it, Diana, but you don't know how much I resent him behaving as if you were still in love with him.

DIANA. But I can't tell him—not yet, anyway. (*Gently.*) Surely you must see how cruel that would be?

ROGERS. This is a case where you must be cruel only to be kind.

DIANA. Yes, Bill, that's true. Terribly true. But you know, cruelty is something that's physically impossible to me. I'm the sort of person who's miserable if I tread on a snail.

ROGERS. You must tell him, Diana. Otherwise it's so unfair on him. Tell him now.

DIANA. (*Quickly.*) No, not now.

ROGERS. Well, this evening.

DIANA. Well, I'll try. It's a terribly hard thing to do. It's like
—it's like kicking someone when he's down.

ROGERS *puts his arms round her.*

ROGERS. I know, old girl, it's a rotten thing to have to do. Poor
little thing, you mustn't think I don't sympathize with you,
you know.

DIANA. (*Laying her head on his chest.*) Oh, Bill, I do feel such a
beast.

ROGERS. Yes, yes, of course. But these things happen, you know.

DIANA. I can't understand it even yet. I loved Kit—at least I
thought I did, and then you happened—and—and—Oh,
Bill, do you do this to all the women you meet?

ROGERS. Er—do what?

DIANA. Sweep them off their feet so that they forget everything
in the world except yourself.

ROGERS. Diana, will you give me a truthful answer to a question I'm going to ask you?

DIANA.. Yes, of course, Bill.

ROGERS. Is your feeling for me mere—infatuation, or do you
really, really love me?

DIANA. Oh, you know I do, Bill.

ROGERS. (*He kisses her.*) Oh, darling. And you really don't love
Kit any more?

DIANA. I'm still fond of him.

ROGERS. But you don't love him?

DIANA. No, Bill, I don't love him.

JACQUELINE *comes in through the window.* ROGERS, *his back to
her, doesn't see her.* DIANA *breaks away.*

ROGERS. And you *will* tell him so?

DIANA. Hullo, Jacqueline.

JACQUELINE. Hullo, Diana. Rather warm, isn't it?

She walks across the room and into the kitchen.

DIANA. (*Alarmed.*) You don't think she saw anything, do you?

ROGERS. I don't know.

DIANA. She may have been standing outside the window the
whole time. I wouldn't put it past her.

ROGERS. What does it matter anyway? Everyone will know
soon enough.

DIANA. (*Thoughtfully.*) She's the sort of girl who'll talk.

ROGERS. Let her.

DIANA. (*Turning to him.*) Bill, you don't understand. Our feelings for each other are too sacred to be soiled by vulgar gossip.

ROGERS. Er—yes, yes. But, dash it, we can't go on keeping it a secret for ever.

DIANA. Not for ever. But don't you find it thrilling to have such a lovely secret just between us and no one else? After all, it's our love. Why should others know about it and bandy it about?

ROGERS. Yes, I know, but——

KIT *comes in through window. He glances moodily at* DIANA *and* ROGERS *and throws himself into an armchair, picking up a paper and beginning to read.* ROGERS *points significantly at him and frames the words 'Tell him now' in his mouth.* DIANA *shakes her head violently.* ROGERS *nods his head urgently.* KIT *looks up.*

DIANA. (*Hurriedly.*) You people have got a lecture now, haven't you?

KIT. In about five minutes.

DIANA. Oh. Then I think I'll go for a little walk by myself. (*Going to window.*) We'll have our bathe about four, don't you think, Bill?

ROGERS. Right.

DIANA *goes out. Pause.*

(*Breezily.*) Well, Neilan, how's the world treating you these days.

KIT. Bloodily.

ROGERS. I'm sorry to hear that. What's the trouble?

KIT. Everything. (*He takes up a paper.*)

ROGERS. (*After a pause.*) This show tonight at the Casino ought to be rather cheery, don't you think?

KIT *lowers his paper, looks at him, and raises it again.*

Who are you taking?

KIT. (*Into the paper.*) Jacqueline.

ROGERS. Jacqueline?

KIT. (*Loudly.*) Yes, Jacqueline.

ROGERS. Oh. (*Cheerfully.*) That's a charming girl, I think.

D

Clever. Amusing. Pretty. She'll make somebody a fine wife.

KIT *emits a kind of snort.*

Did you say anything?

KIT *doesn't answer.*

She's what the French call a sympathetic person.

KIT. Do they? I didn't know.

ROGERS. Oh, yes they do. Much nicer than most modern girls. Take some of these English girls, for instance——

KIT. You take them. I want to read.

He turns his back. ROGERS, *annoyed, shrugs his shoulders.* BRIAN'S *car is heard outside in the road.* ROGERS *goes to the bookcase and takes out his notebook.*

BRIAN'S *voice can be heard in the garden singing 'Somebody Stole my Girl'.*

KIT *gets up.*

(*Shouting through the window.*) Blast you, Brian.

BRIAN. (*Appearing at window.*) What's the matter, old boy? Don't you like my voice?

KIT. No, and I don't like that song.

BRIAN. 'Somebody Stole my Girl'? Why, it's a—— (*He looks from* KIT *to* ROGERS.) Perhaps you're right. It's not one of my better efforts. (*He puts a parcel on the table.*) This has just come for Alan. It feels suspiciously like his novel. (*He goes to bookcase and takes out his notebook.*) You won't believe it, but I used to sing in my school choir. Only because I was in the rugger fifteen, I admit. (*Sits next* KIT.) What's the old boy lecturing on today?

KIT. The Near East, I suppose. He didn't finish it yesterday.

BRIAN. Good lord! Was it the Near East yesterday? I thought it was the Franco-Prussian War.

KIT. You must get a lot of value out of these lectures.

BRIAN. Well, I only understood one word in a hundred.

ROGERS. It's rather the same in my case.

BRIAN. Give me your notes in case the old boy has the impertinence to ask me a question.

He takes KIT'S *notes and starts to read them.* ALAN *comes in through door at the back, followed by* KENNETH.

ALAN. (*Going to table and picking up parcel.*) Ah, I see the novel has come home to father again.

BRIAN. Open it, old boy. There may be a marvellous letter inside.

ALAN. There'll be a letter all right. But I don't need to read it.

He sits down at table and pushes the parcel away.

BRIAN. Bad luck, old boy.

KENNETH *grabs the parcel and unties the string.*

You mustn't give up hope yet, though. First novels are always refused hundreds of times. I know a bloke who's been writing novels and plays and things all his life. He's fifty now, and he's still hoping to get something accepted.

ALAN. Thank you, Brian. That's very comforting.

KENNETH *has extracted a letter from the parcel and is reading it.*

ROGERS. (*Amicably.*) Will you let me read it some time?

ALAN. (*Pleased.*) Would you like to? I'm afraid you'd hate it.

ROGERS. Why? What's it about?

KENNETH *hands down the letter to* ALAN.

ALAN. (*Glancing over letter. He crumples the letter up and throws it away.*) It's about two young men who take a vow to desert their country instantly in the case of war and to go and live on a farm in Central Africa.

ROGERS. (*Uncomfortably.*) Oh.

ALAN. War breaks out and they go. One of them takes his wife. They go, not because they are any more afraid to fight than the next man, but because they believe violence in any circumstances to be a crime and that, if the world goes mad, it's their duty to remain sane.

ROGERS. I see. Conchies.

ALAN. Yes. Conchies. When they get to their farm one of them makes love to the other's wife and they fight over her.

ROGERS. Ah. That's a good point.

ALAN. But in fighting for her they are perfectly aware that the motive that made them do it is as vile as the impulse they feel to go back and fight for their country. In both cases they are letting their passions get the better of their reason —becoming animals instead of men.

ROGERS. But that's nonsense. If a man fights for his country or his wife he's—well, he's a man and not a damned conchie.

ALAN. The characters in my book have the honesty not to rationalize the animal instinct to fight, into something noble like patriotism or manliness. They admit that it's an ignoble instinct—something to be ashamed of.

ROGERS. (*Heated.*) Ashamed of! Crikey!

ALAN. But they also admit that their reason isn't strong enough to stand out against this ignoble instinct, so they go back and fight.

ROGERS. Ah. That's more like it. So they were proved wrong in the end.

ALAN. Their ideal wasn't proved wrong because they were unable to live up to it. That's the point of the book.

KIT. (*From his corner, morosely.*) What's the use of an ideal if you can't live up to it?

ALAN. In a hundred years' time men may be able to live up to our ideals even if they can't live up to their own.

KENNETH. (*Excitedly.*) That's it. Progress.

KIT. Progress my fanny.

ROGERS. But look here, are you a pacifist and all that?

ALAN. I am a pacifist and all that.

ROGERS. And you're going into the diplomatic?

ALAN. Your surprise is a damning criticism of the diplomatic. Anyway, it's not my fault. My father's an ambassador.

ROGERS. Still, I mean to say—— Look here, supposing some rotter came along and stole your best girl, wouldn't you fight him?

KIT. (*Looking up.*) You'd better ask me that question, hadn't you?

ROGERS. (*Swinging round.*) What the devil do you mean?

KIT. (*Getting up.*) And the answer would be yes.

ROGERS. (*With heavy sarcasm.*) That's very interesting, I'm sure.

ALAN. (*Enjoying himself.*) By the way, I forgot to tell you, in my novel, when the two men go back to fight for their country they leave the woman in Central Africa. You see after fighting over her they come to the conclusion that she's a bitch. It would have been so much better, don't you think, if they had discovered that sooner?

KIT. All right, you asked for it.

He raises his arm to hit ALAN, *who grapples with him and holds him.*
ALAN. Don't be a damned fool.

ROGERS *strides over and knocks* ALAN *down.*
KIT. (*Turning furiously on* ROGERS.) What the hell do you think
you're doing?

KIT *aims a blow at* ROGERS, *who dodges it, overturning a chair.*
KENNETH *runs in to attack* ROGERS. BRIAN, *also running in, tries
to restrain both* KENNETH *and* KIT.
BRIAN. Shut up, you damned lot of fools. (*Shouting.*) Kit, Babe,
show some sense, for God's sake! Look out—Maingot!

ALAN *gets up and is about to go for* ROGERS *when* MAINGOT *comes
in from the garden, carrying a large notebook under his arm.* KIT,
KENNETH, *and* BRIAN *sit down.* ROGERS *and* ALAN *stand glaring
at each other.* MAINGOT *picks up the chair that has been knocked
over, pulls it to the table, sits down, and spreads his notebook out
on the table.*
MAINGOT. Alors, asseyez-vous, Messieurs. Le sujet cet après-
midi sera la crise de mille huit cent quarante en Turquie.

ALAN *and* ROGERS *sit down, still glaring at each other.*
Or la dernière fois je vous ai expliqué comment le gouver-
neur ottoman d'Egypte, Mehemet Ali, s'était battu contre
son souverain, le Sultan de Turquie. Constatons donc que la
chute du Sultanat . . .

CURTAIN

ACT II

SCENE 2

SCENE: *The same.*
TIME: *About six hours later.*
  DIANA *is discovered sitting in one armchair, her feet up on the other.
She is smoking a cigarette and gazing listlessly out of the window.*
JACQUELINE *comes in through door at back, dressed in a Bavarian
costume.*
JACQUELINE. Hullo! Aren't you getting dressed?
DIANA. (*Turning her head. She gets up and examines* JACQUELINE.)
Darling, you look too lovely.

JACQUELINE. Do you like it?

DIANA. I adore it. I think it's sweet. (*She continues her examination.*) If I were you, dear, I'd wear that hat just a little more on the back of the head. Look, I'll show you. (*She arranges* JACQUELINE'S *hat.*) No, that's not quite right. I wonder if it'd look better without a hat at all. (*She removes hat.*) No, you must wear a hat.

JACQUELINE. I suppose my hair's wrong.

DIANA. Well, it isn't quite Bavarian, is it, darling? Very nice, of course. (*Pulling* JACQUELINE'S *dress about.*) There's something wrong here. (*She kneels down and begins to rearrange the dress.*)

Pause.

JACQUELINE. I've got something to say to you, Diana. Do you mind if I say it now?

DIANA. Of course not. (*Tugging dress.*) Oh, lord, there's a bit of braid coming off here.

JACQUELINE. Oh!

DIANA. I'll fix it for you.

JACQUELINE. If you look in that basket over there you'll find a needle and thread. (*She points to a work-basket which is lying on the seat of one of the chairs.*)

DIANA. Right. (*She goes to basket.*)

JACQUELINE. But you needn't trouble——

DIANA. (*Extracting needle and thread.*) That's all right. It's no trouble. I enjoy doing this sort of thing. (*Threading needle.*) Well, what was it you wanted to say to me?

JACQUELINE. I overheard your conversation with the Commander this afternoon.

DIANA. (*Making a bad shot with the thread. She turns to the light.*) All of it, or just a part of it?

JACQUELINE. I heard you say that you were in love with the Commander and that you didn't love Kit.

DIANA. Oh! (*Kneeling at* JACQUELINE'S *feet.*) Now, scream if I stick a needle into you, won't you? (*She begins to sew.*) Is that what you wanted to tell me?

JACQUELINE. I wanted to know if you were going to tell Kit that you didn't love him.

DIANA. (*Sewing industriously.*) Why?

JACQUELINE. Because if you don't tell him, I will.

DIANA. (*After a slight pause.*) My poor Jacqueline, I never knew you felt like that about Kit.

JACQUELINE. Yes, you did. You've known for some time, and you've had a lot of fun out of it.

DIANA. Well, I wish you the best of luck.

JACQUELINE. Thank you. (*Starting.*) Ow!

DIANA. Sorry, darling, did I prick you?

JACQUELINE. Are you going to tell him?

DIANA. I don't think so.

JACQUELINE. I shall, then.

DIANA. My dear, I think that would be very silly. He won't believe you, it'll make him very unhappy, and, worst of all, he'll be furious with you.

JACQUELINE. (*Thoughtfully.*) Yes, that's true, I suppose.

DIANA. (*Biting off the thread and standing up.*) There. How's that?

JACQUELINE. Thank you so much. That's splendid. So you won't leave Kit alone?

DIANA. Now, let's be honest, for a moment. Don't let's talk about love and things like that, but just plain facts. You and I both want the same man.

JACQUELINE. But you don't——

DIANA. Oh yes, I do.

JACQUELINE. But what about the Commander?

DIANA. I want him too.

JACQUELINE. Oh!

DIANA. Don't look shocked, darling. You see, I'm not like you. You're clever—you can talk intelligently, and you're nice.

JACQUELINE. That's a horrid word.

DIANA. Now I'm not nice. I'm not clever and I can't talk intelligently. There's only one thing I've got, and I don't think you'll deny it. I have got a sort of gift for making men fall in love with me.

JACQUELINE. Oh, no. I don't deny that at all.

DIANA. Thank you, darling. I didn't think you would. Well, now, you have been sent into the world with lots of gifts, and you make use of them. Well, what about me, with just my one gift? I must use that too, mustn't I?

JACQUELINE. Well, what you call my gifts are at any rate social. Yours are definitely anti-social.

DIANA. Oh, I can't be bothered with all that. The fact remains that having men in love with me is my whole life. It's hard for you to understand, I know. You see, you're the sort of person that people *like*. But nobody *likes* me.

JACQUELINE. Oh, I wish you wouldn't keep harping on that. I wouldn't mind if everybody hated me, provided Kit loved me.

DIANA. You can't have it both ways, darling. Kit looks on you as a very nice person.

JACQUELINE. (*With sudden anger.*) Oh, God! What I'd give to be anything but nice!

DIANA. In a way, you know, I envy you. It must be very pleasant to be able to make friends with people.

JACQUELINE. You could be friends with Kit if you were honest with him.

DIANA. Darling! And I called you intelligent! Kit despises me. If he didn't love me he'd loathe me. That's why I can't let him go.

JACQUELINE. (*Pleadingly.*) Oh, Diana, I do see your point of view. I do see that you must have men in love with you, but couldn't you, please, couldn't you make the Commander do?

DIANA. No—I always act on the principle that there's safety in numbers.

JACQUELINE. Well, there's this Lord Heybrook arriving to-morrow. Supposing I let you have the Commander and him.

DIANA. No, darling. I'm sorry. I'd do anything else for you, but if you want Kit, you must win him in fair fight.

JACQUELINE. (*A shade tearfully.*) But I don't stand a chance against you.

DIANA. To be perfectly honest, I agree with you, darling.

JACQUELINE. I only hope you make some awful blunder, so that he finds out the game you're playing.

DIANA. (*With dignity.*) I don't make blunders. He's taking you to the Casino tonight, isn't he?

JACQUELINE. Yes, but he's so furious because you're going with the Commander that he'll give me the most dreadful evening.

DIANA. That's all right. I'm not going. I don't feel like it, as a matter of fact.

JACQUELINE. But have you told the Commander?

DIANA. Yes; he's furious, poor poppet, but it's very good for him.

JACQUELINE. (*After a pause.*) I wonder if you realize the trouble you cause? You know there was a fight about you this afternoon?

DIANA. Yes. I hear Alan was in it. That's *very* interesting.

JACQUELINE *is surprised.* DIANA *smiles.* KIT's *voice is heard off, calling 'Jack, where are you?'* JACQUELINE *turns to* DIANA *in sudden fright.*

JACQUELINE. Does Kit know you're not going tonight?

KIT *comes in through door at back. His lower half is enclosed in the frilly skirt of a Greek Evzone, beneath which can be seen an ordinary pair of socks with suspenders. In addition he wears a cricket shirt and tie. He carries the tunic over his arm.*

KIT. Jack, I can't get into this damned coat.

DIANA *bursts into a shriek of laughter.*

DIANA. Kit, you look angelic! I wish you could see yourself.

KIT. You shut up.

JACQUELINE. I told you it might be rather a tight fit.

KIT. But it's miles too small. Your brother must be a pygmy.

JACQUELINE. Take that shirt off and then try.

KIT. Jack, would you mind terribly if I didn't come? I can't go dressed as an inebriated danseuse.

DIANA *shrieks with laughter again.*

JACQUELINE. Don't be silly, Kit. It's going to look lovely.

KIT. Honestly, though, I don't think I'll come. You wouldn't mind?

JACQUELINE. I'd mind—awfully.

KIT. Alan's not going. I don't think I can face it really. I've asked Babe if he'll take you, and he says he'd love to. (*Turning to* DIANA—*offhandedly.*) I hear you're not going, Diana.

DIANA. No. I feel rather like you about it.

KIT. (*To* DIANA.) You know, they have dancing in the streets tonight. We might get rid of the others later and go out and join in the general whoopee—what do you say?

DIANA. Yes, that's a lovely idea, Kit.

KIT. (*Turning to* JACQUELINE.) I'm awfully sorry, Jack, but honestly——

JACQUELINE. It's all right. I'll have a lovely time with Kenneth. (*She goes out quickly through door at back.*)

KIT. She seems rather odd. You don't think she minds, do you?

DIANA. Well, how on earth should I know?

KIT. Darling, if we go out tonight, you will get rid of the Commander, won't you? If he comes I won't be answerable for the consequences.

DIANA. He's not so easy to get rid of. He clings like a limpet. Still, I'll do my best.

KIT. I can't understand why you don't just tell him to go to hell.

DIANA. (*Gently.*) That'd be a little—cruel, wouldn't it, Kit?

KIT. As someone said once, why not be cruel only to be kind?

DIANA. Yes, that's true, but, you know, Kit, cruelty is something that's physically impossible to me. I'm the sort of person who's miserable if I tread on a snail.

KIT. But can't you see, darling? It's unfair on him to let him go on thinking he's got a hope.

DIANA. Poor old Bill. Oh, well, darling, come and give me a kiss and say you love me.

ROGERS *comes in through garden door.*

KIT. With pleasure. (*He kisses her, although she tries to push him away.*) I love you.

ROGERS. (*To* KIT) What the devil do you think you're doing?

KIT. I'll give you three guesses.

ROGERS. I've had enough of this. I'm going to give this young puppy a good hiding.

DIANA. (*Trying to separate them.*) Don't be silly, Bill.

ROGERS. Out of the way, Diana.

KIT. Do what the Commander says, Diana.

DIANA. (*Still separating them.*) You're both quite mad.

MAINGOT *comes in through door at back dressed in Scottish High-land costume.* BRIAN *and* ALAN *follow, gazing at him with rapture.* KIT *and* ROGERS *and* DIANA *break apart.*

ALAN. (*Clasping his hands in admiration.*) Mais c'est exquis, Monsieur! Parfait!

MAINGOT. N'est-ce pas que c'est beau? Je l'ai choisi moi-même. Ça me va bien, hein?

ALAN. C'est tout ce qu'il y a de plus chic.

BRIAN. Vous ne pouvez pas dire le différence entre vous et un réel Highlander.

MAINGOT. Mais oui. Ça—c'est un véritable costume écossais.

DIANA. Oh, yes, that is formidable.

MAINGOT. (*Crossing to* DIANA) Vous croyez? Et aussi je connais quelques pas du can-can écossais.

ALAN. Amusez-vous bien, Monsieur.

MAHNGOT. Merci.

BRIAN. J'espère que vous baiserez beaucoup de dames, Monsieur.

MAINGOT. (*Turning appalled.*) Ha? Qu'est qu'il dit, ce garçon là?

BRIAN. Ai-je dit quelque chose?

MAINGOT. Une bétise, Monsieur. On ne dit j'amais baiser—embrasser. Il ne faut pas me donner des idées.

He goes out chuckling. ALAN, BRIAN, *and* DIANA *go to the window to watch him go down the street.* KIT *and* ROGERS *stand looking at each other rather sheepishly.*

ALAN. My God! What *does* he look like?

DIANA. He looks perfectly sweet.

JACQUELINE *comes in, followed by* KENNETH, *in sailor costume.*

BRIAN. Your father's just gone off, Jack. If you hurry you can catch him.

JACQUELINE. Right. (*Gaily.*) Goodbye, everyone. You're all fools not to be coming. We're going to have a lovely time.

KENNETH. (*To* ALAN.) Alan, do change your mind and come.

ALAN. No, thank you, Babe—have a good time.

KENNETH. Alan——

ALAN. Well, I'm going to have a drink. Anyone coming with me?

BRIAN. I'm ahead of you, old boy.

DIANA. Yes, I'm coming.

ALAN. I suppose that means I'll have to pay for both of you.

DIANA. Yes, it does.

ALAN. Are you two coming?

ROGERS *and* KIT *look at each other and then shake their heads.*

ROGERS AND KIT. No.

DIANA *and* BRIAN, KENNETH *and* JACQUELINE *all go out, talking.*

ALAN. Oh, no. I see you're going to have a musical evening! (*He follows the other two out.*)

KIT. Now we can have our little talk.

ROGERS. I don't mean to do much talking.

KIT. But I do. Diana has just this minute given me a message to give you. She wants you to understand that she knows what you feel about her, and she's sorry for you. But she must ask you not to take advantage of her pity for you to make her life a burden.

ROGERS. Right. Now that you've had your joke, let me tell you the truth. This afternoon Diana asked me to let you know, in as kindly a way as possible, that her feelings for you have changed entirely, and that she is now in love with me.

KIT. (*Astounded.*) God! What nerve! Do you know what she's just said about you? (*Shouting.*) She called you a silly old bore, who stuck like a limpet and weren't worth bothering about.

ROGERS. Oh, she did, did she?

KIT. Yes, she did, and a lot more besides that wouldn't bear repeating.

ROGERS. All right, you lying young fool. I've felt sorry for you up to this, but now I see I've got to teach you a lesson. Put your hands up.

KIT. (*Putting up his fists.*) It's a pleasure.

They stand facing each other, ready for battle. Pause. ROGERS *suddenly begins to laugh.*

ROGERS. (*Collapsing, doubled up with laughter, into a chair.*) You look so damned funny in that get-up.

KIT. (*Looking down at his legs, and beginning to giggle.*) A little eccentric, I admit.

ROGERS. Like a bedraggled old fairy queen.

KIT. I'll go and change.

ROGERS. (*Becoming serious.*) No, don't. If you do I'll have to fight you. I can't when you're looking like that, and if you go on looking like that it'll save us from making idiots of ourselves.

KIT. You know, that's rather sensible. I am surprised.

ROGERS. You know, I'm not quite such a damned fool as you youngsters seem to think. As a matter of fact, I'm a perfectly rational being, and I'm prepared to discuss this particular situation rationally. Now, I'm ready to admit that you have a grievance against me.

KIT. But I haven't—speaking rationally.

ROGERS. Oh, yes. Rationally speaking, you might say that I've alienated the affections of your sweetheart.

KIT. (*Smiling.*) But you haven't done anything of the sort.

ROGERS. (*Raising his hand.*) Please don't interrupt. Now, I'm perfectly ready to apologize for something that isn't altogether my fault. I hope you will accept it in the spirit in which it is offered.

KIT. (*Incredulous.*) But do you really think Diana's in love with you?

ROGERS. Certainly.

KIT. Why do you think that?

ROGERS. She told me so, of course.

KIT. (*Laughing.*) My poor, dear Commander——

ROGERS. I thought we were going to discuss this matter rationally?

KIT. Yes, but when you begin with a flagrant misrepresentation of the facts——

ROGERS. You mean, I'm a liar?

KIT. Yes, that's exactly what I do mean.

ROGERS. (*Jumping to his feet.*) Come on. Get up. I see I've got to fight you, skirt or no skirt.

KIT. No, no. Let reason have one last fling. If that fails we can give way to our animal passions. Let me tell you my side of the case.

ROGERS. (*Sitting.*) All right.

KIT. I've just had a talk with Diana. She said you were in love with her. I suggested to her that it was only fair to you to let you know exactly where you stood—in other words, that she was in love with me and that you had no chance. She answered that, though what I'd said was the truth——

ROGERS. She never said that.

KIT. (*Raising his hand.*) Please don't interrupt. (*Continuing.*) Though what I'd said was the truth, she couldn't tell you because it would be too cruel.

ROGERS *starts slightly.*

I then said, rather aptly, that this was a case where she should be cruel only to be kind.

ROGERS. You said what?

KIT. Cruel only to be kind.

ROGERS. What did she say?

KIT. She said she found it physically impossible to be cruel. She said she was the sort of person who was miserable if she trod on a snail.

ROGERS. What? You're sure of that?

KIT. Certainly.

ROGERS. She said she was miserable if she trod on a snail?

KIT. Yes.

ROGERS. (*With a world of feeling.*) Good God!

KIT. What's the matter?

ROGERS. It's awful! (*Rising and walking about.*) I can't believe it. I don't believe it. This is all a monstrous plot. (*Swinging round.*) I believe you listened in to my conversation with Diana this afternoon.

KIT. Why?

ROGERS. Because I also told her she ought to be cruel only to be kind, and she made precisely the same answer as she made to you.

KIT. (*After a pause.*) You mean about the snail?

ROGERS. Yes, about the snail.

KIT. In other words she's been double-crossing us. No, you've made all that up.

ROGERS. I only wish I had.

KIT. How do I know you're telling the truth?

ROGERS. You'll have to take my word for it.

KIT. Why should I?

ROGERS. Do you want to make me fight you?

KIT. Yes, I do.

Pause.

ROGERS. Well, I'm not going to.

KIT. (*Sitting down suddenly.*) I wonder why it's such a comfort to get away from reason.

ROGERS. Because in this case reason tells us something our vanity won't let us accept.

KIT. It tells us that Diana's a bitch.

ROGERS *half moves out of his chair.*

Reason! Reason!

ROGERS *subsides.*

ROGERS. You're right. We'd better face it. Diana's in love with neither of us, and she's made a fool out of both of us.

KIT. We don't know that—I mean that she's in love with neither of us. She may be telling lies to one and the truth to the other.

ROGERS. Is that what your reason tells you?

KIT. No.

Pause. They are both sunk in gloom.

I feel rather sick.

ROGERS. I must have a stronger stomach than you.

Pause.

I suppose you loved her more than I did?

KIT. Loved her? I still do love her, damn it.

ROGERS. But you can't, now that you know what you do.

KIT. What difference does that make? I love her face, I love the way she walks, I love her voice, I love her figure. None of that has changed.

ROGERS. (*Sympathetically.*) Poor boy. It's simpler for me though it's far more of a shock. You see, what I loved about her was her character.

Pause.

KIT. You used to kiss her, I suppose?

ROGERS. (*Sadly.*) Oh, yes.

KIT. You didn't—you didn't——?

ROGERS. (*Severely.*) I loved her for her character. (*After a pause.*) Did you?

KIT. Well, no, not really.

ROGERS. I see.

Pause.

KIT. What are we going to do?

ROGERS. We'd better face her together. We'll ask her point-blank which of us she really does love.

KIT. If she says me, I'm done for.

ROGERS. But you won't believe her?

KIT. I'll know she's lying, but I'll believe her all the same.

ROGERS. Well, supposing she says me?

KIT. That's my only hope.

ROGERS. Then, for your sake, I hope she says me.

KIT. That's terribly kind of you, Bill. I say, I may call you Bill, mayn't I?

ROGERS. Oh, my dear Kit.

Pause.

You know, what I feel like doing is to go out and get very drunk.

KIT. Suppose we go and throw ourselves into the sea instead.

ROGERS. I think my idea is better.

KIT. Yes, perhaps you're right. Then let's start now.

ROGERS. You can't go out like that, my dear Kit.

KIT. Then let's go to the Casino.

ROGERS. I haven't got anything to wear.

KIT. (*Holding out tunic.*) Wear this over your flannels.

ROGERS. All right. Help me put it on.

ALAN *and* BRIAN *come in.* KIT *is buttoning up* ROGERS' *tunic. They both stop in amazement.*

ALAN. What on earth——?

KIT. (*Excitedly.*) Bill and I are going to the Casino, Alan. You've got to come, too.

ALAN. Bill and you? What is this? Some new sort of game?

KIT. Go and put something on. You come, too, Brian.

BRIAN. No, old boy. Not me.

KIT. Go on, Alan. We want to get out of the house before Diana arrives. Where is she, by the way?

ROGERS. Who cares!

KIT *laughs.*

ALAN. (*Scratching his head.*) Let me get this straight. You want me to come to the Ball with you and the Commander——

KIT. Don't call him the Commander, Alan. His name is Bill.

ALAN. Bill?

KIT. Yes, Bill. He's one of the best fellows in the world.

ROGERS. We're going to get drunk together, aren't we, Kit?

ALAN. Kit?

KIT. Screaming drunk, Bill.

ALAN. (*Dashing to door.*) I won't be a minute.

Exit ALAN.

BRIAN. This sounds like a party.

KIT. Brian, tell me how I can get hold of your Chi-Chi? Is she going to the Casino tonight?

BRIAN. Yes, old boy.

KIT. How can I recognize her?

BRIAN. I don't think you can miss her. She's not likely to miss you, anyway, if you go into the bar alone.

KIT. Has she got a good figure.

BRIAN. I like it, but I'm easy to please. From sideways on it's a bit S-shaped, if you know what I mean.

ALAN *comes down, wearing his German coat.*

ALAN. I shall probably be lynched in this thing.

KIT. Come on. Let's go.

They go to the window. KIT *with his arm across* ROGERS' *shoulder.*

BRIAN. Hi! Wait a minute. What am I to tell Diana?

They stop.

ROGERS. Tell her we're being cruel only to be kind.

KIT. Tell her to be careful she doesn't go treading on any snails.

ALAN. Just tell her to go to hell. That leaves no room for doubt.

They go out. BRIAN *gazes after them as the*

CURTAIN FALLS

ACT III

Scene i

SCENE: *The same.*

TIME: *A few hours later.*

The curtain rises to disclose ALAN *on the sofa,* KIT *in the armchair,* ROGERS *on the floor by the end of the sofa, each smoking a cigar. They are still in the clothes in which they had gone to the Casino.* ROGERS *is half asleep.*

KIT. (*Drowsily.*) I don't agree with you. I don't agree with you at all. You can't judge women by our standards of Right and Wrong.

ALAN. They have none of their own, so how can you judge them.

KIT. Why judge them at all. There they are—all of them, I grant you, behaving absolutely nohow—still, that's what they're for, I mean they're built that way, and you've just got to take them or leave them. I'll take them.

ROGERS. (*Murmuring dreamily.*) I'll take vanilla.

KIT. Now, you tell me that Diana's a cow. All right, I shan't deny it. I shall only say that I, personally, like cows.

ALAN. But you can like them without loving them. I mean, love is only sublimated sex, isn't it?

ROGERS. (*Rousing himself a little.*) Devilish funny thing—my old friend Freud, the last time I met him, said *exactly* the same thing. Bill, old man, he said, take my word for it, love is only sublimated sex. (*Composing himself for sleep again.*) That's what Old Freudie said.

ALAN. I fear that Bill is what he'd describe himself as half seas over.

KIT. He's lucky. The more I drank up at that foul Casino the more sober I became. What were you saying about sublimated sex?

58

ALAN. Only that if that's what you feel for Diana, why sublimate?

KIT. Ah! Because she's clever enough to give me no choice.

ALAN. How simple everything would be if that sort of so-called virtue were made illegal—if it were just a question of will you or won't you.

ROGERS' *head falls back on to the chair.*

No one ought to be allowed to get away with that—'I'd like to but I mustn't'. It's that that leads to all the trouble. The Commander has now definitely passed out. You know (*excitedly*) I like him, Kit. It's quite amazing how pleasant he is when you get to know him.

A slight smile appears on ROGERS' *face.*

KIT. Yes, I know.

ALAN. Do you realize that if it hadn't been for Diana, we'd probably have gone on disliking him for ever?

KIT. Yes. We've got to be grateful to her for that.

ALAN. I wonder *why* we disliked him so much before tonight.

ROGERS. (*From a horizontal position.*) I'll tell you.

ALAN. Good lord! I thought you'd passed out.

ROGERS. Officers in the Royal Navy never pass out.

ALAN. They just fall on the floor in an alcoholic stupor, I suppose?

ROGERS. Exactly.

KIT. Well, tell us why we disliked you so much.

ROGERS. Right.

ALAN helps him to a sitting position.

Because you all made up your mind to dislike me before I ever came into this house. All except Diana, that's to say. From the moment I arrived, you all treated me as if I were some interesting old relic of a bygone age. I've never known such an unfriendly lot of blighters as you all were.

ALAN. We thought you were a bumptious bore.

ROGERS. Oh, I may have seemed a bortious bump, but that was only because I was in a blue funk of you all. Here was I who'd never been away from my ship for more than a few days at a time, suddenly plumped down in a house full of strange people, all talking either French, which I couldn't understand, or your own brand of English, which was almost as hard, and all convinced I was a half-wit. Of course I was in a blue funk.

ALAN. Well, I'm damned.

ROGERS. As a matter of fact, I liked you all.

ALAN. Oh, that's very gratifying.

ROGERS. I didn't agree with most of your opinions, but I enjoyed listening to them. I wanted to discuss them with you, but I was never given the chance. You all seemed to think that because I was in the Navy I was incapable of consecutive thought—I say, whisky doesn't half loosen the old tongue.

ALAN. But you always seemed so aggressive.

ROGERS. I was only defending myself. You attacked first, you know.

ALAN. (*Contritely.*) I'm terribly sorry.

ROGERS. That's all right. As a matter of fact it's done me a lot of good being here. One gets into a bit of a rut, you know, in the Service. One's apt to forget that there are some people in the world who have different ideas and opinions to one's own. You'll find the same in the diplomatic.

ALAN. I know. That's one of the reasons I want to chuck it.

ROGERS. Will you let me give you a bit of advice about that? I've been wanting to for a long time, but I've always been afraid you'd bite my head off if I did.

ALAN. Of course.

ROGERS. Well, chuck it. Go and do your writing.

ALAN *looks surprised. He takes a deep puff at his cigar.*

ALAN. I'd go back to England tomorrow, only—— (*He stops.*)

ROGERS. Only what?

ALAN. I don't know if I can write, for one thing.

ROGERS. It's ten to one you can't, but I shouldn't let that stop you. If it's what you want to do, I should do it.

ALAN. That isn't the real reason.

ROGERS. You haven't got the guts, is that it?

ALAN. That isn't quite my way of putting it, but I suppose it's true. I can't bring myself to make a definite decision. I'm afraid of my father, of course. But it's not only that. I admit

that there are a dozen things I'd rather do than the diplomatic. It's an exciting world at the moment. Do you know,
sometimes I think I'll go and fight. There must be a war on
somewhere.

ROGERS. I thought you were a pacifist?

ALAN. Oh, what the hell?—I shall become a diplomat.

ROGERS. You'll be a damned bad one.

ALAN. I can adapt myself.

ROGERS. (*Rising, yawning.*) Well, I've given you my advice for
what it's worth. I shall now go to bed to sleep the sleep of
the very drunk.

ALAN. You mustn't go yet. You've got to wait for Diana.

ROGERS. (*With a magnificent gesture.*) Diana—pooh!

ALAN. It's all very well for you to say 'Diana—pooh', but
this weak-kneed, jelly-livered protoplasm here is still in her
clutches.

KIT. (*Who has been musing.*) Are you referring to me?

ALAN. Diana's only got to raise her little finger and he'll go
rushing back to her, screaming to be forgiven.

ROGERS. Then we must stop her raising her little finger.

ALAN. Exactly. That's why we must face her together.

ROGERS. (*Sitting heavily.*) The United Front. We must scupper
her with a plunging salvo.

ALAN. Oh, no, don't let's do that.

KIT. (*Dismally.*) She's only got to say she still loves me.

ALAN. My dear Kit, if she has to choose between you and Bill,
she'll choose you. You're younger, you're better-looking,
and you've got more money. Don't you agree, Bill?

ROGERS. He's certainly younger and he's certainly got more
money.

ALAN. (*To* KIT.) You must be firm, you must be strong. If you
show any weakness, you'll be a traitor to our sex.

ROGERS. By jove, yes. We must put up a good show in this
engagement.

KIT. It's all very well for you to talk. You don't know——

ALAN. Haven't I resisted her attacks for a whole month?

KIT. They were only little skirmishes. You don't know what it
is to receive the whole brunt of her attack. It's quite hope-

less. You can help me as much as you like, but if she attacks me directly, I shall go under, I know that.

ALAN. Do you hear that, Commander? I submit that he be tried for Extreme Cowardice in the face of the Enemy.

ROGERS. The Court finds the prisoner guilty. (*Rising with dignity.*) Mr. Neilan, I must call upon you to surrender your trousers. Ah? I see you have come into court without them. Very well, I have no option but to ask you for your skirt.

KIT. Come and get it.

ROGERS. I've been longing to get my hands on that damn thing all the evening. Come on, Alan.

KIT leaps out of his chair, and runs across the room pursued by ROGERS and ALAN. He is cornered and there is a scuffle. DIANA, stately and sad, comes through the french windows. She stands in the doorway for some five seconds before ROGERS sees her.

ROGERS. Crikey! (*He taps the two others on the shoulders and they straighten themselves.*)

There is a rather nervous silence.

DIANA. (*Coming into the room.*) Well—I hope you all enjoyed yourselves at the Casino.

ROGERS. (*After glancing at the others.*) Oh, yes. Thanks very much.

DIANA. Brian gave me a message from you which I found rather hard to understand. Perhaps you'd explain it now.

Pause. ALAN looks inquiringly from KIT to ROGERS. ROGERS looks appealingly at ALAN.

ALAN. Well, who is to fire the first shot of the salvo?

No answer.

Come, come, gentlemen.

No answer.

Very well, I must engage the enemy on your behalf. Diana, these two gentlemen have good reason to believe that you have been trifling with their affections. You have told Kit that you are in love with him and are bored by Bill, and you have told Bill that you are in love with him and are bored by Kit. So now they naturally want to know who exactly you are in love with and who exactly you are bored by.

ROGERS. (*Nodding vigorously.*) Yes, that's right.

DIANA. (*With scorn.*) Oh, do they?

ALAN. Are you going to answer their question?

DIANA. Certainly not. Whom I love and whom I don't love is entirely my own affair. I've never heard such insolence.

ALAN. (*Turning to* ROGERS *and* KIT, *chuckling.*) Insolence! She's good, this girl, she's very good.

DIANA. (*Patiently.*) May I please be allowed to go to my room?

ALAN. (*Barring her way.*) Not until you've answered our question.

DIANA. I think you'd better let me go.

ALAN. Just as soon as you've given a straight answer to a straight question.

Pause. DIANA *at length takes a step back.*

DIANA. All right. You want to know who I'm in love with. Well, I'll tell you. (*To* ALAN.) I'm in love with you.

ALAN *recoils. There is a dead silence.*

DIANA *brushes past* ALAN. *He seizes her wrist.*

DIANA. Good night!

ALAN *drops his hands and steps back. He falls limply into a chair.* DIANA *goes out.*

ROGERS. (*Scratching his head.*) Now will someone tell me, was our engagement a success?

ALAN. (*Bitterly.*) A success? (*Groaning.*) Oh, what a girl, what a girl!

KIT. (*Gloomily.*) It was a success as far as I'm concerned.

Pause.

ALAN. I'm frightened. I'm really frightened.

ROGERS. What? (*Sternly.*) Alan, I never thought to hear such words from you.

ALAN. I can't help it. I shall fall. Oh, God! I know it, I shall fall.

ROGERS. You must be firm. You must be strong. The United Front must not be broken.

ALAN. I want you to promise me something, you two. You must never, never leave me alone with that girl.

ROGERS. That sounds like rank cowardice.

ALAN. Cowardice be damned! You don't realize the appalling danger I'm in. If I'm left alone with her for a minute, I shudder to think what might happen. She might even (*in a whisper*) marry me.

ROGERS. Oh, not that.

ALAN. It's true. God help me. I think she may easily try to marry me. (*Turning imploringly to the others.*) So you see, you can't desert me now. Don't let me out of your sight for a second. Even if I beg you on my knees to leave me alone with her, don't do it. Will you promise?

ROGERS. I promise.

ALAN. And you, Kit?

KIT. (*Nods.*) All right.

ALAN. Thank you. I've only got three weeks before the exam., but that's a long time with Diana in the house.

ROGERS. I think your hope lies in this Lord Heybrook fellow who's coming tomorrow. She may easily find that a peer in hand is worth more than one in the vague future. (*Getting up.*) I shall go to bed. Good night, Alan. You have my best wishes. (*At door.*) Don't go down to breakfast tomorrow until I come and fetch you. Good night, Kit. (*He goes out.*)

ALAN. There's a real friend. I hope you're going to show the same self-sacrifice.

KIT. I don't know what you're making all the fuss about. You ought to be very happy.

ALAN. Happy? (*Sarcastically.*) I've noticed how happy you've been these last few weeks.

KIT. I have in a way.

ALAN. That's not my way. Damn it, Kit, I'm a man with principles and ideals. I'm a romantic. Let me give you a little word-picture of the girl I should like to fall in love with. Then you can tell how far it resembles Diana. First of all, she must not be a cow.

KIT. (*Shrugging indifferently.*) Oh, well, of course——

ALAN. Secondly, she will be able to converse freely and intelligently with me on all subjects—Politics—Philosophy—Religion—— Thirdly, she will have all the masculine virtues and none of the feminine vices. Fourthly, she will be physically unattractive enough to keep her faithful to me, and attractive enough to make me desire her. Fifthly, she will be in love with me. That's all, I think.

KIT. You don't want much, do you? I admit it isn't a close

description of Diana, but where on earth do you expect to
find this love-dream?

ALAN. They do exist, you know. There's someone here, in this
house, who answers to all the qualifications, except the last.

KIT. (*Sitting forward.*) Good lord! You don't mean Jack, do
you?

ALAN. Why not?

KIT. But—but you couldn't be in love with Jack.

ALAN. I'm not, but she's exactly the sort of girl I should like
to be in love with.

KIT. (*Smiling.*) Love and Jack. They just don't seem to connect.
I'm frightfully fond of her, but somehow—I don't know—I
mean you couldn't kiss her or make love to her.

ALAN. Why not try it and see?

KIT. Who? Me? Good lord, no.

ALAN. Don't you think she's attractive?

KIT. Yes, I suppose she is, in a way, very attractive. But don't
you see, Alan, I know her far too well to start any hanky-
panky. She'd just scream with laughter.

ALAN. Really? She'd just scream with laughter? (*Turning on
him.*) You poor idiot, don't you realize the girl's been madly
in love with you for two months now?

KIT. (*After a pause, derisively.*) Ha, ha!

ALAN. All right. Say ha, ha! Don't believe it and forget I ever
said it. I promised her I'd never tell you.

Pause.

KIT. What did you have to drink up at the Casino?

ALAN. Less than you.

KIT. Are you stone-cold sober?

ALAN. As sober as ten Lady Astors.

KIT. And you sit there and tell me——

Voices heard outside.

KIT. (*Getting up in alarm.*) Oh, lord!

MAINGOT *comes in, followed by* JACQUELINE *and* KENNETH.

MAINGOT. Aha! Le Grec et l'Allemand. Vous vous êtes bien
amusés au Casino?

JACQUELINE. Hello, Kit.

ALAN. Très bien, Monsieur. Et vous?

KIT *is gaping open-mouthed at* JACQUELINE.

MAINGOT. Ah, oui! C'était assez gai, mais on y a mangé excessivement mal, et le champagne était très mauvais et m'a couté les yeux de la tête. Quand même le quartorze ne vient qu'une fois par an. Alors je vais me coucher. Bonsoir, bonne nuit et dormez bien.

ALL. Bonsoir.

MAINGOT *goes out through door at back, carrying his Highland shoes which he has changed for slippers.*

JACQUELINE. Why did you all leave so early?

KIT. (*Gaping.*) Oh, I don't know.

JACQUELINE. Your costume caused a sensation, Kit. Everyone was asking me what it was meant to be.

KIT. (*Nervously.*) Really.

ALAN. Did you have a good time, Kenneth?

KENNETH. Oh, all right. I'll say good night. I've got an essay to finish before tomorrow.

JACQUELINE. Good night, Kenneth, and thank you.

KENNETH. Good night.

KENNETH *goes out, looking sulky, through door at back.*

ALAN. You must have had a wonderful time with the Babe in that mood.

JACQUELINE. What's the matter with him, Alan?

ALAN. He's angry with me for not doing his essay for him. I think I'd better go and make my peace with him. (*At door.*) Don't go to bed for a few minutes. I want to talk to you, Jack.

He goes out. There is a pause. KIT *is plainly uncomfortable.*

KIT. Jack?

JACQUELINE. Yes?

KIT. Did you have a good time tonight?

JACQUELINE. (*Puzzled.*) Yes, thank you, Kit.

KIT. Good. I—er—I'm sorry I couldn't take you.

JACQUELINE. That's all right. (*Smiling.*) That was Brian's girl you and Alan were dancing with, wasn't it? What's she like?

KIT. Pretty hellish.

Pause.

Jack?

JACQUELINE. Yes?

KIT. Oh, nothing. (*He gets up and wanders forlornly about the room.*) Was it raining when you came back?

JACQUELINE. No, it wasn't raining.

KIT. It was when we came back.

JACQUELINE. Really?

Pause.

KIT. Yes, quite heavily.

JACQUELINE. It must have cleared up, then.

Pause. KIT *is fiddling with a box of matches.*

KIT. (*Turning with sudden decision.*) Jack, there's something I must—— (*In turning he upsets matches.*) Damn, I'm sorry.

JACQUELINE. I've never seen a clumsier idiot than you, Kit. (*She goes on her knees.*) I seem to spend my life cleaning up after you. There!

She gets up. KIT *kisses her suddenly and clumsily on the mouth. She pushes him away. They are both embarrassed and puzzled.*

(*After a long pause.*) You smell of whisky, Kit.

Enter ALAN.

ALAN. Oh!

KIT. I'm going to bed. Good night. (*He goes out.*)

JACQUELINE. What's the matter with him? Is he drunk?

ALAN. No, Jack, but I've a confession to make to you.

JACQUELINE. (*In alarm.*) You haven't told him?

ALAN. I couldn't help it.

JACQUELINE. Oh, Alan, no.

ALAN. Will you forgive me?

JACQUELINE. I'll never forgive you. It's ruined everything. (*A shade tearfully.*) He's just been talking to me about the weather.

ALAN. Well, he's a bit embarrassed. That's natural.

JACQUELINE. But he'll spend all his time running away from me now, and when he is with me he'll always be wondering if I want him to kiss me, and he'll go on talking about the weather, and—(*turning away*)—oh, it's awful!

ALAN. I'm sorry, Jack. I meant well.

JACQUELINE. Men are such blundering fools.

ALAN. Yes, I suppose we are. Will you forgive me?

JACQUELINE. (*Wearily.*) Of course I forgive you. (*After a pause.*) I'm going to bed.

ALAN. All right. We'll talk about it in the morning. I may be able to persuade Kit I was joking.

JACQUELINE. (*At door.*) No. Please don't say anything more to Kit. You've done enough harm as it is. (*Relenting.*) Good night, Alan. You're just a sentimental old monster, aren't you?

ALAN. Who, me?

JACQUELINE. Yes, you. Good night.

She goes out. ALAN, *left alone, lights a cigarette. Then he goes to door at back and opens it.*

ALAN. (*Calling.*) Jack?

JACQUELINE. (*Off.*) Yes?

ALAN. Will you see if Brian's in his room. I want to lock up.

JACQUELINE. (*Off.*) Right. (*After a pause.*) No, he must still be out.

ALAN. I'll leave a note for him.

He closes the door, takes an envelope from his pocket, and unscrews his pen. While he is writing DIANA *comes in softly and stands behind him. He doesn't hear her.*

DIANA. (*Gently.*) Alan.

ALAN. (*Jumping up.*) Oh, God!

DIANA. Do you mind if I speak to you for a moment?

ALAN. (*Pointing vaguely at the ceiling.*) Well, I was just going to bed. (*Dashes to garden door.*)

DIANA. (*Inexorably.*) I suppose you didn't believe what I told you just now. (*She catches him.*)

ALAN. (*Looking despairingly round for help.*) No, I didn't believe it.

DIANA. (*With quiet resignation.*) No. I knew you wouldn't, and, of course, after what's happened I couldn't expect you to. But, whether you believe me or not, I just want to say this.

ALAN. (*Wildly.*) In the morning, Diana, say it in the morning. I'm frightfully tired and——

DIANA. Please listen to me. I just wanted to say that it's been you from the first moment we met. Kit and Bill never meant a thing to me. I let them think I was in love with them. But it was only because I had some idea it might make you jealous.

ALAN. It's a pity you didn't succeed.

DIANA. Oh, I know what you think of me, and you're quite right, I suppose. (*Pathetically.*) I've told so many lies before that I can't expect you to believe me when I'm telling the truth.

ALAN. Poor little Matilda.

DIANA. (*Comes back to* ALAN.) But this is the truth, now. This is the only completely sincere feeling I've ever had for anyone in all my life. (*Simply.*) I *do* love you, Alan. I always have and suppose I always will.

ALAN. (*In agony.*) Oh, go away. Please go away.

DIANA. All right. I know you have every right to think I'm lying, but I'm not, Alan, really, I'm not. That's what's so funny.

ALAN. (*Imploringly.*) Oh, God help me!

DIANA. (*At door.*) Good night, Alan. (*Simply.*) I do love you.

She smiles tearfully at him. He throws away his cigarette, and walks over to her.

ALAN. Say that again, blast you!

DIANA. I love you.

He embraces her fervently.

DIANA. (*Emerging from embrace, ecstatically.*) I suppose this is true.

ALAN. You know damn well it is.

DIANA. Say it, darling.

ALAN. (*Hedging.*) Say what?

DIANA. Say you love me.

ALAN. Must I? Oh, this is hell! (*Shouting.*) I love you.

DIANA. (*Turning back rapturously.*) Alan, darling——

BRIAN *comes in through window.*

BRIAN. Hello, Alan, hello, Diana, old thing.

DIANA *looks through* BRIAN *and turns hurriedly to the door.*

DIANA. (*Softly.*) Good night, Alan. I'll see you in the morning.

She goes out. ALAN *sinks into a chair.*

BRIAN. Did you see that, old boy? She cut me dead. She's furious with me. I must tell you about it, because it's a damned funny story. After you boys had gone I took Diana to have a bite of dinner with me. Well, we had a bottle of wine and got pretty gay, and all the time she was giving me the old green light.

ALAN. The green light?

BRIAN. Yes. The go-ahead signal. Well, after a bit I rather handed out an invitation to the waltz, if you follow me.

ALAN. Yes. I follow you.

BRIAN. I mean, everybody being out, it seemed an opportunity not to be missed. Well, do you know what she did then, old boy?

ALAN. No.

BRIAN. She gave me a sharp buffet on the kisser.

ALAN. What did you do?

BRIAN. I said, well, if that isn't what you want, what the hell do you want? Then she got up and left me. I never laughed so much in all my life.

ALAN. (*Dazedly.*) You laughed?

BRIAN. Wouldn't you, old boy?

ALAN *gazes at him with amazed admiration.*

Well, I'm for bed. I say, I met the most charming little girl just now on the front—fantastic piece she was. She gave me her card—yes, here it is. Colette, chez Mme Pontet, Rue Lafayette, 23. Bain 50 francs. I think I shall pop round tomorrow and have a bain.

ALAN. (*Rising and gazing at* BRIAN *with awe.*) Oh, Brian! How right-minded you are!

BRIAN. Me?

ALAN. Thank God you came in when you did. You don't know what you've done for me with your splendid, shining example. I now see my way clear before me. A great light has dawned.

BRIAN. I say, old boy, are you feeling all right?

ALAN. Listen, Brian. You weren't the only person to get the old green light from Diana tonight. I got it, too.

BRIAN. Doesn't surprise me. I should think she's pretty stingy with her yellows and reds.

ALAN. Yes, but I didn't respond to it in the same glorious way as you. However, what's done can be undone. (*Going to door.*) I am now going upstairs to put the same question to Diana that you did earlier in the evening.

BRIAN. I shouldn't, old boy. She'll say no, and believe me, she's got rather a painful way of saying it.

ALAN. If she says no, then, lacking your own sterling qualities, I shan't pay a visit to Rue Lafayette 23. No. I shall run away. I shall go back to London tomorrow.

BRIAN. But what about your exam. and so forth?

ALAN. I shall chuck that. Well (*opening door*) I am now about to throw my future life into the balance of fate. Diplomat or writer. Which shall it be? Diana shall choose.

ALAN *goes out.*

BRIAN. (*To himself.*) Crackers!

He shakes his head wonderingly. After a bit he rises, crosses to table, and stops to think.

BRIAN. (*Musing*). Bain 50 francs! (*Fumbles for money and starts to count.*) Ten, twenty—thirty—forty—forty-one, forty-two —forty-three—forty-three—— Damn.

Slamming of door is heard. ALAN *comes in.*

ALAN. I'm going to be a writer. Come and help me pack.

He disappears. BRIAN *follows him out murmuring expostulations as the*

CURTAIN FALLS

ACT III

SCENE 2

SCENE: *The same.*

TIME: *The next morning.*

MARIANNE *is clearing away the breakfast,* JACQUELINE *helping her.*
KENNETH *enters from window,* MAINGOT *following. They have evidently just finished a lesson.*

MAINGOT. (*At window.*) Dîtes à Monsieur Curtis que je l'attends. Il ne vaut pas la peine de continuer. Vous n'en saurez j'amais rien.

KENNETH. (*Sadly.*) Oui, Monsieur.

MAINGOT. Je serai dans le jardin. Oh, ma petite Jacqueline, que j'ai mal à la tête ce matin.

JACQUELINE. Pauvre, papa! Je suis bien fâchée.

MAINGOT. Ça passera—ça passera. Heuresement le quatorz ne vient qu'une fois par an.

He goes back into garden.

KENNETH. (*Calling.*) Brian.

BRIAN. (*Off.*) Yes, old boy?

KENNETH. Your lesson.

BRIAN. (*Off.*) Won't be a second.

KENNETH *closes the door and wanders mournfully over to the book-case.*

JACQUELINE. Why so sad this morning, Kenneth?

KENNETH. You've heard the news about Alan.

JACQUELINE. Yes, my father told me.

KENNETH. Don't you think it's awful?

JACQUELINE. No. For one thing, I don't believe for a moment he's serious.

KENNETH. Oh, he's serious all right. What a damn fool! If I had half his chance of getting in the diplomatic I wouldn't go and chuck it up.

Enter BRIAN, *carrying a notebook.*

BRIAN. 'Morning all. Where's Maingot Père?

KENNETH. He's waiting for you in the garden.

BRIAN. Oh. (*Anxiously.*) Tell me, old boy, how is he this morning? Gay, happy—at peace with the world?

KENNETH. No. He's got a bad headache, and he's in a fiendish temper. (*He goes out.*)

BRIAN. Tut, tut. Couple of portos too many last night, I fear.

JACQUELINE. Why this tender anxiety for my father's health, Brian?

BRIAN. Well, Jack, I'm afraid I may have to deliver a rather rude shock to his nervous system. You see, I'm supposed to have done an essay on the Waterloo campaign, and what with one thing and another I don't seem to have got awfully far.

JACQUELINE. How far?

BRIAN. (*Reading.*) La bataille de Waterloo était gagnée sur les champs d'Eton.

JACQUELINE. And that's the essay, is it?

BRIAN *nods.*

Well, if I were you, I shouldn't show it to him. I'd tell him you did one of five pages and it got lost.

BRIAN. (*Doubtfully.*) Yes, but something seems to tell me he won't altogether credit that story.

Enter MAINGOT.

MAINGOT. Eh bien, Monsieur Curtis, qu'est-ce qu'on attend? Vous êtes en retard.

BRIAN. (*Affably.*) Ah, Monsieur, vous êtes bon—ce matin, j'espère?

MAINGOT. Non, j'ai affreusement mal à la tête.

BRIAN. (*Sympathetically.*) Oh. C'est trop mauvais. A trifle hung-over, peut-être? Un tout petit peu suspendu?

MAINGOT. Vous êtes fou ce matin?

They go out together, MAINGOT *heard expostulating.*

BRIAN. (*Off, his voice coming faintly through the window.*) Il est très triste, Monsieur. J'ai perdu mon essai . . .

JACQUELINE *smiles. Having finished her clearing away, she takes off her apron and the handkerchief that covers her hair. She looks at herself in a pocket-mirror. The door at the back opens very slowly and* ALAN's *head appears.*

ALAN. (*Whispering.*) Jack!

JACQUELINE. (*Turning.*) Hallo, Alan.

ALAN. Is Diana about?

JACQUELINE. She's in the garden. She wants to speak to you.

ALAN. I bet she does. But I'm taking good care she doesn't get a chance.

He comes cautiously into the room. He is dressed in a lounge suit preparatory for going away.

I want to get my books together. (*He goes to bookcase.*)

JACQUELINE. Alan, you're not serious about this, are you?

ALAN. Never more serious in my life, Jack. (*He is collecting books from the bookcase.*)

JACQUELINE. You're breaking Diana's heart, you know.

ALAN. Ha! Is that what she told you?

E

JACQUELINE. Oh, no. She wouldn't give herself away to me, but I honestly think she is rather in love with you, Alan.

ALAN. Yes, that's just what I'm afraid of.

JACQUELINE. You know, you're the only man in the world who's ever got away from Diana unscathed.

ALAN. (*Turning quickly.*) Don't say that! It's unlucky. I'm not out of the house yet.

He turns back to the bookcase as DIANA *comes quietly into the room from the garden.*

JACQUELINE. (*Quickly.*) Look out, Alan.

ALAN. (*Seeing* DIANA.) Oh, my God!

He darts out of the room, dropping all his books as he does so. DIANA *follows him out purposefully, but is too late. After a second she re-appears.*

DIANA. It's no good, he's sure to have locked the door of his room. (*She sits down mournfully.*) I'm afraid he's quite deter-mined to go. I feel dreadfully bad about it, because I'm responsible for the whole thing. All this talk of writing is just nonsense. He's only running away from me.

JACQUELINE. I don't altogether blame him.

DIANA. I suppose it's a wonderful compliment for a man to throw up his career just for my sake, but I can't see it that way. I'm really frightfully upset.

JACQUELINE. You don't look it.

DIANA. But I am, honestly I am. You see, I can't understand why he should want to run away from me. I can't see what he's got to be frightened of.

JACQUELINE. Can't you?

DIANA. If only I could get a chance to talk to him alone, I'm sure I could persuade him not to go.

JACQUELINE. I'm sure you could, too. So is Alan. But I don't think you'll get the chance.

Enter MARIANNE *from kitchen.*

MARIANNE. (*To* JACQUELINE.) S'il vous plaît, M'mselle, voulez vous venir voir la chambre de Lord Heybrook? Je l'ai préparée.

JACQUELINE. Bien, Marianne. Je viens tout de suite.

Exit MARIANNE, *and* JACQUELINE *follows her to the door.*

DIANA. Oh, does this Lord Heybrook arrive this morning?

JACQUELINE *has turned back to the kitchen door as the other door opens and* ALAN *comes in.* JACQUELINE *is momentarily alarmed for his safety, but sees* ROGERS, *who strolls in behind* ALAN, *and is reassured. She smiles and goes out.*

ALAN, *studiously avoiding looking at* DIANA, *goes over to the book-case and picks up the books he has dropped.* ROGERS *takes a position between him and* DIANA, *nonchalantly looking up at the ceiling.*

DIANA. (*Quietly.*) Bill, please go away. I want to talk with Alan alone.

ROGERS. Well, it's . . .

DIANA. (*Shortly.*) Bill, did you hear me? I asked you to go.

ROGERS. (*Firmly.*) I'm sorry, I can't.

DIANA. (*Realizing the situation, steps back with dignity.*) Do you think it's necessary to behave like this?

ALAN. You can say anything you want to say in front of Bill.

DIANA. No, thank you. I'd rather not.

ALAN. Then you don't say it.

DIANA. (*After a slight pause.*) All right, if you're determined to be so childish. This is all I want to say. (*With great sincerity.*) Alan, you know your own mind. If you feel you must run away from me, go ahead. I won't try to stop you. I only hope you'll be happy without me. I know I shan't be happy without you.

ALAN. (*Beginning to fall.*) You'll get over it.

DIANA. Oh, I expect so. You'll write to me occasionally, won't you?

ALAN. Oh, yes, every day, I expect.

DIANA. I'd like to know how you're getting on in your new career. I wish you the very, very best of luck.

ALAN. Thank you.

DIANA. I'll be thinking of you a lot.

ALAN. That's very kind of you.

DIANA. Well, that's really all I wanted to say, only . . . (*falteringly*) I would rather like to say goodbye, and that's a bit hard with Bill standing there like the Rock of Gibraltar.

There is a long pause.

ALAN. (*Suddenly.*) Bill, get out.

ROGERS *doesn't budge.*

ALAN. Get out, Bill.

ROGERS *seems not to have heard.* ALAN *approaches him menacingly.*
Get out, blast you!

ROGERS. (*Slowly.*) Is that the voice of reason, my dear fellow?
ALAN *stares at him and suddenly collects himself.*

ALAN. Oh, thank you, Bill. Come on, help me carry these books
upstairs, and don't leave my side until I'm in that damned
train.

They go towards the door.

DIANA. So you don't want to say goodbye?

ALAN. (*At door.*) Yes, I do. Goodbye.

He goes out, followed by ROGERS.

DIANA, *in a sudden rage, hurls some books through the door after
them.*

DIANA. You forgot some.

She goes to kitchen door.

(*Calling.*) Marianne, à quelle heure arrive ce Lord Heybrook?

JACQUELINE. (*Calling from the kitchen.*) Lord Heybrook's arriving
at ten-fifteen. (*She appears in the doorway.*) He'll be here any
moment now.

DIANA. (*Annoyed.*) Oh, thank you very much.

JACQUELINE. Well, any luck with Alan?

DIANA. (*Shortly.*) No.

JACQUELINE. He wouldn't listen to reason?

DIANA. Do you mind, Jacqueline? I'm really too upset to talk
about it.

JACQUELINE. Why don't you go to England with him, if you
feel like that?

DIANA. How can I go chasing him across half a continent? One
has a little pride after all.

JACQUELINE. Yes, I suppose one has.

DIANA. Besides, if Alan really feels he'll be happier without me,
there's nothing I can do about it.

JACQUELINE. No, I suppose there isn't. (*Inconsequentially.*) Poor
Lord Heybrook!

DIANA. What's Lord Heybrook got to do with it?

JACQUELINE. Nothing. (*She wanders over to the window.*) It's a

lovely morning for a bathe, don't you think? There's a cold
wind and the sea is rough, but I shouldn't let that stop you.

DIANA. Really, Jacqueline, you're becoming quite nice and
catty in your old age. (*Defiantly.*) As a matter of fact, I think
I will have a bathe. Why don't you come with me?

JACQUELINE. Oh, no. My bathing dress isn't nearly attractive
enough. Besides, I'm giving lessons all the morning. (*Looking at her watch.*) I'm supposed to be giving one now. Kit's
late as usual.

DIANA. By the way, how are you getting on in that direction?

JACQUELINE. Not very well, I'm afraid.

DIANA. Oh, I'm sorry. I suppose Kit's terribly upset about me?

JACQUELINE. You needn't worry. I shall do my best to console
him.

DIANA. I've been horribly unkind to him. After Alan's gone I
shall have to be specially nice to him to make up for it.

JACQUELINE. (*Alarmed.*) Oh, no.

DIANA *raises her eyebrows.*

Oh, why don't you go to England with Alan? Heaven
knows Alan's never done me any harm, but I can feel quite
ruthless about anything that will get you out of this house.

DIANA. Excitable race, you French—I always say.

Enter KIT.

KIT. (*Ignoring* DIANA.) Sorry, Jack. I'm late.

JACQUELINE. All right, Kit.

DIANA. Well, I don't want to disturb you. (*Going to door.*) I'm
going to have a bathe.

DIANA *goes out.* KIT *stands shyly, holding a notebook.*

JACQUELINE. (*Adopting a schoolmistress manner.*) Sit down, Kit.
Have you done that stuff?

They sit at table. KIT *hands her his notebook.*

Good. You must have worked quite hard.

She bends her head over the notebook. KIT *gazes at her.*

KIT. (*Suddenly.*) Jack, I want to say——

JACQUELINE. (*Hurriedly.*) This is wrong. (*She underlines a word.*)
You can't say that in French. You have to turn it. (*She writes
something in the book.*) Do you see?

KIT. (*Looking over her shoulder.*) Yes, I see.

JACQUELINE *continues to read.*

JACQUELINE. My dear Kit—— (*Reading.*) Une pipe remplie avec du tabac. What ought it to be?

KIT. Remplie de tabac, of course.

JACQUELINE. Why didn't you write it, then? (*She underlines another word.*) Kit, this whole exercise is terrible. What on earth were you thinking of when you did it?

KIT. You.

JACQUELINE. Well, you'd better do it again.

KIT. (*Annoyed.*) What! Do it all again?

JACQUELINE. Yes. (*Weakening.*) Why were you thinking of me?

KIT. Not the whole damn thing?

JACQUELINE. Certainly. Why were you thinking of me?

KIT. (*With dignity.*) Shall I translate you some 'La Bruyère'?

JACQUELINE. All right.

KIT. Page one hundred and eight.

They take up their books in a dignified silence.

JACQUELINE. If I let you off, will you tell me?

KIT. I might.

JACQUELINE. Very well. You're let off. Only mind you, if you do another exercise as bad as that I'll make you do it again, and three more besides. Now, why were you thinking of me?

KIT. I was wondering whether I ought to tell you I was sorry for—for what happened last night, or whether I ought to pass it off with a gay laugh and a shrug of the shoulders.

JACQUELINE. Which did you decide?

KIT. I decided to leave it to you.

JACQUELINE. I think I'd rather have the gay laugh and the shrug of the shoulders.

KIT. You shall have it. (*He gets up.*)

JACQUELINE. No, you needn't bother. We'll take the gay laugh, etcetera, for granted.

KIT. (*Sitting.*) Very well. The incident is now closed, permanently and perpetually closed. (*He opens his book.*) Chapter four. Of love. There is a fragrance in pure friendship——

JACQUELINE. (*Puzzled at his attitude.*) I don't know why you should have thought I wanted you to apologize. After all, what's a kiss between friends?

KIT. Alan told me this morning that you were in a steaming fury with me about it, so I thought——

JACQUELINE. Oh, I see. Alan's been talking to you about me this morning, has he? Come on, tell me, what's he been saying now?

KIT. I don't see why I shouldn't tell you. You see, last night, when Alan was a bit drunk, he played a stupid practical joke on me. He told me (*covering his face with his hands*)—this is a bit embarrassing, but it's a good laugh—he told me that you had been madly in love with me for two months. (*He uncovers his face and waits for the laugh, which doesn't come.*) Well, I, being also rather drunk, believed him, and so, as I was feeling rather sentimental, I—kissed you, as you remember; and of course I couldn't understand why you didn't fall into my arms and say, 'At last, at last!' or some such rot. However, this morning Alan told me the whole thing had been a joke, and that you were really rather angry with me for—well—spoiling a beautiful friendship, and all that nonsense. So that's why I thought I'd better apologize.

JACQUELINE. (*With sudden violence.*) What a blasted fool Alan is!

KIT. Yes, it was a damn silly trick to play. Not at all like him.

JACQUELINE. Kit—supposing I—had fallen into your arms and said, 'At last, at last!' or some such rot, what would you have done?

KIT. Oh, I should have kissed you again and said: 'I've loved you all the time without knowing it,' or some such idiocy.

JACQUELINE. Oh, Kit. You wouldn't.

KIT. (*Apologetically.*) Well, I told you I was feeling sentimental last night, and what with seeing what a fool I'd been over Diana and trying to forget her, and suddenly hearing that you were in love with me, and being drunk——

JACQUELINE. You don't feel sentimental this morning, do you?

KIT. Lord, no. You don't have to worry any more. I'm quite all right now.

He takes up his book and tries to concentrate.

JACQUELINE. Isn't there any chance of your feeling sentimental again, some time?

KIT. Oh, no. You're quite safe.

JACQUELINE. If I gave you a drink or two, and told you that what Alan said last night was the truth? And that I *have* been in love with you for two months and that I've been longing for you to kiss me every time I'm with you, would that make you feel sentimental?

KIT. There's no knowing what it mightn't make me feel.

Pause.

JACQUELINE. I haven't got any drink, Kit. Or must you have drink?

She stands up and KIT *embraces her.*

(*A little hysterically.*) At last! At last!

KIT. I've loved you all the time without knowing it.

JACQUELINE. Or some such idiocy.

KIT. I mean that, Jack.

JACQUELINE. Don't get serious, please, Kit. This is only a joke. It's only because we are both feeling a bit sentimental at the same time. (*Holding him away.*) Or are you?

KIT. Would I be behaving like this if I weren't?

JACQUELINE. I don't know. I wouldn't like to have played a sort of Diana trick on you. You haven't got that trapped feeling, have you?

KIT. I've got a peculiar feeling in the stomach, and an odd buzzing noise in the head. I think that must mean I'm in love with you.

JACQUELINE. You mustn't talk about love.

KIT. But you do.

JACQUELINE. I've got two months' start of you. I'm not going to let you mention the word 'love' for two months. Oh, Kit, do you think there's a chance you may be feeling sentimental in two months' time?

KIT. I'll take ten to one.

JACQUELINE. Well, go on being beastly to me in the meanwhile, because I should hate it if you didn't.

KIT. I'll try, but it won't be easy.

ALAN *pokes his head cautiously round the door.*

ALAN. Is Diana about?

JACQUELINE. Come in, Alan. You're quite safe, and I've got some news.

ALAN *comes in, followed by* ROGERS.

ALAN. What news?

JACQUELINE. I don't want the Commander to hear it. (*To* ROGERS.) Do you mind awfully?

ROGERS. Oh, no. Not at all. Tell me when you're finished.

He goes out.

ALAN. Well, what's the news?

JACQUELINE. Kit says it's just possible that in two months' time he may feel quite sentimental about me.

ALAN. Well, well, well. You could knock me over with a feather.

KIT. You've got a lot to explain, Alan. What the hell do you mean by telling me a whole packet of lies?

ALAN. Is that the proper way to speak to one, who, by a series of tortuous ruses, has at last brought you two love-birds together?

JACQUELINE. We're not love-birds. We're friends.

KIT. Sentimental friends.

JACQUELINE. No. Friends who sometimes feel sentimental.

ALAN. Well, make up your minds what you are, and I'll give you my blessing. Time presses. I came in to say goodbye.

ROGERS. (*Appearing in doorway.*) I can come in now, can't I?

JACQUELINE. How did you know?

ROGERS. Male intuition as opposed to female. I listened at the keyhole.

ALAN. Do you know, Jack, the only reason I'm sorry to be going is having to leave Bill just when I'd discovered him.

ROGERS. We'll see each other again, don't you worry. We're brothers under the skin.

ALAN. Tell me, Jack, did Diana say anything about coming to England with me?

JACQUELINE. No, she's definitely staying here. She says your happiness comes first.

ALAN. For my happiness read Lord Heybrook. Thank God for his lordship.

Enter KENNETH.

KENNETH. Alan, must you go?

ALAN. Yes, Babe, I must. There's a load off my mind, and I don't only mean Diana.

KENNETH. I don't think you know what you're doing.

ALAN. Oh, yes, I do.

A car noise is heard outside. MAINGOT *appears at window.*

MAINGOT. Jacqueline! Jacqueline! Je crois que c'est Lord Heybrook qui arrive. Es-tu-prête?

JACQUELINE. Oui, Papa.

MAINGOT. Bien! (*He darts out again.*)

JACQUELINE. (*Excitedly.*) Lord Heybrook! Oh, go and tell Diana, someone, or she'll miss her entrance.

KIT. (*Running to door.*) Diana, Lord Heybrook!

JACQUELINE. What does he look like, Kenneth?

KENNETH. I can't see. Your father is in the light.

ALAN. Oh, sit down, all of you. Give the man a chance.

MAINGOT. (*Calling off.*) Marianne! Les bagages!

Enter DIANA, *in her bathing dress. She takes up a position of non-chalance, with her back to the garden door.*

MAINGOT. (*Off.*) Par ici, Milord!

Enter LORD HEYBROOK *and* MAINGOT *from window.* LORD HEY-BROOK *is a bright young schoolboy, about fifteen years old.*

(*Escorting* LORD HEYBROOK *across the room.*) Alors vous êtes arrivé. J'espère que vous avez fait bon voyage . . . etc.

LORD HEYBROOK, *after smiling around shyly, goes out followed by* MAINGOT. JACQUELINE *collapses with laughter on* KIT's *chest. The others begin to laugh also.*

DIANA. Come and help me pack, someone. I'm going to catch that London train or die.

She disappears through door at back.

ALAN. (*Pursuing her despairingly.*) No, no, oh, God, no! (*Turning at door.*) Stop laughing, you idiots. It isn't funny. It's a bloody tragedy.

But they only laugh the louder as the

CURTAIN FALLS

FLARE PATH

TO
KEITH NEWMAN

Characters:

PETER KYLE
COUNTESS SKRICZEVINSKY (DORIS)
MRS. OAKES
SERGEANT MILLER (DUSTY)
PERCY
FLYING-OFFICER COUNT SKRICZEVINSKY
FLIGHT-LIEUTENANT GRAHAM (TEDDY)
PATRICIA GRAHAM
MRS. MILLER (MAUDIE)
SQUADRON-LEADER SWANSON
CORPORAL JONES

ACT I   SATURDAY, ABOUT 6 P.M.
ACT II   SCENE 1 ABOUT THREE HOURS LATER
         SCENE 2 SUNDAY MORNING, ABOUT 5.30
ACT III   SUNDAY, ABOUT NOON

The action passes in the Residents' Lounge of the Falcon
Hotel at Milchester, Lincs.

Flare Path was first produced at the Apollo Theatre, London, on August 13th, 1942, with the following cast:

COUNTESS SKRICZEVINSKY ...	*Adrianne Allen*
PETER KYLE	*Martin Walker*
MRS. OAKES	*Dora Gregory*
SERGEANT MILLER	*Leslie Dwyer*
PERCY	*George Cole*
COUNT SKRICZEVINSKY ...	*Gerard Hinze*
FLIGHT-LIEUTENANT GRAHAM	*Jack Watling*
PATRICIA GRAHAM	*Phyllis Calvert*
MRS. MILLER	*Kathleen Harrison*
SQUADRON-LEADER SWANSON	*Ivan Samson*
CORPORAL JONES	*John Bradley*

The play directed by ANTHONY ASQUITH

ACT 1

SCENE: *The residents' lounge of the Falcon, at Milchester, Lincs.*

Downstage, L., a door marked 'Lounge Bar'. Upstage, L., a curved counter marked 'Reception', behind which is a door bearing the label 'Private'. Back, L., swing doors leading on to road. Large bow windows at back, with window seats. Staircase, R., leading to a small landing at back and thence out of sight. Downstage, R., a door marked 'Coffee Room'. Centre, R., a fireplace with fire burning.

On the rise of the curtain the sole occupant of the room is DORIS SKRICZEVINSKY, *a carelessly dressed woman in the early thirties, inclined to fat. She has fallen asleep in a large armchair, a copy of Everybody's open on her lap. A wireless at her side is emitting, at intervals, the trumpeted call sign of the B.B.C.*

PETER KYLE, *a man of about thirty-five, dressed in correct country attire—too correct to be convincing—comes in from the road, carrying a suitcase. He looks round, then goes up to the reception desk and rings a small handbell. Nothing happens. He rings again.* DORIS *wakes up.*

DORIS. (*Calling.*) Mrs. Oakes!

MRS. OAKES *comes in from the door marked 'Private', her office. She is a tall, angular woman of middle age.*

MRS. OAKES. Yes? (*Seeing* PETER.) Yes? What can I do for you?

PETER. I'd like a room, please.

MRS. OAKES. Single or double?

PETER. Single.

MRS. OAKES. Quite impossible. I'm sorry.

PETER. Oh.

There is a pause broken by the voice of the B.B.C. announcer.

ANNOUNCER. Hullo, Forces! Round the World in Eighty Days. A dramatization of the novel——

DORIS *switches it off.* MRS. OAKES, *paying no further attention to* PETER, *has come from behind her counter to collect a tea-tray.*

DORIS. (*Derisively.*) Round the world in eighty days! They do think up some queer ones, I must say.

87

MRS. OAKES. I never listen these days, except to the news. Finished with your tea, Countess?

DORIS. Yes, thank you, Mrs. Oakes.

MRS. OAKES takes up the tray. PETER is watching her, exasperated.

MRS. OAKES. Of course, I'm not saying it would be easy to think up new things all the time——

PETER. (*Loudly.*) What about a double?

MRS. OAKES. You said you wanted a single.

PETER. Yes, but if you haven't got a single, I'd like a double.

MRS. OAKES. I'm sorry. We're full right up.

PETER. Then why did you give me the choice of asking for a single or a double?

MRS. OAKES. You might have been a married couple.

PETER. I might have been a sultan and full harem, but I don't see that makes any difference. If you haven't got a room, you haven't got a room, have you?

MRS. OAKES. (*Unmoved.*) No. We haven't got a room. (*She goes into her office.*)

PETER turns round.

PETER. God, what a——

DORIS. (*Excitedly.*) Why, it is!

PETER. I beg your pardon.

DORIS. You're Peter Kyle, aren't you?

PETER. Yes, I am. (*Politely.*) I'm afraid——

DORIS. Oh, no. You wouldn't know me. I saw 'Light of Love' in Milchester only yesterday. Isn't that funny?

PETER. (*Abstractedly.*) Yes, it is. (*He makes an obvious effort to be polite.*) It's over two years old now—'Light of Love'.

DORIS. Oh, we only get the old ones in Milchester. Well, I never—this is a thrill!

PETER. It wasn't a good picture either, I'm afraid.

DORIS. Oh, it was quite good, really. One or two bits were rather silly, I thought. You were ever so good, though.

PETER. Thank you very much.

DORIS. Not at all. I always think you're good.

PETER. I'm so glad.

She stares at him in wonder and awe. PETER is evidently not unaccustomed to this. He walks forward and extends his hand graciously.

How do you do?

DORIS. Oh, how do you do. My name's Doris. I won't tell you the other name, because you'd never be able to pronounce it. (*She hastily tidies her crumpled frock.*) You came over here to arrange about your new picture, didn't you? I read all about it in the *Express*.

PETER. Yes.

DORIS. And you're giving all your salary to the Red Cross. I do think that's fine. Of course, you're English, aren't you?

PETER. By birth, yes. But I've been an American citizen for the last seven years.

DORIS. Well, well, well! Peter Kyle! Would you believe it— drifting into the old Falcon—just like that—and asking for a room.

PETER. And not getting it.

DORIS. Oh, don't you worry about that. The idea! (*Calling.*) Mrs. Oakes!

MRS. OAKES *emerges from her office.*

MRS. OAKES. Yes? (*Glaring at* PETER.) I thought I told you——

DORIS. (*Excitedly.*) Mrs. Oakes, don't you know who this gentleman is?

MRS. OAKES. No.

DORIS. Look at him carefully and then tell me if you don't recognize him.

MRS. OAKES *stares at* PETER.

MRS. OAKES. (*At length.*) No, I can't say I do.

DORIS. Look again. Look at him side-view, then you'll see. (*To* PETER.) Turn round.

PETER. (*Embarrassed.*) I think if you don't mind——

DORIS. There! You must know that smile. Who does it remind you of?

MRS. OAKES. (*At length.*) Mabel Smart's brother.

PETER. I think I'd better tell you my name straight away, otherwise this might go on all night. I'm Peter Kyle.

MRS. OAKES. Peter Kyle?

DORIS. Yes, you know. The film actor.

MRS. OAKES. An actor?

DORIS. (*Frenziedly.*) You must have seen him, Mrs. Oakes. He's at the Palace this week in 'Light of Love'.

MRS. OAKES. I don't go to the Palace. (*To* PETER.) Have you been at the Odeon in Skillingworth?

PETER. I've really no idea.

DORIS. Of course he has. He's very famous—so please, Mrs. Oakes, do try and fix him up if you can.

MRS. OAKES. (*To* PETER.) How long did you want to stay?

PETER. Just the one night.

MRS. OAKES. Just the one night. Well, Countess, seeing that the gentleman is a friend of yours I'll see what I can do.

PETER. That's terribly kind of you.

MRS. OAKES. Now, let me see. I could put up a bed for him in the attic—only I don't like to do that because of fire bombs.

PETER. I don't mind——

MRS. OAKES. No, but I do. I don't want my hotel burnt down.

PETER. But I'm not particularly inflammable.

MRS. OAKES. Possibly not—but the bed is. I know! There's Number Twelve. Wing-Commander Taylor. He's Duty Defence Officer, so he'll be sleeping up at the Station to-night. You can go in there. (*She opens the register.*) Will you register, please? And fill in this form.

PETER. I'll fill it in and give it to you later.

MRS. OAKES. I can't send you up at once, because the Wing-Commander might want to use his room before dinner.

PETER. That's quite all right.

MRS. OAKES. You must be careful not to touch any of the Wing-Commander's things. He's most particular. Oh! (*She examines the printed form.*) I see you're an alien.

PETER. (*Nervously.*) Er—yes, I am——

MRS. OAKES. (*Coldly.*) Dinner is at half-past seven. (*She goes into her office.*)

PETER. Evidently she thinks I'm a spy.

DORIS. Oh, no, I'm sure she doesn't. It's only that we get so few civilians round here. There's only the aerodrome, you see, and nothing else at all. We're all Air Force here, you know. I suppose you came to see someone up at the station?

PETER. Well—I——.

DORIS. I don't want to be inquisitive. I mean, curiosity killed the cat. But I just thought it was a funny place for a gentleman like you to come to, and I——

PETER. (*Deliberately.*) I was on my way to town. I passed this place and thought it might be fun to stay the night. That's all.

DORIS. Fancy. Well, I'm glad you did, I must say.

PETER. (*With automatic gallantry.*) So am I.

DORIS. (*Simpering.*) Silly.

PETER. (*Hastily.*) When you say you're Air Force, does that mean you work up at the aerodrome?

DORIS. Oh, no. I'm no W.A.A.F. I haven't the figure for it. No—my husband's a pilot.

PETER. Fighter pilot?

DORIS. (*Shocked.*) Oh, no, Bombers. Wellingtons. You must have seen them when you passed the aerodrome.

PETER. I'm not very good about aeroplanes——

DORIS. Aircraft. Yes, he's second pilot in a Wellington, is my Johnny. He's done quite a lot of raids. He's only got a few to go before they give him a rest. After a fixed number of operational trips they get given a rest, you know—put on to something safer—like teaching or groundwork. (*She delves in her bag.*) Have one of these. They're called Summer Crop. I should think they're pretty awful, but it's all they've got here.

PETER. You have one of these. They're Chesterfields.

DORIS. Oo, lovely! (*She takes one.*) However did you get them?

PETER. I smuggled over two thousand in with me from America.

DORIS. Naughty! Do tell me all about Hollywood. Do you know Carmen Miranda or Bing Crosby?

While she is speaking there is the sound of aircraft—heavy bombers— passing overhead. The noise is momentarily very loud. PETER *looks up.*

PETER. What are they?

DORIS. (*Casually.*) Stirlings, I expect. They're four-engine aircraft, anyway. Probably from Shepley. Been a day raid most likely. The boys'll know. Tell me, did you meet Carmen Miranda or Bing Crosby?

PETER. I've never met Carmen Miranda, but I know Bing Crosby fairly well.

DORIS. Fancy! Whatever's he like?

Another aircraft can be heard passing overhead. This time it is DORIS *who looks up.*

PETER. He's very nice. As a matter of fact, our houses are quite near each other and——

DORIS. (*Sharply.*) Sh! (*She jumps up and listens intently.*) There's something wrong with that one. (*She runs to the window, opens it, and sticks her head out.* PETER *follows her.*) There she is! See?

PETER. (*Looking out.*) Yes. God, what an enormous thing. It looks all right to me.

DORIS. She's flying on three engines. Been shot up, I expect. (*The sound passes into the distance.*) (*Suddenly.*) Oh, lor!

PETER. What's the matter?

DORIS. She's landing. Look! They've put the undercarriage down. She's going to land on our aerodrome.

PETER. My God, so it is. It's coming in.

There is a pause, while DORIS *and* PETER *stare intently out of the window. The sound of the aircraft engines fades suddenly as they are throttled back.* DORIS *turns quickly away from the window.* PETER *continues watching.*

DORIS. Is she down?

PETER. Yes, I think so. It's gone out of sight behind those hangars. (*He turns round from the window and moves as if to close it.* DORIS *stops him with a quick gesture. She is still listening intently. There comes the sound of the aircraft engines.*)

DORIS. It's all right. She's taxi-ing back. (*She nods to* PETER *to close the window.*)

PETER. It was in trouble all right. It was flying all lop-sided.

DORIS. Probably flown by the famous Chinese pilot—Wun Wing Low. (*She titters expectantly, but* PETER *does not laugh.*) Not my joke, Teddy Graham's. He's a flight-loot up at the Station. Ooo!—I've suddenly thought—you must know Mrs. Graham, Teddy Graham's wife—Patricia Warren, the actress, you know. She was in a play of yours in New York.

The part was only a—cough and a spit, she says, but you might remember her. She's staying here.

PETER. Really?

DORIS. Do you remember her?

PETER. Yes, I do.

DORIS. She's ever so nice, I think. Don't you?

PETER. Yes. Charming.

DORIS. She won't half be surprised when she sees you. She went up for a nap. Shall I call her down?

PETER. No, please don't. I'll see her later, anyway.

DORIS. She's only been here since yesterday morning. It's the first chance she's had of coming to see her hubby, as the play she was acting in in London only came off last week. He's just been made captain of a Wellington, too—she's as proud as proud of him. It's a treat to see them together—it is really.

PETER. (*Abruptly.*) I feel it's time for a drink. Can I get you one?

DORIS. Thank you, Mr. Kyle. I'll have a gin and lime. There's the bell by the door.

PETER *presses a bell. A man in the uniform of a Sergeant Air Gunner comes in from the road. He is about thirty-five, small, dark, and insignificant. His name is* DAVID MILLER, *and he is known, naturally, as* DUSTY.

DUSTY. Evening, Countess.

DORIS. Hullo, Dusty.

DUSTY. Spotted my wife anywhere?

DORIS. I don't think she's come yet, Dusty. She was coming by 'bus, wasn't she?

DUSTY. Four-twenty-five from Lincoln—so she should 'ave been 'ere twenty minutes ago. She's a proper mucker-upper though—she'll go and catch the wrong bus, you see—end up in Grimsby, and then blame me. (*While he is speaking he is taking off his overcoat. He now turns and sees* PETER.) Oh, excuse me——

PETER. We were just going to have a drink. Will you join us?

DUSTY. Thank you, sir. I don't mind.

PETER. I've rung the bell, but nothing seems to happen. (*To*

DUSTY.) What does A.G. stand for?

DUSTY }
DORIS } *(Simultaneously.)* Air gunner.

DORIS. Didn't you know that? You are ignorant.

PETER. Yes, I am, I'm afraid. So you're the man who sits in the rear turret?

DUSTY. That's right. Tail-end stooge—that's me.

PETER. What's it like being a tail-end stooge?

DUSTY. Oh, not so bad. Gets a bit cold sometimes.

PETER. A bit cold is an understatement, isn't it?

DUSTY. Don't know. Depends, really. Some nights it's all right. Other nights you come down and you got to get a bloke with a 'ammer and chisel to get you off of the seat.

A boy of about fifteen, PERCY, *wearing an apron, comes through the door marked 'Lounge'.*

PERCY. Anybody ring?

PETER. Yes, I rang. I want a gin and lime—— *(To* DUSTY.) What's yours?

DUSTY. Beer, please, sir.

PETER. A beer and a whisky and soda.

PERCY. *(With a broad smile.)* There's no whisky.

PETER. Then I'll have a gin and tonic.

PERCY. *(With a broader smile.)* There's no tonic.

PETER. Then bring me a pink gin.

PERCY. *(Disappointed.)* Yes, you can have that. *(To* DUSTY.) Was that a Stirling come down 'bout ten minutes ago, Sergeant?

DUSTY. That's none of your business what it was, Nosy.

PERCY. Garn, I knows a Stirling when I seen one. Anyone hurt inside?

DUSTY. *(With dignity.)* I've no idea, I'm sure.

PERCY. *(With relish.)* Bet there was. I saw an ambulance driving out. *(He goes out.)*

DORIS. Was anyone hurt?

DUSTY *nods.*

Bad?

DUSTY. Two bumped off—tail gunner and wireless op. Cannon shells. Other gunner caught it—not bad, though.

DORIS. Been a daylight do, has there?

DUSTY. Big one. (*With a glance at* PETER.) Talk about careless talk!

DORIS. Oh, don't mind him. You don't know who he is, do you?

DUSTY. No. Can't say I do.

DORIS. It's Peter Kyle.

DUSTY. (*After a pause.*) Cor! (*He gazes awestruck at* PETER.)

PETER. What's *your* name, Sergeant?

DUSTY. Miller, sir.

PETER. I'm glad to meet you. (*He shakes hands.*)

DUSTY. Peter Kyle. Well, I'm a—— Do you know Dorothy Lamour?

PETER. No. I can't say I do.

DUSTY. (*Plainly disappointed.*) Oh!

PERCY *comes in with the drinks.*

PERCY. It *was* a Stirling come down. Fred in the bar seen 'er, too.

DUSTY. Fred in the bar can be wrong sometimes, I presume, or is he omnificent?

PERCY. I don't know what he is, but 'e knows it was a Stirling. Shot up something terrible it was, 'e says.

PETER *pays him.*

PETER. Keep the change.

PERCY. (*Surprised.*) Thank you, sir. Thank you. (*At door.*) Where's it tonight, Sergeant? Berlin?

DUSTY. It'll be a clip on the ear-'ole for you, my lad, if I 'ave any more of your lip. Beat it!

PERCY *goes. His voice can be heard in the lounge before the door closes behind him.*

PERCY. (*Off.*) Sergeant says it's Berlin tonight.

DUSTY. Cor! Did you hear that?

DORIS. Needs a good spanking. (*To* DUSTY, *in a low voice.*) Nothing on tonight, is there, dear?

DUSTY. Not so far as I know.

DORIS. (*Cheerfully.*) Tinkerty-tonk, Mr. Kyle!

PETER. Good health!

They drink. There is the sound of a car drawing up in the road out-

side, and a Flying-Officer (COUNT SKRICZEVINSKY) *comes in. He wears the Polish Air Force eagle over the left breast, and the word 'Poland' on his shoulders. He is over forty, tall and thin, with a permanent and slightly bewildered smile.*

DORIS. Hullo, Johnny ducks, you're early. (*She comes forward, kisses him lightly on the cheek, and brings him forward to* DUSTY *and* PETER.) Is Teddy with you?

COUNT. 'E—poots—car—garage. (*He speaks English with the greatest difficulty, always retaining his bewildered expression.*)

DUSTY. Evening, sir.

COUNT. Good—evening.

DORIS. Johnny, I want you to meet a very famous man.

COUNT. Pardon?

DORIS. (*Pointing at* PETER.) Very—famous—man. Film star. Understand? Peter Kyle.

COUNT. (*Not having understood.*) Oh, yes—please.

PETER. How do you do? (*He shakes hands. The* COUNT *clicks his heels slightly.*)

DORIS. Isn't he sweet when he does that? First time I met him he kissed my hand. Of course, I had to fall for him after that, didn't I, Johnny ducks?

The COUNT *smiles at her vaguely and she squeezes his hand.*

You must excuse his English, Mr. Kyle. It's not up to much, but it's getting better. He's having English lessons up at the Station—aren't you, Johnny ducks?

COUNT. Please?

DUSTY. English—lessons, sir. Your wife says you are having English lessons.

COUNT. (*With a sudden burst of loquacity.*) Oh, yes. English lessons. I learn much. 'Ow are you today, Mrs. Brown, please? Se Eiffel Tower is se towellest beelding in se vurruld.

DORIS. World, Johnny, world. Not vurruld.

COUNT. World. World.

MRS. OAKES *appears at the office door.*

MRS. OAKES. Good evening, Count.

COUNT. Good evening, missus.

MRS. OAKES. You'll be in to dinner, I presume?

COUNT. Oh, yes, sank you, please.

MRS. OAKES. And you'll be staying the night? No early break-
fasts or late suppers? (*She winks heavily.*)

COUNT. No, please. Tonight I stye wiss my vife.

MRS. OAKES *nods and goes out.*

DORIS. (*To* COUNT.) Not stye. Stay. Tonight I stay with my
wife.

DUSTY (*Calling.*) Oh, Mrs. Oakes!

MRS. OAKES' *head reappears.*

MRS. OAKES. Yes?

DUSTY. It's all right about that double room for tonight,
isn't it?

MRS. OAKES. Yes. You've got Number 2. Do you want to go
up now.

DUSTY. No, thanks. The wife's not come yet. Should've been
'ere an hour ago. (*Gloomily.*) Just like her, I will say.

MRS. OAKES. She'll turn up—you'll find.

Her head disappears as TEDDY GRAHAM *comes in through the front-
door. He is a Flight-Lieutenant, and wears the D.F.C. His age is
twenty-four.*

TEDDY. Hullo, Doris, my beautiful. How's every little thing?
Evening, Sergeant. Where's the wife?

DUSTY. Don't know, sir. Gone off course a bit—looks like.

TEDDY. You told me her navigation was pretty ropy.

DUSTY. It's lousy. If she don't come soon I'll post her as missing—believed got in the wrong 'bus.

TEDDY. I should. Johnny, you clot! What about that beer you
were going to get me?

COUNT. I not forget. (*He rings bell.* TEDDY *suddenly sees* PETER *and
approaches him cautiously.*)

TEDDY. Good God! It's—not—Peter Kyle—is it?

DORIS. Yes it is, Teddy. It really is. Isn't it wonderful?

TEDDY. Pukka gen?

DUSTY. Pukka gen, sir.

TEDDY. Good lord! I say—I mean—Good lord! I say, I'm
most awfully glad to meet you, sir, and all that.

PETER. Must you call me 'sir'?

TEDDY. No, I suppose not—I mean—Peter Kyle! Well, well,

well! (*He shakes* PETER's *hand energetically.*) This calls for a party, don't you think, boys and girls? (*Calling.*) Percy!

COUNT. Please—I wish——

TEDDY. All right, Johnny—these are mine. (*Pointing at* PETER.) Very famous bloke here, Johnny.

COUNT. Oh, yes, sank you.

PERCY *appears promptly, his manner, when he speaks to* TEDDY, *surprisingly deferential.*

PERCY. Yes, Flight-Lieutenant Graham, sir?

TEDDY. Where have *you* been? We've been ringing for half an hour.

PERCY. Sorry, sir. Didn't know it was you, Flight-Lieutenant Graham.

TEDDY. Another round for these people, whatever they're having, Percy, and pints for the Count and me.

PERCY. Yes, sir. Berlin tonight, Flight-Lieutenant Graham?

TEDDY. What? No, Percy. Home, Sweet Home, tonight.

PERCY'S *face falls. He goes out.*

TEDDY. I say, this has rather shaken me—you know—I mean your being here, in the old Falcon—just like—I mean—a commercial traveller or something. No offence, or any- thing——

PETER. That's all right.

TEDDY. Good lord, you must know Pat. That's my wife. Patricia Warren. She was—still is—I mean she still uses the name and all that. (*Calling.*) Pat! Pat! Are you upstairs?

PATRICIA. (*Her voice coming from upstairs.*) Hullo, Teddy. I heard you come in.

TEDDY. Come on down. There's something down here that's going to shake you considerably.

PATRICIA. Oh? Just coming.

TEDDY. I say, I suppose you do know her. I mean, she was in a play of yours, you know—tiny part, but she shoots a line about your having been very kind to her and all that——

PETER. Does she? Yes, I remember her well.

TEDDY. Look—you go there—(*He points to a place directly beneath the stairs.*)—so she won't see you as she comes down——

PETER. (*Protestingly.*) No, I think——

DORIS. (*Pushing him.*) Go on, silly! Look out!

PATRICIA GRAHAM *comes down the stairs. She is about* TEDDY'S *age, perhaps a year or two older.*

PATRICIA. What's all this about my being shaken?

TEDDY. Nothing, darling. Just to get you to come down.

PATRICIA. Hullo, Johnny. Good evening, Doris.

TEDDY. This is Sergeant Miller—my tail gunner. A very bad type——

PATRICIA. He doesn't look it. How do you do? (*Brightly.*) It's funny the loose way you Air Force people use your slang. For instance, to shake someone or to be shaken seems to cover anything from crashing in flames to seeing a caterpillar or something.

PETER *emerges from the recess under the stairs.* PATRICIA *is facing him. She stands quite still.* PETER *smiles, but she does not smile in return. She turns her head quickly to look at* TEDDY, *who is gazing at her, smiling expectantly. Then she looks back at* PETER.

PETER. Hullo.

PATRICIA. Hullo. (*They shake hands.*)

TEDDY. Well, darling, are you shaken, or are you shaken? Now, be honest.

PATRICIA. I'll be honest. I'm shaken.

PERCY *comes in, staggering under the weight of a loaded tray.* Which of these is for me?

TEDDY. Well—as a matter of fact——

PATRICIA. Teddy, you don't mean to tell me you've left me out? I'll have a pink gin.

TEDDY. Another pink gin, Percy.

PERCY. Yes, sir.

TEDDY. Come on, everybody.

PERCY *goes out.*

PATRICIA. (*To* PETER.) When did you arrive?

DORIS. Only a few minutes ago. Just fancy—Peter Kyle blowing into the old Falcon—just like that. Happened to be passing and thought it would be fine to stay the night. You should have seen my face.

PATRICIA. (*Brightly.*) Yes. What's the news from the aerodrome, Teddy?

TEDDY. Nothing much. (*Raising his glass.*) Cheers, everybody!

PATRICIA. There must be some news, or are you going all careless talk on me?

TEDDY. First time I've ever known you take an interest in what's going on at the aerodrome. As a matter of fact, it's been a quiet day, hasn't it, Sarge?

DUSTY. Pretty quiet, sir.

TEDDY. A Stirling force-landed a few minutes ago. You probably saw it.

PETER. The Countess and I saw it.

DORIS. Don't call me Countess, please, Mr. Kyle. Or, if you do, give me my full name, which is Countess Skriczevinsky. (*She screws her face up in a mock effort to pronounce the name.*)

COUNT. (*Correcting her gently.*) Please Countess Skriczevinsky.

DORIS. Get Johnny correcting me for a change!

There is a general laugh. The COUNT *looks slightly more bewildered.* Sorry, ducks. I can say it. I was only fooling. (*Correctly.*) Countess Skriczevinsky.

The COUNT *smiles.*

PATRICIA. What was the matter with the Stirling that force-landed?

TEDDY. Been shot up in a raid. Big raid, too, I believe. I can't tell you where, of course.

PERCY *comes in with* PATRICIA's *pink gin.*

PERCY. 'Ell of a do on Kiel this afternoon.

TEDDY. (*Startled.*) Come here, Percy. (*Regarding him sternly.*) Who told you that?

PERCY. Just come through on the six o'clock.

TEDDY. Oh, the laugh's on me.

PERCY. 'Ell of a do it must 'ave been. Blenheims, Wimpeys, 'Alifaxes, and Stirlings. We lost seventeen. Shot down twenty-two of theirs, though. (*He goes out.*)

TEDDY. Seventeen? Not too good. (*He meets* DUSTY's *eye.*) I reckon the squadron's done pretty well up to now to keep out of these daylight do's, don't you?

DUSTY. (*Fervently.*) You're telling me.

COUNT. (*Suddenly.*) I—have—wish to go on sese daylight do's.

TEDDY. You mean you don't have wish.

COUNT. No, no. I *do* have wish. I have wish to see my bombs to fall——

There is a slight pause.

TEDDY. I see what you mean, Johnny old boy.

PATRICIA. I want another drink.

TEDDY. Good lord! You haven't finished that one already?

PATRICIA. Yes.

PETER. (*Calling.*) Percy!

PERCY *appears at door.*

(*Politely.*) What were you drinking, Mrs. Graham?

PATRICIA. Thank you, Mr. Kyle. It was a pink gin.

PETER. A pink gin for Mrs. Graham—and the same again for the others.

PERCY *goes out.*

DORIS. My Johnny'll be getting tinky-boo. He can't stand more than a couple, can you, ducks?

COUNT. Yes, please.

DORIS. You mean, no, thank you.

COUNT. No, sank you.

DORIS. Thank you, Johnny. Thank. Th-ank.

COUNT. Sank you. Sank you.

TEDDY. Good old Johnny. Keep cracking—it'll come.

PERCY *comes in with new drinks.*

PERCY. (*Off.*) Hurry up with those pints, Fred.

TEDDY. Just as well we've got tonight at home, eh, Dusty?

DUSTY. (*Gloomily.*) I wouldn't put it past 'em to send us out now. They done it before.

TEDDY. Dusty's the world's prize moaner. He even moaned to me over the intercomm. because he'd shot down a Messerschmitt. Tell them about it, Dusty.

DUSTY. (*Alarmed.*) No, Mr. Graham, sir, please. Not now.

PATRICIA. (*Politely.*) Do tell us, Sergeant.

DUSTY. It's nothing, mum, really. Mr. Graham's told you it's only I shot down a Messerschmitt, I think.

TEDDY. What do you mean, you think? It was at night, Patricia. Nothing else in the sky for miles around except us and this 110,.and he still thinks someone else might have shot it down. Tell 'em, Dusty.

DUSTY. They'll think it's a line, sir.

PATRICIA. Why don't *you* tell the story, Teddy?

TEDDY. I didn't see it. We were stooging along over the Dutch coast somewhere, and suddenly I hear Dusty's voice over the intercomm., saying: (*Imitating* DUSTY's *gloomy voice.*) "'Ullo, skipper. Tail calling. Me. 110's just been at us. Sod's gone into the drink on fire. Over.'

There is a general laugh. DUSTY *looks acutely uncomfortable.*

'Gone' is the operative word.

PATRICIA. (*To* DUSTY.) You did shoot at it, though, didn't you?

DUSTY. Oh, yes, mum. I shot at it all right. Bright moon there was. Saw it as clear as I'm seeing you. He opens up 'bout five 'undred yards with 'is cannons, and I've got 'im in my sights, and 'e's getting bigger all the time, and I press the triggers and there's a ruddy great glow all of a sudden and down 'e goes into the drink turning and twisting. I thought——

There is a pause. Everyone, including the COUNT, *is listening intently.*

DUSTY. Crikey!

PATRICIA. That's not what I'd have thought.

DUSTY. First time I'd ever seen a Messerschmitt, and down he goes—just like that. (*He clicks his teeth unbelievingly.*)

TEDDY. Good show, Dusty. You get another beer for that.

A small woman, much muffled up, enters from the road and comes down R. DUSTY *puts his beer down and walks forward.*

DUSTY. 'Ullo, Maudie.

MAUDIE. Hullo, Dave.

They do not kiss. The others have politely turned their backs.

DUSTY. Got on the wrong bus, did you, Maudie?

MAUDIE. (*Accusingly.*) You said the Skillingworth bus, Dave.

DUSTY. Yes, that's right. Four-twenty-five from Lincoln.

MAUDIE. Well, I went to Skillingworth and you weren't there.

DUSTY. Lor, Maudie, I didn't tell you to go to Skillingworth. You should 'ave got off at Milchester.

MAUDIE. (*Still accusingly.*) You said the Skillingworth bus, Dave.

DUSTY. Yes, but the Skillingworth bus goes through Milchester; you should 'ave got off at Milchester.

MAUDIE. You never said nothing about Milchester. You don't
look very well, Dave. Have you been getting those backaches?

DUSTY *looks round hurriedly at the others.*

DUSTY. (*Hastily.*) Here, Maudie! You sign your name here.

MAUDIE. (*Not to be put off.*) Because if you have, I've brought
that medicine you left behind last leave—the one your
doctor gave you——

DUSTY. All right, Maudie. Here's where you sign. Here.

TEDDY *detaches himself from the other group.*

TEDDY. So she got in to base at last, Dusty.

DUSTY. Yes, sir. Brought her in on the beam.

TEDDY. How do you do, Mrs. Miller?

DUSTY. This is Flight-Lieutenant Graham, Maudie—you
know—the one I was telling you about. He's my
skipper.

MAUDIE. Pleased to meet you.

TEDDY. How do you think he's looking?

MAUDIE. A bit peaky, I told him. I think he must have been
getting those backaches of his——

DUSTY. (*Hastily.*) If you'll excuse us, sir, we'll be nipping upstairs——

TEDDY. See you both later.

DUSTY *shepherds* MAUDIE *across the room to the stairs, carrying her
small suitcase.*

MAUDIE. (*On the stairs.*) The man at Skillingworth said I should
have caught the four-forty-five from Lincoln.

DUSTY. (*Heatedly.*) He doesn't know what he's talking about.
Four-twenty-five's all right, if you done what I told you.

MAUDIE. He said the four-forty-five doesn't go through Skillingworth at all, and all I had to do was to change into a Milchester bus at Windowbrook—you did say the Skillingworth
bus, Dave. (*They pass out of sight.*)

PETER. The henpecked hero.

DORIS. Dusty's not henpecked, believe me. I bet he gives as
good as he gets. Shall *we* go upstairs, Johnny ducks? I must

tidy up a bit and dinner's quite soon, and you'll want a shave.

COUNT. Please?

DORIS. Shave, dear. (*She strokes his chin.*)

COUNT. Oh, yes. Not—shave—sis—morning. Very—pricky.

DORIS. Prickly, duckie.

PATRICIA. Perhaps he meant pretty.

DORIS. He meant prickly—and he's right. I don't like my beautiful going about looking like an old porcupine. Come on, Johnny. Upstairs.

COUNT. (*With a great effort.*) Yes. Excuse, please. I must go up to my room where I will shave.

TEDDY. Terrific, Johnny! Well done!

COUNT. (*Delighted.*) That was good how I am saying him?

DORIS. Yes, my precious, but that wasn't. That was bloody awful how you were saying him. (*They pass out of sight.*)

TEDDY. Talk about henpecking—Doris rules her old Count with a rod of iron.

There is a pause. Neither PATRICIA *nor* PETER *answer him.* PATRICIA *is occupied in not looking at* PETER.

PETER. What's that? I'm sorry.

TEDDY. I said Doris rules her old Count with a rod of iron.

PETER. Yes. I feel awfully sorry for him.

TEDDY. Why? Doris is all right.

PETER. Yes. She seems charming. Only—well, of course, it may be that he doesn't speak any English.

TEDDY. Even if he didn't speak a word of English, I don't think he'd run any risk of mistaking Doris for the Duchess of Dillwater.

PETER. No, I suppose not. How long have they been married?

TEDDY. I don't know. He was married to her when they formed the Polish Squadron on the Station. He's good value, old Johnny. (*He finishes his beer.*) I'm going to have a bath before dinner. (*He strolls to the stairs.*) I'm sure you two are longing to get down to a nice theatrical gossip match.

PETER. We'll have quite a lot to talk about, I expect.

TEDDY. (*On the stairs.*) I bet you will. All about Angel Fanny and Sweetie-pie Cyril. Darling, can I borrow your eau-de-Cologne?

PATRICIA. Yes, but don't take too much—it's absolutely priceless.

TEDDY. I'm going to pour it on with a bucket. If I can't look like the screen's great lover, I can at least smell like a glamour boy. So long. (*He goes out of sight, whistling. There is a pause.*)

PETER. He's nice, but what a baby!

PATRICIA *looks angrily at him.*

Darling, don't be angry, please.

PATRICIA. Angry? (*Wearily.*) Oh, lord, what an idiot you are!

PETER. I don't see that I've done anything so wrong in coming down to face the music.

PATRICIA. Face the music? How beautifully Hollywood! What was your idea? To get Teddy alone and say 'I love your wife'?

PETER. If you must know, yes.

PATRICIA. (*Bitterly.*) How did you visualize the scene after that? Was it like your last film, when you let Spencer Tracy knock you down, and saved each other's lives just before the fade-out? (*She turns away from him.*) And you call Teddy a baby!

PETER. (*Stubbornly.*) I'm sorry, but I've never been able to see why you should have to do the telling alone.

PATRICIA. Because this isn't a film, and there's no need for you to worry about whether you're playing a sympathetic part.

PETER. You're being rather brutal.

PATRICIA. (*Near tears.*) I'm trying to be.

PETER. (*Approaching her.*) Pat, darling.

PATRICIA *turns quickly away,* PETER *staring at her, bewildered.*

PETER. This hasn't made any difference, has it?

PATRICIA. Of course it hasn't made any difference.

PETER. (*After a pause.*) I'll go away tonight.

PATRICIA. What's the use? He's seen you and spoken to you. He's heard us calling each other Mr. Kyle and Mrs.

F

Graham. You've quite quietly reduced the whole thing to the level of a rather nasty little intrigue.

PETER. (*Obstinately.*) You'd much better let me tell him. I can explain——

PATRICIA. (*Violently.*) I'm the one to tell him—the only one, Pete.

PETER *looks at her in silence, then shrugs his shoulders and turns away. There is a pause. Then* PATRICIA *follows him and puts her hand on his arm.*

PATRICIA. (*With a change of tone.*) Sorry, Pete. Oh, darling. (*Kisses him.*) I am hating all this, you see.

PETER. I know. Are you sure I can't help?

PATRICIA. I'm afraid you can't. Nobody can.

PETER. What are you going to tell him?

PATRICIA. Everything.

PETER. Starting way back?

PATRICIA. Way back. It *is* way back, I suppose?

PETER. April twenty-seventh, nineteen thirty-eight.

PATRICIA. You always did have a date complex.

PETER. So did you. What about our celebrations on the twenty-seventh of every month? You can't have forgotten them?

PATRICIA. (*Nodding.*) Fifteen altogether.

PETER. I wish you'd told him that part of it when you married him. Then this wouldn't be so difficult now.

PATRICIA. In films the wife always tells her husband about her past affairs—doesn't she?

PETER. Shut up about films, darling. Why didn't you tell him? Funk?

PATRICIA. No, I didn't see why I should.

PETER. Yes, but I still think it would have been better——

PATRICIA. Pete, don't be so dense. If I'd told him anything about you at all, I'd have had to admit that I was still in love with you when I married him—and that was something I didn't want to admit even to myself.

Pause.

PETER. You *were* a fool to run out on me, weren't you?

PATRICIA. You *were* a fool to let me go.

PETER. Well, I couldn't very well have stopped you, could I?

PATRICIA. You could have come over here a bit sooner than you did. I couldn't go to you after the war—or a letter would have been rather nice.

PETER. I was making a big experiment, darling, you know that—trying to live without you. It wasn't a success.

PATRICIA. Nor was mine.

Pause. PETER *looks at her for a moment, then turns away.*

PETER. (*In a deliberately casual voice.*) When you married Teddy, how much did you feel for him?

PATRICIA. I don't know, Pete; he didn't give me much chance. He was on a week's leave, and we were married before he went back to his Squadron. What the papers would call a whirlwind wartime romance.

PETER. But now you do know, don't you?

PATRICIA. Yes, I know now.

PETER *turns to her.*

PETER. Tell me, then, how much do you feel for him now?

PATRICIA *smiles.*

I'm horribly jealous of him. You know that.

PATRICIA. I'd be angry if you weren't. You can't know anyone as well as that without feeling something, and something rather strong.

PETER. Is there much to know?

PATRICIA. Not much—but what there is, is—well—just terribly nice. (*After a slight pause.*) But in the sense which you mean, I don't feel anything for him at all.

PETER. That's true, isn't it, Pat?

PATRICIA. Yes, it's true. I'd have given quite a lot to have said to you the other day, 'Go back to America, Mr. Kyle. I'm married and in love, and I don't want you.' It's a pity I couldn't, isn't it?

PETER. I suppose you might say it's a pity for both of us, but somehow I don't think so. (*They embrace.*) You won't run out on me again, will you?

PATRICIA. You know why I did, don't you?

PETER. Because of the row——

PATRICIA. Not because of the row. If it hadn't been over that, it would have been over something else. I ran out purely and simply because I couldn't bear not being married to you.

PETER. (*Laughing*.) Considering we'd been living—as you might say—in sin—for well over a year——

PATRICIA. I know. I hated Rita for not giving you a divorce, but you see even after we'd been living together for months and months people still behaved to me as the latest Peter Kyle girl friend. In the end it made me so frightened of losing you that I ran away from you. D'you understand that?

PETER. No.

PATRICIA. (*Smiling*.) Of course you don't. It's mad, isn't it?

PETER. Absolutely batty—anyway, now that Rita has given in.

PATRICIA. Don't worry. All the Ritas in the world wouldn't get me to make the same mistake again—or any mistake again. (*After a pause*.) I'll tell Teddy tonight. Ring the bell; I want another drink.

PETER *does so*.

PETER. Why didn't you last night?

PATRICIA. There was a party. They were all very sweet, and they all had gallons of beer, and they all sang songs, very bawdy most of them—and finally two or three of them passed out like logs.

PETER. What about Teddy? Did he pass out, too?

PATRICIA. Yes. I had to put him to bed, poor lamb.

PETER. Charming for you.

PATRICIA. No, it wasn't—I mean, it was, rather.

PETER. It couldn't have been.

PATRICIA. I don't know. I quite enjoyed it. Perhaps because I was so relieved that I hadn't got to tell him.

Enter PERCY.

PERCY. You rang?

PETER. Yes, Percy. I want a pink gin for Mrs. Graham.

PERCY. Coo! That's the third, isn't it?

PETER. Yes, Percy. That's the third.

PERCY. Coo! (*He turns to go*.)

TEDDY *appears on the landing*.

TEDDY. Hey, Percy! (*To the others.*) You've ordered, haven't you?

PETER. Yes, we have.

PERCY. Yes, sir?

TEDDY. Get me a beer.

PERCY. O.K., Flight-Lieutenant Graham, sir. (PERCY *goes out.*)

PATRICIA. You've been very quick.

TEDDY. As far as a bath went, I've had it.

PETER. You had a bath?

TEDDY. No. The water was cold.

PETER. But you said you had it.

TEDDY. I had it—meaning I didn't have it.

PETER. How can you have had it when you didn't have it? I don't understand.

PATRICIA. You're being very dense. It's Air Force slang.

PETER. Oh, I see. So you're still unbathed?

TEDDY. Yes, but I smell gorgeous. Smell!

PETER. Gorgeous.

TEDDY. (*To* PATRICIA.) Smell!

PATRICIA. Gorgeous, Teddy.

PETER. How long have we got before dinner?

TEDDY. About half an hour, if it's not out on its E.T.A.

PETER. E.T.A.?

TEDDY. Estimated time of arrival.

PETER. Oh, I see. Well, I think *I'll* go up now. I haven't even seen my room yet. (*He walks up the stairs.*)

TEDDY. Did you have a nice bee, you two?

PETER. (*On the stairs.*) Yes, thank you, Teddy. (*He leans over the banisters.*) Do you mind me calling you Teddy?

TEDDY. Good lord, no! It's an honour.

PETER. An honour? Thank you, Teddy. (*He goes out.*)

TEDDY. Nice bloke, considering.

PATRICIA. Considering what?

TEDDY. He's an actor.

PATRICIA. Thank you for the comment on my profession.

TEDDY. Darling, don't be a clot. I didn't mean you. You're the old exception that proves the old rule, if you see what I mean.

PATRICIA. What old rule is that?

TEDDY. Well, actors are funny blokes. They never seem to be themselves. They only worry about what sort of effect they're having on other people.

PATRICIA. They act—in other words?

PERCY *comes in with the drinks.*

TEDDY. Yes, I suppose that's it. They never seem to do or say anything naturally. They're always thinking of an invisible audience. I bet they even act in the bathroom. (*He takes a beer from* PERCY, *who goes out giggling.*)

PERCY. (*Off, in the lounge.*) Do you know what Flight-Lieutenant Graham just said? He said——

The door closes.

TEDDY. Percy'll get me a bad reputation. Don't you agree, though, darling?

PATRICIA. (*Lightly.*) Not altogether. I think they feel things like other people, you know—although, I admit, they're inclined to act what they feel rather than just—feel.

TEDDY. Oh, well. Perhaps you're right. Don't let's argue, anyway. We never have and we never will. (*He raises his glass.*) Cheers, darling!

PATRICIA. Cheers! (*She gulps her drink, and makes a wry face.*)

TEDDY. I say. That went down the old hatch pretty quick, didn't it?

PATRICIA. Teddy——

TEDDY. Darling, I've just thought. Talking about actors acting and all that. We all act, in a way. At least, I know I do.

PATRICIA. (*Smiling.*) Do you, Teddy?

TEDDY. (*Seriously.*) Yes, I do. I don't mean with you, so much. Up in the mess, with the blokes. They call me P. O. Prune —he's a character in the Training Manual—sort of crazy, good-tempered, half-witted sort of bloke—you know the type—and I—well, I kind of act P.O. Prune for them. Yesterday, for instance, I was up on an air test, and I saw the C.O.'s car pulling out of the gate, so I put the old Wimpey into a dive and beat him up—you know, pulled out only a few feet above his head and stooged round him. I didn't particularly like doing it, and I had the hell of a strip torn off about it afterwards—but—well—I was being P.O. Prune, you see, and the blokes had a good laugh.

PATRICIA *is staring at him. When he finishes she turns her head away quickly.* TEDDY *notices the movement.*

Sorry. I'm being a bore.

PATRICIA. (*Uncertainly.*) No, you're not. Go on.

TEDDY. I say, Pat, is anything the matter?

PATRICIA. (*Wipes her eyes quickly.*) Nothing. I'm being an actress, that's all.

TEDDY. (*Puzzled.*) Did I say anything?

PATRICIA. No. I'm a bit tight, I think. When I'm tight I get weepy. I'm all right now.

TEDDY. Lesson to me not to talk about myself. I'm ashamed of you, Graham, making a woman cry. (*There is an awkward pause.*) Oh, by the way. Have you any plans for tomorrow evening?

PATRICIA. (*Uncertainly.*) No—I—that's to say, I don't think so.

TEDDY. Let's go over to Lincoln and beat up the Saracen's Head a trifle, shall we?

PATRICIA. If you like.

TEDDY. We might take old Johnny and Doris along with us, too. I've got an idea this hole is getting you down a bit. We'll make a night of it tomorrow.

PATRICIA. (*Impulsively.*) Teddy——

TEDDY. Yes?

PATRICIA. I've got something I must tell you.

TEDDY. All right. Don't look so serious about it. What is it?

PATRICIA. Not here. Shall we go upstairs?

TEDDY. This sounds awful. You look like our C.O. at his worst. Are you going to tear me off a strip?

PATRICIA *is already walking up the stairs.*

PATRICIA. Don't talk, Teddy, please.

TEDDY. I know. You want me to pay a dress bill.

PATRICIA. (*Violently.*) Don't talk!

An Air Force officer, SQUADRON-LEADER SWANSON, *comes in quickly. He is about fifty-five, and wears last war medals, but no wings.*

SWANSON. Teddy—thank the Lord I've found you.

TEDDY. Hullo, Gloria.

SWANSON. Come here, quick. (*Seeing* PATRICIA.) Oh, excuse me.

TEDDY. This is my wife. Squadron-Leader Swanson—our adjutant—a shocking type.

SWANSON. Good evening, Mrs. Graham. Can you spare me your husband for a moment?

TEDDY. Is it anything important? We were just——

SWANSON. Yes, it is. Damned important.

Pause. TEDDY *nods.*

TEDDY. Oh. Oh, I see. (*To* PATRICIA.) You'll have to excuse me, darling. Go along to our room.

PATRICIA *looks from one to the other. Then without a word she goes along the passage.*

SWANSON. (*Sternly.*) What's the idea of marrying a glamour girl? She's far too good-looking for a type like you.

TEDDY. I could marry Garbo if I tried. What's the trouble, Gloria?

SWANSON. You know.

TEDDY. (*Simply.*) Damn!

SWANSON. Just come through from Group.

TEDDY. What time take-off?

SWANSON. 22.00 hours. Briefing 19.45.

TEDDY. This is a hell of a time to let us know. Who's going? Everyone?

SWANSON. No. A Apples, L London, U Uncle. And a kite from the Polish Squadron—S Sugar.

TEDDY. Johnny's. What's the job?

SWANSON. Special. Very hush-hush. Not exactly a piece of cake, I believe. What in hell was the idea of pooping off the Station like that? They told you this morning something might still come through.

TEDDY. They knew where to find me. I went up to ops. at five-thirty. There was nothing on then—and, Christ, if Group can't make up their minds by five-thirty——

SWANSON. I wouldn't have put it past you, P. O. Prune, to have gone roaring off to Brighton or somewhere for the weekend, and then we'd have had a pretty little court-martial on our hands.

TEDDY. You'd have got me out of it, Gloria.

SWANSON. I bloody well wouldn't. What have you done with your crew?

TEDDY. They're all up at the station except Miller, the gunner. He's here. His wife's come down, poor blighter. I suppose we can't find a relief for him, can we?

SWANSON. No, it's too late. I gather you brought old Count Kiss-me-Quick down with you?

TEDDY. Yes. He's here.

SWANSON. Then you'd all better get cracking. You can use my car.

TEDDY. I'll use my own. (*He goes to foot of stairs. Calling.*) Johnny! Sergeant Miller! What's the met. report like?

SWANSON. All right, I think.

COUNT *appears, followed by* DORIS.

COUNT. What is, please?

TEDDY. Come on down. Sorry, Doris. No wives.

DORIS. Oh, I get you. O.K., ducks. (*She goes back up the stairs, meeting* DUSTY *on the landing.*) You're wanted, Dusty. (*She goes out.*)

DUSTY *looks down at the group below, then frames an inaudible but obvious expletive.*

DUSTY. (*Calling.*) Stay there, Maudie. I'll be back in a tick. (*He comes downstairs.*)

TEDDY. (*In a low voice.*) We've got some nice cheerful news for you boys. It's going to make your evening.

DUSTY. Didn't I tell you this'd happen?

TEDDY. You did, Dusty.

COUNT. We—go out tonight?

TEDDY. Yes, Johnny. Take-off 22.00. Briefing 19.45.

DUSTY. 'Ell of a time to tell us, I must say. Caught us bending proper this time. Group must be fair busting their stays with laughter.

TEDDY. I bet they are. Are you all ready, Johnny?

COUNT. I go upstairs. One minute only.

TEDDY. Go and say goodbye to your wife, Dusty. I'm sorry this had to happen. I'll drive you both up. I'll just go and get the car out.

SWANSON. I'll follow you later. I'm not going away from here without a drink.

SWANSON *goes into lounge.* TEDDY *goes out at back.* MAUDIE *has come quietly down the stairs.*

DUSTY. Maudie, I told you to stay in the room.

MAUDIE. What's up, Dave?

DUSTY. Bit of bad luck, Maudie. I got to leave you tonight.

MAUDIE. I only got one night. Don't go out tonight, Dave.

DUSTY. It's not my doing, old girl. Been a bit of a muck-up at Group.

MAUDIE. What's Group?

DUSTY. Group headquarters. Where the orders come from.

MAUDIE. Why don't you tell them your wife's come down, and she's only got the one night? They might send one of the other boys instead.

DUSTY. No go, Maudie.

MAUDIE. Oh, Dave.

DUSTY. I tell you what. After you've had your supper—good supper they give you 'ere, too—you go up to bed, see, and get some sleep. I'll be back 'bout four or maybe five, and we'll still have some time together. Your bus don't go till one tomorrow.

MAUDIE. All right, Dave. If they tell you you've got to do it, you've got to do it, I suppose. Try and get back soon.

DUSTY. 'Course I will. I'll be back before you know I'm gone. I got the best skipper in England, and I'll tell him to step on it tonight.

TEDDY *has come in quickly in time to hear the last sentence. He waits a second, then walks forward.*

TEDDY. Oh, Mrs. Miller, I'm terribly sorry about this—it's the cruellest bad luck.

MAUDIE. I was asking Dave, Mr. Graham, if it wouldn't do no good to tell this Group that his wife's come down?

TEDDY. (*Gently.*) I'm afraid not. You see, there wouldn't be time.

MAUDIE. Oh, I see. (*To* DUSTY.) You going now?

DUSTY. This minute, Maudie.

MAUDIE. Goodbye, Dave.

DUSTY. Goodbye, old girl. You do what I told you, now. Get some sleep.

TEDDY. If there's anything you want, Mrs. Miller, I know my wife would be only too glad——

MAUDIE. No, thank you, Mr. Graham. There won't be nothing. (*She goes up the stairs.*)

DUSTY *blows a kiss to* MAUDIE, *and goes out quickly.*

(*On the stairs.*) Take care of him, sir. Don't let him go doing none of those silly tricks like he was telling me about— shooting at searchlights and such.

TEDDY. No, I won't. I promise you.

MAUDIE *goes out, passing the* COUNT, *who comes running down the stairs.*

COUNT. I am most happy. It is two weeks we have not go out.

TEDDY. You're a glutton for trouble, aren't you?

COUNT. Please?

TEDDY. Doesn't matter. Jump in the car, Johnny. I'll follow you.

COUNT *goes out.*

(*Calling.*) Pat!

PATRICIA *appears on landing.*

PATRICIA. (*Descending the stairs.*) You're going up to the Station, aren't you.

TEDDY. Yes. I've got to rush. I just want to say goodbye. I hoped this wasn't going to happen while you were here. I'm awfully sorry.

PATRICIA. It's a raid, I suppose.

TEDDY. It's not exactly a practice stooge-around.

PATRICIA. (*Helplessly.*) Teddy, I don't know what to say.

TEDDY. Happy landing—or just—come back.

PATRICIA. Come back.

He kisses her.

TEDDY. Goodbye, darling. God willing, I'll be waking you up at the hellish hour of five or so tomorrow morning. (*He goes abruptly to the door.*) Oh, by the way, whatever it was you had to tell me will have to wait till I get back. I suppose that's all right with you?

PATRICIA. Yes. That's all right with me.

He smiles at her and goes out.

> DORIS *is on the stairs, coming down. She passes* PATRICIA *and pats her arm comfortingly, without saying anything. Behind her* MAUDIE *appears and quietly descends the stairs.*

The sound of a car moving away breaks the silence.

CURTAIN

END OF ACT I

ACT II

Scene 1

Scene: *The same, about three hours later.*

PETER *is sitting on the fender, and* PATRICIA *is sitting above the fire.* MAUDIE *is in a chair, R., apart from them. Coffee things are on the table, R. The wireless is going.*

ANNOUNCER. . . . . at the controlled price of two and ten a pound, and will shortly be obtainable throughout the United Kingdom. (*Pause.*) That is the end of the nine o'clock news. Tonight's talk is by a sergeant wireless operator from one of the Stirlings which took part in this afternoon's strikingly successful raid on the harbour and docks of Kiel.

PATRICIA. Turn it off. (PETER *does so.*) You don't mind, do you, Mrs. Miller?

MAUDIE. No, thank you. I wasn't listening, anyway.

The lounge door opens and DORIS *appears, accompanied by a rattle and hum of voices. She has a drink in her hand and a set of darts.*

DORIS. Anyone hear the nine o'clock? I clean forgot the time.

PATRICIA. We've just turned it off.

DORIS. There wasn't anything fresh, I suppose. No pincers on anything anywhere?

A R.A.F. corporal appears at the door.

CORPORAL. Come on, Countess. We still want a double-two.

PATRICIA *shakes her head.*

DORIS. (*To* CORPORAL.) Take my turn, Wiggy. I'll be back in a minute. (CORPORAL *goes out.*) Why don't you all come in here? We're having a slap-up do.

PATRICIA. I don't think so, if you don't mind.

DORIS. Perhaps you're right. The boys are a bit noisy.

PATRICIA. (*Hastily.*) It's not that.

DORIS. I know, ducks. You don't have to tell me. Do you

remember the old joke about wives waiting up for their husbands at five in the morning with a rolling-pin? Makes me laugh sometimes when I think of it, it does, really. There's a full moon tonight. I think I'll just go and have a look.

She goes out of the front-door.

PETER. I've rather taken to the Countess. What's going to happen to her after the war, I wonder?

PATRICIA. Oh, she'll go to Poland with her Johnny, and find herself mistress of an enormous estate, with thousands of serfs, or moujiks, or whatever they are. She'll probably make a big success of it.

PETER. Supposing there is an after the war.

PATRICIA. Or supposing there's a Johnny.

DORIS *re-enters and stands by inside door.*

PETER. (*Slowly.*) Or supposing he wants to take her.

PATRICIA. Yes, that's rather a point, I admit.

PETER. I'm afraid it's *the* point. Our Countess has a personal interest in the war continuing.

DORIS. The sirens have just gone in Skillingworth.

CORPORAL. (*Off.*) What's yours, Countess?

DORIS. (*Over her shoulder.*) Gin and ginger. (*To* PATRICIA.) It's on Hull, I believe, but they may drop a couple on the aerodrome. They do sometimes. Tinkerty-tonk, Mrs. Miller!

MAUDIE. Tinkerty-tonk.

DORIS *disappears into lounge.*

PETER. Purely as a matter of idle interest—is there a shelter here?

PATRICIA. I don't know. If there is I don't suppose anyone would bother to use it.

PETER. I suppose if I'd been in England longer than a mere three months, I might become as blasé about raids as you are. (*Sharply.*) Listen! Those ours?

MAUDIE. (*Breaking a long pause.*) Theirs.

PETER. Oh, are they? How do you know?

MAUDIE. I lived in London till we were bombed out.

PATRICIA. I live in London, too, but I can never tell the difference.

MAUDIE. Perhaps you don't listen for it like what I do.

There are three muffled explosions.

PETER. Bombs?

PATRICIA. (*Smiling.*) No—guns. You've got a lot to learn.

PETER. Superior beast. (*He touches her hand, and both look round at* MAUDIE.)

PATRICIA. (*She gets up and goes over to* MAUDIE.) Is there anything you'd like, Mrs. Miller? Some coffee or something?

MAUDIE *looks up.*

MAUDIE. No, thank you, Mrs. Graham.

PATRICIA. That's not a very comfortable chair you've chosen. Wouldn't you like to come over by the fire?

MAUDIE. I'm quite comfy here, thank you.

PATRICIA. It's rotten luck, your having only the one night.

MAUDIE. I'll have a bit of tomorrow before the bus goes.

PETER. Do you have to go far?

MAUDIE. Only to St. Albans.

PATRICIA. Can't you possibly stay another night?

MAUDIE. No, I must be to work seven o'clock Monday. It's a laundry, you see.

PETER. Couldn't you ring your people up and explain? I'll ring them up for you, if you like.

MAUDIE. Oh, no, please. You mustn't.

PETER. Why not?

MAUDIE. They wouldn't like it. I'd be losing my job, and that'd never do—not now it wouldn't. Besides, I must be to work Monday morning. There's a lot to be done Mondays.

PATRICIA. I'm sure if you'd let Mr. Kyle explain——

MAUDIE. (*Firmly.*) No, Mrs. Graham. Thank you all the same.

Pause.

PETER. How do you like your work in the laundry, Mrs. Miller?

MAUDIE. Oh, it's not so bad. I'm new to it, of course.

PETER. You haven't always done that kind of work?

MAUDIE. Oh, no. Not peace time, I didn't. I didn't have to work peace time. Dave had a good job, you see, and we had our own home in Eccleston Bridge Road—nice place it was. Of course, it's down now. Dave worked in London

Transport—conductor—might have been inspector quite soon.

PATRICIA. And now he's a rear gunner in a Wellington bomber, shooting down Messerschmitts. (*To* MAUDIE.) Don't you ever find it unreal, what's happened to your husband and yourself?

MAUDIE. Unreal? No, I don't see it's unreal. It's happened, hasn't it?

PATRICIA. Yes, it has.

MAUDIE. Mind you, I'm not saying I like him being a gunner; it's not good for him in those turret things. They're wickedly cold. He told me so himself—and he gets horrible backaches. He used to get them when he was working on the buses. Besides, it's no good saying they always get back from these raids, because they don't—not all of them. Then I'm not saying I liked being bombed out and going to live in St. Albans with Dave's Aunt Ella, who I've never got on with and never will—and working at the Snowflake—but what I say is, there's a war on, and things have got to be a bit different, and we've just got to get used to it—that's all.

PETER. Yes, I see. Very sensible.

There is a sudden burst of voices as the lounge door opens and DORIS *comes in. From the lounge we can hear the* BARMAN'S *voice shouting:* Time, gentlemen, please. It's gone half-past nine. Time, gentlemen, please.

DORIS. (*Humming to herself.*)

>   I don't want to join the Air Force,
>   I don't want to go to war.

Phew! The Countess Skriczevinsky is a teeny bit tippy-o. (*Seeing* MAUDIE.) Hullo, Mrs. Miller, dear. Everything O.K.?

MAUDIE. (*With dignity.*) Yes, thank you for asking.

DORIS. Nothing you'd like me to get you? A little dinky, or anything?

MAUDIE (*Cuttingly.*) It's very kind of you, I'm sure, but I won't have a little—dinky. (*She sniffs contemptuously and gets up from her chair.*) Good night, Mrs. Graham.

PATRICIA. Good night, Mrs. Miller.

MAUDIE. Good night, Mr. Kyle.

PETER. Good night.

Without saying good night to DORIS *she begins to mount the stairs.*

MAUDIE. (*On the stairs.*) Oh, by the way, Mrs. Graham, on account of my Dave is rather funny about me not mentioning his backaches to nobody, please don't say nothing to him about me having told you about them.

PATRICIA. All right, Mrs. Miller. I won't say a word.

DORIS. (*Calling.*) Good night, Mrs. Miller, ducks. Sleep tight.

MAUDIE. I'd say you were more likely to do that than what I am, Countess. (*She goes out.*)

DORIS. Oo, did you hear that? I bought that properly, didn't I? Sleep tight! I'll give her sleep tight!

PATRICIA. I shouldn't brood on it, Doris.

DORIS. I suppose she thinks it's common for a countess to have a few drinks with the boys.

PATRICIA. (*Soothingly.*) I'm sure she doesn't.

PETER. As a matter of fact, I know lots of countesses who don't stop at having a few drinks with the boys.

DORIS *turns slowly in his direction. She glares at him.*

DORIS. Now you're making fun of me, Mr. Peter Kyle, and I don't like it.

PETER. (*Contrite.*) I'm sorry.

DORIS. Now don't blame me for being a countess. It's not my fault. I didn't want it. I'd much rather be plain Mrs.— but Johnny likes people to call me Countess, so I've got to let them, see. But don't you be funny about me just because of that.

PATRICIA. (*Hastily.*) He wasn't being funny about you, Doris.

PETER. Of course I wasn't——

DORIS. And another thing—I overheard everything you said about me and my Johnny just now. How I had a personal interest in the war going on.

PETER *and* PATRICIA *start. There is a pause.*

PETER. I think you misheard me.

DORIS. Misheard my eye. That's what you said all right.

PETER. If I did, I've no idea what I meant.

DORIS. I know what you meant. You meant my Johnny's going to leave me flat the minute the war's over. That's what you meant. I'm only all right for him as long as the war goes on, and as soon as it's over and he gets back home he'll realize he's made an awful muck-up in marrying me and he'll—he'll—— (*She chokes and turns her back quickly.* PATRICIA *goes up to her.*)

PATRICIA. Doris, my dear, don't be so idiotic. Even if Mr. Kyle did say that—and he didn't—it doesn't matter, because you know perfectly well it isn't true.

DORIS. I don't know it isn't true. I wish I did. I think it *is* true. (*She turns round. Defiantly.*) But I don't want the war to go on—just because of that.

PETER. (*Simply.*) Please believe me. I never said you did.

Pause.

DORIS. Oh, dear. I've gone and made a fool of myself again. Sorry, dear. Sorry, Mr. Kyle. Oh, dear—Peter Kyle! I've been longing to meet him all my life! Then when I do, I go and snap his head off.

PETER. I really *am* most terribly sorry if I said anything to make you think——

DORIS. Oh, for heaven's sake! I'd no business to listen, anyway. Forget it. Wonder if it's clouding over at all. (*She goes to the window.*) Turn out the light for a sec, will you, ducks?

PETER *turns the light out.* DORIS *sticks her head out of the window.* No, it's a lovely night, I'm afraid.

PATRICIA. Why afraid?

DORIS. If the weather was dud they might call it off. They won't, though. There's a lovely moon. What's the time?

PETER. A quarter to ten.

DORIS. They haven't lit the flare path yet.

PATRICIA. What's the flare path?

DORIS. Lights in a line—so that they can see when they're taking off. You ought to know that, married to a flight-loot.

MRS. OAKES *comes in from her office and turns on the light.*

MRS. OAKES. (*With a scream.*) My black-out! (*She turns off the lights again.*)

DORIS. All right. We'll do it, Mrs. Oakes.

PETER *turns on the lights.*

MRS. OAKES. Have they gone yet?

DORIS. You shouldn't know they were going at all.

MRS. OAKES. Well, something made them all go back to the aerodrome in an awful hurry. (*With a heavy wink.*) I suppose it could have been an ENSA show. What time are they going to be back? That's all that concerns me.

DORIS. (*Returning the wink.*) My guess is the ENSA show will be over about five in the morning.

MRS. OAKES. Your guess is as good as anyone's, Countess. Will the last one up please turn off the lights. I'm going to bed. Breakfast is at eight-thirty, Mr. Kyle—tomorrow being Sunday, we don't serve it in the bedrooms, as we are so shockingly understaffed.

PETER. That's quite all right. I don't have breakfast.

MRS. OAKES, *on her way to the stairs, stops dead.*

MRS. OAKES. (*Appalled.*) You don't have breakfast?

PETER. (*Nervously.*) No. I—er—just a cup of tea, I mean—but as a general rule I—er—well—(*Defiantly.*) I don't have breakfast.

DORIS. He's an actor, you see, Mrs. Oakes. He has to keep his figure.

MRS. OAKES. His figure. I see. I'm afraid I can make no reduction in the price of the room.

PETER. That's quite all right.

MRS. OAKES. (*Severely.*) It's not all right at all, Mr. Kyle. I'm sure I don't like to charge people for what they don't have. But, you see, there *is* a war on, and if you don't have breakfast you must just take the consequences, that's all. Good night. (*She goes out.*)

PETER. What consequences? Duodenal ulcer?

PATRICIA. (*Laughing.*) No, darling. Paying for it.

There is a slightly awkward moment following this slip.

DORIS. Wonderful the way you stage people darling each other. To hear you sometimes, you'd think you were passionately in love. (*Suddenly.*) There's the All Clear—can you hear it?

PATRICIA. (*After listening.*) Yes, I can—just. Good.

DORIS. (*Almost simultaneously.*) Damn! (*Answering* PATRICIA'S *unspoken inquiry.*) They wouldn't take off with Jerry overhead. They couldn't light the flare path, you see. Of course, sometimes old Jerry hangs about over the aerodrome for hours, and they don't know he's there. Then, just when they've lit the flare path and the boys are taking off—or coming in, more likely—he'll swoop down on them and shoot them up. You're a sitting target when you're coming in—so Teddy says—and you're dead beat probably and thanking God you've got back, and then suddenly—— (*She stops.*) Filthy trick, I think. Of course, we do the same over on their aerodromes. What's the time, Mr. Kyle? Sorry to keep troubling you.

PETER. Twelve minutes to ten.

DORIS. I'll go and watch the take-off from my room. You see better from up there. It won't be for a bit yet, of course. Good night. (*She goes to the stairs.* PATRICIA *and* PETER *say good night.*)

DORIS. (*To* PETER.) Sorry, ducks.

PETER. (*Imploringly.*) Please!

DORIS. (*Laughing.*) Please! You sound like my Johnny. (*On the stairs.*) If there's anything you want in the middle of the night, Pat dearie, can't sleep, or anything—don't worry about waking me up. I'll be quite glad to have company. Nighty night. (*She goes out.*)

There is a silence between PETER *and* PATRICIA *for a moment.*

PETER. (*With a sudden explosion.*) God damn it!

PATRICIA *goes to him, but says nothing.*

What right has she to go listening at doors? It wouldn't have been so bad if she didn't know it was true.

PATRICIA *puts her hand out and touches his. He takes it and looks down at it, examining a ring on her finger.*

I had rather a good taste for a film star in those days, hadn't I?

PATRICIA. It was very good taste.

PETER. Dripping with the wages of sin.

PATRICIA. I suppose I should have sent them all back to you. That's what a nice girl would have done.

PETER. A nice girl wouldn't have had anything to do with me in the first place.

PATRICIA. Oh, I think she would, Pete. (*As an afterthought.*) Not that I'm claiming to be a nice girl.

PETER. Why did you have anything to do with me?

PATRICIA. I had my reasons.

PETER. What were they? The reasons?

PATRICIA. You do like to be told, don't you?

PETER. I've had to do without being told for over a year now.

PATRICIA. And whose fault was that?

PETER. (*Promptly.*) Mine.

PATRICIA. That's a surprise.

PETER. (*Invitingly.*) So now . . .

PATRICIA. All right. I loved you first for being kind to a shy and imported small-part actress in your play.

PETER. I had my reasons.

PATRICIA. I know you did. I loved you for that, too—because when the reason was removed you went on being kind.

PETER. Perhaps I still had hope.

PATRICIA. Perhaps. You certainly had cause for it, hadn't you?

PETER *nods smilingly.*

I'm not going on with a long catalogue of your virtues.

PETER. I'm glad to know that it would be long.

PATRICIA. Only long because what are virtues to me are perhaps vices to other people. No, Pete, I don't suppose other people think you're very nice. They see through your act quite easily, I think—it's not awfully difficult to see through.

PETER. That's what you've always said, but I think it's a very good act.

PATRICIA. The modest, shy, quiet, cultured, self-possessed film star? It never has made sense, Pete. People see through it at once, and they take it for granted that what's underneath must be nasty because what's on top is so nice. Whereas I know what's underneath, and I love it because it's simple and childish and—I don't know—just rather helpless.

PETER. Do you remember that awful row we had in Jack and Charlie's when you first said that?

PATRICIA. It wasn't a row—not one of our real ones—just a sulk.

PETER. We were both extremely dignified with each other for about a week, I remember that.

PATRICIA. Very hoity-toity until we met each other under a bed playing sardines in that awful woman's house in Long Island.

PETER. My God, yes, I remember. (*They laugh—gravely.*) What fools we were to miss a whole damned year.

PATRICIA *nods without speaking.*

Pat, don't bully me if I say something to you, will you?

PATRICIA. No, darling.

PETER. Well, I'm getting old, Pat.

PATRICIA. Old? You're thirty-nine.

PETER. Thirty-nine when you left me, forty-one now. Not old, really; just a nice, ripe, fruity middle-age. Perfectly all right if I were a good enough actor to play middle-aged parts.

PATRICIA. But you are.

PETER. The Studio doesn't think so. After my next picture I'm out. Oh, well, it's not only that, Pat, and this will sound (*he smiles at her shamefacedly*) funny, I suppose, if you happen to look at it like that. It's the war, you see. I don't understand it, Pat—you know that—democracy—freedom—rights of man—and all that—I can talk quite glibly about them, but they don't mean anything, not to me. All I know is that my own little private world is going—well, it's gone really—and the rest of the world—the real world—has turned its back on me and left me out, and though I want to get into the circle, I can't. I hate that, Pat—I hate being left out in the cold. I know it's a selfish way of looking at it, but I don't care. So you see—I do—what with one thing and another—I do happen to need you. (*His voice trails away into an embarrassed silence.*)

PATRICIA. (*Uncertainly.*) Yes, you do, Pete. I'm glad that you do.

PETER. All very shy-making. I'm sorry.

PATRICIA, *saying nothing, puts an arm round his shoulder.*

It's only that I worry sometimes.

PATRICIA. You don't need to. You should know that by now.

PETER. Things can happen.

PATRICIA. Not to me.

PETER. (*Lightly.*) You're a faithful type?

PATRICIA *winces slightly.*

PETER. (*Quickly.*) Damn! I'm awfully sorry.

PATRICIA. It's all right. It's only that I'd forgotten him for the moment.

PETER. After tomorrow——

There is a noise at the front-door. SWANSON *comes in.*

SWANSON. (*Jovially.*) Hullo—'ullo. Mrs. Graham, eh? Thought I'd find you up. (*He looks at* PETER.)

PATRICIA. Good evening, Squadron-Leader. This is Peter Kyle —Squadron-Leader Swanson.

SWANSON. Oh, yes. You're the actor type, aren't you? I heard all about you from Teddy. He's been burbling about meeting you all the evening. Shooting a terrific line.

PETER *smiles politely.*

I say, I suppose you wouldn't like to come up to the Station tomorrow? Say a few words or something. Give the blokes a hell of a thrill—something to write to their girl friends about, instead of official secrets.

PETER. I'd love to, but as a matter of fact I'm leaving for London tomorrow.

SWANSON. (*Hangs up his coat.*) Oh, pity. Well, perhaps some other time. Waiting up for the take-off, eh? Won't be long now. After they've gone take my advice—toddle off to bed and get some sleep. Won't seem any time before he's back again. As a matter of fact, old Teddy asked me to come along and see if you were all right and all that.

PATRICIA. It's very kind of you.

SWANSON. Not at all. (*Apologetically.*) As a matter of fact, I'm not much good as a comforter on these occasions. I get so damned nervous myself.

PETER. (*Making conversation.*) You're not flying tonight yourself?

SWANSON. Good lord—I don't fly. Look. Nothing up here. (*He flicks his breast.*) Just an old wingless wonder. Adjutant. Combination nurse and maid of all work to the Squadron. No business in the Air Force at all, really. Ought to be in the Army, like I was in the last war. (*He is piling up cushions to form a pillow.*) My bed for tonight.

PETER. My God! It isn't *your* room I've taken, is it?

SWANSON. Lord, no. I sleep up at the station as a rule. But when the boys are out on a job I like to be up when they come in, and I can't trust that damn fool of a batman to wake me. It's warmer down here, too.

PATRICIA. Let me help.

SWANSON. Oh, please don't bother.

PATRICIA. It's not an awfully good fire.

SWANSON. It'll burn up. Teddy calls me Gloria, you know. No respect for senior rank. Shocking.

PETER. Mrs. Graham, are you going to take the Squadron-Leader's advice, or are you going to wait up? If you are, I'd be very happy to——

PATRICIA. I'll go to bed. I think it's better.

PETER. I see. Well, good night.

PATRICIA. Good night.

PETER. (*On the stairs.*) Good night, sir.

SWANSON, *who has been blowing away at the fire, straightens himself.*

SWANSON. What's that? Oh, are you off to bed? Good night. Oh, I say.

PETER. Yes?

SWANSON. Have you met Alice Faye?

PETER. Yes. Once.

SWANSON. Good lord! (*He returns to the fire.*)

PETER. Good night, Mrs. Graham.

PATRICIA. Good night, Mr. Kyle.

PETER *goes out.*

PATRICIA *is still kneeling beside* SWANSON, *who is puffing away at the fire without effect.*

PATRICIA. You'll never get it to go like that. Here, let me. (*She takes a sheet of newspaper and uses it to draw the fire.*)

SWANSON. Takes a woman to think of that. (*He looks at his watch. Pause.*)

PATRICIA. You're very fond of Teddy—Squadron-Leader?

SWANSON. Who isn't? Look out. That'll burn. (*He pulls the paper away. The fire is glowing.*)

PATRICIA. Who isn't?

SWANSON. Of course, I'm fond of 'em all, if it comes to that,

but I don't know the others as well as I know old P.O. Prune.
We call him that, you know.

PATRICIA. Yes, he told me.

SWANSON. He's not quite so prunish as he lets on. I've seen
him sometimes—— (*He breaks off.*) Dammit, you're his wife.
You must know him better than I do.

PATRICIA. Yes, of course.

SWANSON. I hate all this patriotic bilge in the newspapers, but,
my God, we do owe these boys something, you know.

PATRICIA. Yes.

SWANSON. It's going pretty well now. Thank you. (*He stands
up.*) You've been married a year or so now, haven't you?

PATRICIA. Just under a year.

SWANSON. He's damned lucky, if I may say so. I was scared
stiff when I heard he'd married an actress. He's the type
who might have fallen for some awful bottle-party floosie
who'd have let him down with a wallop. (*He fumbles in his
pocket and produces a slip of paper.*) Oh, by the way, I knew I
had something to show you. Some joker put this in the Mess
Suggestion Book. I copied it out. Thought it might amuse
you. (*He hands it to her.*) Read it out.

PATRICIA. (*Reading.*) Suggested that Flight-Lieutenant Graham
shall in future be permitted to mention his wife's name not
more than ten times per diem; and that on each subsequent
mention of the said wife's said name—to wit, Patricia, or
Pat, Paddy, Paddykins, and other such nauseating diminu-
tives—over and above the allotted ten times per diem,
Flight-Lieutenant Graham shall forfeit to all officers within
hearing a pint of beer. (*She finishes reading.* SWANSON *chuckles
delightedly.* PATRICIA *continues staring at the slip of paper.*)

SWANSON. You see. Practically everyone in the mess has signed
it—even little Tinker Bell, the Signals Officer—who dies of
fright if you speak to him.

PATRICIA *hands it back.*

SWANSON. Go on, keep it. I thought it might be fun for you to
have—with all the names on it——

An aircraft's engines can be heard. SWANSON *turns abruptly to the
window.*

Turn off the light.

PATRICIA *turns out the lights.* SWANSON *pulls back the curtains, allowing the moonlight to illumine the room.* PATRICIA *joins him at the window.*

There's the flare path—do you see? Those little points of light. There's one taking off now.

The noise of the aircraft's engines increases.

They're making their run from the far side of the field, across this way. There's one off, thank God!

The noise passes directly overhead and fades.

It's a hellish tricky business, taking off on a night like this, with no wind and a full load of bombs. Hellish tricky. Worse than landing. Here's the next just starting his run.

PATRICIA. Which is Teddy's?

SWANSON. Can't tell. They don't take off in any particular order. There are only four aircraft flying tonight—A Apple, L London, U Uncle—that's Teddy—and S Sugar from the Polish Squadron. (*Sharply.*) God!

PATRICIA. What's the matter?

SWANSON. It's all right. He's off. I thought he wasn't going to make it. He must have cleared that fence by inches.

The noise passes overhead and fades.

Next one's coming up. (*Sharply.*) Hullo! What's that? The first one seems to be circling round up there. Can you hear him?

PATRICIA. No. Do you think it might be a German?

SWANSON. I hope to God it's not. There is one circling round up there. Ah, there he goes, the next one—do you see? You can just pick him up. That dark shape.

PATRICIA. (*In alarm.*) His engines are on fire.

SWANSON. (*Laughing.*) No. That's the exhaust. It always looks like that. You can see it miles away. Useful to night fighters. Good boy! Nice take-off. One more to go. (*He listens intently again.*) Ah, here he comes. Here's the last one starting his run. See him?

PATRICIA. Yes, I see him.

SWANSON. God!

PATRICIA. (*Almost simultaneously.*) Why have they turned out the flares?

There is a sudden rattle of machine-gun fire, followed by three loud but dull-sounding explosions.

They're bombing the aerodrome. It was a German.

SWANSON. (*Shouting.*) Brakes, you idiot, brakes! Don't take off.

There is another rattle of machine-gun fire, followed by another explosion, sharper than the bomb bursts and with a tearing, rending sound following it. PATRICIA *stifles a scream. A dull red glow appears at the window.* SWANSON *pulls the curtains to violently.*

(*Quietly.*) Put the lights on.

PATRICIA. (*In a panic.*) I can't find the switch. I can't find the switch. I can't——

DORIS. (*In matter-of-fact tones.*) It's on the left of the door, by the hall.

The room is suddenly flooded with light. PATRICIA *is standing by the switch.* DORIS *is at the foot of the stairs, fully dressed. She is standing quite still.*

SWANSON *goes over to telephone and lifts receiver.*

SWANSON. Milchester 23.

PETER *appears in a dressing-gown. He runs downstairs.*

PETER. What happened?

SWANSON. An aircraft crashed or was shot down, taking off.

PETER *walks across to* PATRICIA *and takes her hand.* MAUDIE *has come down the stairs behind him in time to hear* SWANSON's *last line.*

MAUDIE. It's not Dave, is it?

DORIS. We don't know who it is, dear. The Squadron-Leader's finding out for us. (*She puts an arm round* MAUDIE.)

SWANSON. (*At telephone.*) Hullo. Put me through to Controller —Squadron-Leader Swanson . . . Hullo, Manning! Swanson here . . . Yes, I saw it. What happened? . . . No, no, of course not, but at least you know which aircraft it was. . . . Yes. . . . I see. . . . All right. (*He rings off and turns round.*) The crashed aircraft is A Apples.

MAUDIE. Dave?

DORIS. No, dear. We're all right.

SWANSON. L London, U Uncle—that's Teddy's—and S Sugar are all airborne, and are now on their way——

There is a pause. Nobody moves. SWANSON *turns abruptly and goes out.*

CURTAIN

NOTE: *While the curtain is lowered, denoting the passing of time, the sound of an aircraft's engines in flight continues to be audible until some seconds after the raising of the curtain on Scene 2.*

ACT II

SCENE 2

SCENE: *The same, about 5.30 the following morning.*

The sound of an aircraft's engines can be heard. SWANSON *and* DORIS *are at the window, outlined against the faint light of early dawn. The sound of the engines ceases as they are throttled back.*

SWANSON. (*At length.*) He's down all right.

DORIS. It's Johnny's, I'm almost sure. I recognized the engines.

SWANSON. That's absurd, my dear Countess, if you don't mind my saying so. All Wellingtons sound alike.

DORIS. Not to me they don't.

PATRICIA *appears on the stairs.*

PATRICIA. Is that one of them back?

SWANSON. Morning, Mrs. Graham. Yes, it's the second to come in. The first one landed about twenty minutes ago.

PATRICIA. I must have been asleep. Are either of them Teddy's?

SWANSON. Don't know yet. Don't like to keep on ringing Ops.

DORIS. (*Cheerfully.*) We'll know soon enough, anyway.

MRS. OAKES *comes out of the coffee-room with a loaded tray. She is in a rather elaborate déshabillé.*

MRS. OAKES. May I have the curtains drawn, please? I want to switch on the lights.

SWANSON. It's still black-out, I suppose.

He pulls the curtains to, blacking out the room. DORIS *switches on the lights.*

MRS. OAKES. It's black-out until five fifty-two. Will you give me a hand with this table?

SWANSON. Of course. What's the time now?

MRS. OAKES. Just gone half-past. I thought I'd lay a table in here. It's warmer with that fire. (*She puts the tray on a table. Acidly.*) I must say I can't quite understand how it has kept in all this time. I usually have to relight it.

SWANSON. (*Embarrassed.*) Well, as a matter of fact——

MRS. OAKES. Quite, Squadron-Leader. I see. (*To* PATRICIA.) Shall I lay a place for you, Mrs. Graham? I expect you'll want to have breakfast with your husband, won't you—now that you're up?

PATRICIA. I don't want much to eat.

MRS. OAKES. There isn't much to eat. Now let me see—Flight-Lieutenant Graham, Flying-Officer Count Skriczevinsky, Sergeant Miller—that'll be five with you, Countess, I'm afraid I can't provide for casuals like you, Squadron-Leader.

SWANSON. That's all right. I'm going home, anyway, as soon as they come.

MRS. OAKES. I won't wake Mrs. Miller up. I peeped into her room as I came past, and she was sound asleep. (*She is laying the table.*)

PATRICIA. Can I help you?

MRS. OAKES. No, thank you, Mrs. Graham. I can manage very well.

PATRICIA. Do you always do this yourself?

MRS. OAKES. Well, I haven't got five hundred servants, Mrs. Graham, and the ones I have got wouldn't stay long if I made them work at this time in the morning. (*She elbows* PATRICIA *out of the way and goes out into the coffee-room.*)

PATRICIA. There's one more to come in yet, isn't there?

DORIS. Yes, ducky.

PATRICIA *looks down at the neatly-laid table.*

PATRICIA. Five places! How horribly smug and complacent it looks.

DORIS. (*Soothingly.*) After flying all night they've got to have something to eat when they come back.

PATRICIA. Supposing they don't come back?

Pause.

DORIS. Poor dearie. This is the first time you've been here for a do, isn't it?

PATRICIA. A do. Oh, God, how I hate all this polite Air Force understatement. Isn't there a more dignified word for it than a do?

SWANSON. Come and sit over here, Mrs. Graham. Quite a good fire, you know—thanks to me.

PATRICIA *looks from* DORIS *to* SWANSON.

PATRICIA. I think I will. (*She sits down by the fire.*) I'm sorry. I didn't sleep much. (*She looks up at* DORIS, *who is fully dressed.*) You didn't sleep at all—either of you.

DORIS. Oh, I went off now and then. Didn't I, Squadron-Leader?

SWANSON. You snored once.

DORIS. Oh, I didn't. You fibber! (*She giggles.*) I'm sure I don't know what Johnny would say—the Squadron-Leader and me down here together all night and no chaperon.

SWANSON. Probably challenge me to a duel or something. Rapiers at dawn behind the Admin. Block.

DORIS. Serve you right for smirching my honour. Snored! I never snored in my life.

PATRICIA. (*Staring at* DORIS.) I wish I understood. (*She stops.*) You're very brave.

There is the sound of a car in the road outside. DORIS, PATRICIA, *and* SWANSON *all rise abruptly and face the front-door. The car draws up outside the hotel. A door bangs and the car moves on. There is a pause. Then* DUSTY *enters. He wears Air Force battle-dress and a high-necked jumper.*

DUSTY. Morning, all.

PATRICIA. (*Quickly.*) Teddy——?

DUSTY. Putting the car away, mum. (*Seeing the fire.*) Cor! Give me a piece of that. (*He walks to the fire, passing* SWANSON *on the way.*) Morning, sir.

SWANSON. Morning, Sergeant. Good trip?

DUSTY. (*Gloomily.*) Proper muck-up from beginning to end.

DORIS. S Sugar back yet?

DUSTY. Not yet, Countess.

SWANSON. You and L London are back, then. You were the first to land, I suppose?

DUSTY. Yes, sir. About half an hour ago. (*Exclamatorily.*) What about A Apples? Shook us considerable, that did.

SWANSON. You saw the crash?

DUSTY. Yes, I was in the tail, you see, sir. I called up the skipper and we circled round her for a bit. Cor! what a blaze. Nobody got out, did they, sir?

SWANSON. (*Shortly.*) One man was thrown clear. The navigator.

DUSTY. Old Ginger Walsh, that is. Good old Ginger! Is he hurt bad?

SWANSON. They think he'll recover.

DUSTY. I'll trot along and see him tomorrow. How's the wife been behaving herself, Countess? O.K.?

DORIS. O.K., Dusty. She went up to bed early, and she's still asleep.

DUSTY. This fire don't half feel good on my behind.

TEDDY *enters. His wrist has been bound up with a handkerchief. He is similarly dressed to* DUSTY.

SWANSON. Hullo, Prune. Trust you to get down first. What did you do—drop your bombs on Bognor and dash for home?

TEDDY. That's about it—only it wasn't Bognor, it was Little-hampton—wasn't it Sarge?

DUSTY. That's right, sir. All our bombs fell in the target area.

TEDDY. (*Turns to* PATRICIA.) Hullo, darling.

PATRICIA. Hullo, Teddy.

TEDDY. You shouldn't have got up.

SWANSON. What have you done to your wrist, Teddy?

TEDDY. What? Oh, that. It's nothing at all. It got into the way of a flame float I was throwing out.

SWANSON. Let's have a look. (*He undoes the handkerchief.*) You ought to have it seen to.

TEDDY. (*Crosses to fire.*) I'll take it along to the M.O. tomorrow. Hullo, Doris.

DORIS. Hullo, Ted.

SWANSON. What sort of a trip did you have? Sergeant's just said it was a proper muck-up.

TEDDY. He's prejudiced. I wouldn't let him shoot up a train he'd taken a dislike to.

DUSTY. It looked so blooming pleased with itself, puffing along down there.

TEDDY. Wonderful moon. You could see everything. Not even our navigator could go wrong.

SWANSON. Any incidents?

TEDDY. Turned intelligence officer on me, have you, Gloria?

SWANSON. If you don't want to tell me——

TEDDY. No incidents, Gloria, if you exclude the fact that we had half our tail-plane shot away.

DUSTY. Wallowing about we were, coming home, like a fat old woman learning to swim. Fair turned me stomach.

TEDDY. Catted—did you, Dusty?

DUSTY. Wasn't so bad for you, sir, up front.

TEDDY. It's never so bad for the driver, they say.

MRS. OAKES *comes in with a loaded tray.*

MRS. OAKES. (*Politely.*) Good morning, gentlemen.

TEDDY. Morning, Mrs. Oakes. What have you got there for us? (*He lifts the cover off the dish. Joyfully.*) Eggs and bacon!

MRS. OAKES. I'd be glad if you wouldn't shout it to the entire hotel. I'm infringing regulations.

TEDDY. Mrs. Oakes, I could kiss you from head to foot.

MRS. OAKES. I trust you'll do nothing of the sort.

TEDDY. Eggs, Dusty. Eggs! You know what eggs are, don't you, or have you forgotten?

DUSTY. You mean those round things that used to come out of hens in peace time?

TEDDY. That's right. Come and sit down, Pat. I could eat a house. I could eat you, Mrs. Oakes.

DORIS. (*Sharply.*) Sh! Quiet! (*She listens intently.*) Sorry. Thought I heard a Wimpey.

MRS. OAKES. Is the Count not in yet?

DORIS. No, not yet. I think if you don't mind, duckies, I'll go up to my room. I can hear better from up there. (*She goes up the stairs. An uncomfortable silence has fallen on the room.*) (*From the landing.*) Save Johnny and me one of those eggs, won't you, dear?

TEDDY. You bet.

DORIS *goes out.*

SWANSON. Any news of S Sugar?

TEDDY. No. They're worried at Ops. They were over the target twelve minutes before us—but they've heard nothing from them since.

Pause.

MRS. OAKES. I'll put this over here, by the fire. . . . If he comes in very late, knock on my door and I'll come down and make him some more. (*She puts a covered dish by the fire—she goes up the stairs.*)

TEDDY. As usual, I can't thank you enough.

MRS. OAKES. Don't be ridiculous. I dare say some people would be glad to have the chance of doing it. I'm going to bed now. Good morning.

TEDDY. Good morning, Mrs. Oakes.

MRS. OAKES *goes out.*

SWANSON. Me for bed, too. Good show, Prune. Glad to see you back. Good night.

TEDDY. Good night, Gloria. (*Severely.*) I take an extremely poor view of your waiting up like this. Don't let it occur again.

SWANSON. God, you don't think I waited up for you, do you? Keeping the women company, that's all.

TEDDY. Then you're a dirty old man.

SWANSON. (*To* PATRICIA.) What did I tell you? No respect. Shocking. (*He goes out.*)

TEDDY. Come and sit down, boys and girls.

PATRICIA *sits between* TEDDY *and* DUSTY.

Did you see the take-off?

PATRICIA. Yes.

TEDDY. That crash was a bit of bad luck. It doesn't happen very often, you know. Plate, darling?

PATRICIA. I don't want anything to eat, thanks awfully.

TEDDY. On the level?

PATRICIA. On the level. I couldn't, really.

TEDDY. All the more for us, eh, Dusty?

DUSTY. Well, sir, between you and me, I don't feel any too peckish myself.

G

TEDDY. (*Quickly.*) Anything wrong?

DUSTY. No, sir. Just that ride home. Cor, I still feel it down in the old darby kel. If you don't mind, sir, I think I'll go up and have a bit of shut-eye.

TEDDY. Poor old Dusty! I'm awfully sorry. I *did* try and keep her steady, you know, but——

DUSTY. (*Strenuously.*) Cor, stuff me! Going to say it's your fault now, I suppose?

TEDDY. Well, it is, in a way.

DUSTY. Cor, stone me up an apple. (*To* PATRICIA.) Isn't a skipper in the world would've brought us 'ome safe tonight, bar 'im, and he goes and apologizes for giving me stummick trouble. Cor, stuff me sideways, what a man!

TEDDY. Good night, Dusty.

DUSTY. Good night, sir. (DUSTY *goes out.*)

TEDDY *is standing at the foot of the stairs.* PATRICIA *is still sitting at the table, her back to him.*

TEDDY. (*Murmuring.*) Good old Dusty! Don't you like old Dusty, darling?

PATRICIA. Yes, Teddy. Very much.

TEDDY. Darling!

PATRICIA. Yes, Teddy?

TEDDY. I said, didn't you like old Dusty?

PATRICIA. Yes, I said I did very much.

TEDDY. Did you? Darling——

PATRICIA. Yes?

TEDDY. Where are you?

PATRICIA *turns her head sharply and looks at him for the first time.*

PATRICIA. Here, Teddy.

TEDDY. Where? I can't see. Pat, come here. I want you.

PATRICIA. I'm here, Teddy. (*She kneels down beside him and tries to support him.*) I'm here, beside you. (*She looks round for help.*) Oh, God!

TEDDY. It's funny. I couldn't see you. I don't think I feel very well. It's nothing. Just a bit tired, that's all. (*He fumbles at his breast pocket, and pulls out a flask. He tries to open it, but fails.* PATRICIA *takes it from him.*)

It twists sideways.

PATRICIA *opens it. He tries to take the flask from her, but she restrains him. She holds it while he drinks. He coughs and splutters.*

TEDDY. Cherry brandy. Filthy stuff. Keeps you warm, though. (*He shakes his head.*) What are we doing—kneeling down? We look as if we were praying or something. (*He struggles to his feet, supported by* PATRICIA.) God, what an exhibition! I'm sorry.

PATRICIA. Do you feel well enough to go up to bed?

TEDDY. I feel well enough, but I'm not going to. With eggs and bacon on the old menu—what an idea!

PATRICIA. You're ill. You're not just tired. You're ill. I'm going to ring up a doctor.

TEDDY. I'll murder you if you do. Come on. (*He crosses to the table—his hands are still shaking.*) You watch me make a pig of myself. (*He picks up a knife and fork. Then he suddenly puts them down with a clatter and pushes the dish away.*) No good.

PATRICIA *walks towards telephone.*

What are you doing?

PATRICIA. I'm going to get a doctor.

TEDDY. No, you don't. (*He grasps her hand.*)

PATRICIA. I'm sorry, Teddy. I must. (*She shakes her hand free and walks towards the telepone.*)

TEDDY. (*Imploringly.*) Don't, Pat, please.

PATRICIA. It's much better, Teddy. (*She lifts the receiver.*) Hullo . . . hullo . . .

TEDDY. (*In a hard voice.*) Do you want to get me chucked out of the Air Force.

PATRICIA. What do you mean?

TEDDY. Put that receiver down.

PATRICIA *replaces receiver.*

Come here.

PATRICIA *walks slowly up to him. He puts his hand on her shoulder.* They always say a man should have no secrets from his wife, don't they?

PATRICIA. Yes. Tell me.

TEDDY. All right. Do you know what's the matter with me?

Funk. Just ordinary, common or garden, plain bloody funk.

PATRICIA. Don't be absurd.

TEDDY. If a doctor examined me now, his diag—whatever it is —would be simply this. Here's a bloke who doesn't like flying.

PATRICIA. (*Stares at him, then smiles.*) What about this? (*She touches his D.F.C. ribbon.*)

TEDDY. The doc would say to himself—bloke's got the D.F.C. Must have been all right once. Then he'd ask me—how many ops. have you done, my lad? Seventeen, sir. Doc says to himself—bloke packs up after only seventeen trips, eh? Just couldn't take it, I suppose.

PATRICIA. Don't talk like that, Teddy. It's sheer nonsense. The doctor would say—this man's ill. Probably nothing to do with flying at all. He ought to have a rest.

TEDDY. (*Bitterly.*) A rest?

PATRICIA. What's wrong with that?

TEDDY. There's nothing wrong with it. It's very nice—for some people. Ground job. Promotion probably. I'd have a fine time as a Squadron-Leader admin. at a training school flaunting a D.F.C. and shooting a line with the pupils. The only thing is, some of the pupils might wonder why I'd only done seventeen trips before being grounded, and a few of them might guess.

PATRICIA. In a case like this nobody would dare say a thing.

TEDDY. Only my friends. They'd say: Oh, yes—Teddy Graham —not a bad bloke. Didn't like flying, that's all. And on my confidential report they'd put—grounded. Lack of moral fibre. That's the official phrase for—no guts.

PATRICIA. (*Angrily.*) Listen, Teddy. There's no sense in all this. If you're too ill to fly——

TEDDY. I'm not too ill to fly. I fly all right. You heard what Dusty said.

PATRICIA. Yes, but it may not always be like that.

TEDDY. It will always be like that.

PATRICIA. What about your crew? Is it fair on them?

TEDDY. (*Clenching his fists.*) What's fair on my crew is my business.

PATRICIA. It's their lives you're risking as well as yours.

TEDDY. I'm their captain. Their captain. I wouldn't risk their lives.

PATRICIA. You are.

TEDDY. Don't, Pat, don't. You don't know—I can't bear it——

PATRICIA. I'm sorry, Teddy. (*She puts her hand on his arm. He falls at her feet. He lays his head on her lap and sobs.*)

PATRICIA. Oh, my dear, my dear.

TEDDY. (*His voice muffled by sobs.*) A bloody Messerschmitt put a cannon shell in our tail-plane—we went straight down in a dive—I heard Dusty on the intercomm.—He said—I thought I'd bought it, Skipper, but I'm all right—I'm all right! We were in a vertical dive and I couldn't pull out—I couldn't pull out, and Dusty said he was all right. (*He is shaken by a further outburst of sobbing.* PATRICIA *strokes his head, saying nothing.*) All the way back I had to fight to keep her on course—every one of them must have known it was odds against our getting home—but they trusted me—they trusted me—I heard the wireless op.—say to the navigator —he's only just come on the crew—he said—don't worry, windy. Skipper'll get us home. Oh, my God! Skipper'll get us home. . . .

PATRICIA. You got them home.

TEDDY. You don't know what it's like to feel frightened. You get a beastly, bitter taste in the mouth, and your tongue goes dry and you feel sick, and all the time you're saying— This isn't happening—it can't be happening—I'll wake up. But you know you won't wake up. You know it is happening, and the sea's below you, and you're responsible for the lives of six people. And you have to pretend you're not afraid, that's what's so awful. Oh, God, I was afraid tonight. When we took off and saw that kite on fire, I didn't think: There are friends of mine in that. I thought (*slowly*): That might happen to us. Not very—pretty, is it?

He recovers himself slowly, PATRICIA *watching him in silence. Then he turns away from her.*

TEDDY. Now you know it. Lack of moral fibre. I'm glad I
told you.

PATRICIA. I'm glad, too.

TEDDY. Lend me a handkerchief.

PATRICIA gives him one from her pocket. TEDDY *takes it, turns his
back on her, and wipes his eyes. Sits on the sofa.*

God, what you must think of me!

PATRICIA. (*Sits next to him.*) Teddy, look at me.

He turns reluctantly to face her.

Why didn't you tell me all this before?

TEDDY. I didn't want you to know you'd married a twerp.

PATRICIA. You damned little fool! (*She snatches the handkerchief
back from him.*)

TEDDY. Now, don't *you* start. One exhibition's enough for tonight.

PATRICIA. (*Fiercely.*) I'm all right.

TEDDY. Thank God I've had the courage to tell you. I couldn't
tell anyone else in the world. I couldn't. But you help me,
you see, so much.

PATRICIA. (*Angrily.*) I don't help you at all. I've never tried
to. How could I, when you keep these things from me?

TEDDY. You do help me—just by being—well—you—and,
incidentally, by being my wife. It was you who got us home
tonight. Not me.

PATRICIA. (*Desperately.*) That's not true, Teddy. You're just
saying that because you think I like to hear it. But it's not
true.

TEDDY. Try leaving me and see what happens. (*Pause.*) I
admit you've got every reason to now. You must think
you got married under false pretences.

PATRICIA. (*Quietly.*) No. I don't think that.

TEDDY. Thank you, Pat.

Pause

PATRICIA. (*Gently.*) I still think you should see a doctor.
Someone who'll understand, and try and help you.

TEDDY. I don't need any help. Except yours. I do need that.

PATRICIA. (*After a pause.*) Why go on with it, Teddy? You've
done your share. More than your share.

TEDDY. (*Slowly.*) I have got quite a few more trips to do before I get given a rest.

PATRICIA. But there's no magic in any particular number. It may be more for some and less for others.

TEDDY. It may be more for me. It's not going to be less. We've got to win this war somehow, you know. God, how *Daily Mail*! I'm glad nobody heard it but you. (*He gets up.*) You know, I feel better now than I've felt for months. I feel almost well enough to cope with Mrs. Oakes' bacon and eggs. (*He raises cover and looks.*) No. I spoke too soon.

PATRICIA. (*Dully.*) They must be cold by now.

TEDDY. They are. I say, darling.

PATRICIA. Yes?

TEDDY. Poor old Mrs. Oakes is going to be rather upset when she comes down in the morning and finds her precious eggs haven't been touched. (*He brings the dish over to her.*) I'd hate to hurt the old thing's feelings. (*He looks round.*) I know. The coal shovel. (*He is staring at the dish by the fire.*) I'd forgotten about old Johnny. (*He looks at his watch.*) If anything has happened to him, be kind to old Doris, won't you? I'm not much good at saying the right things on these occasions. We'd better leave it there, just in case. (*He takes the shovel from* PATRICIA.) I won't be long. I'm just going to have a look at the garden. (*He goes out with the shovel and the covered dish.* PATRICIA *sits, without moving, her chin resting on her hands.* PETER *comes down the stairs in a dressing-gown.*)

PETER. I heard his voice. He got back all right, then?

PATRICIA. Yes.

PETER. I'm glad. Poor Pat! You must have had a rough night. (*He takes her hand. She withdraws it sharply. He stares at her, surprised. She stands up. There is a pause. Then* TEDDY *comes in with the dish in his hands.*)

TEDDY. Hullo!

PETER. Hullo! I'm glad to see you back.

TEDDY. Thanks.

PETER. (*Indicating dish.*) What are you doing with that?

TEDDY. I've been burying six fried eggs and twelve rashers of bacon in a flower bed. Crazy type, you see, old Graham. By the way, it's broad daylight. Look. (*He pulls back the window curtains, admitting the morning sun.*) Come on, darling. Time we were in bed. (*He takes her hand and leads her up the stairs.* PETER *watches them from below.*)

CURTAIN

END OF ACT II

ACT III

SCENE: *The same, about* 12 *noon the same morning.*

DORIS *is on the window-seat, a Sunday paper on her lap, gazing out of the window.* PERCY *comes in from the lounge.*

PERCY. Twelve o'clock, Countess. Bar's open.

DORIS. (*Abstractedly.*) What? Oh, thank you, Percy.

PERCY. Fun and games last night, eh? That Wiggy Jones. He's a one, eh? That song: I don't want to join the Air Force. That's a song, eh? Been trying to remember it all morning.

DORIS. You'd better forget it, Percy. It's not a song for little boys.

PERCY. Garn with your little boys! Bit of a do up at the aerodrome last night, eh? Did you 'ear 'bout it? One got shot down taking off.

DORIS. I saw it.

PERCY. Did you? Coo, wish I 'ad. Saw the wreckage this morning, though. Burnt right out, it was. 'Orrible! (*In a confidential whisper.*) Where was it last night, do you know?

DORIS. Eight o'clock news said it was the Rhineland.

PERCY. Rhineland, eh? It was Rhineland last time they went. I knew something was up when they didn't come down to dinner. Flight-Lieutenant Graham, 'e tried to fox me. Nothing on tonight, Percy, 'e said. 'Ome sweet 'ome tonight. I knew 'e was keeping something up 'is sleeve. Count went too, didn't 'e?

DORIS. Yes. He went.

PERCY. 'Ow is 'e this morning? All right?

DORIS. He hasn't come back yet.

There is a pause. PERCY *stares at her unbelievingly.*

PERCY. Not come back?

DORIS. Of course, they may have force-landed somewhere.

PERCY. That's what 'appened, you mark my words. Count's not one to get 'imself shot down by those dirty 'uns.

DORIS. I'm afraid though, Percy, if they had force-landed, they'd have let Milchester know.

There is another pause.

PERCY. Coo, I'm sorry, Countess.

DORIS. That's all right, Percy.

PERCY. I seen 'em go off night after night, and they always got back. Never thought they wouldn't, some'ow. Course you'd 'ear it on the wireless: 'Some of our aircraft failed to return.' Never thought it'd 'appen to us, though. Coo! Makes yer think, don't it? (*He stands uncertainly at the door.*) Anything I can get you, Countess? Gin and lime or anything?

DORIS. No thanks.

PERCY. I'll see it's on the 'ouse.

DORIS. No, Percy. Ta, all the same.

MRS. OAKES *comes in from the coffee-room.* PERCY, *seeing her, darts out into the lounge.*

MRS. OAKES. Any news, Countess?

DORIS. No, not yet. The Squadron-Leader is going to let me know as soon as he hears anything.

MRS. OAKES. I expect he'll come back all right. Do you feel it cold in here, Countess? Would you like a fire?

DORIS. No, thanks. It's a lovely day, really. Like summer.

PETER *comes in through the front-door.*

MRS. OAKES. I saw you admiring our garden, Mr. Kyle. How do you like it?

PETER. (*Perfunctorily.*) Very much. Is Mrs. Graham still not down?

MRS. OAKES. I don't think so. I haven't seen her.

PETER. But it's nearly lunch time.

MRS. OAKES. Just gone twelve.

PETER. I suppose you couldn't—— (*He stops.*)

MRS. OAKES. Couldn't what, Mr. Kyle?

PETER. It doesn't matter. I'll wait. (*He sits down.*)

MRS. OAKES *goes to the door of her office.*

(*Brusquely.*) Get me a whisky and soda, please.

MRS. OAKES. That's hardly my province. (*She goes to the lounge door. Calling.*) Percy!

PERCY. (*Appearing at lounge door.*) Yes, mum?

MRS. OAKES. A whisky and soda for Mr. Kyle.

PERCY. Yes, mum. There's no whisky, mum.

MRS. OAKES. (*To* PETER.) There's no whisky.

PETER. Is there any brandy?

MRS. OAKES. (*To* PERCY.) Is there any brandy?

PERCY. Yes, mum.

PETER. Brandy and soda, then.

MRS. OAKES. Brandy and soda, Percy.

PERCY. Yes, mum.

PERCY'S *head disappears.*

MRS. OAKES *walks to the door of her office.*

MRS. OAKES. The next time you're requiring a drink, will you be good enough to press the bell marked 'Waiter'?

PETER *does not answer.*

MRS. OAKES *goes out.*

PETER *is engaged in reading some pencilled sheets of paper, which look as if they had been torn from a pocket-book.* PERCY *comes in with a brandy and soda.*

PERCY. Brandy and soda, sir. Two and ten.

PETER. (*Looking up.*) What? Oh, all right. (*He throws two coins on to the tray with a clatter.*) Keep the change.

PERCY. Thank you, sir. Thank you. (*He goes up to* DORIS *and puts something into her hand.*)

PERCY. Countess.

DORIS. What's this, Percy?

PERCY. Bele. An Indian god. Bought 'im at a fair. You hold 'im in your right 'and, and whatever you wish comes true.

DORIS. Oh. (*She puts it in her right hand, holds it a second and returns it to him.*) Thanks, Percy.

PERCY. No. You keep 'im. It don't work if it's not yours.

DORIS. Don't you want him?

PERCY. No. You keep him. Just been thinking. Count might 'ave baled out over the other side, then 'e'd be a prisoner of war.

DORIS. I'd rather anything than that.

PERCY. Why? It's not so bad.

DORIS. The Germans don't treat Poles as prisoners of war.

PERCY. (*After a pause.*) Cor! They're proper swine, aren't they?

PERCY *goes out.*

PETER *stuffs the sheets of paper into his pocket and stands up. He looks up at the stairs, and then impatiently at his watch. He appears suddenly to notice* DORIS *for the first time. He clears his throat.*

PETER. I heard about your husband from Mrs. Oakes. I'm most terribly sorry——

DORIS. Thank you, Mr. Kyle, but I've not given up yet. What I always say is, while there's life there's—hope.

SWANSON *has come in quickly, and* DORIS *speaks the last word looking straight at him over* PETER'S *shoulder. Her voice falters.* PETER *turns round.*

SWANSON. Morning, Kyle. Do you mind if I see the Countess alone for a moment?

PETER. No. Not at all. (*He goes to the lounge door.*) If Mrs. Graham comes down will you tell her that I want to see her—most urgently. It's very important.

SWANSON. Right. I'll tell her.

PETER *goes into lounge.*

SWANSON *does not look at* DORIS, *who has not taken her eyes off his face.*

DORIS. (*At length.*) Come on, dear. Tell us.

SWANSON. Well, I'm afraid it may be rather a shock——

DORIS. That's all right. I've had the shock. Tell us.

SWANSON. Your husband's aircraft did send out a signal this morning, at approximately 04.25. It said simply: Am force-landing on the sea. Then they sent out call signs for about ten minutes, and the D.F. stations got a pretty accurate fix on them. Then nothing more was heard. Since daylight this morning aircraft and power boats—the Air Sea Rescue chaps—have been out looking for them, and about half an hour ago they signalled us that the wreckage of a Wellington bomber had been found—within three miles of the spot fixed by the D.F. people. So I'm afraid it looks—— (*He stops.*) They're continuing the search: they had a rubber dinghy on board, and it's just possible they might have been picked up by some vessel which hadn't a wireless or any way of letting us know.

DORIS *shakes her head.*

DORIS. It's better not to think of loopholes. I'm quite ready to face it. Johnny's dead.

SWANSON. (*Automatically.*) You're very brave.

DORIS. That's the second time that's been said to me since last night. It isn't true. I'm just—ready, that's all.

PATRICIA *comes down the stairs.*

Thanks for taking all this trouble, Squadron-Leader. I know what a bind it must be, breaking bad news to people.

She turns towards the stairs and comes face to face with PATRICIA.

Hullo, ducks.

PATRICIA. I overheard what you said. Is it—Johnny?

DORIS. Yes, dear. They found bits of poor old S Sugar floating in the drink. It looks as if he's bought it all right.

PATRICIA. I'm terribly sorry——

DORIS. I know you are.

PATRICIA. Is there anything I can do.

DORIS. No, dear. Thanks all the same.

DORIS *goes up the stairs and out.*

PATRICIA. Isn't it awful how hopelessly inadequate the ordinary social phrases are at a moment like this? (*Bitterly.*) I'm terribly sorry.

SWANSON. That's all one can say, I think.

PATRICIA. Is there no hope?

SWANSON. Officially, yes. Unofficially—— (*He shakes his head.*) She prefers to take the unofficial view, and I dare say it's better she should. (*Pause.*) Well, I must be going. Sunday papers haven't come, and I've volunteered to go down to the village to collect them.

PATRICIA. Is there a chemist in the village that's open on Sunday?

SWANSON. We can beat one up for you, if you like—why?

PATRICIA. I want to get some stuff for Teddy's wrist. Are you driving in? Will you give me a lift?

SWANSON. Yes, but do you mind waiting five minutes? I've got to dash up to the station first.

PATRICIA. That's all right. Whenever you're going.

SWANSON. I'll get cracking. (*At door.*) How is his wrist?

PATRICIA. Oh, it's all right, but it looks as if he might have got some dirt in it.

SWANSON. How is he apart from that this morning?

PATRICIA. A bit tired, I think. They had rather a shaky do last night.

SWANSON. Shaky do? Learning the old vernacular, eh? Well, I'll dash. Oh, by the way, Kyle's waiting for you in there. (*He points to the lounge.*) Says it's most important.

PATRICIA. Oh, thank you.

SWANSON. Won't keep you long.

> SWANSON *goes out.*
>
> PATRICIA *looks, undecided, at the lounge door. Then she turns quickly to go back upstairs. The lounge door opens and* PETER *comes out.* PATRICIA, *halfway up the stairs, turns slowly.*

PATRICIA. Peter—please—I don't want to see you. I told you——

PETER. You're going to see me.

PATRICIA. Not now. I'll come up to London. I'll see you there. I'll explain——

PETER. Explain what?

> PATRICIA *slowly nods towards the letter in his hand.*

Five little bits of paper dumped on my bed with my morning tea, and you expected me to jump on the first train up to London and fade quietly out of your life muttering, 'It's a far, far better thing'—— (*Bitterly.*) Who's living in a film world, you or me?

PATRICIA. I was coming to see you in London. I had to write it down because it helped me to think. I couldn't have said it. I can't say it now. I'm sorry I wrote it though, Pete, it wasn't awfully brave.

PETER. You really want me to take this letter seriously?

PATRICIA. Yes, Pete.

PETER. This is how seriously I take it. (*He tears the letter up into small pieces.*) Never play this sort of trick on me again as long as you live. If you have any more of these bouts of conscience, or—whatever it is—come and tell me—but for the love of God don't send me any more notes by any more chambermaids. I've had the worst morning of my life.

(*He turns his back on her and lights his cigarette with unsteady fingers.*)

PATRICIA. Try and understand, Pete, I'm not doing this for fun.

PETER *turns*.

PETER. Doing what?

PATRICIA. Leaving you.

There is a pause. PETER *stares at her unbelievingly.*

PETER. Shut up, Pat, don't talk nonsense.

PATRICIA. I'm leaving you, Pete.

PETER *puts his cigarette out and takes a step towards her.*

PETER. Why?

PATRICIA. I've told you. Teddy needs me.

PETER. Do you think I don't?

PATRICIA. He's my husband.

PETER. (*Bitterly.*) That's very good. (*He turns away, obviously trying hard to control himself. When he turns back to face her, he tries to smile.*) In your letter you say that it's your duty to stay with your husband. You did say duty, didn't you?

PATRICIA. I don't know, I can't remember.

PETER. You did say duty. Your duty to him, or to me, or to yourself, or to your country, or to what—what does duty mean anyway? I'm sorry, Pat, I don't understand, really I don't.

PATRICIA. I didn't think you would, Pete.

PETER. I know you don't feel anything for him, you've told me so.

PATRICIA. Did I?

PETER. (*He looks at her startled, then walks up to her.*) What was it you found out last night?

PATRICIA. I can't tell you. It wasn't only about Teddy, it was something about myself too, something I didn't know before. (*Desperately.*) I can't explain myself, Pete, I told you I wouldn't be able to.

PETER. (*Urgently.*) You've got to try.

PATRICIA. I can't—I can't.

She turns to go. PETER *goes quickly up to her and turns her round to face him.*

PETER. You must explain yourself. You're leaving me. Why?

PATRICIA *says nothing.*

You're leaving me. Do you understand what that's going to mean to me? This isn't some ordinary little intrigue that can be smashed in a second, this is something that's vitally important.

PATRICIA. No!

PETER. What?

PATRICIA. This isn't important. We thought it was, but it isn't, not now anyway. That's one of the things I found out last night. (*She stops uncertainly.*)

PETER. (*Quietly.*) Go on.

PATRICIA. I was awfully sure about things until last night. I had made a fool of myself once before, that time I ran away from you, because of conventions and what other people said and thought. I made up my mind, never again. You know that. I used to think that our private happiness was something far too important to be affected by outside things, like the war or marriage vows.

PETER. Yes it is, Pat, far too important.

PATRICIA. No, it isn't, Pete, beside what's happening out there; (*She points to the window*) it's just tiny and rather—cheap— I'm afraid. I don't want to believe that. I'm an awful coward. It may be just my bad luck, but I've suddenly found that I'm in that battle, and I can't——

PETER. Desert?

PATRICIA. Yes, desert.

PETER. Very heroic.

PATRICIA. I'm sorry if it sounded like that. Heaven knows it's far from the truth.

PETER. (*After a pause.*) Pat, listen to me. You say you love me. I know that's true. I love you too, but more than that, I need you so much that if you go away from me now I just don't know what I'm going to do. That's not a line, Pat, the sort of thing one says at a moment like *this*, it's true—I just don't know what I'm going to do.

PATRICIA. Oh, Pete—— (*She takes his shoulders.*)

PETER. Come with me, Pat, we'll go away, we'll forget about
Teddy——

PATRICIA. (*Moves away.*) No.

There is a long pause.

PETER. (*At length.*) Haven't you forgotten something?

PATRICIA. What?

PETER. I'm desperate, Pat. I'll do anything in the world to
stop you leaving me.

PATRICIA. (*Stating a fact.*) No, Pete, you wouldn't do that.

PETER. Where's Teddy?

PATRICIA. Upstairs.

PETER. Will you go up now and tell him that you're coming
away with me? (*Calling.*) Percy!

PERCY appears.

PERCY. Sir?

PETER. Go and tell Flight-Lieutenant Graham that I'd like to
see him.

PERCY. Yes, sir. (*He goes to the stairs.*)

PETER. Tell him that it's important.

PERCY. Yes, sir, I'll tell him.

PERCY goes out.

PATRICIA. (*Quietly.*) I could deny it, you know.

PETER. It won't be difficult to prove.

PATRICIA. Whatever you tell him won't force me to leave
Teddy.

PETER. Won't it? I think that's for Teddy to say.

There is a pause.

PATRICIA. You won't do it, Pete.

SWANSON comes in through the front-door.

SWANSON. All ready, Mrs. Graham? Haven't been long, have I?

PATRICIA, staring at PETER, turns her head slowly.

PATRICIA. What? No, you've been very quick.

PERCY runs down the stairs.

PERCY. Flight-Lieutenant Graham's in his bath, sir. Says he'll
be down directly.

PETER. Right. Thank you. (*He throws him half-a-crown.*)

PERCY. Thank you, sir. Thank you.

PERCY goes out.

SWANSON. Well, we'd better get weaving, or we'll find this chemist feller has gone to lunch.

PETER. I don't think Mrs. Graham's going with you, after all. Are you, Mrs. Graham? Didn't you say you had to stay in?

Pause. PATRICIA *reaches for her coat.*

PATRICIA. No, I'm not staying in. I must get that stuff for Teddy.

SWANSON, *a little puzzled, holds the door open for her.*

SWANSON. I can get it for you, quite easily, you know—if you'd rather stay behind.

PATRICIA. Thank you, but I'd rather come with you.

PETER *is staring at her. She meets his eyes for a brief instant, then turns and goes out quickly.* SWANSON *follows her.*

PETER, *left alone, lights a cigarette.* DUSTY'S *and* MAUDIE'S *voices can be heard outside.* PETER *goes to the window-seat.* DUSTY *and* MAUDIE *come in.*

DUSTY. Aunt Ella's all right if you treat 'er all right. There's nothing wrong with Aunt Ella.

MAUDIE. *You* don't have to live with her, Dave.

DUSTY. You need tact, Maudie, that's all, just a bit of tact.

MAUDIE. (*Firmly.*) You need a frying-pan—that's what you need.

DUSTY. That's the wrong attitude. What I say is—— (*He catches sight of* PETER *in the corner.*) Oh, good morning, sir.

PETER. (*Shortly.*) Good morning.

DUSTY. Nice day, isn't it?

MAUDIE *has walked across the stage towards the stairs, which she is now mounting.*

Where are you going, Maudie?

MAUDIE. Up to our room. I've got my packing to do.

DUSTY. Heavens, Maudie, you don't want to pack yet. You've got loads of time. Bus doesn't go till one.

MAUDIE. I don't want to miss it, Dave.

DUSTY *chases her up the stairs.*

DUSTY. You won't miss it, Maudie, that I promise.

MAUDIE. If I don't get packed I will miss it.

DUSTY. But you 'aven't got nothing to pack, bar one nightie and a toothbrush——

MAUDIE *disappears.*

(*To* PETER.) Women!

DUSTY *goes out.*

PETER *gets up and walks across to the lounge door.* DORIS *appears on the landing.*

DORIS. Mr. Kyle?

PETER *turns.*

PETER. Yes?

DORIS. Are you good at languages?

PETER. I know French and Spanish and some German. Why?

DORIS. Can you tell me what language this is written in? (*She hands him a letter.*) It isn't Polish, that's all I know.

PETER. (*Glancing at letter.*) It's French. (*He hands the letter back.*)

DORIS. Yes, of course. He spoke French like he spoke Polish. I suppose he thought it'd be easier for me to get translated.

PETER. It's from your husband?

DORIS. He left it with me. I was only to read it if something happened to him. Funny—it's the only letter I've ever had from him. (*She looks at letter, knitting her brows.*) You know French. Will you read it for me?

PETER. Do you mind? I'd rather not.

DORIS. Oh, don't worry. I'll get someone else.

PETER *takes the letter from her.*

PETER. Sorry.

DORIS. Thanks, Mr. Kyle, dear. Sorry if it's a bother. If there's anything in it that's—well—you know—you won't tell anyone, will you?

PETER. No.

DORIS. Of course you wouldn't. O.K., dear. Go ahead.

PETER. It begins: 'It will be necessary for you——'

DORIS. Doesn't he start with dear Doris, or anything?

PETER. No.

DORIS. The French for dear is chère, isn't it? That's the only French word I know. All right, go on.

PETER. (*Translating slowly.*) 'It will be necessary for you to translate'—no—'to have this letter translated. I do not yet express myself in your language well enough to say what I wish to say to you. I am not able to leave you without telling you what your kindness and devotion have meant to me——'

DORIS. Silly.

PETER. —'Since the murder of my wife and boy in Varsovie'—that's Warsaw.

DORIS. The Nazis machine-gunned them on the road, just as they were leaving——

PETER. 'I did not think to feel'—it's rather difficult this. I think he means: 'I did not think I would feel any human emotion again'—that's not quite right, I'm afraid.

DORIS. I know what he means. Go on.

PETER. 'I came to your country with only one thought, to continue to fight against the Germans until I myself found the death in battle which I—have—sought—for a long time. It was not always easy, living in a strange country whose manners—whose customs and language and humour I could not understand. At first it seemed intolerable—and would have been so if I had not had the—blessed—good fortune to meet you, my beloved wife——'

DORIS. Chère?

PETER. No. Bien-aimée—well-loved.

DORIS. I see. Go on.

PETER. 'I found in you what I had lost in Warsaw—I had thought for ever—an—understanding and a sympathy'—sympathie means something a little different to sympathy. It's rather hard to translate.

DORIS. I think I know what it means.

PETER. '—an understanding and a sympathy so strong'—powerful—'that the words we neither of us could speak did not need to be spoken. I can only thank you with a full heart—and it is with real sorrow that I take my leave of you now. I would have so much wished to have repaid you for the sacrifice you made for my sake, in giving up your career—as hotel-keeper——'

DORIS. Hotel-keeper?

PETER. Hotelière.

DORIS. I was a barmaid, dear. I was behind the bar when I first met him. The Crown at Pulborough. He came into the public bar one night and said he was lost, only nobody could understand him. I walked with him as far as where he was going. When he said good night he kissed my hand. He came into the Crown a lot after that—always the public bar, I don't know why. Hotel-keeper. That's Johnny all over. Sorry, dear. Go on.

PETER. 'I would have so much wished to have repaid you for your sacrifice—by taking you with me, after the war, to Poland, where I might in some very small measure, have been able to make a return to you of the material debt I owe you: the other debt I can never repay. Goodbye, my dear, dear wife. I love you for ever.'

PETER *finishes translating, folds the letter up, puts it back into the envelope and returns it to* DORIS.

DORIS. Ta. *She puts the letter in her bag and gets up. She blows her nose furtively, and walks to the stairs.* PETER *lights another cigarette, purposely not looking at her.*

DORIS. I shan't forget the way you did that. You made it sound very nice. (*She reaches the landing.*) You didn't make up that last bit, did you?

PETER. No. It's in the letter. You can get anyone to translate it for you.

DORIS. Thanks, dear. Just so long as I know.

DORIS *goes out.*

MRS. OAKES *enters from coffee-room, some sheets over her arm. She bends down at the foot of the stairs and picks up the scraps of paper which* PETER *had torn up in his scene with* PATRICIA.

MRS. OAKES. (*Clicking her teeth disapprovingly.*) What's this? A paper-chase?

PETER. They're mine. (*He takes the scraps of paper from her and stuffs them in his pocket.*)

MRS. OAKES. Waste-paper receptacles are provided, Mr. Kyle. Besides, there's such a thing as salvage, you know.

PETER. I'm sorry. It was very untidy of me.

MRS. OAKES *goes up the stairs, meeting* TEDDY, *who comes running down, dressed in ordinary uniform—not battledress.*

TEDDY. Hullo, you old dusky enchantress. We made rather a hole in your bacon and eggs last night, eh?

MRS. OAKES *glances round hurriedly at* PETER.

MRS. OAKES. By which you mean the sausages, I suppose.

TEDDY. That's right. The sausages. Delicious.

MRS. OAKES. I'm glad you liked them, I'm sure.

MRS. OAKES *goes up the stairs and out.*

TEDDY. (*To* PETER.) You wanted to see me about something, didn't you?

PETER. Yes, I did.

TEDDY. Any objection if I order a beer first. I've got a thirst on.

PETER. Go ahead.

TEDDY. Anything for you?

PETER. No, thank you.

TEDDY *goes to lounge door.*

TEDDY. A somewhat boozy type, old Graham, I'm afraid. (*Calling.*) Hey, Percy. Bring me a beer, and jump to it!

PERCY. (*Off.*) Yes, Mr. Graham, sir.

TEDDY. (*To* PETER.) Bad show about Johnny, isn't it?

PETER. Yes. I'm very sorry.

TEDDY. He was good value, old Johnny. One of the very best. (*Pause.*) They're a bit different from us, these Poles, you know. Crazy types, most of them. They're only really happy when they're having a crack at Jerry.

PETER. The same doesn't apply to you?

TEDDY. Not exactly. I'm quite ready to admit we sometimes find it a bit of a bind.

PERCY *comes in with a half-pint of beer.*

Well, bung-ho! (*He takes a gulp of beer.*) Chalk it up, Percy.

PERCY. Yes, sir.

PERCY *goes out.*

TEDDY. O.K., Kyle. Shoot. Give us the five-second burst.

PETER *does not reply.*

Go ahead. What have you got to say to me?

PETER. Nothing.

TEDDY. What do you mean—nothing?

PETER. Nothing. Just goodbye. I'm leaving this morning.

TEDDY. Oh, sorry to hear it. Percy told me it was something important.

PETER. He must have got it wrong. It's quite unimportant.

TEDDY. (*Contrite.*) I say, I'm most frightfully sorry. I didn't mean that, you know. I mean, you'll be coming down again, won't you?

PETER. No. I'm leaving on the Clipper within a few days. You won't see me again.

TEDDY. Wish I was a film star.

PETER. Do you?

TEDDY. Dashing madly about all over the world, pursued by fans, making pots of money, glamorous females hurling themselves at you wherever you go.

PETER. It's not so much fun as it sounds.

TEDDY. Not exactly a bind, though. I say, I nearly forgot. (*He fumbles in his pockets and produces a notebook.*) You've got to write something in my book.

PETER. I'd rather not, if you don't mind.

TEDDY. What do you mean, you'd rather not? I'll take it as a personal affront.

PETER. It's only that I don't know what to say.

TEDDY. Say anything—preferably something I can shoot a line about. You know—to my life-long buddy—or—to the whitest man I ever knew—no, what about—to Teddy Graham, dauntless eagle of the skies, from his humble admirer and friend——

PETER. (*Suddenly losing control.*) For God's sake, shut up!

TEDDY *starts. There is a pause.*

TEDDY. Sorry. Only my warped sense of humour, you know.

PETER *snatches the book, scribbles something in it hurriedly, and returns it to* TEDDY.

TEDDY. Thanks a lot. (*He reads it.*) Oh, thanks. Between you and me I never know what that means, although it's the Air Force motto.

PETER. I don't know what it means, either.

TEDDY *puts the notebook away.*

Sorry for the outburst. I don't feel too well this morning.

TEDDY. (*Sympathetically.*) You don't look any too well. Hardly the smooth, glamorous lover of the screen. (*He puts a hand over his mouth.*) Sorry. Is that a brick?

PETER. Yes. I'm getting old, you see, Teddy, and that's something I don't care to be reminded of.

A car door slams outside, and PATRICIA *comes in. She stands just inside the door.*

TEDDY. Hullo, darling. Did you get that stuff?

PATRICIA. Yes. It wasn't what you asked for, but the chemist said it was just as good. (*She hands him a packet.*)

TEDDY. Thanks most awfully. Kyle's leaving us this morning. Did you know?

PATRICIA *looks at* PETER.

PATRICIA. Yes. He told me.

TEDDY. He's off on the Clipper in a couple of days. Lucky type, isn't he?

PATRICIA. Yes.

TEDDY *occupies himself with his beer. There is a pause.* PETER *turns abruptly and makes for the stairs.* MRS. OAKES *comes down simultaneously.*

PETER. (*To* MRS. OAKES.) Can you get me a car?

MRS. OAKES. Yes, Mr. Kyle. When do you want it?

PETER. As soon as possible.

MRS. OAKES. I'll do my best.

PETER *goes out.*

He looks ill—Mr. Kyle. Is anything the matter with him?

TEDDY. It's that dinner you gave him last night, I expect.

MRS. OAKES. Indeed it isn't. I had the rissoles myself, and there's nothing wrong with me.

TEDDY. We haven't all got your cast-iron stomach.

MRS. OAKES. Flight-Lieutenant Graham!

MRS. OAKES *goes out.*

TEDDY *kisses* PATRICIA *on the cheek.*

TEDDY. You don't look any too well yourself this morning. Do you feel all right?

PATRICIA. Oh, I'm all right. When will you be flying again?

TEDDY. Don't know. Not for two or three days, anyway. They'll be working on that tail-plane of ours. Next time I go on a trip, I suppose you'll be back in London.

PATRICIA. No, I won't.

TEDDY. (*Spluttering into his beer.*) Don't give me heart failure. You mean you're going to stay down here?

PATRICIA. Yes, Teddy, if you want me to.

TEDDY. Don't be an utter clot, darling! If I want you to! God, how marvellous! How long will you stay?

PATRICIA. For good.

TEDDY. For good—but what about your new play? Aren't you starting rehearsals next week?

PATRICIA. No, I'm not going to do it. I'm turning it down.

TEDDY. You'll give up the flat?

PATRICIA. Yes.

TEDDY. Oh, boy! Yippee! (*He vaults into the sofa.* PATRICIA *watches him, unsmiling.* TEDDY *pulls himself up short, a trifle crestfallen.*) I say, Pat—you're not doing this because of— because of——

PATRICIA. No, Teddy. I want to stay with you. (PATRICIA *has been unwrapping the parcel from the chemist. She approaches* TEDDY *now with a bandage and a bottle of iodine.*) I think I'd better do this now.

TEDDY. All right, nurse. (*He bares his wrist.*) I warn you I shall scream.

PATRICIA *dabs iodine on his wrist.*

PATRICIA. Sorry.

TEDDY. It doesn't hurt at all. (*Suddenly.*) Ow! D.A.

PATRICIA. D.A.?

TEDDY. Delayed action.

PATRICIA *begins to bandage the wrist.*

PATRICIA. I'm not very good at this, I'm afraid.

TEDDY. You're much too beautiful to be good at bandaging.

PATRICIA. Teddy?

TEDDY. Yes, darling?

PATRICIA. You have been rather a fool, you know.

TEDDY. Have I?

PATRICIA. We've been married nearly a year now.

TEDDY. You're telling me.

PATRICIA. We don't know each other awfully well, do we?

TEDDY. No, I suppose we don't—at least I know you all right

—every little bit of you—but I admit I have been a bit of a dark horse with you. But now, after last night——

PATRICIA. Last night isn't enough. It's not enough unless you go on telling me things—unless you——

TEDDY. What?

PATRICIA. Unless you treat me more like a wife and less like a show-piece.

TEDDY. (*Shocked.*) Show-piece?

PATRICIA. (*Slowly.*) Suggested that Flight-Lieutenant Graham shall in future be permitted to mention his wife's name not more than—how many times—per diem—ten—was it?

TEDDY. Oh, Gawd! How did you hear about that?

PATRICIA. It doesn't matter.

TEDDY. I'll kill Gloria.

PATRICIA. No, don't. He thought—I'd be pleased. I was too—in a way—but—well, you see what I mean, don't you?

TEDDY. God! Tear me off a strip, I deserve it.

PATRICIA. No, you don't. It's not really been your fault; at least it's been much more mine than yours.

TEDDY. Oh, darling, what utter bilge! It's not been your fault at all.

PATRICIA. It doesn't much matter whose fault it's been, Teddy, does it, provided we both make a bit of an effort from now on? There—— (*She finishes bandaging and stands up.*)

TEDDY. Thanks awfully. Darling, talking about show-piece. Well, when I first asked you to marry me, I never thought you'd say yes, and when you did I could never quite believe there hadn't been a mistake somewhere. And so I've always been a bit scared of you. And when we've been together, I've always been afraid of boring you—and so I tried awfully hard not to bore, and so, of course, I always did bore you—and that is why show-piece is just about right, I suppose. But now, after last night, well——

PATRICIA. Go on, Teddy.

TEDDY. Well, it's just that I do love you—and I don't know—somehow, I'm not scared of you any more.

DUSTY *and* MAUDIE *come down the stairs,* DUSTY *carrying* MAUDIE'S *suitcase.*

TEDDY. Morning, Sergeant. How's the old tum?

DUSTY. Not so bad, sir. Feels 'ellish empty, though.

TEDDY. Needs refuelling, I expect. Hullo, Mrs. Miller. How are you this morning?

MAUDIE. Very well, thank you, Mr. Graham. Dave and I went for a walk, and he showed me your Wellington.

TEDDY. (*Startled.*) What? How did you get her past the guards?

DUSTY. She only saw it from the road, sir. It's still out at dispersal.

MAUDIE. (*Accusingly.*) Did you know that it's got a big hole in its tail?

DUSTY. (*Hastily.*) 'Course he knew, Maudie. He's only the jolly old skipper.

MAUDIE. (*Firmly.*) Yes, but you told me that he sits up there in front. He might not have known what was going on at the back.

TEDDY. I don't usually, Mrs. Miller, but as a matter of fact I did know about the hole.

MAUDIE. I thought you ought to know, Mr. Graham; that's why I told you. It looks very dangerous—a great big hole like that.

TEDDY. Thank you, Mrs. Miller. You were quite right to tell me. We're going to have it seen to.

MAUDIE. I'm very glad to hear it.

DUSTY. You must forgive my wife, sir. I'm afraid she don't know much about aircraft.

TEDDY. That's all right, Dusty. My wife doesn't either.

MAUDIE. I do know about aircraft—I know which are ours—which are theirs.

TEDDY. I wish Dusty—Dave—were as hot on aircraft recognition.

During the last few lines the front-door has opened quietly and the COUNT *has been standing just inside the door, taking off his flying-jacket. He is in full flying-kit, dishevelled, dirty, and damp. He waits patiently for a lull in the conversation before launching himself into speech.*

COUNT. Is—please—my wife—in home?

TEDDY. (*With a shout.*) Johnny!
They all move towards him.

Johnny, you old sod! Is it really you? Are you all right?

COUNT. Yes—please—sank you.

DUSTY. (*Shaking his hand.*) Good show, Count, old cock, old cock! Good show, sir!

TEDDY. (*Calling.*) Doris——

PATRICIA. (*Stopping him quickly.*) Don't! I'll go and tell her. It's better. (*She runs up the stairs.*)

TEDDY. (*Deliriously.*) Johnny, you wicked old Pole! What in hell have you been up to? Tell us what happened, Johnny. Where have you been?

COUNT. Please—we fall in se drink.

TEDDY. Yes, I know you fall in the drink. How did you get out of the drink? That's what I want to know.

COUNT. Please—I tell you——

SWANSON *comes bursting in through the front-door.*

SWANSON. (*Shouting.*) Johnny, you old bastard! Are you all right? What happened? (*To* TEDDY.) The whole of his ruddy crew are just piling off a lorry at the guard room—all jabbering like monkeys—and the only thing we can get out of any of them is—'Please we fall in se drink'.

TEDDY. That's all we can get out of Johnny up to now.

DUSTY. We haven't given him much of a chance yet, sir.

TEDDY. Quite right. Quiet, everyone! Come on, Johnny. The floor is yours. You fall in the drink. What happened then?

COUNT. We—land—pumkek.

TEDDY. Pancake. Yes——

COUNT. We—not hurt—not much. We go pouf——

SWANSON. You go pouf?

COUNT. (*Helplessly.*) We go pouf.

TEDDY. I've got it. They inflate their rubber dinghy.

COUNT. Dinghy—yes. We—— (*He makes gesture of rowing.*)

TEDDY. Spot a ship?

COUNT. No.

DUSTY. Swim.

COUNT. (*Repeating gesture.*) No, we——

SWANSON. Ah, row.

COUNT. Yes, sank you—we raow sree hour—see Lysander—far—far—make hola!—No good.

TEDDY. Pilot was having his lunch.

COUNT. We—raow—anosser two hour—sen—get out——

SWANSON. Get out? Out of the dinghy? Why?

COUNT. We walk, please.

SWANSON. You can't ruddy well walk. You're in the ruddy water.

COUNT. Yes, please. We walk in se ruddy water.

DUSTY. They wade ashore, sir.

COUNT. We see—a pheasant.

SWANSON. What's a pheasant got to do with it? You saw a pheasant on the beach?

COUNT. Not—on—beach. By—gottage.

SWANSON. I still don't see——

TEDDY. He means peasant.

COUNT. Yes, please—in gottage—no telephone. At first—pheasant—peasant—not—understand—'e sink we 'ave parachutes—se enemy—but when 'e see Poland (*he points to the lettering on his arm.*) 'e find anosser peasant——

SWANSON. Pheasant.

COUNT. —anosser pheasant wiss big motor. 'E drive us. I see telephone near road. I make to stop and try telephone se aerodrome. I say—please Milchester 23. Zey say—please, sree hour delay, Winchester. I say—Milchester, please. Zey say—yes, please, Winchester. I say—bloody nuts and we go on.

TEDDY. And here you are, please?

COUNT. Yes, sank you.

TEDDY. Good old Johnny!

DORIS *comes down the stairs. The* COUNT *walks across to her and kisses her.*

DORIS. Hullo, ducky. So you've come back to me.

COUNT. (*Kisses her hand.*) You worry, no?

DORIS. (*Smiling.*) Oh, no. Where have you been?

COUNT. Please—I fall in se drink.

DORIS. Yes, I know, but what happened then?

TEDDY. (*Imploringly.*) Doris—have a heart. He's only just finished telling us the story.

SWANSON. Yes. They all went pouf, and were picked up by pheasants. All sorts of fun and games.

DORIS. I'll make him tell me the story later. Only it had better be good, Johnny ducks, after all you've done to me.

There is a sudden shriek from MAUDIE.

MAUDIE. My bus! I missed it.

DUSTY. Cor! So you 'ave.

SWANSON. Doesn't matter, Mrs. Miller. We can't bother about buses at a moment like this.

MAUDIE. But I have to bother——

SWANSON. I'll drive you into Lincoln this afternoon.

MAUDIE. That's very kind of you, I'm sure, but I'm going to St. Albans.

SWANSON. Or, better still, Grantham. Plenty of trains from there.

TEDDY. Don't worry, Mrs. Miller. We'll get you to St. Albans, if we have to fly you there and drop you by parachute.

MAUDIE. (*Doubtfully.*) I'd rather have gone by bus.

TEDDY. This calls for the party of the century. Percy!

PERCY *enters.*

PERCY. Cripes, the old Count! (*Rushes to him.*) Coo, I'm glad you're back. Where have you been?

COUNT. Please, I fall——

TEDDY.
SWANSON. } He fall in se drink.

TEDDY. Percy! Pints for everyone. We'll come and help you. Come on, Dusty. Come on, Gloria.

SWANSON, TEDDY, *and* DUSTY *make for the bar.*

DUSTY. (*Going.*) I won't be a tick, dear.

MAUDIE. But, Dave, my bus!

DUSTY. As far as your bus goes, you've had it.

DUSTY *goes into bar.*

DORIS *and* COUNT *go towards bar. They stop to kiss.* MRS. OAKES *comes out of her office.*

MRS. OAKES. Good gracious, the Count! Well, this is a nice surprise. We'd quite given you up.

They shake hands.

TEDDY. (*Coming out.*) Gin and lime for you, Doris?

DORIS. Yes, please.

They move to the bar.

COUNT. Please, I am dirty to go in there.

DORIS. You're filthy to go anywhere, Johnny. But I shouldn't worry just this once.

PERCY *has come out with two pints. He puts them on table, R.*

PERCY. Countess, what about Bele now?

DORIS. Of course it was Bele. Thank you ever so much. (*She hugs* PERCY *and cries on his shoulder.*) Silly, crying when he's come back.

PERCY. 'Course not, it's only natural.

DORIS. Well, here he is.

PETER *appears on the landing and begins to come downstairs.*

PERCY. No, you keep him. Never did me any good.

DORIS. Thanks, Percy. I think I will. You never know. (*They go into bar.*)

DUSTY *and* SWANSON *come from bar, each carrying a pint, and* DUSTY *has a port for* MAUDIE. PETER *has got to the desk.* MRS. OAKES *appears.*

MAUDIE. Dave, I don't think I should.

DUSTY. Go on, Maudie. You'll need a few ports if you're going to be dropped by parachute. Won't she, sir?

SWANSON. Well, Mrs. Miller, here's fluff in your latchkey!

MAUDIE. Fluff in yours!

TEDDY *runs in from bar to foot of stairs.*

TEDDY. Pat! Pat! Come on down. You don't know what you're missing. Come on, Kyle! (*He runs back to bar.*)

DUSTY *and* SWANSON *are whispering together.*

MRS. OAKES. (*To* KYLE.) You'll notice I haven't charged you for the breakfast after all.

PETER. Yes, I see. Thank you very much. (*Pays bill.*)

MRS. OAKES. By the way, I trust you left the Wing-Commander's things just as they were?

PETER. Yes, I was very careful.

PATRICIA *appears on landing.*

MRS. OAKES. You could have had No. 2 for tonight. I'm sorry you're leaving us so soon.

PETER. I'm afraid (*pauses as he sees* PATRICIA) I had no choice. (*He gets his hat off stand.*)

MRS. OAKES. Goodbye and thank you.

PETER. Thank you.

MRS. OAKES *goes into office.*

PATRICIA. (*From stair.*) Goodbye.

PETER. Goodbye, Mrs. Graham. (PETER *goes out.*)

SWANSON *whispers to* MAUDIE. *She giggles.* PERCY *enters with another port for* MAUDIE. *Singing is heard in the bar.*

PERCY. Talk about George Formby!

MAUDIE. (*Taking port.*) Tinkerty-tonk!

SWANSON. Tinkerty-tonk!

TEDDY. (*Enters from bar.*) We're making old Johnny sing. Come on, Johnny!

DORIS *pushes him into room.*

TEDDY. Go on, Johnny. Try again.

COUNT. Oh, no, please. I sing so bad.

DORIS. (*Calls out.*) Come on, Percy! Come on, Fred! Come and hear Johnny sing.

ALL *come on, carrying pints.*

SWANSON. Go on, you old clot.

DUSTY. Go on, sir.

TEDDY *makes* JOHNNY *get up on centre table.*

COUNT. (*Sings, helped for the first line by the others.*)

>   I don't want to join the Air Force,
>   I don't want to go to war.
>   I'd razzer hang around
>   Piccadilly Underground,
>   Living on ze earning of a 'igh-born lady . . .

MRS. OAKES *comes in.* JOHNNY *fades on* "'igh-born lady".

MRS. OAKES. (*Severely.*) Quiet, Count!

COUNT. (*Gets off the table.*) Beg pardon, please. Sey make me sing.

TEDDY. Where's old Kyle? Let's make him join the party.

PATRICIA. (*From the window.*) He's gone.

TEDDY. Gone? Oh, pity! Still, we can do all right without him. Come on, darling. (*He holds out his arm to her to join the circle.*)

SWANSON. Now, then, boys and girls! All together. Never mind
Mrs. Oakes. She's heard it before.

> We don't want to join the Air Force,
> We don't want to go to war . . .

They sing in unison. PATRICIA *stands still for a moment, watching.
Then she walks forward to join the group.* TEDDY, *singing lustily,
puts an arm around her.*

CURTAIN

WHILE THE SUN SHINES

TO
ANTHONY ASQUITH

Characters:

HORTON
THE EARL OF HARPENDEN
LIEUTENANT MULVANEY
LADY ELISABETH RANDALL
THE DUKE OF AYR AND STIRLING
LIEUTENANT COLBERT
MABEL CRUM

ACT I   MORNING

ACT II   NIGHT

ACT III SCENE 1 LATE NIGHT
            SCENE 2 MORNING

The action passes in the sitting-room of Lord Harpenden's chambers in Albany, London.

While the Sun Shines was first produced at the Globe Theatre, London, on December 24th, 1943, with the following cast:

HORTON	*Douglas Jeffries*
THE EARL OF HARPENDEN ...	*Michael Wilding*
LIEUTENANT MULVANEY ...	*Hugh McDermott*
LADY ELISABETH RANDALL ...	*Jane Baxter*
THE DUKE OF AYR AND STIRLING	*Ronald Squire*
LIEUTENANT COLBERT	*Eugene Deckers*
MABEL CRUM	*Brenda Bruce*

The play directed by ANTHONY ASQUITH

ACT I

SCENE: *The sitting-room of Lord Harpenden's chambers in Albany, London. A large, square room, furnished solidly with late eighteenth-century mahogany furniture. Double doors back centre lead into the bedroom; a single door, L., into the hall. Large windows take up most of the right wall.*

HORTON, *Lord Harpenden's manservant, comes in. He is carrying a breakfast tray, which he puts down on a table. He is a thin, gloomy-faced man of about fifty. He knocks gently on the bedroom door. Receiving no reply, he opens the door and goes in—to emerge instantly. He closes the door again, ponders a second, and then knocks loudly. There is still no answer. He knocks again.* LORD HARPENDEN *comes out, looking tousled and sleepy. He is a young man of twenty-three or twenty-four, of rather frail appearance.*

HARPENDEN. What's the matter?

HORTON. Your breakfast is ready, my Lord.

HARPENDEN. Yes. So I see—but why did you dart in and out like that, like a scared rabbit?

HORTON. I—beg your pardon, my Lord.

HARPENDEN *surveys his appearance in a wall mirror, and gives a faint shudder of disgust. He begins to comb his hair with a small pocket-comb.*

HARPENDEN. Oh, Horton, bring another breakfast, will you?

HORTON. Yes, my Lord.

HARPENDEN. What have you got?

HORTON. Well, there's some spam.

HARPENDEN. No, don't waste the spam; it's too useful for sandwiches, late at night. What about sausages?

HORTON. I can manage one, my Lord.

HARPENDEN. That'll do.

HORTON. It's tea and not coffee, isn't it, my Lord?

HARPENDEN. What do you mean? (*He has picked up* The Times *and is glancing through it.*)

175

HORTON. Miss Crum prefers tea to coffee for breakfast.

HARPENDEN. Miss Crum? Who said anything about Miss Crum?

HORTON. Isn't it Miss Crum?

HARPENDEN. No, it is not Miss Crum.

HORTON. (*Doubtfully.*) It looked like Miss Crum.

HARPENDEN. (*Raising his voice.*) I don't care who it looked like —it is not Miss Crum. As a matter of fact it isn't Miss Anything——

HORTON. Mrs. Chappel?

HARPENDEN. Horton—you haven't by any chance forgotten that I'm getting married tomorrow?

HORTON. No, my Lord.

HARPENDEN. Very well, then. Now, will you kindly go into that room, draw the curtains, take a good look around, and then come out and tell me how sorry you are.

HORTON. I hardly like to do that, my Lord.

HARPENDEN. Go on.

HORTON *goes into the bedroom. There comes the sound of curtains being drawn, then* HORTON *reappears and closes the door.*

HORTON. I'm extremely sorry, my Lord.

HARPENDEN. Thank you, Horton.

HORTON. Funny, it looked just like Miss Crum, the way she sleeps all curled up with her arm over her face——

He is interrupted by a wail from HARPENDEN, *who has taken the cover off his breakfast dish.*

HARPENDEN. Horton—what's happened to my grandmother's other egg?

HORTON. Well, my Lord——

HARPENDEN. There were two—you know there were. She sent me two, and I had one yesterday—now where's the other?

There is a slight pause before HORTON *can gain enough courage to answer.*

HORTON. There was an accident, my Lord.

HARPENDEN. Oh, no!

HORTON. I'm afraid so, my Lord.

HARPENDEN. (*With a wealth of reproach.*) Oh, Horton!

HORTON. I had taken the egg out of the refrigerator, and I

was just going to break it on the side of the frying-pan when——

HARPENDEN. Please, Horton, this is too painful. I'd rather not hear anything more about it.

HORTON. No, my Lord. I'm very sorry.

The telephone rings. HORTON *goes to answer it.*

Hullo . . . Yes, m'lady. (*He puts the receiver down.*) Lady Elisabeth.

HARPENDEN *gets up and takes the receiver.* HORTON *goes out.*

HARPENDEN. Hullo, darling. How are you? Have a good journey? . . . Not the whole night? . . . Couldn't you get a sleeper? . . . Well, surely your father could have fixed it for you . . . through the Air Ministry. . . . Yes, but I consider coming up to marry me is work of national importance . . . How are you? . . . Yes I know, but apart from that, how are you? . . . Good. You didn't have any trouble about leave? . . . When? . . . Wednesday? . . . Well, that gives us six days . . .

MULVANEY, *a young American in the late twenties, appears at the bedroom door. He has swathed an eiderdown round his otherwise naked body.*

(*To* MULVANEY.) Good morning.

MULVANEY. Good morning. (*He looks round the room, blinking in the daylight.*)

HARPENDEN. (*Into telephone.*) No, darling, nobody you know . . . Well, not this morning, darling, because I've got an interview at the Admiralty. Let's meet for lunch. One o'clock at Pruniers. All right? Where are you staying? Brown's? . . . How did you get in? . . . Three weeks ago? . . . No, I had a very quiet evening, in bed at ten . . . All right, don't believe it . . . it's true . . . See you at lunch then . . . Goodbye. (*He replaces the receiver. To* MULVANEY.) Let me get you a dressing-gown.

He goes into the bedroom. MULVANEY *continues his bewildered scrutiny of the room.* HARPENDEN *comes out with a dressing-gown, which he gives to* MULVANEY, *who nods his thanks.*

MULVANEY. Pardon me—where am I?

HARPENDEN. You're in my chambers in Albany.

MULVANEY. What are chambers?

HARPENDEN. Flat. Apartment.

MULVANEY. What's Albany?

HARPENDEN. It's a sort of block of chambers—apartments—off Piccadilly.

MULVANEY. And, if you'll pardon me again, who are you?

HARPENDEN. My name's Harpenden.

MULVANEY. Mine's Mulvaney. Glad to know you.

They shake hands.

HARPENDEN. How do you do? Do you mind if I start my breakfast? Yours is on the way.

MULVANEY. Go right ahead. Was that your bed I slept in?

HARPENDEN *sits down to his breakfast.*

HARPENDEN. Yes.

MULVANEY. Oh. Have I been there since ten, last night?

HARPENDEN. What? Oh, no. You see, I didn't see any point in volunteering the information to one's strictly brought up fiancée that one spent half the night in the Jubilee.

MULVANEY. The Jubilee? Now, that name seems to pull a plug. Was I there last night?

HARPENDEN. Well—you looked in——

MULVANEY. (*Nodding.*) And looked out?

HARPENDEN. Shall we say your exit was more involuntary than your entrance?

MULVANEY. It's coming back to me. They gave me the bum's rush, didn't they?

HARPENDEN. You could put it that way, I suppose. I didn't really see it. One minute you were there, doing a pas seul in the centre of the floor, and the next minute you were in the street.

MULVANEY. What's a pas seul?

HARPENDEN. A little dance on your own.

MULVANEY. Was that what I was doing?

HARPENDEN. That is the charitable view of what you were doing.

MULVANEY. What's the uncharitable view?

HARPENDEN. Pinching Mrs. Warner's behind.

MULVANEY. Who's Mrs. Warner?

HARPENDEN. The proprietress of the Jubilee.

MULVANEY. Oh, my aching back! So I'm in the street. What happens then?

HARPENDEN. Well, when I left the place, about half an hour later, I tripped over you in the black-out.

MULVANEY. Gee, was I lying there unconscious all that time?

HARPENDEN. Semi-conscious.

MULVANEY. Knocked out, huh?

HARPENDEN. No. Passed out.

MULVANEY. Say, listen—how could you tell the difference?

HARPENDEN. I'd rather not go into that at the moment.

MULVANEY. O.K. O.K. Only let me tell you, concussion can take some funny forms.

HARPENDEN. I doubt if concussion would take the form of breathing gin fumes in my face and calling me Dulcie.

MULVANEY. Did I call you Dulcie?

HARPENDEN. Amongst other things.

MULVANEY. Gosh! How did I come to do that, I wonder?

HARPENDEN. Not knowing Dulcie, it's hard for me to say.

MULVANEY. She's my girl friend back home.

HARPENDEN. So I gathered.

MULVANEY. You don't look a bit like her.

HARPENDEN. That's too bad.

MULVANEY. Well, go on. What happened then?

HARPENDEN. You wouldn't tell me where you lived. At least you gave your address as 856 Orinoco Avenue, Elizabeth City, Ohio.

MULVANEY. Yeah. That's where I live all right.

HARPENDEN. Yes, but it didn't help the immediate problem of finding you a bed.

MULVANEY. You could have taken me to the Jules Club or somewhere.

HARPENDEN. I thought of that, but not knowing the customs of the American Army I wasn't sure how they would view the parking on their doorstep at four o'clock in the morning of a very pickled lieutenant, inclined to embrace everyone he saw and call them Dulcie.

MULVANEY. (*After a moment's thought.*) It would have been O.K.

HARPENDEN. I didn't like to risk a court-martial.

MULVANEY. So you brought me here.

HARPENDEN. The porter and I carried you up and put you to bed.

MULVANEY. Say, I hope I didn't disgrace you.

HARPENDEN. Oh, that's quite all right. The porters here have been used to putting people to bed for well over a hundred years. Lord Byron had chambers in Albany.

MULVANEY. (*Interested.*) Did he now? Say, isn't that something? It is kind of old world, this place, at that.

HARPENDEN. Yes, it is. I like it very much. My family have always lived here.

MULVANEY. Do they live here now?

HARPENDEN. No, I haven't any family—at least, I'm an orphan.

MULVANEY. Tough. Gee, it gives one quite a kick to have slept in a place Byron used to sleep in. Did he write any of his poetry here, do you think?

HARPENDEN. I expect so.

MULVANEY. (*Quoting.*)

> So we'll go no more a-roving
> So late into the night,
> Though the heart . . . (*Falters.*)

How does it go on?

HARPENDEN. I'm afraid I don't know. I don't read Byron.

MULVANEY. (*Remembering.*)

> Though the heart be still as loving
> And the moon be still as bright.

Imagine your not reading Byron.

HARPENDEN. Imagine.

MULVANEY. That's funny, you know.

HARPENDEN. (*Piqued.*) I don't see why it's funny—quite a lot of people don't read Byron.

MULVANEY. Yeah. But—hell—you live here.

HORTON *comes in with another breakfast tray.*

HARPENDEN. Here's your breakfast.

MULVANEY. (*To* HORTON.) Take it away, Buddy. I couldn't use it.

HORTON *looks at* HARPENDEN *in doubt.*

HARPENDEN. You'd better try and eat something. It's supposed to be good for—er—for concussion.

MULVANEY. O.K. I'll try a cup of coffee.

HORTON *begins to pour out a cup of coffee.*

Gee, I almost forgot to thank you for being my good Samaritan.

HARPENDEN. Oh, that's all right. I hope you'll do the same for me one day.

MULVANEY. You bet, in the event you ever come to Elizabeth City and get yourself thrown out of Smoky Joe's.

HARPENDEN. All right, Horton. You can clear this away now. (*He indicates his tray.*)

HORTON. Very good, my Lord.

MULVANEY *starts, looks at* HORTON *and then at* HARPENDEN, *as if at a strange animal.*

HARPENDEN. You're in the Air Corps, aren't you?

MULVANEY. (*Still staring at* HARPENDEN.) That's right.

HARPENDEN. Pilot?

MULVANEY. Bombardier.

HARPENDEN. Liberators?

MULVANEY. Forts.

He continues to scrutinize HARPENDEN, *who becomes conscious of his gaze and looks uncomfortable.* HORTON, *meanwhile, has collected* HARPENDEN's *breakfast tray.*

HORTON. Will you be wearing your uniform, my Lord?

HARPENDEN. Yes. My best one. I'm going to the Admiralty.

MULVANEY *puts his coffee cup down with a clatter.*

MULVANEY. (*To* HORTON.) You wouldn't fool me, would you?

HORTON. No, sir.

MULVANEY. (*To* HARPENDEN.) Are you a lord?

HARPENDEN. Er—yes——

MULVANEY. You said your name was Harpenden.

HARPENDEN. That's right.

MULVANEY. You mean you're Lord Harpenden?

HORTON. The Earl of Harpenden.

HORTON *goes out.*

MULVANEY. So you're an earl?

HARPENDEN. Er—yes—I'm afraid so!

There is a pause while MULVANEY *gazes at* HARPENDEN *intently.*

MULVANEY. You're the first earl I ever saw.

HARPENDEN. Oh, they're quite common, really, you know——

MULVANEY. It's funny. You seemed quite an ordinary sort of guy.

HARPENDEN. I am quite an ordinary sort of guy.

MULVANEY. Don't give me that. You're an earl. Say, listen, what do I call you?

HARPENDEN. My friends usually call me Bobby.

MULVANEY. I wouldn't call you that.

HARPENDEN. Why not?

MULVANEY. It doesn't seem right.

HARPENDEN. Last night you called me Dulcie.

MULVANEY. (*Ashamed.*) Gosh! So I did.

HARPENDEN. What's your Christian name?

MULVANEY. Joe.

HARPENDEN. Right. It's Joe and Bobby from now on. Now listen—I've got to go and dress. How long is your leave?

MULVANEY. Seven days.

HARPENDEN. Where are you staying in London?

MULVANEY. Nowhere yet. I only got up yesterday.

HARPENDEN. Well, you can stay here if you like.

MULVANEY. Hell, no—I couldn't do that.

HARPENDEN. That's all right. I won't be here after tomorrow. I'm getting married, you see, and we're spending our leave together in Oxford.

MULVANEY. Gee—congratulations!

HARPENDEN. Thanks, Joe.

MULVANEY. What's that going to make her? I mean, what's the feminine of earl?

HARPENDEN. Countess.

MULVANEY. (*Disappointed.*) Oh, Countess. I knew a girl became a countess. She married an Italian.

HARPENDEN. Really?

MULVANEY. She got herself a divorce, and now she's back in Elizabeth City, but she's still a countess.

HARPENDEN. Well, of course, Italian countesses don't mean very much—I don't mean to be rude to your friend.

MULVANEY. That's O.K.—Elly's a good girl, but she's not one of nature's countesses.

HARPENDEN. So much for Elly. Well, now, it's settled, isn't it? You're going to stay here for your leave?

MULVANEY. Well, it's darned kind of you, Bobby.

HARPENDEN. My man, Horton, will look after you.

MULVANEY. (*Giggling.*) Your man, Horton. Gee, this slays me!

HARPENDEN *smiles politely.*

HARPENDEN. Well, I must go and dress.

MULVANEY. Just a minute. Before I finally accept your very kind invitation, would it be all right to—well, you know, a guy might feel kind of lonely at times, and——

HARPENDEN. Yes, that's all right. Horton's very discreet.

MULVANEY. It's a kind of hypothetical question, anyway. I don't know a darned soul in this town.

HARPENDEN. Don't you? Oh, well, we'll soon fix that. What's your type—anything special?

MULVANEY. Under fifty.

HARPENDEN *has begun to dial a number.*

HARPENDEN. I'm ringing up someone who's very good-looking, very amusing, and mad about Americans. (*Into receiver.*) Hullo. Extension 5651 please. Thanks. (*To* MULVANEY.) She works at the Air Ministry . . . Typist . . .

MULVANEY. A what?

HARPENDEN. Typist. Stenographer, you know.

MULVANEY. Oh . . .

HARPENDEN. (*Into receiver.*) Hullo. Could I speak to Miss Crum, please? Lord Harpenden . . . (*To* MULVANEY.) I'll ask her round for a drink and then you could invite her to dinner or something . . . (*Into receiver.*) Hullo, Mabel . . . Bobby . . . How are you? . . . Well, I've told you before not to go out with Poles . . . Yes, I know they're pets, but that's not the point . . . Look, darling, what time is that horrible old Sir Archibald letting you off today? . . . Well, what are you doing at the office if it's your day off? . . . Oh, I see. What about coming round here for a drink? . . . Albany . . .

In about an hour . . . There's an American I want you to meet . . . yes, a pet . . . he's a Bombardier . . . he's got the most wonderful story about a raid on Bremen that'll thrill you to the marrow . . . All right, darling . . . I may be out, but he'll be here anyway . . . Yes, I'll try to be in, but I've got an interview at the Admiralty . . . I don't suppose it'll take long . . . That's the girl . . . yes, tomorrow . . . St. George's, Hanover Square. You're coming, aren't you? . . . Yes, you did. You met her at a cocktail party, about a year ago . . . Yes, that's right. Brown hair and grey eyes . . . Darling, you are speaking of the woman I love . . . Yes, I do, really I do . . . Yes, of course I love you too, but in a different way . . . All right. Bless you.

He rings off.

She's coming round this morning. She's got the day off, so you can ask her to lunch.

MULVANEY. I've never done a raid on Bremen.

HARPENDEN. (*Vaguely.*) Haven't you? Oh well, I don't suppose she'll mind.

MULVANEY. Say, this is darned kind of you.

HARPENDEN. Oh, that's all right. Just look on it as a bit of reciprocal lease-lend.

He goes into the bedroom.

MULVANEY. (*Calling.*) Say, Bobby—can I use your 'phone?

HARPENDEN. (*Off.*) Yes—of course.

MULVANEY *goes to the telephone. He dials a number.*

MULVANEY. Hullo. Can I speak to Colonel Murphy, please? Lieutenant Mulvaney . . .

HORTON *comes in and crosses the room to the bedroom door.*

HORTON. (*At door.*) Was your breakfast to your liking, sir?

MULVANEY. (*With an air of dignity.*) Yes, thank you, Horton.

He giggles suddenly. HORTON *raises his eyebrows and goes into the bedroom.*

(*Into receiver.*) Hullo, Spike? . . . Say, listen, what happened to you guys last night? . . . Yeah, I remember as far as that, but how come I got to a joint called the Jubilee all by myself? . . . Oh, what was she like? . . . O.K., I'll tell you, but you won't believe me. I slept in the same bed with an

earl . . . No, not a girl, stupid, an earl. E-A-R-L. An earl
. . . Hell, no, I wouldn't kid you, Spike. (*Angrily.*) Because
he says he's an earl . . . Well, you got to believe a guy when
he says a thing like that . . .

HORTON *comes out of the bedroom, with* MULVANEY'S *uniform over
his arm.*

No, they don't wear crowns. Only when they go to Westminster Abbey—I know that——(*He catches sight of* HORTON.)
Hey, where are you going with my uniform?

HORTON. I was going to brush it, sir. If I may say so, it needs
a good brushing badly.

MULVANEY. Righty-oh, old fellow. (*He giggles again.*)

HORTON *goes out.*

MULVANEY. (*Into receiver.*) That was his man, Horton. Doesn't
it slay you? . . . The earl? Well, he's young—younger than
me . . . You can, too, be an earl when you're young.
Remember little Lord Fauntleroy . . . Well, the little
Duke, then . . . you're a disbelieving son of a bitch . . . A
place called the Albany . . . Sort of old-fashioned apartment
house, only the apartments are called chambers . . . Wise
guy . . . Yeah, Lord Byron lived here . . . Lord Byron . . .
No, he's dead, you ignorant bastard. Don't you know anything except how to drive a B.17? . . .

HORTON *comes in.*

This guy's called Harpenden—the Earl of Harpenden . . .
Not a bad little guy. (*He catches sight of* HORTON.) A cracking
good sort . . . See you tonight at the Club . . . O.K. Goodbye.
(*He rings off.*)

HORTON. Excuse me, sir, did you want your buttons cleaned?

MULVANEY. Er—no thanks. We don't clean our buttons.

HORTON. Very good, sir. (*He turns to go.*)

MULVANEY. Say, don't go for a minute. Stay and talk.

HORTON. Sir?

MULVANEY. How long have you been the earl's man?

HORTON. I've been with his Lordship all his life. Before that I
was with his father.

MULVANEY. You're not the only man he's got, I suppose?

HORTON. No, sir. We have two large country estates, and

before the war they needed a very big staff to keep them up.

MULVANEY. Before the war? What's happened to them now?

HORTON. One is a hospital, and the other has been taken over by the Air Force.

MULVANEY. That's tough.

HORTON. Tough, sir?

MULVANEY. Well, I've read a lot about how these English aristocrats are being ruined by the war——

HORTON. Oh, no, sir. We are far from being ruined. Luckily our money doesn't come from our estates, which were always run at a loss, even before the war.

MULVANEY. What does it come from, then?

HORTON. Ground rents, sir—in London, mostly.

MULVANEY. Real estate, huh? That's pretty valuable, I guess——

HORTON. Yes, sir. We must be worth all of two million pounds, sir.

MULVANEY. Holy smoke! Eight million dollars!

HORTON. Yes, sir. Probably a good deal more than that.

MULVANEY. Gee!

He ponders for a second. HORTON *waits patiently for his next question.*
You know, it doesn't seem right to me that a guy should be worth all that money and not to have had to work for it.

HORTON. It happens in your country, too, sir.

MULVANEY. Yeah, I suppose it does. Still, we don't call them earls.

HORTON. No, sir.

MULVANEY. You mustn't mind me. I'm just an ignorant American.

HORTON. I'm an American myself, sir. I was born in America, and had an American father.

MULVANEY. Is that so?

HORTON. My mother went to New York before I was born. She was a housemaid with the Morgan family there. She married an American opera singer.

MULVANEY. She did? Well, how come you're not at the Metropolitan yourself?

HORTON. I fancy I inherited my mother's talents rather than my father's. Anyway, I understand he was not a very good opera singer. Well, now, sir, if you'll excuse me, I'd better be getting on with my work.

MULVANEY. Sure thing. Sorry to have kept you.

HORTON. Not at all, sir. Very glad to have a chat with a fellow citizen.

He goes out. Left alone, MULVANEY *looks around the room with a new expression on his face.*

MULVANEY. (*Muttering to himself.*) Eight million bucks!

HARPENDEN *comes out of the bedroom. He is dressed as an ordinary seaman, less boots.* MULVANEY *does not see him.* HARPENDEN *goes up to him, making no sound in his stockinged feet.*

HARPENDEN. Do I need a shave?

MULVANEY *turns and starts when he sees the uniform.*

MULVANEY. Gosh Almighty!

HARPENDEN. What's the matter?

MULVANEY. Is that fancy dress or are you really a gob?

HARPENDEN. I'm really a—gob. Tell me, do I need a shave?

MULVANEY. (*Examining his chin.*) I guess it'll pass all right.

HARPENDEN. (*Doubtfully.*) It's got to pass a lot of lynx-eyed old admirals. (*He strokes his chin.*) Damn! I think I do need a shave.

MULVANEY. Why don't you have a shave, then?

HARPENDEN. I've only got one saw-toothed old razor blade, and I can't get another.

MULVANEY. Not even for eight million dollars?

HARPENDEN. (*Opening the hall door and calling.*) Horton. Bring my boots down, will you? (*He surveys himself critically in the mirror.*)

MULVANEY. Can you beat that—an earl being a gob.

HARPENDEN. Do you mind not using that revolting word. We say 'matelot'.

MULVANEY. O.K., matelot. Say, what sort of ship are you in?

HARPENDEN. Destroyer.

MULVANEY. Seen any action?

HARPENDEN. Not much. We sink the odd submarine from time

to time. We did have a bit of nonsense at Narvik once—a long time ago.

MULVANEY. Say, that *was* a long time ago. How long have you been in this racket?

HARPENDEN. Three years.

MULVANEY. Gosh! And they haven't made you an officer yet?

HARPENDEN. Not yet. They may this morning, though; that's what my interview at the Admiralty is about.

MULVANEY. How come you haven't been up for an interview before?

HARPENDEN. I have been—three times. This is an annual ceremony.

MULVANEY. And they turned you down—each time?

HARPENDEN. Flat, my dear Lieutenant, as a pancake.

MULVANEY. How come—you being his earlship and all that?

HARPENDEN. His earlship and all that I may be, but, as I am reluctantly forced to conclude, I am also an extremely incompetent sailor.

HORTON *comes in with his boots.*

HORTON. Your boots, my Lord.

HARPENDEN. Thank you, Horton.

HARPENDEN *sits down, and* HORTON, *kneeling before him, helps him on with them.* MULVANEY *watches the scene incredulously.*

MULVANEY. For Pete's sake!

HARPENDEN. You'd better get dressed, unless you want to receive Mabel Crum in your negligée.

MULVANEY. O.K.

He walks towards bedroom door, passing HARPENDEN's *chair as he does so, where he halts abruptly.*

(*Mocks sternly.*) Isn't it customary in the British Navy for a rating to stand up when an officer passes him?

HARPENDEN, *grinning, rises smartly and stands to attention.*

HARPENDEN. I'm very sorry, sir.

MULVANEY. So I should hope. (*He inspects him.*) All right. Carry on, my Lord. (*Chuckling.*) Gee, wouldn't it slay you——

He goes into the bedroom. HARPENDEN *sits down again, while* HORTON *helps him on with his other boot.*

HORTON. High-spirited young gentlemen, these Americans.

HARPENDEN. Yes, Horton, very. By the way, you've got to look after him, after to-morrow. I'm lending him these chambers.

HORTON. (*After a slight pause.*) Is that wise, my Lord? You have some very breakable things here, and——

HARPENDEN. Don't worry about that, Horton. He appreciates my things much better than I do.

There is a ring at the front-door.

HORTON. Very good, my Lord.

He goes out into the hall, and after a moment we can hear him greeting someone at the front-door.

ELISABETH. (*Off.*) Good morning, Horton.

HORTON. (*Off.*) Good morning, m'lady.

HORTON *re-enters.*

Lady Elisabeth.

HARPENDEN *gets up, surprised.* ELISABETH *comes in.* HORTON *goes out.* ELISABETH *is very young, and seemingly quite unconscious of the fact that she is very beautiful. She is in W.A.A.F. (corporal) uniform.*

HARPENDEN. Hullo, darling. (*He kisses her on the cheek.*) I told you—I've got to dash off to this interview in a second.

ELISABETH. I'm sorry, Bobby, but I just simply had to fly in and wish you luck.

HARPENDEN. That's very sweet of you. I need it. Well, how are you? Poor little thing. Did you have an awful journey?

ELISABETH. Awful.

HARPENDEN. Didn't you sleep at all?

ELISABETH. Not a wink.

HARPENDEN. You look very well on it, I must say. (*He points to her arm.*) Hullo, haven't you gone down one? You were a sergeant last time I saw you.

ELISABETH. Yes, I know.

HARPENDEN. What's the trouble?

ELISABETH. My C.O.'s a cat.

HARPENDEN. So's my captain if it comes to that. Funny, we're neither of us awfully good at our jobs, are we?

ELISABETH. Oh, I'm quite good at mine. I just have bad luck. That's all.

HARPENDEN. What did you do this time?

ELISABETH. I lost the plans of the Station Defence.

HARPENDEN. Good Lord!

ELISABETH. Well, we found them again all right. I'd only left them in the Ladies.

HARPENDEN. But that's nothing at all. What bad luck!

ELISABETH. You're a beast, but I love you.

HARPENDEN. Do you really?

ELISABETH. Oh, I don't know about really.

HARPENDEN. You're not beginning to have doubts on our wedding-eve?

ELISABETH. No, Bobby, it's just that it's easier for you to know about these things than it is for me.

HARPENDEN. Why, may I ask?

ELISABETH. Well, I've practically never known any other man in my life, except you—living up in that awful old Northern fastness of ours. I've always loved you, though, especially since you've been a sailor, because you look so beautiful in that uniform, with those lovely baggy trousers and that low neck——

HARPENDEN. Your view seems to be shared by their Lordships at the Admiralty.

ELISABETH. Now you—you've known hundreds of girls—thousands probably.

HARPENDEN. No, darling. Just hundreds.

ELISABETH. So it's easier for you to judge.

HARPENDEN. Judge what?

ELISABETH. Whether you love me really or not.

HARPENDEN. I love you really. (*He kisses her.*)

ELISABETH. More really than you love Mabel Crum?

HARPENDEN. Who's Mabel Crum?

ELISABETH. Darling, you know very well who Mabel Crum is. So do I, too. We hear things, you know, even up in Inverness.

HARPENDEN. I have simply no idea what you're talking about.

ELISABETH. Oh, yes, you have. (*Reproachfully.*) Oh, darling, how could you?

HARPENDEN. How could I what?

ELISABETH. Mabel Crum. But she's awful.

HARPENDEN. How do you know?

ELISABETH. Why, even Daddy knows her.

HARPENDEN. I don't see why the fact that she's an acquaintance of Colonel the Duke of Ayr and Stirling should necessarily damn this lady, whoever she is.

ELISABETH. Well, you know what Daddy's like.

HARPENDEN. Darling, you shock me—really you do.

ELISABETH. Do you remember I met this Mabel Crum at a party when you were on leave, about a year ago? I pretended not to know anything about it then, because we weren't even officially engaged. But I hear now you've been seeing her again.

HARPENDEN. Your gossip, my sweet, is as untrustworthy as your father's racing tips. I haven't seen Mabel Crum for months and months. In fact, I've really no idea what can possibly have happened to her. (*He glances furtively at the door, then at his watch.*)

ELISABETH. (*Reproachfully.*) Bobby!

HARPENDEN. What do you mean—Bobby?

ELISABETH. I always know when you're lying. You give yourself away every time.

HARPENDEN. How?

ELISABETH. I'm not going to tell you how. It's a little trick that's going to come in very useful after we're married. After we're married I shall know the exact minute when you start seeing Mabel Crum again.

HARPENDEN. Elisabeth! I consider that a perfectly revolting thing to say. Have you no moral standards of any sort?

ELISABETH. (*Sincerely.*) I don't know. I've never had a chance of finding out.

HARPENDEN. And this is the girl I am marrying!

ELISABETH. Oh. You don't have to worry about me. It's you I'm worrying about. I have a logical mind, and I can't see why, if you see Mabel Crum before we're married, you shouldn't see her after we're married, too.

HARPENDEN. Shall I tell you why? A little bagatelle called the marriage vow.

ELISABETH. Do you mean to keep that little bagatelle?

HARPENDEN. I do.

ELISABETH *stares at him.*

ELISABETH. Yes, I can see you do. You're not lying now. All right, darling, I'm sorry. (*She puts her head on his shoulder.*) It's only because I don't know anything about men. I've only got Daddy to go by.

HARPENDEN. For the sake of the future of the human race, I trust that that is a misleading model.

ELISABETH. He's coming round to see you this morning—on business, he says.

HARPENDEN. Oh God! Doesn't he ever do any work at the War Office?

ELISABETH. Not much. I think they only gave him the job because the army wanted to take over Dunglennon.

HARPENDEN. What is the job?

ELISABETH. Liaison Officer to the Poles.

HARPENDEN. Oh, does he speak Polish?

ELISABETH. No, but he says he understands their point of view.

HARPENDEN. I should have thought a little ready cash would have been more acceptable.

ELISABETH. Oh, he got that, too. The bookies have got it by now. Which reminds me, darling, don't put any money into Zippy Snaps, will you?

HARPENDEN. It's easy for you to sit there and say don't put any money into Zippy Snaps. Anyway, thank God, he'll miss me. I've got to go out. (*He gets up from the sofa.*)

ELISABETH. Oh, Bobby, I've just remembered. Oh, how awful! I should have told you before. There's someone else coming round to see you this morning.

HARPENDEN. Yes, darling? Who's that?

ELISABETH. Well, I haven't only asked him to come round, either.

HARPENDEN. What do you mean?

ELISABETH. I told you I had to sit up all night in the train, didn't I? Well, we were eight in the carriage, and next to me there was the most enchanting little Free French Lieutenant. Wasn't that funny?

HARPENDEN. Hilarious.

ELISABETH. Well, anyway, we talked all night, in French mostly, so the others couldn't hear what we were saying.

HARPENDEN. Darling, am I to understand that for ten hours you regaled each other with a selection of smutty stories?

ELISABETH. No, darling, but you know what Frenchmen are. We talked of all sorts of things—his private life, my private life, General Giraud——

HARPENDEN. Darling, will you stop burbling and come to the point.

ELISABETH. Oh, yes, all right. Well, anyway, he was going up to London on leave and the poor little man had no idea where he was going to stay, so I said—— (*Noticing* HARPENDEN *start.*) What's the matter?

HARPENDEN. So you said he could stay here?

ELISABETH. Yes, Bobby. I hope you don't mind, but I knew you wouldn't be using the flat after tomorrow, and I thought just for the one night you wouldn't mind him bunking in that bed with you. (*She points to bedroom door.*)

HARPENDEN. Darling, there is already a vast American bombardier bunking in that bed with me. He's in there now, dressing. I refuse point blank, for you or for Free France, to sleep three in a bed.

ELISABETH. Oh, dear! Who's the American?

HARPENDEN. It's rather a long story to tell you now. You say this is a little Frenchman?

ELISABETH. Quite little. Of course I only saw him sitting down.

HARPENDEN. Would he fit on the sofa, do you think?

ELISABETH. Yes, I should think so.

HARPENDEN. All right. Well, you'd better stay here and explain the situation to him when he arrives. I've got to go. See you at lunch. Goodbye.

A thought strikes him. He looks nervously at the door.

Or perhaps, now I come to think of it, it would be better
if I just left a message for him with Horton. I mean I don't
want to keep you——

ELISABETH. That's all right. I'd like to stay here. I've got
nothing to do all morning.

HARPENDEN. Oh! Splendid.

Pause.

Darling, do you mind if I make a 'phone call?

ELISABETH. I thought you were in a hurry.

HARPENDEN. Yes, but this is something I've just thought of
that's got to be done. Official business—for my Captain.
(*He is dialling as he speaks. Into receiver.*) Hullo, Air Ministry.
Extension 5651 please . . . Hullo—Oh—this is Lord Harpenden here. Could I possibly speak to the young lady I
spoke to earlier this morning . . . I forget her name . . . Oh,
yes, of course, how stupid of me. (*To* ELISABETH.) Terrible
head for names. (*Into receiver.*) Oh, hullo . . . Yes, this is
Lord Harpenden. You may remember I spoke to you earlier
on a certain matter. I see that you've taken no steps to
expedite delivery . . . Yes, I'm glad of that . . . Well, the
fact is that something has come up that renders the immediate project temporarily inoperative . . . Yes, that's exactly
it . . . Exactly . . . I'll ring you later. Goodbye.

ELISABETH. (*Without suspicion.*) What have you got to do with
the Air Ministry, darling?

HARPENDEN. Oh, we work a lot with the R.A.F., you know—
Coastal Command—flying boats—co-operation's all the
thing these days. (*He looks at his watch.*) Oh, Lord, I'm late.
Goodbye, darling.

He kisses her. There is a ring at the front-door.

Oh, Lord! Here's your Frenchman. You can entertain him.

There is the sound of voices in the hall.

DUKE. (*Off.*) Good morning, Horton.

HORTON. (*Off.*) Good morning, your Grace.

ELISABETH. No, it's not. It's Daddy.

HARPENDEN. Damn!

HORTON *opens the door.*

HORTON. His Grace.

The DUKE *comes in. He is in Colonel's uniform, about fifty-five, rather portly, but with the remnants of great good looks.*

DUKE. Ah, hullo, my boy. I've caught you in. Good. How are you? Looking well, anyway. All that ozone, I expect, isn't that it?

HARPENDEN. Yes, sir. Thank you.' If you'll excuse me, I must——

DUKE. That's all right, my boy; I won't keep you a second. Just wanted a little chat on certain rather pressing matters —business, you know—awful bore and all that, but it's no good shirking these things, what?

ELISABETH. Daddy—Bobby's got an interview at the Admiralty, and if he doesn't start soon he'll be late.

DUKE. What's that? Mustn't be late for the Admiralty, my boy. That'll never do.

HARPENDEN. No, sir. I quite agree.

DUKE. So I'll come straight to the point. I've just come from your solicitors. We've been looking over that marriage settlement. Well, now, that's a very handsome document, I must say—very handsome indeed. There's just one thing——

HARPENDEN. Do you mind, sir, if we discuss it some other time? If I'm late for this interview——

DUKE. Quite so, my boy, but this won't take a minute. Who's the president of your interviewing board?

HARPENDEN. I've really no idea.

DUKE. Well, find out his name and if you're late I'll give him a tinkle this afternoon and explain you were with me.

HARPENDEN. Thank you, sir. That's very kind of you, but——

DUKE. That's all right, my boy. No trouble at all. I know all these old Admirals—do anything for me, most of 'em. They're ten a penny at the Turf. Now where were we—ah yes—the settlement. Now, here's where I think it falls down. I notice that no provision whatever has been made for your wife's family.

HARPENDEN. That was agreed, sir.

DUKE. Agreed by whom? Not by me.

HARPENDEN. No, sir. You weren't consulted. By your daughter's solicitors.

DUKE. Quite so—but I must say they seem to me to have slipped up badly there. Now, there are one or two most deserving cases in our family that need attention—for instance, Elisabeth's Aunt Amy.

ELISABETH. Daddy—Aunt Amy's perfectly happy in that nursing home—and she's got plenty of money of her own——

DUKE. Quite so, my dear, but she could always do with a little more.

ELISABETH. I can't see why, seeing that she thinks she's Karl Marx.

DUKE. That hallucination is unfortunate, I know, but should not, I feel, preclude her ending her days in a manner fitting to her true estate. However, if you like, we can leave Aunt Amy out. Now—coming a little nearer home——

HARPENDEN. I made no provision for you, sir, because, as you know, I had anyway agreed to make you an allowance.

DUKE. Quite so, my boy, quite so, but these things are better on paper. On paper, my boy, signed, sealed, and delivered.

HARPENDEN. I can't see why——

DUKE. My dear fellow, these days we must face facts——

ELISABETH. (*Sharply.*) Bobby? (*She shows him her watch.*)

HARPENDEN. Oh, Lord! I'm really going to be late. Please, sir, could we face them some other time?

DUKE. I'll tell you what. I've got a car; I'll drive you round to the Admiralty, and we can talk some more about it on the way. What do you say?

HARPENDEN. Thank you, sir, only we must start now.

DUKE. Yes, yes. That's all right.

HARPENDEN *dashes into hall. The* DUKE *gets up, has a sudden thought, and goes to telephone.*

By Jove, I nearly forgot.

ELISABETH. (*Frantically.*) Oh, Daddy, do please hurry——

DUKE. That's all right, my dear. It'll only take a second.

ELISABETH. But Bobby's got an interview at the Admiralty.

HARPENDEN. (*Re-appearing.*) Oh Lord, what's happened now?

DUKE. Just a little tinkle, my boy. I won't keep you a jiffy.

ELISABETH. Don't worry, darling.

DUKE. (*Into receiver.*) Hullo—is that Macdougall and Steinbeck? . . . This is Primrose Path speaking . . . Primrose Path . . . I want fifty pounds each way . . . What's that? Oh, well, it's in the post. Yes, posted it myself . . . My dear sir, I can assure you. The old account? . . . Ah well, there was a little mistake over that. My servant forgot to post it . . . Yes, devilish stupid of him . . . My good man, I presume you know who I am? . . . Oh, you do . . . Well, really, that's nice treatment, I must say . . . Very well, then. I shall remove my custom elsewhere . . . And a very good day to you, sir. (*He rings off, furiously.*) Bolsheviks! (*He begins to dial another number.*)

HARPENDEN. Oh, God!

ELISABETH. (*Taking his hand. To the* DUKE.) Daddy——

DUKE. (*Muttering.*) Damned lot of Yahoos—Macdougall and Steinbeck. (*Into telephone.*) Hullo—Give me the hall porter, please . . . Hullo, Barker—this is the Duke of Ayr and Stirling . . . Will you put on half-a-crown each way on Bernadotte in the three-thirty for me . . . That's right. (*Impatiently.*) Yes, yes, yes . . . When I see you . . .

He rings off. There is a ring at the front-door.

All right, my boy. Now we can go off. Quite ready?

HARPENDEN. Yes, sir, quite. (*He moves to the door.*)

DUKE. Hey, wait a minute! You can't go to the Admiralty looking like a scarecrow.

He pulls his collar about. HARPENDEN *gives a wail and runs to* ELISABETH.

HARPENDEN. Here, you fix it.

ELISABETH *smoothes out his collar.*

ELISABETH. There, darling. It looks sweet.

HORTON *comes in.*

HORTON. Lieutenant Colbert.

HARPENDEN. God in heaven!

COLBERT *comes in. He is a small, clean-shaven, very neat-looking officer in the Fighting French Forces.* HARPENDEN *dashes up to him.* Hullo. How are you? Lovely to see you. Make yourself at home. I've got to go.

He disappears into the hall. COLBERT *looks after him, rather surprised. Then he bows to* ELISABETH.

ELISABETH. Hullo. This is my father—Lieutenant Colbert. Daddy, hurry up.

She runs out after HARPENDEN.

DUKE. (*With an atrocious accent.*) Enchanté, Monsieur, enchanté. (*Shakes hands.*) Il fait chaud aujourd'hui, n'est-ce-pas?

COLBERT. Oui, Monsieur. Je l'ai remarqué moi-même.

DUKE. Votre figure me semble familière. Vous connaissez Paris?

COLBERT. Oui, Monsieur, je connais Paris.

DUKE. I haven't been to Paris since the Duc de Caze won the Grand Prix. How I used to love Paris . . . Paris in the spring . . . The restaurants . . . the cafés . . . the boulevards . . .

COLBERT. Et les jolies femmes, mon Colonel?

DUKE. Ah, les jolies femmes . . . I remember as a boy, there was the most charming little thing . . .

COLBERT. Comment?

DUKE. Un charmant petit morceau . . .

HARPENDEN *and* ELISABETH *dash in.*

HARPENDEN. Oh, for heaven's sake, sir!

DUKE. All right, my boy, I'm coming. (*To* COLBERT.) We must meet again, monsieur. Vous devez venir avoir un morceau à manger avec moi, a mon club . . . Turf.

COLBERT. Avec plaisir.

DUKE. Capitale. (*To* ELISABETH.) Goodbye, my dear. I'll pick you up later. Now, my boy——

He goes out, followed by HARPENDEN.

HARPENDEN. (*Following him out.*) Oh, God!

DUKE. (*Off, his voice coming from the hall.*) The point about this settlement, my boy, is that it's a form of insurance——

ELISABETH. Sit down, won't you?

COLBERT. Thank you. (*He sits down.*)

ELISABETH. It's all right about using this flat, except that you'll have to sleep on the sofa, just for tonight.

COLBERT. That is very kind. Who was that sailor?

ELISABETH. That was my fiancé—Bobby Harpenden.

COLBERT. Your fiancé?

ELISABETH. You're surprised?

COLBERT. You told me he was an earl. I had not expected to see him dressed in that manner.

ELISABETH. You pictured him with a little coronet and an ermine cloak?

COLBERT. Hardly, milady. But I imagined him a little older and with big moustache and a hooked nose—I do not know why.

ELISABETH. He's very good-looking, don't you think?

COLBERT. Not for me. He is altogether too—qu'est ce que c'est fâde?

ELISABETH. Insipid.

COLBERT. Yes. Too insipid.

ELISABETH. Oh.

COLBERT. I am sorry, milady, but I must say what I think.

ELISABETH. That's quite all right, only do you mind not calling me milady.

COLBERT. I beg your pardon. What must I call you, then?

ELISABETH. Well, later on last night we were calling each other Elisabeth and René.

COLBERT. Last night was—last night.

ELISABETH. And today's today. I don't see what difference . . .

COLBERT. Milady—Elisabeth—I made one of two errors last night. Either I said to you too much—or I did not say enough.

ELISABETH. Well, you didn't say too much.

COLBERT. Then I did not say enough.

ELISABETH. What more did you have to say?

COLBERT. Very much more indeed.

ELISABETH. Then say it now.

COLBERT. You would be very angry with me, if I did. No. It is better I keep silent.

ELISABETH. Very well. Just as you please.

Pause. COLBERT *suddenly slaps his knee and gets up.*

COLBERT. I shall say it. I must say it. Elisabeth—do not marry this man.

ELISABETH. Not marry Bobby? Why ever not?

COLBERT. I implore you. Turn back before it is too late.

ELISABETH. But—but I love him. Why should I——

COLBERT. You love him. Yes. You told me so last night. But you also told me what is the truth—you told me you had for him no—no passion, no white-hot burning of the heart.

ELISABETH. Oh, dear! Did I really say that?

COLBERT. You did not employ those words, but that is never-theless what you said. You love him—oh, yes, we will agree. So does one love one's brother or one's little puppy dog. But you are not *in love* with him. No, no, no, milady, Elisabeth. Not in a thousand years.

ELISABETH. But I may be in love with him. It's just that I don't know, that's all. Anyway, ordinary, quiet, restful love is a much better basis for marriage than this white hot burn-ing passion of the heart—or whatever you call it.

COLBERT. Oh, no, Elisabeth. Oh, no. That is where you make such a terrible mistake. Ah, I see it all so clearly. Two great English houses, the alliance planned from an age when you were both little children, obedient little children——

ELISABETH. No, no, it's not like that at all. Both of us have always been perfectly free to choose——

COLBERT. That is what your families have allowed you to believe——

ELISABETH. But—but even if I'm not in love with Bobby—and I don't admit that for a minute, mind you—but even if I'm not, at least he's in love with me.

COLBERT. Is he? And what about the woman Crum?

ELISABETH. Oh, dear! Did I tell you that?

COLBERT. Turn back, Elisabeth. Turn back, or you will ruin two lives.

ELISABETH. But this is ridiculous! What right have you to say these things to me?

COLBERT. There! I told you you would be angry.

ELISABETH. I'm not in the least angry, but the whole thing is quite absurd. Supposing I don't marry Bobby—what then? I'll go back to Inverness, and after the war I'll go on living in Dunglennon, and I'll never meet anybody again as nice or as good-looking or as—all right—as rich as Bobby; and I'll just be an old maid and sink into a decline.

COLBERT. You will not be an old maid. Nor will you sink into a decline. It is not in your face. (*He comes closer to her.*) You are very beautiful, but that is nothing. You have in your eyes a joy, a desire, a voluptuous flame of life, that will not be quenched.

ELISABETH. Have I?

COLBERT. Wait, Elisabeth. Wait, and one day you will find a lover worthy of those eyes.

ELISABETH. How do you know I will?

COLBERT. I know it. That is all. You have only to wait. And I know, too, that you will not have to wait for very long.

There is a pause, while ELISABETH *evidently ponders what line she ought to pursue.*

ELISABETH. Look here, what reason have you got for saying all this to me?

COLBERT. That is a question I do not wish to answer.

ELISABETH. I believe you're making love to me.

COLBERT. You have the right to believe that, milady.

ELISABETH. I'm going to tell Bobby every single thing you've said.

COLBERT. Very well. He will strike me with a right hook, and that is unfortunate, but——

ELISABETH. I hope he does strike you with a right hook—and a left hook too——

COLBERT. (*Resignedly.*) You see how angry I have made you. If what I said was not the truth you would not be angry; you would merely laugh.

ELISABETH. I do laugh. I think everything you've said is frightfully funny. (*Rather tearfully*) I may not be laughing outside, but I am laughing inside—like mad.

Pause.

COLBERT. I will go. (*He turns at the door.*) I repeat. Turn back, Elisabeth, before it is too late. Leave this earl who does not love you to his title, his riches, and his Crums.

ELISABETH. Oh, go away!

COLBERT *goes.* ELISABETH *is plainly upset. She blows her nose violently, then goes to a big radiogram in the corner, L., opens it, and switches it on. After a slight pause there comes the strains of a dance band playing a soft and sentimental air.*

I

MULVANEY *comes out of the bedroom, whistling cheerfully. He is dressed in American Army uniform, with wings. He stops short at sight of* ELISABETH. *He looks her up and down appraisingly, and a slow smile of satisfaction spreads across his face.*

MULVANEY. Well, well, well. So you finally showed up?

ELISABETH. (*Nervously.*) Hullo.

MULVANEY. I guess I'd better introduce myself. My name's Mulvaney—Lieutenant Mulvaney.

ELISABETH. How do you do. I'm——

MULVANEY. (*Shaking hands.*) That's O.K. You don't have to tell me who you are. Your pal the earl told me all about you——

ELISABETH. (*Politely.*) He told me about you, too.

MULVANEY. Yeah, I know. (*He stares at* ELISABETH *with undisguised admiration.*) Well, well, well. I'm telling you that son of a gun didn't exaggerate one little bit. In fact, he didn't tell me the half of it. (*After another appraising stare.*) Zowie!

ELISABETH. (*Smiling nervously.*) Thank you very much.

MULVANEY. Amongst other things, he said you had a soft spot for Americans.

ELISABETH. Did he? Well, of course, I like Americans very much.

MULVANEY. Then I can see you and me are going to be friends.

ELISABETH. I hope so.

MULVANEY. Strictly between ourselves, I got a soft spot, too— for babes who look like you.

ELISABETH. That's splendid.

MULVANEY. It's terrific. Say, listen, how about a little drink? I could use one myself.

ELISABETH. (*Faintly.*) So could I.

MULVANEY. I wonder where the earl keeps his liquor— if any.

ELISABETH. (*Pointing.*) In that cupboard over there.

MULVANEY. Yeah. You'd know a thing like that, wouldn't you? Who better? (*He opens the cupboard.*) Hot dog! There's some Scotch.

ELISABETH. Isn't there any sherry?

MULVANEY. Sherry? You wouldn't fool me, would you, Babe? You'll take Scotch and like it. (*He pours out a very large measure in a tumbler and takes it across to her, neat.*)

ELISABETH. Oh, I couldn't possibly drink that. Would you mind——

MULVANEY. Spoiling it for you? O.K.

He squirts a minute portion of soda water into the glass, and brings it back to her. He has poured himself another glass, neat.

ELISABETH. But it's much too strong.

MULVANEY. Aw, go on. It won't hurt you. (*He raises his glass.*) Here's to Anglo-American relations.

ELISABETH. (*After a pause, muttering.*) Anglo-American relations.

They drink. MULVANEY *throws his back at a gulp.* ELISABETH *takes one sip of hers and makes a wry face.*

MULVANEY. What's the matter?

ELISABETH. It's so strong.

MULVANEY. Aw, now, you wouldn't want me to think you a cissy, would you—in that uniform? Go on, drink it—for the honour of the R.A.F.

ELISABETH, *obeying a sudden impulse, swallows the whole of the drink. She splutters.* MULVANEY *takes the glass from her hand and puts it down.*

That's better.

ELISABETH. (*Weakly.*) I'm not used to drinks as strong as that at this time in the morning.

MULVANEY. (*Smiling.*) Yeah, yeah. I know, I know. Well, well. Now what shall we do?

ELISABETH. I don't know.

MULVANEY. You haven't any etchings to show me?

ELISABETH. Bobby has some in his bedroom.

MULVANEY. Yeah, I bet he has.

He laughs, as if she has made a joke. ELISABETH *laughs too, politely, but puzzled.*

MULVANEY. He didn't tell me you'd be in uniform. It suits you, though. Gosh, that blue brings out the colour of your eyes.

ELISABETH. Oh! Do you think so?

MULVANEY. I certainly do think so. That's one fine little pair of eyes you got yourself there, Sergeant. (*Looking at her arm.*) Are you a sergeant?

ELISABETH. No. Just a corporal.

MULVANEY. Not for long, I'll bet. Say, aren't all the Air Marshals crazy about you?

ELISABETH. They don't appear to be.

MULVANEY. They must be a lot of blind old sourpusses. Now, if you were in the Army Air Corps——

ELISABETH. What would happen?

MULVANEY. You'd be a General.

ELISABETH. I wish I were in the Army Air Corps.

MULVANEY. You're not the only one who wishes that. Tell me, Babe, what do you like most about Americans?

ELISABETH. Well, I've met so awfully few, working where I do. But if you're typical of them, then I've got to admit that—— (*She stops.*)

MULVANEY. Go ahead. Admit whàt?

ELISABETH. Well—that they're a bit—different from other men.

MULVANEY. Different in a good way or a bad way?

ELISABETH. (*After a slight pause.*) In a good way.

There is a pause. MULVANEY *jumps up.*

MULVANEY. O.K. So let's have another drink.

ELISABETH. Oh, no—please——

MULVANEY *has risen and is on his way to the drink cupboard.*

MULVANEY. Say, listen—you're not fooling anyone, Babe, but yourself with this Polyanna stuff. I want another drink, you want another drink, so we both have another little drink. It's good stuff, too—pre-war, by the smell of it. (*He comes back to her with another large whisky, and one for himself.*) Bottoms up, this time—or as you say—no heel taps.

ELISABETH. Oh, dear. I'd much rather not.

MULVANEY. Now, listen, if you haven't finished that drink by the time I've finished mine I'll put you over my knee and spank the life out of you.

ELISABETH. I believe you would, too.

MULVANEY. You bet your sweet life I would. Now (*he extends his glass*) here's to even closer Anglo-American relations.

ELISABETH. (*Muttering.*) Even closer Anglo-American relations.

She closes her eyes and gulps it down quickly, even before MULVANEY
has finished his.

(*Proudly.*) There! (*She suppresses a belch.*) Who's a cissy now?

MULVANEY. (*Admiringly.*) Not you, Babe.

He takes her glass and puts it down. ELISABETH *sits bolt upright on
the sofa, staring straight ahead.* MULVANEY *sits beside her.*

O.K. Shall I shall you about Bremen?

ELISABETH. (*Turning her head slowly, and smiling.*) Oh, yes, do.

MULVANEY. Well—there we were, upside down, nothing on
the clock, enemy fighters swarming all around us.

ELISABETH. Oh, how awful!

MULVANEY. So what did we do?

ELISABETH. What?

MULVANEY. Come a little closer and I'll tell you.

ELISABETH *moves a little closer to him.*

ELISABETH. (*A trifle thickly.*) What did you do?

MULVANEY. We righted the ship, beat off the fighters, and
returned to our base.

ELISABETH. Riddled with holes?

MULVANEY. Riddled with holes.

ELISABETH. How wonderful!

MULVANEY. Aw, it didn't mean a thing.

ELISABETH. Oh, but it was. It was wonderful. Did you get the
—the congresh—congrenshanell thing?

MULVANEY. Come again?

ELISABETH. (*Carefully.*) The Congressional Medal of Honour.

MULVANEY. Oh, that? No. They're thinking up something else
for us, as a matter of fact.

ELISABETH. Isn't that wonderful?

MULVANEY. Why, it was nothing.

*She beams at him, and then appears to be conscious for the first time
of* MULVANEY's *hand on her knee. She stares at it, more puzzled
than angry.* MULVANEY *jumps up and goes to the radiogram.*

How do you work this thing? You should know.

ELISABETH. Oh, yes, I do. I'll show you.

*She makes her way, a trifle unsteadily, to the radiogram and switches it
on.* MULVANEY *holds out his arms to her in invitation to dance and
she goes to him. They begin to sway together in unison.*

MULVANEY. Gosh, Baby, you're one of the loveliest things I ever saw in all my life, and I'm not kidding.

ELISABETH. (*After a faint pause, looking up at him.*) You're rather lovely, yourself.

MULVANEY *hugs her closer, still in the attitude of the dance. Then he tilts her face up and kisses her. She struggles violently for a second, then succumbs and finally contributes. It is a long kiss. The telephone rings two or three times, unnoticed. Then* MULVANEY *breaks away.*

MULVANEY. I suppose I'd better answer that.

He goes to the telephone. ELISABETH *stands in apparent ecstasy, staring straight ahead of her.*

MULVANEY. (*Into receiver.*) Hallo. No, he's out. Who? . . . Mabel who? . . . (*A look of horror crosses his face.*) Yeah, I'll tell him. What was the name again? . . . Yeah. That's what it sounded like . . .

He rings off, and stares at ELISABETH *with horror and perplexity.*

ELISABETH. (*Drowsily.*) Who was that?

MULVANEY. No one. No one at all.

ELISABETH. Don't you want to go on dancing?

MULVANEY. (*Burbling.*) Well, as a matter—I've got to rush, you know—this minute—see my Colonel—I'm late——

He darts out into the hall. ELISABETH *sits down abruptly on the sofa, smiling contentedly. The* DUKE *comes in.*

DUKE. Ah, there you are, my dear. I'm sorry I kept you waiting. I hope you haven't been bored.

ELISABETH. (*Drowsily.*) No, Daddy. I wasn't bored. Not bored at all. Not even the teeniest little bit bored. (*She turns over on her side.*) Good night, Daddy, I'm going to sleep.

The DUKE, *puzzled and alarmed, approaches the sofa and looks down at his daughter, already asleep.*

DUKE. God bless my soul! What an astonishing thing!

CURTAIN

END OF ACT I

ACT II

SCENE: *The same. About 11 p.m. the same night.*

Curtain rises to disclose a man and a woman, sitting together in the same armchair. The man can be recognized as JOE MULVANEY.

HARPENDEN *enters from the hall, putting his latchkeys away in his pocket as he does so. He has his sailor's hat on the back of his head.*

HARPENDEN. (*Carelessly, as he passes the chair.*) Hullo, Mabel.

MULVANEY *jumps up hastily, almost spilling* MABEL CRUM *on to the floor. She is a little older than Elisabeth, but with an even wider, an even more innocent, stare of her eyes.*

MABEL. Hullo, darling.

HARPENDEN *gives her a peck on the cheek and makes his way to the drink cupboard.*

MULVANEY. (*Embarrassed.*) I didn't think you'd be back till later.

HARPENDEN. I'm sorry, Joe. I went on a pub-crawl all by myself and got bored.

He pours himself a whisky and soda.

All my friends are out of town.

MABEL. What about Freddy Dawson?

HARPENDEN. His leave's been cancelled. He went dashing back this afternoon.

MABEL. Wasn't he going to be your best man?

HARPENDEN. Yes, he was. I knew it was a mistake to choose a Commando. Joe, what about you deputizing for him?

MULVANEY. (*Uncomfortably.*) Well—it's darned kind of you, Bobby—and I sure appreciate the compliment—but maybe I'd better not.

HARPENDEN. Why not?

MULVANEY. Well—I'm an American, and perhaps your family wouldn't like it.

HARPENDEN. I told you I haven't got any family, except a very

207

old grandmother who can't move out of her bed and sends me an egg from time to time.

MULVANEY. It's your wife's family I meant.

HARPENDEN. They won't mind. In fact, they'd be delighted.

MULVANEY. (*Nervously.*) No, Bobby. I don't think they'll be delighted.

HARPENDEN. Why not? It's an excellent gesture towards closer Anglo-American relations.

MULVANEY. Yeah. You're telling me. Hell, Bobby, I'd just love to do it ordinarily, and I'm sure grateful for you asking me, but count me out, there's a good guy.

HARPENDEN. Oh, all right. What about you, Mabel? I could dress you as a sailor.

MABEL. Darling, I couldn't trust myself. I'd break down and cry and tear the bride's eyes out.

HARPENDEN. (*Putting his arm round her waist.*) Isn't she a nice girl, Joe? Don't you adore her?

MULVANEY. (*Without enthusiasm.*) Yeah. I sure do.

MABEL. He doesn't. He thinks I'm torture.

HARPENDEN. That wasn't exactly what he appeared to be thinking when I came in.

MABEL. Darling, he was getting something out of my eye.

HARPENDEN. For a girl who takes care of her appearance, Mabel, you manage to get an inordinate amount of things in your eye.

MULVANEY. Now listen—what do you mean I think you're torture? I don't know what——

MABEL. He's fallen in love with a girl he met this morning.

MULVANEY. (*Alarmed.*) Hey! That's not true. Whatever gave you that idea?

MABEL. He won't stop talking about how lovely she was, and how melting and soft and alluring; and then apparently he made an awful boob, because he blushes scarlet whenever he thinks of it.

MULVANEY. Hey, listen——

HARPENDEN. Who was she?

MULVANEY. Oh, no one. No one at all. I was making it all up.

MABEL. It was a W.A.A.F.

HARPENDEN. Tell us about it, Joe.

MULVANEY. Listen, Bobby. Have a heart, will you? Don't ask me about it. It's something I'm trying to forget.

MABEL. Not very hard.

HARPENDEN. He probably fell for the old confidence trick— you know—the furious father or the enraged fiancé or something.

MULVANEY. Stop it, will you. Tell us about yourself. How did the interview go? I forgot to ask you when I phoned.

HARPENDEN *shakes his head gloomily.*

What went wrong?

HARPENDEN. I was quarter of an hour late in the first place, then found myself overdoing the free, frank, open boyish manner, and got the jitters and became far too cringing and servile, and my hair was too long and I hadn't shaved and I didn't know how many tuppenny-halfpenny stamps I could buy for half a crown. In short, for the fourth time in this war, I proved conclusively to the Admiralty and to myself that I am not the officer type.

MULVANEY. Too bad. (*Cautiously.*) Tell me. Did you see your fiancée today?

HARPENDEN. Only for a few seconds—at Brown's about drink time. I was supposed to meet her for lunch, but she rang up to say she had a headache and had gone to bed.

MULVANEY. (*Straightening his tie.*) Headache, huh? (*Heartily.*) Well, well. Do you know what I think I'm going to do? I'm going bye-byes myself.

HARPENDEN. And leave me alone with this man-eater on my wedding-eve?

MULVANEY. Aw, she's no man-eater. You don't get real man-eaters this side of the Atlantic.

HARPENDEN. (*To* MABEL.) If I were you, darling, I'd resent that.

MABEL. Americans always fall for the obvious. They don't appreciate subtlety.

MULVANEY. If you want to see a real man-eater you come to Elizabeth City, and I'll show you one.

HARPENDEN. Dulcie?

MULVANEY. Hell, no. Not Dulcie. I meant—Elly.

HARPENDEN. Oh, Countess Elly.

MULVANEY. Dulcie's a good girl. I'm in love with Dulcie— (*As an afterthought.*)—I hope.

He goes into the bedroom. His head appears again after a second.

(*Contritely, to* MABEL.) Gee—Miss Crum—I must be going nuts. I forgot all about seeing you home.

MABEL. That's all right, Lieutenant. I can easily see myself home.

MULVANEY. But—hell—you live outside London—in a village called Kensington or something, don't you?

HARPENDEN. All right, Joe, don't worry, I'll see she gets home all right. You go to bed.

MULVANEY. O.K. Good night, folks.

He goes into bedroom. HARPENDEN *goes to door and opens it.*

HARPENDEN. (*Calling through door.*) Use the side nearest the window. And don't take up all the bed, like you did last night. I spent most of the night squashed against the wall, struggling for breath.

MULVANEY's *head appears at the door.*

MULVANEY. Last night I thought you were Dulcie.

HARPENDEN. Well, tonight you would oblige me by thinking I'm Hitler.

MULVANEY. O.K. Just so long as I know.

His head disappears. HARPENDEN *closes the door.*

HARPENDEN. What do you think of him?

MABEL. He's a pet.

HARPENDEN. That is a term you apply without discrimination to any member of the Allied Forces who happens to look your way. I asked you what you thought of him.

MABEL. Why so interested?

HARPENDEN. Because, if you must know, I think it's time you settled down and took to yourself a nice husband.

MABEL. Darling—not an American.

HARPENDEN. Why not?

MABEL. You don't *marry* Americans.

HARPENDEN. Don't you. Oh, well—you know best.

MABEL. Besides—what about Dulcie?

HARPENDEN. Dulcie's three thousand miles away.

MABEL. (*Sincerely.*) Poor Dulcie.

HARPENDEN. Poor Dulcie. Did you have a good time tonight? What did you do?

MABEL. Oh, we went to the Hippodrome and had dinner at the Savoy. He was really awfully sweet. Very distrait, though. I think he really did have some rather shattering experience this morning.

HARPENDEN. Really?

MABEL. The poor pet was in such a state about it—whatever it was—that he wanted to go dashing off after dinner to the park, or somewhere, to think things out, he said.

HARPENDEN. Isn't that typically American—to go to the park to think things out?

MABEL. He didn't want to come back here at all—until I said you'd be awfully offended with him if he just faded away without saying a word. And even then he was terribly nervous and jumpy. I couldn't get him to settle down at all.

HARPENDEN. Sorry to have come barging in on you like that.

MABEL. Oh, that's quite all right, darling. Between you and me I think we were both of us delighted to see you barge in.

HARPENDEN. I'm sorry about that. Why?

MABEL. Well—he—because he doesn't like me so much and I —because I love you so much.

HARPENDEN. I bet you say that to all the sailors.

He kisses the top of her head.

MABEL. Not every sailor is as sweet as you are. And not every sailor has two million pounds tucked away in his ditty box.

HARPENDEN. Only until nasty Mr. Gallacher takes it out of my ditty box.

MABEL. Yes, but think what fun you can have with it until he does. What fun you *have* had.

HARPENDEN. That'll be my epitaph when I swing from the lamp-post outside Albany.

MABEL. You have a morbid sense of humour, darling.

Pause.

HARPENDEN. Look—it wasn't only because I was bored that I came back early tonight. I wanted to see you.

MABEL. Did you, darling?

HARPENDEN. (*Embarrassed.*) Yes. First I thought I'd write you
—then I thought that was a bit—you know—then I thought
I ought to tell you—myself—although it isn't awfully easy
—so——

MABEL *looks up at him sympathetically.* HARPENDEN *turns away,
in order not to meet her eyes.*

You see, we've always been good friends and I'd hate anything—Oh, God! I wish I could come to the point.

MABEL. (*Quietly.*) You don't have to, darling. I know what the
point is. After tonight you don't want to see me any more.
That's it, isn't it?

There is a pause.

HARPENDEN. You're an angel.

MABEL. But—darling—don't be silly. I knew it perfectly well.
I don't see you very often—you get so little leave, anyway,
and when I read you were getting married I thought, well,
that's that. He'll just fade quietly away and I won't ever see
him again. I didn't even expect a letter—because anyway
you're not a very good letter-writer, are you? I must say
I'm rather grateful you told me, though.

HARPENDEN. I didn't tell you. You told me.

MABEL. You tried to, anyway. Can I get myself another
drink?

HARPENDEN. Yes, of course.

*She walks away from him to the drink cupboard and pours herself a
drink.* HARPENDEN *goes to the desk and takes an already written
cheque out of the drawer. He gazes at* MABEL's *back in indecision,
then takes her bag off the sofa, and stuffs it inside.* MABEL *turns in
time to see him.*

MABEL. What are you up to?

HARPENDEN. Nothing.

MABEL, *drink in hand, snatches up her bag and looks inside. She
takes the cheque out.*

(*Nervously.*) Just your taxi-fare home.

Pause, while MABEL *examines the cheque.*

MABEL. (*At length.*) My God! Darling, you *are* a bloody fool!
(*She folds it up deliberately.*) The correct thing for me to do
now, I suppose, is to tear it up, grind the pieces into the

carpet with my heel, burst into tears, and say you've insulted me.

HARPENDEN. I hope you don't.

MABEL. I won't. That's the sort of insult I appreciate. (*She gazes at it enthralled.*) Those noughts make me dizzy.

HARPENDEN. Don't spend it all at once.

MABEL. (*Musingly.*) I'll pay a quarter's rent in advance, I'll pay my dentist—he'll have a stroke—poor little man—I'll pay that swine Bojo Sprott back every cent I owe him, plus interest—I'll buy that mink coat—pay for that gin—buy that sapphire brooch and—oh, yes—I'll pay for Brenda's operation. What's left can go into war-savings. (*She puts it away in her bag.*) Darling, take that smirk off your face, and don't make any of those nasty dry comments. Will you believe me that there's never been any derrière pensée——

HARPENDEN. No, darling, arrière pensée——

MABEL. Arrière pensée, then. There's never been any thought of things like this (*she touches her bag*) behind any little—favours I may have done you in the past. My greed got the better of me just now—otherwise I *would* have torn up that cheque and made a scene. Do you believe me?

HARPENDEN. Yes, darling, I do.

MABEL. That's all—except, well—goodbye.

She puts her arm round his neck, and he kisses her.

MABEL. And thank you—very much. (*She turns quickly. Trying to laugh.*) Something in my eye again.

HARPENDEN. I'll kiss it well.

He is going towards her when there is a ring at the front-door.

Oh, Lord! Now who on earth's that?

MABEL. You don't suppose it's Elisabeth, do you?

HARPENDEN. I'm pretty sure not. She wouldn't come round here alone at this time of night.

MABEL. Why ever not?

HARPENDEN. She's rather—old-fashioned—in these matters.

There is another loud, imperious ring.

Horton's in bed. (*He moves towards the door, then turns.*) Just in case of accidents, would you mind awfully going up to the kitchen for a moment?

MABEL. Why the kitchen?

HARPENDEN. Well, it's the only other room available.

MABEL. All right, darling.

HARPENDEN. Take your drink. Have you got cigarettes?

MABEL *nods.*

Good. Now you go up the stairs and turn to the left—not the right, that's where Horton sleeps. (*He picks up a paper off the table.*) Here's the *New Statesman.* (*He hands it to her.*) Or would you rather I sent a man up to keep you company?

MABEL *glances at the front page of the* New Statesman.

MABEL. What do *you* think?

She goes out. There is another loud, incessant peal of the bell.

HARPENDEN. (*Shouting.*) All right. Just coming. (*He knocks on the bedroom door.*) Joe! Joe! Come out of there.

MULVANEY. What's cooking?

HARPENDEN. That's exactly it. You're to go up to the kitchen, and keep Mabel Crum company.

MULVANEY. The kitchen? Why? What are we going to do up in the kitchen?

HARPENDEN. Do you need me to brief you? Here, take a bottle of gin. (*He pushes him to the hall door.*) Up the stairs and turn to the left.

MULVANEY, *bewildered, allows himself to be pushed out into the hall.* HARPENDEN *follows him out. After a second we hear his voice in the hall.*

(*Off.*) I'm very sorry, sir. I had no idea——

DUKE. (*Off.*) That's all right, my boy.

The DUKE *enters, followed by* HARPENDEN.

I had to see you. It's most urgent. If you hadn't been in I'd have camped on your doorstep all night——

HARPENDEN. (*Patiently.*) Yes, sir. As a matter of fact, I should have rung you up about it. I went to see my solicitors this afternoon——

DUKE. (*Testily.*) What the dickens are you talking about?

HARPENDEN. The marriage settlement, sir, I've had them insert that clause you wanted.

DUKE. Oh, you did? Oh, well, that was good of you, my boy, extremely good of you.

HARPENDEN. Not at all, sir.

DUKE. (*Explosively.*) Damnation!

HARPENDEN. (*Startled.*) I beg your pardon?

DUKE. My boy, are you feeling strong enough to stand a shock?

HARPENDEN. Yes—I think so, sir—why?

DUKE. I've just come from seeing Elisabeth. I was with her for over four hours, but she's adamant, I'm afraid—adamant.

HARPENDEN. Adamant about what?

DUKE. My boy—brace yourself.

HARPENDEN. Yes, sir. I have braced myself.

DUKE. She says she's not going to marry you.

Pause.

HARPENDEN. Oh.

DUKE. (*Testily.*) Did you hear what I said?

HARPENDEN. Yes. I heard what you said. Why isn't she going to marry me?

DUKE. That's just it. I don't know.

HARPENDEN. Oh.

DUKE. She talked a lot of gibberish about planned alliance and wrecking two lives and your not having any white-hot burning thingamagig about you—or something——

HARPENDEN. What was that about white-hot burning thinga-magig?.

DUKE. Well, I can't remember the words exactly—there was something about a voluptuous flame of something or other —I remember that—and then there was this white-hot poppycock and then—well, to cut a long story short, she says she's not in love with you any more.

HARPENDEN. Oh.

DUKE. (*Testily.*) Don't keep on saying Oh.

HARPENDEN. There doesn't seem much else to say, except Oh.

DUKE. Good God, man! You're not going to let it rest at that, are you?

HARPENDEN. Well, if she feels she doesn't love me——

DUKE. (*Shocked.*) Good Lord! I'm amazed at you, Robert, my boy. I really am. Why, if I were in your shoes, do you know what I'd do?

HARPENDEN. No. What?

DUKE. I'd raise heaven and earth to make her change her mind. I'd put up such a shindy they'd hear me in Timbuctoo.

HARPENDEN. You suggest I should stand outside Brown's Hotel and make a disturbance?

DUKE. (*Impatiently.*) No, no, no. You misunderstand me. I mean storm her—woo her—take her by force.

HARPENDEN. That's not quite my line, I'm afraid.

DUKE. Good Lord! I thought you were a man.

HARPENDEN. What is your definition of a man, Duke?

DUKE. Someone who does something at a moment like this, instead of just standing there, wilting like a swooning lily.

HARPENDEN. Who's wilting like a swooning lily?

DUKE. You are. Why, good Lord, man, look at you——

HARPENDEN. I take it, sir, that in spite of the fact your daughter says she doesn't love me, you're still in favour of this match?

DUKE. Of course I'm in favour of this match—it's a damned good match.

He collects himself, goes up to HARPENDEN *and puts his arm round his shoulders.*

I'm fond of you, my boy—you know that. I feel about you as I'd feel about my own son.

HARPENDEN. Thank you, sir.

DUKE. Well—what are you going to do about it, eh?

HARPENDEN. (*After a pause.*) I'm going to have a drink.

He goes to the drink cupboard.

DUKE. Robert—I'm disappointed in you.

HARPENDEN. Anything for you?

DUKE. I'll have a pint of Pommery. Got any Pommery?

HARPENDEN. No.

DUKE. Whisky and soda.

HARPENDEN. What on earth made her change her mind like this?

DUKE. Well, I've been thinking it out, and it occurred to me that something that happened this morning might have some connection——

HARPENDEN *gives him his drink.*

(*Automatically.*) Good health. (*He drinks.*)

HARPENDEN. What happened this morning?

DUKE. Something devilish fishy. Deuced odd, the whole thing. After I'd dropped you at the Admiralty—by the way, I suppose there was no trouble about your being late, was there?

HARPENDEN. There was—but it doesn't matter.

DUKE. Sorry, my boy; I'll ring up the First Lord tomorrow. What's his name—Socialist wallah——

HARPENDEN. Alexander—but for God's sake don't. Go on. What was this fishy thing that happened?

DUKE. Well, when I came back here to pick up Elisabeth I found her in a state I can only describe as peculiar.

HARPENDEN. Peculiar? How peculiar?

DUKE. Devilish peculiar. Between you and me, my boy—and don't let it go any further—if it hadn't been Elisabeth I'd have said she was sozzled.

HARPENDEN. Sozzled? Elisabeth——

DUKE. Stinko—profundo.

HARPENDEN. I don't believe it.

DUKE. She insisted on putting her feet up on the sofa and dropping off to sleep, there and then.

HARPENDEN. Well, she had a headache. She told me so when she put me off for lunch.

DUKE. (*Darkly.*) Yes. Later on she did have a headache. Not at the time though. She was as gay as a bee when I found her. (*In a confidential whisper.*) And her breath!

HARPENDEN. Sherry?

DUKE. Whisky.

HARPENDEN. But she hates whisky.

DUKE. My boy—it was unmistakable. You can't deceive me. I've had too much experience of it in our family.

HARPENDEN. Good Lord!

DUKE. But that's not the end of it. Just before I came into the sitting-room, while I was talking to Horton out in the hall, a young man came dashing past me and out through the front-door, going like the wind.

HARPENDEN. Who was it?

DUKE. Never clapped eyes on him before in all my life.

HARPENDEN. Did Elisabeth know who he was?

DUKE. Well, I asked her, and she said—and this is what makes me very suspicious—she said that he'd dropped from the skies. At first I thought she meant one of those parachutist fellows.

HARPENDEN. What did he look like?

DUKE. Well, he was tall and dark—and he was in uniform— not our uniform. As a matter of fact, I think he might have been one of those Americans who are wandering around all over London these days.

HARPENDEN. An American! Then I know who it is.

DUKE. You do? Right, my boy, your duty is plain. You must get in touch with this scallywag——

HARPENDEN. I don't need to get in touch with him. I mean, he's here.

DUKE. Here? Where?

HARPENDEN. In the kitchen.

DUKE. In the kitchen? What's he doing in the kitchen?

HARPENDEN. I tremble to think.

DUKE. Well, good Lord, don't just stand there—get him down from the kitchen.

HARPENDEN. (*Doubtfully.*) Well, I'm not at all sure——

DUKE. Well, if you won't, I will.

He goes to the hall door, opens it, and roars through.

Hey, you! Up in the kitchen—whoever you are. Leave whatever you're doing and come down at once! At once, do you understand? Now we'll see.

HARPENDEN. What am I to say to him?

DUKE. Leave it to me.

MULVANEY *and* MABEL *come in together.*

(*To* HARPENDEN.) What is this woman doing here?

MABEL. (*Brightly,* to DUKE.) Hullo, Tibby, darling. How are you?

DUKE. Oh, it's you, Mabs.

He gives her a quick peck, then turns on MULVANEY.

Now, sir, I must ask you for an explanation——

HARPENDEN. (*Pacifically.*) By the way, this is Lieutenant Mulvaney—the Duke of Ayr and Stirling.

MULVANEY. Holy mackerel! A Duke!

DUKE. I want a straight answer to a straight question. Have you or have you not been making love to my daughter?

MULVANEY. (*After a pause.*) Well, here's the way it is, your—by the way, what do I call you?

DUKE. Never mind what you call me. Answer my question.

MULVANEY. (*To* HARPENDEN.) Is the Duke of Ayr and Whosis your father-in-law?

HARPENDEN. Yes, to be—or rather—not to be.

MABEL. Darling, what a lovely Hamlet you'd make.

DUKE. Stop it, Mabs! You shouldn't be here at all.

HARPENDEN. Darling, go back to the kitchen—do you mind?

MABEL. Oh, no. Please let me stay. This is exciting.

DUKE. (*Thundering.*) Back to the kitchen, Mabs!

MABEL. (*Sulkily.*) Oh, all right. (*At the door.*) If the Lieutenant did make love to your daughter, you might ask her to get in touch with me some time.

She goes out. HARPENDEN *snatches up a paper and hands it to her through the door.*

HARPENDEN. Darling, the *New Statesman.* (*He closes the door.*)

DUKE. Now, sir. Your answer——

MULVANEY. Well, Duke, I guess the answer is yes—I did make love to your daughter.

HARPENDEN. (*Hurt.*) Joe!

MULVANEY. I'm sorry, Bobby. I should have told you, I guess, but I didn't have the nerve. You see, the whole thing was a ghastly mistake.

DUKE. A mistake? You have the confounded impudence to force your attentions on my daughter—after taking good care—mark you—to render her blotto—and then you stand there and tell me it was just a mistake——

MULVANEY. But it *was* a mistake, Duke. You see, I thought your daughter was Mabel Crum.

The DUKE *is rendered temporarily speechless.* HARPENDEN *gives an exclamation.*

HARPENDEN. Oh, God! Of course. I see it all now——

DUKE. You thought my daughter was Mabel Crum?

HARPENDEN. Yes, yes, of course he did. It was a perfectly natural thing for him to do.

DUKE. You will forgive me if I cannot see why it should be a perfectly natural thing for this feller to think my daughter——

HARPENDEN. (*To* MULVANEY.) Joe. I forgive you for everything, but whatever it was you said to Elisabeth has had the effect of making her say she won't marry me——

MULVANEY. (*Looking more pleased than upset.*) It has? Well, can you beat that?

DUKE. (*Returning once more to the attack.*) I may be very obtuse, but I must continue to ask why this gentleman thought my daughter was Mabel Crum?

There is a ring at the front-door.

HARPENDEN. Oh, God! Joe, run and see who that is. I'm out to everybody.

MULVANEY. Sure thing.

He runs out into the hall.

DUKE. You may be satisfied with this feller's explanation, but it seems devilish flimsy to me. Why on earth should he think my daughter is Mabel Crum?

HARPENDEN. Oh, for heaven's sake, sir. He did. Isn't that enough for you?

DUKE. (*Roaring.*) NO!

MULVANEY *comes back.*

MULVANEY. It's a little French guy. He says you promised him he could sleep here.

HARPENDEN. Oh, Lord! Where is he?

MULVANEY. Right here. In the hall.

HARPENDEN *opens the door.*

HARPENDEN. Come in, won't you?

COLBERT *comes in.* HARPENDEN *shakes hands.*

How are you? I'm so glad you came. Nice to see you. I wonder if you'd mind awfully going up to the kitchen for a moment?

COLBERT. The kitchen?

HARPENDEN. Yes. It's up the stairs and turn to the left. You can't miss it.

MULVANEY. It's quite comfortable up there. There are two armchairs and a bottle of gin.

HARPENDEN. And a lady who'll be absolutely delighted to see you.

He steers COLBERT *towards the door and out.*

HARPENDEN. (*To* MULVANEY.) Now listen. You've got to put this right, Joe.

MULVANEY. What do you want me to do, Bobby?

HARPENDEN. The best thing, I should think, would be to go round to see her at Brown's and explain the whole thing.

DUKE. What's the good of that? He'll only start making love to her again.

HARPENDEN. Oh, no, he won't.

MULVANEY. (*Miserably.*) What makes you think I won't?

HARPENDEN. Joe!

DUKE. (*Triumphantly.*) Did you hear that? The feller's not to be trusted an inch.

HARPENDEN. (*Appalled.*) Joe, you're not serious?

MULVANEY. Never more serious in my life, Bobby.

HARPENDEN. But—but you've only known her since this morning.

MULVANEY. While you've known her all your life. What's the difference?

HARPENDEN. Good Lord!

He sinks into a chair.

MULVANEY. I'd never have said a word about this, if Elisabeth hadn't spoken up first.

HARPENDEN. You think she feels the same way about you?

MULVANEY. Doesn't it look that way to you?

HARPENDEN. Yes, I suppose it does. Good Lord!

The DUKE, *who has been glancing from one to the other in bewilderment, now advances on* MULVANEY.

DUKE. Am I to understand, sir, from all this rigmarole that you are now batting on an entirely different wicket?

MULVANEY. (*Politely.*) Come again, Duke?

DUKE. A moment ago you gave as an explanation for your conduct the fact that you mistook my daughter for an unfortunate lady who shall be nameless. Now, as I understand it, you're claiming that your motives are sincere and your intentions are honourable.

MULVANEY. Well, Duke—if you want it in plain English, here it is. I think I love your daughter and I think your daughter loves me.

DUKE. Good God!

MULVANEY. Sorry, Bobby. It does seem one hell of a way to return your hospitality.

HARPENDEN. (*Gloomily.*) For God's sake don't start apologizing. I couldn't bear it.

DUKE. Oh—so you couldn't bear it. Why, good God, man, you're not going to let him snatch the girl you love from under your very nose?

HARPENDEN. How can I stop him?

DUKE. Well—good Lord—at least you can—you can fight him, can't you? Knock him for six through that window!

HARPENDEN, *sunk deep in an armchair, looks up at* MULVANEY.

HARPENDEN. He's too big. Besides, I like him.

DUKE. Like him? What's that got to do with it?

COLBERT *comes in quietly.*

DUKE. (*Testily.*) Go away, Monsieur. Allez-vous-en!

COLBERT. Mademoiselle Crum has told me that something has arisen in connection with milady Elisabeth. Might I ask, is it that milady has decided not to marry milord Harpenden?

HARPENDEN. Yes. That's right.

COLBERT. Then if you are searching for the reason of her decision I think I can give it to you. It is I alone who am responsible.

DUKE. What?

COLBERT. This morning I advised the Lady Elisabeth not to marry this Lord.

DUKE. Wait a minute. Am I to understand that you made love to my daughter, too, this morning?

COLBERT. I cannot deny it, Monsieur.

DUKE. But why, Monsieur? Pourquoi? I suppose because you thought she was Mistinguett?

COLBERT. No, Monsieur. Because I love her.

There is a moment's pause, while everyone stares at COLBERT *wonderingly.*

What is more, if, as you say, your daughter has taken my advice, then it appears probable that she has returned my love.

Another pause. DUKE *suddenly goes to the hall door.*

DUKE. I shall be obliged, gentlemen, if, when in due course you have concluded your deliberations, you would inform me with how many members of the United Nations my daughter is to form an attachment. Personally, I'm going up to the kitchen to have a gin with Mabel Crum.

He goes out. There is a pause, while HARPENDEN *and* MULVANEY *stare, bewildered, at* COLBERT.

COLBERT. (*With quiet martyrdom.*) I suppose you will wish to knock me down, milord.

HARPENDEN. You're certainly smaller than he is—but at the moment I don't see what's to be gained by knocking you down either.

MULVANEY. Considerable satisfaction.

He advances belligerently on COLBERT, *but is restrained by* HARPENDEN.

HARPENDEN. Wait a minute, Joe. Don't start a rough-house yet. If you fight him, then I've got to fight you—and after he's recovered I've got to fight him again. Now that's too much fighting for one night. Let's try a little international arbitration first.

MULVANEY. Aw, hell, Bobby, there's no sense in arbitrating with this guy. He's screwy. He doesn't know what he's talking about. Let's you and me gang up on him and bounce him down the stairs—what do you say?

COLBERT. Tiens! I see I am facing two enemies. That is a surprise. (*To* MULVANEY.) I should have thought you would have been my ally, seeing that my confession has saved you from being falsely accused of stealing this Lord's fiancée.

MULVANEY. (*Hotly.*) Falsely accused nothing! Elisabeth is leaving Bobby because of me—see.

COLBERT. I don't think so, Monsieur. She is leaving him because of me.

HARPENDEN *watches them with raised eyebrows.*

MULVANEY. (*Belligerently.*) Listen, I made love to her.

COLBERT. So did I make love to her.

MULVANEY. I said she was the loveliest thing I ever saw in all my life.

COLBERT. I too, said she was very beautiful.

MULVANEY. Yeah—but I made real love to her—see. I kissed her.

Slight pause.

HARPENDEN. (*Politely.*) Go on, Monsieur. Don't let it rest at that. Tell him what *you* did to my fiancée.

MULVANEY. (*Turning to him, contrite.*) I'm terribly sorry, Bobby —but this guy's got me all balled up.

COLBERT. (*To* MULVANEY.) At what hour did you take these liberties with milord's fiancée?

MULVANEY. What the hell does it matter what hour?

COLBERT. It matters very much. Try, if you will, to remember —was it after eleven o'clock?

MULVANEY. Not much after.

COLBERT. But after, none the less?

MULVANEY. Yeah. I guess so.

COLBERT. What abominable luck! Sacré nom d'une Pipe! And these attentions of yours—she repaid them?

MULVANEY. I'll say she did. (*As an afterthought.*) I'm sorry, Bobby.

HARPENDEN. (*Ironically.*) Not at all. Just imagine I'm not here. I'm going to curl up on the sofa with a good book.

He sits down on the sofa, picks up a book, opens it, and pretends to read.

COLBERT. I am also most sorry, milord, to be forced to say such things before you.

HARPENDEN. Not at all. Don't worry about me. (*He takes his book up and then lowers it again.*) Oh, before you go on—I think I ought to tell you—I hope you won't both be too angry with me—this morning I also made a little love to my fiancée; and at one moment I even went so far as to give her a kiss. I'm most terribly sorry. You must both try to be generous and forgive me.

COLBERT. At what hour was it that you gave your fiancée a kiss, milord?

HARPENDEN. Oh yes, of course, that's very important, isn't it? It was—let me see—about ten minutes to eleven.

COLBERT. Ten minutes to eleven? That is all right then. It was a few minutes after eleven that I advised her not to marry you and to await a lover more worthy of her.

HARPENDEN. Oh, I see. A lover more worthy of her?

COLBERT. Yes, milord. I was naturally referring to myself and had too much delicacy to say so; but I'm afraid that it looks now as if she might have made this ludicrous error of applying my advice to this Lieutenant.

HARPENDEN. (*Rising.*) I'm terribly sorry—you haven't been introduced, have you? Lieutenant Mulvaney—Lieutenant Colbert.

MULVANEY. Aw, nuts! (*To* COLBERT.) Listen, you. What right have you got to go dashing about saying those sort of things to guys' fiancées?

HARPENDEN. (*From the sofa.*) Ha!

MULVANEY. (*To* HARPENDEN.) Well, at least I had some sort of excuse for behaving as I did. He had none.

COLBERT. I have every excuse. Last night, on the train from Inverness to London, I sat next to the most adorable young girl I have yet seen in England. She is merely a Corporal W.A.A.F., so naturally I open conversation——

MULVANEY. You see the sort of guy this is—a railroad menace.

COLBERT. Not at all. When in Rome I do as the Romans, and in English trains I usually try to give the impression of having died in my seat. But this opportunity I could not let to pass. I find my W.A.A.F. is not at all what I imagine. She speaks to me in perfect French, and before long we are telling each other the most intimate details of our private lives. I find she is to marry the following day a young and immensely rich noble whom she patently—from a thousand little hints she gives me—does not love and who, it is equally patent, does not love her.

HARPENDEN *gets up suddenly.*

HARPENDEN. (*Aggressively.*) And why is that so patent?

COLBERT. I find he keeps a mistress.

HARPENDEN. I keep a mistress?

COLBERT. That young woman I have just met in the kitchen—is she not a mistress?

HARPENDEN. No. She's Mabel Crum.

COLBERT. Do not misunderstand me, milord. I am not prudish in these matters. A man can keep a hundred mistresses and still maintain a happy and successful marriage. But when I hear that he keeps a—Mabel Crum—naturally I say—then of course he cannot love Elisabeth as wholeheartedly, as devotedly, with the same white-hot burning passion——

HARPENDEN. Aha! White-hot burning thungummy, eh?

COLBERT. Milord?

HARPENDEN. She mentioned some such idiotic phrase to her father when she told him she wasn't going to marry me.

COLBERT. She did? Splendid! Then perhaps it is still possible she has returned my passion.

MULVANEY. Listen, you little rat—the only way she'd return your passion is through the mail, marked 'Not wanted'.

COLBERT. The situation is not helped by impoliteness, Monsieur. We are at an impasse. You maintain she loves you, I main-she loves me. We must devise a scheme of finding out the truth.

HARPENDEN *goes quickly to telephone and begins to look up a number.*

MULVANEY. Good for you, Bobby—only, say listen—let me talk to her, will you.

COLBERT. If he talks to her it is only fair play I talk to her, too.

HARPENDEN. Look, I am a patient man. I have sat—mainly in silence—while you two gentlemen have gloatingly described in the fullest and most sordid details the vile attentions you have forced on the girl I love. May I remind you, however, that you are under my roof, and you're both very much mistaken if either of you imagines that you're going to have twopence-worth of verbal loveplay with my fiancée on my telephone.

COLBERT. But—milord—since this evening she is no longer your fiancée.

HARPENDEN. We'll see about that. (*Into receiver.*) Hullo, Brown's? Lady Elisabeth Randall, please . . . Yes, darling.

Bobby . . . No, please don't . . . All right, then. I promise not to argue. Just tell me why—I'm surely entitled to know that . . . Yes, but your father wasn't as explicit as I'd like and . . . When will I get it? . . . Tomorrow? Yes, but I want to know tonight . . . Darling, don't cry . . . I only want to know what's happened . . . Why can't you? . . . Yes, but what's the difference between loving someone and being in love with someone . . . All right, then, tell me. Is there someone else? . . . What do you mean, you don't know? . . . Well, let me tell you, I do know——

MULVANEY *makes a grab for the receiver, but* HARPENDEN *nudges him violently away.*

Yes, I know more about it than you think. I know it's one of two men——

COLBERT. (*Urgently.*) The fair play, milord!

HARPENDEN. The fair play, my fanny! . . . Sorry, darling . . . All right, well, let me tell you—so that you'll be warned. One of them is a vicious French snake who goes about bothering young W.A.A.F.s in railway carriages, and the other is a lecherous American who mistook you for a trollop.

MULVANEY. Hey—you little rat!

Again he wrestles with HARPENDEN *to grab the receiver, but is thwarted.*

(*Shouting frantically down receiver.*) Don't believe him, Elisabeth——

HARPENDEN. No, darling, I don't hear anything. Crossed line I expect . . . Yes, darling. A trollop . . . Well, apparently he expected to find a trollop in my sitting-room . . . (*Crossly.*) No, I don't know why . . . Well, you know what these Americans are, they expect to find trollops wherever they go . . . Darling, be reasonable.

MULVANEY *gains the receiver for a moment.*

MULVANEY. (*Frantically.*) Don't believe him, Elisabeth—I don't think you're a trollop—I love you.

COLBERT. (*Grabbing the receiver from* MULVANEY.) Ecoutez Elisabeth . . . I am not a vicious French snake . . . I love you passionately, devotedly, with a burning . . . She has rung off.

HARPENDEN. What did you expect?

COLBERT. Milord, I am astonished with you. Was that what you learnt on the playing-fields of Eton?

HARPENDEN. I was at Harrow.

MULVANEY. (*Displaying his enormous fist.*) I've a good mind to punch you right in the nose.

HARPENDEN. Really! This display of righteous indignation comes a little oddly from you two gentlemen, I must say. Must I remind you that I have known and loved Elisabeth for some twenty years—while you two——

COLBERT. Palsambleu! And so what?

HARPENDEN. I beg your pardon?

COLBERT. The world is no longer what it was when this match between you and Elisabeth was first planned. Les droits de seigneur have gone—never to return. You are a doomed class.

HARPENDEN. All right. I'm a doomed class, but that's no reason I shouldn't marry the girl I love, is it?

COLBERT. Certainly it is, when that girl is Elisabeth. At all costs she must be saved from sharing your doom.

HARPENDEN. Left wing, eh?

COLBERT. Socialiste.

HARPENDEN. Well, I read the *New Statesman* myself.

COLBERT. That will not save you from extinction.

MULVANEY, *who, during all this has been sunk deep in thought, makes a furtive move towards the door.* HARPENDEN *sees him.*

HARPENDEN. (*Sharply.*) Hey! Where do you think you're going?

MULVANEY. (*A trifle shamefacedly.*) Oh, I just thought I'd go out for a little stroll.

HARPENDEN. I suppose your little stroll wouldn't take you anywhere near Brown's Hotel, would it?

MULVANEY. I don't even know where Brown's Hotel is.

HARPENDEN. Then of course you wouldn't think of asking a policeman, would you?

He gets between MULVANEY *and the front-door.*

HARPENDEN. No, you don't go for a little stroll. You're not leaving this flat tonight.

MULVANEY. How do you think you're going to stop me?

HARPENDEN. I don't know—but I'm going to have a good try.

COLBERT. (*To* MULVANEY.) If you attack milord I shall assist him.

MULVANEY. I'm quite ready to take on the two of you.

COLBERT. Without doubt, but have you forgotten that we are guests in milord's flat?

MULVANEY. That's no reason why he should keep me locked up in here all night like a little boy. If I want to go for a stroll, why shouldn't I go for a stroll? I'm a free man, aren't I?

HARPENDEN. If you want exercise I've got a rowing machine in the bathroom.

MULVANEY. Now, Bobby, you don't want to break the poor girl's heart, do you? She loves me, God damn it!

COLBERT. That fact is not yet fully established, Monsieur. It may well be myself she loves.

HARPENDEN. You both forget that several hours have passed since eleven o'clock this morning. All sorts of Poles, Czechs, Belgians and Dutchmen may have made love to her since then—or she may have gone dotty about the night porter at Brown's.

MULVANEY. (*Pleadingly.*) Look, Bobby, be reasonable, will you? I got to get to see Elisabeth tonight.

COLBERT. If he goes, then I go, too.

HARPENDEN. And if you both go, I go with you.

COLBERT. Another impasse. There is only one solution.

HARPENDEN. What's that? The fair play?

COLBERT. Exactly, milord—the fair play. Each man to go round to Brown's Hotel in turn.

MULVANEY. Yeah—but who goes first?

COLBERT. (*Brightly.*) Alphabetical order?

MULVANEY. No, thank you, Mr. Colbert.

COLBERT. Then we must toss up a coin.

HARPENDEN. Hey, wait a minute. I don't think I agree to this.

COLBERT. Where is your spirit of sport, milord?

HARPENDEN. Buried on the playing-fields of Harrow.

COLBERT. If you do not agree to my suggestion, milord, then I shall be painfully compelled to side with this large

Lieutenant against you. You would not then stand much chance.

MULVANEY. I got an idea. Do you guys play craps? (*He brings out some dice from his pocket.*)

COLBERT. Once—a long time ago. I have forgotten.

MULVANEY. Well, it's quite simple. Do you know how, Bobby?

HARPENDEN. (*Sulkily.*) Yes, vaguely. You have to make seven or something, don't you?

MULVANEY. Yeah. A seven or eleven wins straight off—two or three loses. But with anything else—say, a six or an eight— you have to throw until you make that number, when you'd win—or a seven, when you'd lose. Get the idea?

COLBERT. I think so, yes.

MULVANEY. (*To* HARPENDEN.) O.K., Bobby. I'll shoot you first. *The two men kneel down on the floor.*

Now you take one and flip it.

HARPENDEN. Flip it?

MULVANEY. Like that. (*He demonstrates.*) O.K. Mine. I shoot first. (*He rolls the dice.*) Eight. Now I got to roll an eight before a seven.

The DUKE *comes in from the hall, unnoticed, and watches the three men.*

(*Chanting.*) Little eighter from decatur! Little eighter sweet potater! Come up. (*He throws again.*)

DUKE. I trust you are all enjoying yourselves.

COLBERT. Yes, thank you, Monsieur.

DUKE. May I ask what you're doing?

MULVANEY. Shooting craps, Duke.

DUKE. (*Icily.*) I gather you've settled to your mutual satisfaction the unimportant little problem on which you were engaged when I left you?

HARPENDEN. Well—in a sense—this game is going to settle that.

MULVANEY. (*Chanting.*) Come up little five and three—come up little four and four.

DUKE. (*Outraged.*) What? Do you mean to tell me you're playing craps for my daughter?

COLBERT. We are playing to decide who proposes to her first.

DUKE. (*Thundering.*) But this is monstrous, it's unheard of. It's

—it's eighteenth-century. (*He takes a step forward.*) Stop this
obscenity this instant!

MULVANEY. Clear the floor, will you, Duke. You're spoiling
my throw. (*He throws.*) There she is. Four and four. O.K.,
Frenchy. Now it's you and me. Take one and flip.

DUKE. (*Sitting down, aghast.*) Well, would you believe it?

COLBERT, *paying no attention to the* DUKE, *flips a single dice.*

MULVANEY. O.K. That's your throw.

DUKE. (*Roaring.*) May I remind you, gentlemen, that it's my
daughter you're dicing for?

COLBERT. (*Throws.*) Nine. Is that good?

MULVANEY. Not very. Can win, though. Try and throw another
four and five, or six and three.

COLBERT. That won't be easy. (*He throws.*)

The DUKE *comes forward and watches.*

Four. (*He throws again.*) Eight. That's nearer.

MULVANEY. It's near seven, too.

COLBERT. (*Throws.*) Ten. Suite!

DUKE. He has to throw a nine before he throws a seven, is
that it?

MULVANEY. That's it, Duke.

DUKE. (*Thoughtfully.*) You know, poor old Chicken Hartopp
lost a fortune at this game at Miami.

MULVANEY. He's not the only sucker who's done that, Duke.

DUKE. I haven't played craps for years.

The DUKE *kneels down to watch.* COLBERT *throws again.*

SLOW CURTAIN

END OF ACT II

ACT III

Scene 1

SCENE: *The same, about 3 a.m. the following morning. The* DUKE *is engaged in throwing the dice as the curtain rises, while* HARPENDEN *is watching dourly. Both are holding glasses of whisky and soda.* COLBERT *is reclining in the armchair with his feet up on a stool.*

DUKE. Come up, little four and two. Come up for papa. (*He throws again.*) There she is. There's my beauty. Six it is. (*He adds something to a much-scribbled-on score sheet, humming in high good humour.*) That makes you owe me—let me see—now— five hundred and sixty-five pounds ten shillings—do you agree?

HARPENDEN. (*Glumly.*) If you say so.

DUKE. My good child, have a look at the sheet. (*He waves it in his face.*)

HARPENDEN. That's all right. I can't add, anyway. (*He finishes his drink and gets up.*)

DUKE. (*Chuckling.*) Can't add, my boy? No wonder they won't give you a commission. (*He finishes his drink and holds out the glass.*) Here—you might get me one, too, while you're about it.

HARPENDEN *takes his glass.*

Now this time I think I'll put up a pony. (*He glances at the score sheet.*) Twenty-five pounds. Are you on?

HARPENDEN. All right—but don't shoot till I get back.

DUKE. My dear boy—what do you think I am?

HARPENDEN *opens his mouth to tell him, but decides against it.*

COLBERT. Still not returned?

HARPENDEN. No. (*He consults his watch.*) He's now been gone three hours and fifty minutes.

232

COLBERT. (*Unmoved.*) It is nothing. Possibly she will not see him and he is still waiting in the hall of the hotel.

HARPENDEN. (*Gloomily.*) Not Joe. He's the type who breaks down doors and things.

COLBERT. (*Hopefully.*) Then possibly he is in prison.

HARPENDEN. That's too much to hope for.

DUKE. (*Testily.*) Don't stand there chattering. I've put a pony in the pot.

HARPENDEN. (*Coming back to him.*) We were discussing the trivial little matter of your daughter's future, sir.

DUKE. What's that? Oh, yes. This feller's not come back yet?

HARPENDEN *shakes his head.*

Oh, well—I'll lay three monkeys to one against him.

HARPENDEN. I'll take that.

DUKE. (*After a slight pause.*) How long has he been gone?

HARPENDEN. Nearly four hours.

DUKE. Hm. Well, I'm afraid, as a father, it's hardly right for me to accept a wager like that. Sorry, old man. Now, there's twenty-five smackers in the bank, and I'm shooting. (*He rolls the dice.*) Seven. Good Lord! (*Without conviction.*) I hoped you were going to win that time, my boy. (*He adds the score to the sheet.*) That makes you owe me six hundred pounds and ten shillings, exactly.

HARPENDEN. Just a minute. (*He snatches the sheet from him.*) Five hundred and ninety pounds ten shillings.

DUKE. What's that? (*He studies the sheet.*) Yes, that's right. Stupid mistake. What was that about your not being able to add?

The DUKE *studies the score sheet again.* HARPENDEN *suddenly pricks up his ears at a noise outside. He darts quickly into the hall.*

Well—Robert—I'll give you a real chance this time. I'm going to put up fifty. (*Noticing* HARPENDEN'S *absence.*) Where is he?

HARPENDEN *comes back, looking disappointed.* COLBERT *looks at him inquiringly.*

HARPENDEN. People next door.

COLBERT *nods and prepares to go to sleep again.*

K

DUKE. I was saying, Robert, I'm going to give you a real chance this time, and——

HARPENDEN. (*Shortly.*) Thank you, sir, but I'm not playing any more.

DUKE. But, my boy, I've won too much money off you. You'd better let me give you a few more rolls.

HARPENDEN. It's very kind of you, sir, but I'd far rather you didn't give me even one more roll.

DUKE. It's for your own good.

HARPENDEN. I am quite aware of that, sir—but I'm prepared to make that sacrifice.

DUKE. Oh, very well—if you don't want to play any more—I must say I feel very uncomfortable at winning all this money off you. That'll be—let me see now (*he studies the score sheet.*) —five hundred and ninety pounds ten shillings. (*Magnanimously.*) Let's wipe out the ten shillings, shall we?

HARPENDEN. No, sir. Thank you all the same.

DUKE. (*Stretching himself.*) I feel devilish tired. Good Lord! Four o'clock—no wonder. (*Testily.*) What's this damned Yankee Doodle mean by keeping my daughter out all night?

HARPENDEN. The question is not so much what does the damn Yankee Doodle mean, as what does your daughter mean.

DUKE. I'm worried. It shouldn't take her four hours to send this feller packing. (*Turning on* HARPENDEN.) It's all your fault, Robert. You should never have countenanced this diabolical scheme.

HARPENDEN. No, sir.

DUKE. Why don't you ring up Brown's again instead of just standing there——

HARPENDEN. Swooning like a wilting lily?

DUKE. Exactly.

HARPENDEN. I'm not going to ring up Brown's again for the simple reason that, not ten minutes ago, when you were fully absorbed in trying to discover how you had come to cheat yourself of ten bob on the score sheet, I rang up Brown's for the fourth time since one o'clock.

DUKE. (*In kindly tones.*) Bit overwrought, aren't you, old man?

Thought so. Know the signs well, As a matter of fact, I remember your ringing now. What did they say?

HARPENDEN. That Lady Elisabeth left shortly before twelve with an American gentleman and has not yet returned.

DUKE. Hm. Damned impertinence, isn't it? I suppose he's taken her to one of those bottle-party places, like the Jubilee or somewhere.

HARPENDEN. My own guess is Hyde Park.

DUKE. (*Appalled.*) Hyde Park? At four o'clock in the morning? If you believe that why don't you go to Hyde Park and look for them?

HARPENDEN. How? With a torch?

DUKE. Yes, of course, with a torch.

HARPENDEN. I should be lynched, for one thing. Besides, Hyde Park is a very big place, and anyway it might be Green Park.

DUKE. Yes, or St. James's, if it comes to that, with those damned ducks. Well, there's nothing for it but to wait for this feller to come back, I suppose. I'll go and lie down on your bed for a bit, I think. All right?

HARPENDEN. All right.

DUKE. (*He goes to bedroom door.*) Quite sure you wouldn't care for——

HARPENDEN. (*Firmly.*) Yes, sir. Quite sure.

DUKE. (*To* COLBERT,) What about you, Monsieur?

COLBERT *raises himself on his elbow.*

COLBERT. Pardon, Monsieur?

DUKE. Voulez vous rouler avec moi un peu?

COLBERT. Comment?

HARPENDEN. It's all right. The Duke only wants to know if you'd like to throw dice with him.

COLBERT. Ah, I see. Thank you, Monsieur, but I never gamble, I'm afraid.

DUKE. You don't, eh? I noticed a few hours ago you had no qualms about gambling for my daughter.

COLBERT. For such a stake I would gamble all I had in the world.

DUKE. And exactly how much, if I might ask, is that?

COLBERT. In money, about twenty pounds.

DUKE. Twenty pounds. Quite so, Monsieur. (*With dignity.*) I hardly think we need say any more.

He goes out.

COLBERT. He is quaint, the Duke. He is not, I imagine, typical of all your dukes?

HARPENDEN. You imagine right. .

COLBERT. You do not think, by any chance, he is the Duke whom Hess came to see?

HARPENDEN. If he is, then Hess by now is almost certainly the holder of a considerable stock of Zippy-Snaps.

COLBERT. What are Zippy-Snaps?

HARPENDEN. An invention the Duke is interested in. (*He glares at* COLBERT *malevolently.*) It's an excellent scheme, as a matter of fact. Absolutely sure-fire moneymaker. You ought to put your twenty pounds into it.

COLBERT. My friend, you should not bear me a grudge. We must both acknowledge that America has conquered us.

HARPENDEN. I'm damned if I will.

COLBERT. (*Sighing.*) They say it's a virtue in Englishmen not to know when they are beaten. In this case I would call it ridiculous bravado.

Pause. HARPENDEN *continues to stride the room.*

Stop being a tiger in a cage. You make me nervous.

HARPENDEN. Good. (*He continues his walking.*)

COLBERT. Why are you in such a state? You don't really love her——

HARPENDEN. Now look. You've been saying that all the evening. If you say it once more I shall be forced to take steps.

COLBERT. What steps?

HARPENDEN. I'm wearing regulation boots. (*He displays one.*) I do love her, damn it.

COLBERT. And the woman Crum?

HARPENDEN. It might interest you to know that after our marriage I'd arranged never to see the woman Crum again.

COLBERT. Tiens! As a matter of fact, it is among such women that you should choose not only your mistress but your wife.

HARPENDEN. Why, may I ask?

COLBERT. You will need a simple hard-working girl to look

after you—as a mother looks after a child. But the Lady
Elisabeth, it would now appear, is incapable of even looking after herself.

HARPENDEN. Why should I need looking after more than
anyone else?

COLBERT. My good friend, imagine yourself when your millions
are removed from you, as they will be. Look at you now—a
simple sailor. Why do you think you have not yet been made
an officer?

HARPENDEN. Mere class prejudice. I went to a public school.

COLBERT. In the post-war world——

HARPENDEN. Now, don't go on about my being doomed; it's
beginning to depress me. Surely I'd get a pound a week from
Sir William Beveridge? (*He disappears behind the curtain,
emerging after a second. Hopefully.*) The searchlights have suddenly come on. Perhaps the sirens will go in a minute.

COLBERT. They would not hear them. And the searchlights,
crossing and inter-crossing the sky with their delicate tracery,
will only make matters worse.

Pause.

HARPENDEN. (*Violently.*) She can't do this to me, damn it!

COLBERT. My friend, she has already done it to you.

HARPENDEN. I refuse to be treated like an old sock. Why
should she hurl me into the dustbin just because some
rollicking American makes a pass at her? Who the hell does
she think she is?

COLBERT. Ah! Now, this is more the spirit.

HARPENDEN. My God! The nerve of it! The night before our
wedding! No thought for me at all. (*Imitating.*) I'm not in
love with you, Bobby; I love you, but I'm not in love with
you. Just because she has her head filled with some idiotic,
blushmaking, sentimental slush by a ridiculous little French
pick-up——

COLBERT. Bravo! This is magnificent.

HARPENDEN. The utter insane selfishness of it! She knows quite
well I had to go to my Captain and beg him, on my knees
—on my knees, mind you—for special leave to get married.
She knows quite well—because I wrote to her—how difficult

it is for me to get this leave—because of that little trouble over my last forty-eight. On my knees, I beg my Captain. 'Very well, Ordinary Seaman Harpenden,' he says, 'I'll let you have it this time. But, my God, Ordinary Seaman Harpenden,' he says, 'if this is another of your damned tricks and you don't come back to me on time and married, I'll bloody well put you in irons, Ordinary Seaman Harpenden,' he says. She doesn't think of me tossing and groaning and sobbing in irons, does she? Oh, no . . . Oh, dear me, no. There she is—gallivanting about the park like a Bacchante with a great big beefy brute of a bombardier, while I, her true fiancé, am left alone to face disgrace and degradation—my social life ruined, and my naval career blighted before it has begun.

COLBERT. Bravo! Bravo! It is a fine rage. Well done, milord Bobby!

MABEL CRUM *comes in. She looks sleepy and cross.*

MABEL. What's all the noise about?

HARPENDEN. Good Lord! What are you doing here?

MABEL. I don't know. I thought perhaps you could tell me.

HARPENDEN. Do you mean to say you've been up in the kitchen all this time?

MABEL. I suppose I must have been. I've only just come to, to hear this extraordinary roaring coming from down here. Are you still rehearsing Hamlet, darling? Oh, God! (*She rubs her back.*) I've slept in some funny places in my time, but never before in a kitchen armchair. Never again, if it comes to that.

HARPENDEN. Oh, Lord, I'm terribly sorry. I'm afraid I clean forgot about you up there. Where does it hurt? (*He massages her back.*)

MABEL. Just a little bit higher up, ducky. That's right.

HARPENDEN. Do forgive me, won't you?

MABEL. Don't be silly, darling. You've had a lot to cope with tonight, haven't you?

HARPENDEN. Rather more than usual, I admit.

MABEL. Thank you. That's all right now. (*She stretches herself.*) Can I have a drink?

HARPENDEN. Yes, of course. I'll get it. (*He goes to drink table.*)

MABEL. Is Elisabeth leaving you?

HARPENDEN. Looks like it.

MABEL. For that? (*She points to* COLBERT.)

COLBERT. No, Mademoiselle. For Lieutenant Mulvaney.

MABEL. That's one better, I suppose, but she still must be cuckoo.

COLBERT. Perhaps she is not thinking in terms of pounds, shillings, and pence, Mademoiselle.

MABEL. (*With sincerity.*) I never suggested she was. I meant she was cuckoo because the man she's turned down is ten times more attractive than the man she's turned him down for.

COLBERT. Possibly you are prejudiced, Mademoiselle——

MABEL. I'm never prejudiced about men. My God, look at him —(*She points to* HARPENDEN, *who is returning to her with her drink.*)—what more could any girl want?

HARPENDEN. You just like sailors, that's your trouble.

MABEL. Of course I do. (*Taking the drink.*) I'll just finish this, then I'll start my long trek home.

HARPENDEN. How are you going to get to Kensington at this time of night? We'll never get a taxi for you now.

MABEL. That's all right; I can walk.

HARPENDEN. No, of course you can't walk.

MABEL. Darling, I can't stay here, can I? So what else is there?

HARPENDEN. Yes, you can stay here. Certainly you can stay here. Why should I throw open my chambers to any odious Allied officer who likes to take a crack at pinching my girl, and then turn you, my only real friend, out into the night. You're damn well going to stay here.

MABEL. Darling, I'm not going back to that chair——

HARPENDEN. No, of course you're not. I know. You can go in Horton's bed.

MABEL. What about Horton?

HARPENDEN. Oh, I'll get him out first.

MABEL. Darling, of course. I meant, where are you going to put him?

HARPENDEN. He can go on the sofa.

COLBERT. What about myself?

HARPENDEN. H'm. Well, there's nothing else for it. You'd better go in there with me. (*He points to bedroom door.*) It hardly looks as if Lieutenant Mulvaney is going to honour me with his company in my bed tonight.

COLBERT. I am beginning to learn the meaning of the term 'gentleman'.

HARPENDEN. (*To* MABEL.) Just a minute. I'll get you something to sleep in. (*He opens the bedroom door. Looking inside.*) His Grace, thank heavens, is in a repulsive-looking coma.

He goes inside.

MABEL. He's terribly upset, I suppose, about Elisabeth?

COLBERT. Surprisingly so, Mademoiselle.

MABEL. Why surprisingly? He's in love with the girl.

HARPENDEN *emerges with a pair of pyjamas over his arm. He takes them up to her.*

HARPENDEN. (*As he hands her the pyjamas.*) Mabel, my dear, will you marry me?

MABEL *gazes at him, wonderingly. Pause.*

MABEL. Why?

HARPENDEN. Because I love you very much.

MABEL. Why else?

HARPENDEN. Because we get on well together, and I think you'd make me a very good wife.

MABEL. Yes, darling. Why else?

HARPENDEN. Because if I don't marry someone this leave I'm going to get into trouble with my Captain.

MABEL. (*Laughing.*) Oh, Bobby, you are heaven! (*She puts her arms round his neck.*) You don't really want to marry *me*. Can't you think of anyone else?

HARPENDEN. No. There isn't anyone else.

MABEL. With two million and a title you can afford the very best.

HARPENDEN. I don't want the very best. I want you. (*Awkwardly.*) That's to say——

MABEL. (*Stopping his mouth.*) All right, darling. Don't make it worse.

HARPENDEN. I really mean it, you know. I'm asking you to marry me. Of course, if you'd rather not——

MABEL. Bobby, my precious, you don't think any girl in her senses would turn you down, do you?

HARPENDEN. One girl has.

MABEL. But she's not in her senses. I am. Still, before I definitely commit you, hadn't you better think hard and see if there really isn't someone you'd rather marry than me?

HARPENDEN. All right.

He shuts his eyes and ponders for a second. COLBERT, *from the arm-chair, has been watching the scene intently.*

(*At length.*) No. There's only Lucy Scott, and she's taller than I am.

MABEL. She's an awfully nice girl, though.

HARPENDEN. Yes, but I don't think I like her awfully.

MABEL. Well, of course, if you don't like her awfully——

HARPENDEN. No, there really is only you. Do marry me.

MABEL. If I say yes, you won't try and back out, will you?

HARPENDEN. No, of course not.

MABEL. Whatever happens?

HARPENDEN. Whatever happens.

MABEL. Promise?

HARPENDEN. Promise.

MABEL. I don't want to be made what I believe is called the laughing-stock of London. All right, Bobby darling, I'll marry you.

HARPENDEN. Thanks, awfully.

COLBERT *rises from his chair and goes up to them.*

COLBERT. Permit me to congratulate you both.

HARPENDEN. Oh, were you there all the time? I ought to have sent you up to the kitchen.

COLBERT. I am glad you did not. I have never before attended at an English proposal. I would not have missed it for the world.

HARPENDEN. (*To* MABEL.) Is he being rude?

MABEL. Yes, of course he is. (*To* COLBERT, *hotly.*) But let me tell you, Monsieur what's-your-name, I've been proposed to by hundreds of Frenchmen in my time, as well as all sorts of Poles, Czechs, Norwegians and the rest, and I'd far rather have an honest, straightforward English proposal like Bobby's than all that hand-kissing and arm-stroking and 'Oh, but Mademoiselle is so intoxicating' stuff that you people hand out.

She goes out. HARPENDEN *is about to follow her, but stops in the doorway.*

COLBERT. In theory it should work out very well.

HARPENDEN. And in practice?

Pause.

COLBERT. (*With emotion.*) My dear friend, you have my very, very deepest best wishes.

HARPENDEN. Oh! (*He considers for a second.*) Well, anyway, they can't put me in irons now, can they?

He goes out. COLBERT *smiles, shrugs his shoulders, and goes to the telephone, where he looks up a number. He dials.*

COLBERT. (*Into receiver.*) Hullo. Brown's Hotel? . . . Has Lady Elisabeth come in yet? . . . Not yet? . . . No—no message.

HORTON *comes in, looking disgruntled. He is wearing a woollen dressing-gown.*

HORTON. Good morning, sir.

COLBERT. Good morning.

He goes to the sofa, and settles himself down methodically, covering himself with a rug.

HORTON. (*At length.*) Good night, sir.

COLBERT. Good night.

There are voices in the hall. ELISABETH *and* MULVANEY *come in. They are looking exceedingly gay and happy.* HORTON *gets up.*

HORTON. Good morning, my Lady.

ELISABETH. Sorry if we disturbed you.

HORTON. That is quite all right, my Lady. I realize that this is an exceptional evening. Should you want me, I shall be outside in the hall.

He goes out.

MULVANEY. (*Heartily.*) Well, Frenchy! How you been?

COLBERT. Very well, thank you. And you?

MULVANEY. Oh, we've had a wonderful time, haven't we, Liz?

ELISABETH. Wonderful, Joe.

COLBERT. You have been in the park?

MULVANEY. Sure. How did you guess?

ELISABETH. It's the most heavenly night. There's a glorious full moon.

MULVANEY. The searchlights made a swell background.

COLBERT. I know.

MULVANEY. (*To* COLBERT.) Look, Buddy, do you mind fading away for a second? I got a couple of things I still want to say to Liz.

COLBERT. Very well.

He gazes at them for a long time, then sighs deeply, shrugs his shoulders, and goes into the bedroom.

MULVANEY. Well, Liz?

ELISABETH. Well, Joe?

MULVANEY. I guess this is where we say it.

ELISABETH. I guess it is.

MULVANEY. Seems kinda crazy, doesn't it?

ELISABETH. Kinda crazy is an understatement for everything that's happened to me in this last twenty-four hours.

MULVANEY. You're sure this is the way you want it?

ELISABETH. Yes, Joe, and so are you.

MULVANEY. I don't know so much about that.

ELISABETH. (*Smiling.*) Dulcie to you.

MULVANEY. She's a good girl, Liz. Maybe one of these days I'll tell her about you.

ELISABETH. I should be careful about that. You wouldn't want to spoil Anglo-American relations, now, would you?

MULVANEY. Aw, she'd understand. She ought to be darned grateful to you, anyway, all things considered.

ELISABETH. She ought, but I wonder if she would be?

MULVANEY. Do you think Bobby should be grateful to *me*?

ELISABETH. Yes, he should. Of course he should. You've been the little stranger that brings the severed couple together.

MULVANEY. You forget that when this little stranger appeared on the scene the couple wasn't severed anyway.

ELISABETH. Yes, we were, Joe—in a way. I wasn't sure about Bobby. I don't think he was sure about me. We'd have got married all right, but—well, with my urge to experiment, who knows what trouble there might have been later?

MULVANEY. You don't think there'll be trouble now?

ELISABETH. (*Smiling.*) Not if you keep your promise, Joe, and go right out of my life for ever.

MULVANEY. Aw hell, Liz, I'm safe. You should know that by now. How long did we sit on that park bench?

ELISABETH. Nearly four hours.

MULVANEY. Well, in four hours did I once——

ELISABETH. No, but you did an awful lot of arguing.

MULVANEY. Arguing's nothing.

ELISABETH. That rather depends on one's opponent. No, Joe, I'm sorry. You're just a little too attractive to be what you call safe. I'll prefer you as a sentimental but distant memory.

MULVANEY. So this is where we say it?

ELISABETH. This is where we say it. Goodbye, Joe.

MULVANEY. Goodbye, Liz. (*He extends his arms.*)

ELISABETH. No, Joe.

MULVANEY. Aw, come on, Liz. You can't say goodbye for ever to a guy standing fifty feet away from him.

ELISABETH. Have you forgotten I'm getting married today?

MULVANEY. What about yesterday morning then?

ELISABETH. That was different. You thought I was a trollop.

MULVANEY. What did you think I was?

ELISABETH. One day I'll write and tell you. Now I'll just say—goodbye.

She kisses him. COLBERT *appears in the bedroom door.* ELISABETH *breaks away.*

COLBERT. (*To* MULVANEY.) I am most sorry to interrupt, but the Duke is anxious to talk to you. He is in the bedroom.

MULVANEY. O.K. Don't they ever knock on doors in France? *He goes into bedroom.*

ELISABETH. Is Daddy still here? I'd better see him, too.

COLBERT. Wait an instant, milady. I must say it—I shall say it. You are making a hideous, terrible mistake.

ELISABETH. (*Startled.*) What?

COLBERT. Turn back while there is still time—turn back before you ruin yet two more lives——

ELISABETH. Oh, go away, you silly little man!

COLBERT. Silly little man I may be now, milady, but the day will dawn when you will see me in a different light.

MULVANEY *appears at the bedroom door.*

What is this American to you? Nothing. No more than a single evening of voluptuousness——

MULVANEY. (*Advancing on* COLBERT.) Oh, is that all he is?

ELISABETH. Don't pay any attention to him, Joe. Rise above him.

MULVANEY. I got a better idea. I'm going to make him rise above me. (COLBERT *quickly sits down. The* DUKE *comes in.*)

DUKE. I say, this is capital news. Capital. So you've come to your senses at last, have you, my dear? (*He kisses her affectionately.*) I never doubted it. I know you too well. Headstrong—like to kick over the traces once in a while, but no harm done. Just like your mother. There never *was* any truth in that Charley Babington story.

HARPENDEN *comes in from the hall. The* DUKE *advances on him precipitately.*

Ah, Robert, my boy, let me be the very first to congratulate you——

HARPENDEN. (*Bewildered.*) Thank you, sir.

DUKE. (*Jovially.*) You're a sly dog, Robert, I must say. How did you pull it off, eh? That's what I want to know.

HARPENDEN. Well, it wasn't awfully difficult.

ELISABETH. Just a minute, Daddy. I don't think Bobby can possibly know what you're talking about. (*To* MULVANEY.) Joe—you tell him, will you?

MULVANEY. O.K. Bobby, Elisabeth has turned me down flat because she says she's now quite sure she's in love with you.

HARPENDEN. Oh.

ELISABETH. Darling, is that all you're going to say. Just—oh?

DUKE. Don't worry, old girl. That's all he ever says, whatever you tell him. Isn't that so, Robert, my boy?

HARPENDEN. (*With a sickly smile.*) Yes, sir.

DUKE. Go on, Robert—you old stick! Just go ahead and tell her how happy——

MABEL *comes in, in pyjamas.*

MABEL. (*As she enters.*) Darling, you always give me these awful blue pyjamas—— (*She stops at sight of* ELISABETH.)

DUKE. (*Outraged.*) Mabs!

MABEL. Don't tell me. I know. Back to the kitchen.

She goes out.

ELISABETH. That was Miss Crum, wasn't it?

DUKE. (*Uneasily.*) Yes, dear. Little Mabs Crum—very decent sort——

ELISABETH. Oh!

DUKE. Now, you mustn't get hold of the wrong end of the stick, old girl. As a matter of fact, Mabs has been popping in and out all the evening—hasn't she, boys?

COLBERT. Yes, Monsieur.

MULVANEY. Certainly has, Duke.

ELISABETH. Oh?

DUKE. (*Testily.*) Now, don't you start saying 'Oh'! Look here, old girl, I've been in these chambers myself the whole night long. Surely that should reassure you, if nothing else, that there's been no hanky-panky——

ELISABETH. I suppose it should, but, oddly enough, it doesn't.

DUKE. But, my dear, this is a lot of ridiculous moonshine. Mabs is a sweet little child, and we're all very fond of her, but she means nothing in the world to Robert—does she, my boy?

HARPENDEN. Yes, sir—or rather no, sir—I mean——

DUKE. Well, go on, out with it. Does she or does she not?

HARPENDEN. Well, you see—the fact is, I've just asked her to marry me.

DUKE. You what?

COLBERT. It is true, Monsieur. I heard him. I even, I am afraid, encouraged the match.

DUKE. (*Roaring.*) Will you kindly keep out of this, you interfering little jackanapes!

COLBERT. (*Interested.*) Qu'est-ce que c'est jackanapes?

DUKE. Qu'est-ce que c'est jackanapes? C'est—c'est—tell him, someone.

HARPENDEN. Imbécile.

DUKE. You're a damned little interfering imbécile. Allez vous en. Retournez au kitchen!

COLBERT *goes out, muttering.*

Now, Robert, what is this all about? You must be out of your mind. You say you've asked Mabs Crum to marry you?

HARPENDEN. Yes, sir.

DUKE. But in God's name why?

HARPENDEN. (*Forlornly.*) Well, I thought it was rather a good idea.

DUKE..A good idea? A good idea to marry Crum? A woman who's spent her whole life popping in and out of bed with every Tom, Dick, and Harry——

ELISABETH. I thought you said she was such a sweet little child.

DUKE. (*Turning on her.*) You keep out of this, too, Elisabeth. This is a matter for men to handle. Now, look here, Robert——

ELISABETH. Oh, Daddy—there's no point in going on like this. Take me home, please.

DUKE. In a minute.

ELISABETH. (*Shrilly.*) Now! (*To* HARPENDEN.) You had a perfect right to do what you like, I suppose. After all, I did turn you down.

HARPENDEN. Elisabeth, I——

ELISABETH. (*Turning sharply away from him.*) Come on, Daddy.

DUKE. (*With dignity.*) All right, my dear. I'm sure I don't want to stay another minute in the house of a raving madman.

He goes to the door with ELISABETH, *when a thought strikes him, and he turns.*

Oh, just a minute, my dear. (*He returns to* HARPENDEN.) About that money you owe me——

HARPENDEN. What money?

DUKE. The six hundred pounds——

HARPENDEN. You mean the five hundred and ninety pounds ten shillings. Yes, Duke, what about it?

DUKE. It might interest you to know, young man, that I intend to hand over your cheque, when you send it to me, to charity.

HARPENDEN. The charity in question being Messrs. Macdougall and Steinbeck, I presume, sir?

DUKE. (*After a second's speechless pause.*) No, sir. The Society for the marrying-off of fallen women to blithering, nancified nincompoops of earls. (*To* ELISABETH, *with dignity.*) Come. my dear.

ELISABETH *and the* DUKE *go out.*

MULVANEY. I didn't make love to her, you know.

HARPENDEN. (*Listlessly.*) Didn't you? Why not?

MULVANEY. She wouldn't let me.

Pause.

Congratulations on getting yourself engaged again.

HARPENDEN. Thank you.

Pause.

(*Slowly.*) I'm going to murder that bloody little Colbert.

MULVANEY. You and me both, brother.

COLBERT *comes in from the hall, looking delighted with himself. Both* HARPENDEN *and* MULVANEY *turn their heads and glare at him.*

COLBERT. Tiens! I see I am faced by the Anglo-Saxon bloc. (*He stretches himself and yawns.*) It has been a full night. I think, milord Bobby, I shall avail myself of your kind invitation and stake out my claim on your bed.

MULVANEY. (*To* HARPENDEN.) Is he sleeping in our bed?

HARPENDEN. Yes, he is.

A thought seems simultaneously to strike them.

MULVANEY. Hm.

HARPENDEN. Hm.

They go together to bedroom door, which MULVANEY *opens. He sweeps* COLBERT *an elaborate bow.*

MULVANEY. After you, Monsieur.

HARPENDEN *also makes* COLBERT *an inviting gesture towards the bedroom.* COLBERT *hesitates for some time, looking decidedly nervous. Then he straightens his shoulders with a determined air.*

COLBERT. (*Murmuring.*) Vive la France!

He walks into the bedroom with the air of an aristocrat going to the guillotine. MULVANEY *and* HARPENDEN *follow him in and close the door.*

CURTAIN

END OF SCENE I

ACT III

Scene 2

SCENE: *The same, about 10 a.m. that morning.* HORTON *enters from the hall, carrying a large tray. He deposits this on a table, knocks on the bedroom door, and goes in. After a brief pause, he emerges again with the breakfast tray intact and carries it to the hall door, and out. There is a ring at the front-door.*

DUKE. (*Off.*) Good morning, Horton.

HORTON. (*Off.*) Good morning, your Grace.

DUKE. (*Just in door.*) Pay my taxi, will you? I've no change.

HORTON. Very good, your Grace.

DUKE *crosses to window and then to chair.* HORTON *enters.*

DUKE. Is nobody awake?

HORTON. All three young gentlemen were asleep when I went in just now. I shook the shoulder nearest the wall, which I took to be his Lordship's, but which proved to belong to the American gentleman. He told me to scram, which I understood to mean that they had all passed a restless night, did not wish to be disturbed, and required no breakfast.

DUKE. You've heard the news, I suppose, Horton?

HORTON. About his Lordship's engagement to Miss Crum? Yes, your Grace. He told me last night. (*Shakes his head gloomily.*)

DUKE. I agree with you, Horton. It's a shocking business. He seems absolutely set on it, I gather?

HORTON. I'm afraid so, your Grace. I did attempt to indicate my disapproval with one of my looks, but for once he seemed quite unshaken. He said it was the only way he could see to save himself from extinction in the post-war world.

DUKE. Talking like Bevin. Must be off his rocker.

HORTON. I fear so, your Grace.

DUKE. Oh, well, I suppose we must both make the best of a very bad job. Where is Miss Crum?

HORTON. In the kitchen, your Grace.

DUKE. She would be. What's she doing there?

249

HORTON. Having a cup of tea, I fancy, your Grace.

MABEL *comes in, dressed.*

MABEL. Hullo, Tibby, it was you at the door, was it?

DUKE. Yes, Mabs. Good morning. I came round specially to see you.

MABEL. Did you, Tibby? How sweet of you!

DUKE. It's not sweet of me at all. I want to talk to you seriously, on a most urgent matter.

MABEL. All right, then. Fire away.

She sits down. The DUKE sits, too. He seems awkward and embarrassed. MABEL takes a cigarette and the DUKE lights it for her.

Go on, Tibby. Don't keep me in suspense.

DUKE. Well, I hardly know how to begin.

Pause. The DUKE gets up and walks over to MABEL's chair.

(*Urgently.*) Mabs—have you ever heard of Zippy-Snaps?

MABEL. Yes, of course, Tibby. Don't you remember you showed me one once? It didn't work.

DUKE. Didn't it? Astonishing thing. Faulty zipper, I suppose. Anyway, it's a wonderful invention, my dear; it'll revolutionize women's dress. None of this tiresome zipping and unzipping. Just snip snap and there you are, ready to go out. By the way (*Shakes hands.*), before we go any further, let me be the first to congratulate you on your engagement to young Robert.

MABEL. Oh! Did he tell you about it?

DUKE. Yes. Last night. As a matter of fact, we had a few words on the subject, I'm afraid, because at first I naturally felt a bit let down—on my daughter's behalf, you know.

MABEL. Yes, of course, Tibby.

DUKE. Still, thinking things over this morning, I thought— well—these days—it's no good crying over spilt milk, and the best thing I could do would be to come round and congratulate you both on what I am sure will be an excellent match.

MABEL. Thank you so much.

DUKE. He's a blithering young idiot, of course, in many ways, but that's beside the point. Anyway, my dear, I hope you'll both be very happy—Now—returning to Zippy Snaps——

MABEL. Tibby, I've no money at all.

DUKE. (*Testily.*) I know you haven't, my dear—it's not your money that we want—it's you.

MABEL. (*Startled.*) Me?

DUKE. Exactly. Zippy-Snaps will, as we develop, cater mainly for the feminine sex, and I, as Chairman of the Board of Directors, have always maintained that what the Board needs is new blood, and—if possible—new feminine blood——

MABEL. (*Incredulously.*) *You* want *me* on the Board of Directors?

DUKE. We do, my dear. You are exactly the sort of director— or directress, rather—that we require. A smart, young, enterprising girl, with a very well-developed business sense.

MABEL. Yes, and the fact that I'm the future Countess of Harpenden has nothing to do with it, I suppose?

DUKE. Well, of course—it's no good trying to hoodwink you, I can see—that is, I admit, a consideration. A title—and that title especially—will look very well on the prospectus——

MABEL. Supposing I wasn't going to marry Bobby, would you still want me?

DUKE. (*Soothingly.*) Of course, my dear, of course. I've told you —it's your talent and business acumen we want. (*Suspiciously.*) But you *are* going to marry Bobby, aren't you?

MABEL. Well, he's asked me to and I've said yes.

DUKE. Capital. Well now, the whole thing is fixed. I rang up my fellow director this morning and he agreed with the project entirely. The Board, in fact, is unanimous. Well— what do you say?

MABEL. All right, Tibby.

DUKE. We'll get the whole thing signed, sealed, and delivered, and then we'll surprise young Robert with it. My word! Won't he be proud of his little Mabs when he finds out what's happened to her. Let me see now—is there a typewriter here?

MABEL. I don't think so. Why?

DUKE. I thought I'd just type out a couple of letters—perfectly legal—one from me to you—the other from you to me. Then we each sign them and the thing's done. (*Goes to hall, calls off.*) Horton! Horton!

The DUKE *returns.*

MABEL. By the way, Tibby, who's your fellow director?

DUKE. Lord Finchingfield.

MABEL. What? Not poor old Finchy? Is he out again now?

HORTON *comes in.*

HORTON. Yes, your Grace?

DUKE. Oh, Horton, does his Lordship keep a typewriter in his chambers?

HORTON. No, your Grace, but I do.

DUKE. Where is it?

HORTON. Up in the kitchen, your Grace.

DUKE. Lead me to it, then, Horton. Don't go away, now, Mabs, I'll be back in a jiffy.

He goes out. MABEL, *left alone, goes to radiogram and switches it on. She listens to some swing music.* MULVANEY'S *head appears at the bedroom door, his eyes half-closed with sleep. He gropes his way to the radiogram, switches it off, and gropes his way back into the bedroom.*

There is a ring at the front door. MABEL *goes quickly to hall door.*

MABEL. (*Off, calling.*) All right, Horton, I'll answer it.

After a slight pause she returns with ELISABETH.

I thought it was you. Couldn't you get here any sooner?

ELISABETH. I came as quickly as I could. I had to finish my packing.

MABEL. I'm glad you did come, anyway. You were so rude to me on the 'phone I thought you wouldn't. Won't you sit down?

ELISABETH *sits on the sofa.*

ELISABETH. Do you mind saying what you have to say fairly quickly, as I have to catch a train at ten forty-five?

MABEL. (*Looking at her watch.*) I won't keep you more than five minutes. Bobby told you he'd asked me to marry him, didn't he?

ELISABETH. Yes, he did.

MABEL. Did he tell you that I'd accepted him?

ELISABETH. No, but then he hardly needed to tell me that.

MABEL. Well, I did accept him, anyway, and do you know why?

ELISABETH. (*With a faint smile.*) I think I can guess.

MABEL. I doubt very much if you can. Because I'm very fond of him, and because I thought I'd make him a good wife.

ELISABETH. (*Politely.*) Really?

MABEL. He needs someone to take care of him, and I thought I'd be able to do that very well.

ELISABETH. I agree that you've never seemed to find much trouble in taking care of yourself.

MABEL. Yes. Unlike you, I had to, you see.

ELISABETH. You've managed very well.

MABEL. Thank you. I haven't done too badly for myself, I must say.

ELISABETH. To be the Countess of Harpenden is quite an achievement.

MABEL. (*Regretfully.*) Yes, it would have been, I suppose.

ELISABETH. Why, it would have been?

MABEL. Oh, because I'm not going to go through with it. That's what I wanted to tell you.

ELISABETH. Are you serious?

MABEL. Perfectly. I told you I was very fond of him, didn't I? That's why I can't marry him. Does that make sense?

ELISABETH. No, it doesn't.

MABEL. It does, really—if you think it out. Look, ducky—sorry—Lady Elisabeth—you can't imagine anyone behaving as badly—from your standards—as I do, without—well, financial considerations being involved, can you? Oh, hell, this polite beating about the bush gets me down. What I'm saying is, I'm a trollop—let's face it—but not for money.

ELISABETH. What for, then?

MABEL. Men.

ELISABETH. Oh.

MABEL. Now last night, up in the kitchen, I told Bobby that if I married him I'd stay faithful to him, and I meant it. But this morning, in the cold, clear light of dawn, I just knew I couldn't go through with it.

ELISABETH. Perhaps, if you tried very hard——

MABEL. It doesn't matter how hard I tried. No—I can't lie to

Bobby. So regretfully, but firmly, I've got to turn him down
—which, with two million and a title involved, is really
quite something, don't you agree?

ELISABETH. It *is* quite something, I do agree. I must say, I'm
surprised.

MABEL. My dear, I'm amazed.. But there it is. Bobby's too
sweet and he's too easy to cheat. So I can't do it. Of course,
with an old idiot like Tibby——

ELISABETH. You mean my father?

MABEL. Sorry, dear, I forgot he was your father. (*She looks at*
ELISABETH.) I must say you'd never think it. Well, there you
are, Elisabeth. I'm throwing your earl back in your face.
Do you still want him?

ELISABETH. I don't know.

MABEL. He still wants you.

ELISABETH. Is Bobby in there?

MABEL. All the Allies are in there.

ELISABETH. Do you think you could get him out without waking
the others?

MABEL. I'll try, but it won't be easy. By the way, if you're
getting married this morning, it's very unlucky to see him.

ELISABETH. (*Startled.*) Married this morning?

MABEL. Or have you put off all the guests?

ELISABETH. No. We didn't have time. They're going to make
an announcement.

MABEL. Well, that's fine. If you hurry you can still make it. It's
a pity to disappoint all the guests.

ELISABETH. Yes, but—but I don't know. Well, anyway, I must
see him.

MABEL. All right, then. Auntie Mabel will fix it. Now, you
stand there (*she plants* ELISABETH *with her back to bedroom door*)
so you can't see the door, and I'll do the rest.

*She disappears into bedroom, emerging after a few moments with a
very tousled, sleepy, and disgruntled-looking* HARPENDEN, *who is
walking with his eyes closed. He has on his sailor trousers and a vest.*

HARPENDEN. (*Plaintively.*) But why have I got to keep my eyes
closed? Please, may I go back to bed? What is this?

MABEL. I'll tell you all about it in a minute. There. (*She plants him with his back to* ELISABETH.) Now, you can open your eyes.

HARPENDEN *opens his eyes, blinking in the daylight.*

But don't look round. Look straight ahead.

HARPENDEN. All right, I *am* looking. (*Wearily.*) What's it going to be—a lovely choc for baby?

MABEL. Yes, darling. A lovely choc for baby. I'm not going to marry you.

HARPENDEN. (*Eagerly.*) Aren't you? (*Discarding his obvious delight.*) Aren't you, Mabel? Why?

MABEL. There really isn't time to go into that just now. Let's just say that I don't approve of marriage as an institution.

HARPENDEN. Do you really mean you're turning me down?

MABEL. Flat.

HARPENDEN. Oh! I'm very upset.

MABEL. That remark would have more conviction if you could get rid of that joyous gleam in your eye. Goodbye. Bobby, how much do you love Elisabeth?

HARPENDEN. Very much.

MABEL. That's what I thought. (*She walks to the door.*) Don't look round. For the very last time in my life I am going up to your kitchen.

She goes out.

ELISABETH. Bobby?

HARPENDEN. (*Without turning.*) Yes, Elisabeth?

ELISABETH. You knew I was here?

HARPENDEN. I guessed it.

ELISABETH. Is that why you said you loved me very much?

HARPENDEN. No. That's the truth.

ELISABETH. Do you know why we mustn't look at each other this morning?

HARPENDEN. I guessed that, too.

ELISABETH. Do you still want to marry me, darling?

HARPENDEN. More than anything on earth.

ELISABETH. In spite of everything that's happened?

HARPENDEN. If you still want to marry me, that's good enough.

ELISABETH. I do still want to marry you. Much more now than ever before.

HARPENDEN. In spite of having no white-hot burning thing-ummy for me?

ELISABETH. White-hot burning thingummy is a mistake. It may be all right for some people, but not for me.

HARPENDEN. I think I ought to warn you that I'm a doomed man.

ELISABETH. Doomed, darling? To what?

HARPENDEN. Extinçtion, I think.

ELISABETH. I don't mind, provided we both get extinguished together.

HARPENDEN. That's by far the nicest thing you've ever said to me.

ELISABETH. I can think of a nicer thing I might say. It's true, too.

HARPENDEN. What's that?

ELISABETH. I'm in love with you, Bobby.

HARPENDEN. Yes. That's even nicer.

ELISABETH *goes to the door.*

ELISABETH. Don't look round. I'll see you in five minutes' time —in church. Goodbye.

HARPENDEN. Goodbye.

ELISABETH *goes out.* HARPENDEN *stands stock-still until he hears the front door bang. Then he dashes to the bedroom door and opens it.*

HARPENDEN. (*Shouting.*) Hey, you two! Wake up! Help me dress! I'm getting married!

He dashes to the hall door.

(*Shouting.*) Horton, bring my boots down! Iron my collar! And step on it, for God's sake!

He dashes to bedroom door, stops, feels his chin, mutters a curse, and runs to the telephone. He frantically looks up a number. COLBERT *and* MULVANEY *appear at the bedroom. Both are in a state of semi-undress.*

MULVANEY. What's all the noise about?

HARPENDEN. (*Dialling.*) I'm getting married.

MULVANEY. Yeah, I know.

HARPENDEN. You don't know. You can't possibly know. (*Into receiver.*) Hullo, Boots? . . . This is Lord Harpenden—I want

a new razor blade . . . But you must have—I'm getting
married! . . . Oh, all right. . . .

He rings off. HORTON *comes in.*

HORTON. I've had no time to iron your collar, my Lord. Is it
very urgent?

HARPENDEN. Of course it's very urgent. I'm getting married in
five minutes—hell—three minutes. Oh, God! I suppose I
can always say I'm growing a beard.

He darts into the bedroom.

HORTON. Who is his Lordship marrying in three minutes?

MULVANEY. Search me.

HARPENDEN *appears at the door, struggling with his jersey.*

HARPENDEN. Does one get married in a gas-mask?

MULVANEY. It depends who you're marrying, brother.

HARPENDEN. Idiot! I meant, does one carry a gas-mask—full
dress, and all that? Do you know, Horton?

HORTON. I fancy not, my Lord. I am not sure if the rule applies
to ratings, of course, but my brother, who is a Lieutenant-
Commander, did not carry his at his wedding.

HARPENDEN. All right, Horton. Jump to it, man, for heaven's
sake.

MULVANEY. Hey, wait a minute. He wants to know who you're
marrying, and so do we.

HARPENDEN. Oh, didn't I tell you? Elisabeth.

HORTON. I am most relieved, my Lord. You'll be leaving for
Oxford after the wedding?

HARPENDEN. Yes, Horton.

HORTON. Very good, my Lord.

He goes out.

MULVANEY. Gee, Bobby, I don't know what to say.

HARPENDEN. I'll take it as said. (*They shake hands.*) Thanks, Joe.

COLBERT. I, on the other hand, do know what to say. England
has once again muddled through.

The DUKE'S *voice can be heard in the hall.*

HARPENDEN. Oh, God, is that old poop here? Quick, into the
bedroom, both of you! If you're coming to the wedding,
you've got to get dressed.

He pushes COLBERT *and* MULVANEY *into the bedroom, and turns as*

the DUKE *and* MABEL *come in. The* DUKE *is carrying some papers.*
Hullo, sir. See you in church.

He disappears into the bedroom.

DUKE. See me in church? Now what the dickens did he mean
by that?

MABEL. (*Hastily.*) I've no idea, Tibby.

She takes the papers from the DUKE *and carries them over to the desk.*

DUKE. See me in church? Has the boy gone off his rocker?

MABEL. Yes, ducky, I expect so. Where do I sign?

DUKE. At the bottom.

He points. MABEL *quickly signs her name. As the* DUKE *sits down at
the desk* HORTON, *carrying* HARPENDEN's *collar and boots, darts
in from the hall, dashes across to the bedroom door, and disappears
inside.*

God bless my soul! What on earth's the matter with Horton?

MABEL. Darling, I don't know. Sign that nice letter.

He begins to peruse the document. HORTON *emerges from the bedroom
and dashes back into the hall.*

DUKE. Has Horton gone cuckoo, too?

He takes up the pen to sign. MULVANEY, *slightly more dressed than
when last seen, dashes in from the bedroom and goes to the desk,
where he begins to open and close drawers violently.*

MULVANEY.   Pardon me, Duke. (*Calling.*) Hey, Bobby, which
drawer is that ring in?

HARPENDEN. (*Off.*) Right-hand top.

MULVANEY. (*Calling.*) O.K. I got it. Thanks, Duke.

He darts back into the bedroom, carrying a small jewel box. The DUKE,
during MULVANEY's *search, has laid down his pen in disgust.*

DUKE. (*Roaring.*) You infernal cow-puncher. Has everyone gone
raving mad in this house this morning?

MABEL *takes up the pen and puts it into his hand.*

MABEL. Go on, Tibby dear, I'm late for the office already.

DUKE. I've done it. (*He signs.*)

HARPENDEN *comes in, dressed, and runs up to* MABEL.

HARPENDEN. Darling, smooth my collar!

MABEL. (*Doing so.*) There you are. Bobby isn't it lovely? I've
just been made a director of Zippy-Snaps Incorporated.

HARPENDEN. Have you, Mabel? Aren't you a clever girl?

MABEL. I've had the most wonderful time, what with your two thousand and being made a director——

DUKE. (*Chuckling.*) Two thousand, eh? That's a neat little engagement present, I must say.

HARPENDEN. What does he mean?

MABEL. I don't know, darling. I think he's batty, this morning. Goodbye, Bobby.

HARPENDEN. Aren't you coming?

MABEL. No. I've got to go and work.

HARPENDEN. Goodbye, then, darling. (*They kiss.*) You've been an angel.

MABEL. Not really. I'd have made an awful muck of it, I know.

She goes to door.

HARPENDEN. I wish you were coming to the church.

MABEL. Better not. I might suddenly change my mind. Goodbye, Bobby dear. (*She turns to the* DUKE.) Goodbye, Tibby, darling. See you on the Board.

She goes out.

DUKE. Why do you wish she were coming to the church? Why did you say you'd see me in church? What is all this church nonsense?

HARPENDEN. My God, don't you know?

DUKE. Know? Know what?

HARPENDEN. I'm marrying your daughter.

DUKE. Good God! When?

HARPENDEN. (*Looking at his watch.*) Two minutes ago.

The DUKE *stares at* HARPENDEN *for a second, then makes a dash for the hall door.*

DUKE. (*Shouting off.*) Hey, Mabs! Mabs! Wait a minute! I want to see you—Mabs!

MULVANEY *and* COLBERT *come out of bedroom, dressed.*

MULVANEY. Say, listen, Bobby, I'm to be best man, aren't I?

COLBERT. On the contrary, he agreed that it was I who had the first claim.

MULVANEY. (*Hotly.*) First claim! Nothing. I like that, after doing your level best to gum up the entire works.

COLBERT. (*Equally hotly.*) I to gum up the works? Who was it who rendered the bride insensible from drink?

MULVANEY. Say, listen, there's only one way to settle this. (*He brings out his craps from his pockets.*) The fair play.

COLBERT. Very well. The fair play.

They kneel on the floor and each flips one dice. The DUKE *comes back.*

HARPENDEN. Did you catch her?

DUKE. Afraid not. She's caught *me* all right, the little scallywag.

HARPENDEN. I won't hear a word against Mabel Crum.

DUKE. Mabel Crum. What a name on a prospectus!

MULVANEY. (*Chanting, from the floor.*) Little nine for Caroline. Five and four, hit that floor.

DUKE. Hullo! What's going on here? (*He approaches the dice players.*)

HARPENDEN. They're playing to see who's going to be best man.

DUKE. God bless my soul! What next?

MULVANEY. (*Chanting.*) Come up for Baby! Baby wants to be best man!

COLBERT. (*Chanting.*) This Baby wants to be best man.

DUKE. Which do you fancy—France or America?

HARPENDEN. I don't mind.

DUKE. Well, you take America then; I'll take France.

HARPENDEN. All right.

DUKE. Five hundred?

HARPENDEN. Right. Five hundred.

DUKE. Done. (*To* COLBERT.) Monsieur, I've put a monkey on you.

COLBERT. Comment, Monsieur?

DUKE. J'ai metté un singe sur vous. So play up, Monsieur for the sake of the ENTENTE CORDIALE . . .

The four men are now kneeling in a row. The game proceeds to the accompaniment of chants and objurgations, and is still undecided as

THE CURTAIN FALLS

END OF PLAY

LOVE IN IDLENESS

TO
HENRY CHANNON

Characters:

OLIVIA BROWN
POLTON
MISS DELL
SIR JOHN FLETCHER
MICHAEL BROWN
DIANA FLETCHER
CELIA WENTWORTH
SIR THOMAS MARKHAM
LADY MARKHAM

Love in Idleness was first performed on December 20th, 1944, at the Lyric Theatre, London, with the following cast:

OLIVIA BROWN	*Lynn Fontanne*
POLTON	*Margaret Murray*
MISS DELL	*Peggy Dear*
SIR JOHN FLETCHER	*Alfred Lunt*
MICHAEL BROWN	*Brian Nissen*
DIANA FLETCHER	*Kathleen Kent*
CELIA WENTWORTH	*Mona Harrison*
SIR THOMAS MARKHAM ...	*Frank Forder*
LADY MARKHAM	*Antoinette Keith*

The play directed by ALFRED LUNT

ACT I

SCENE: *The sitting-room of a house in Westminster. The furniture and decoration give an impression of tasteful opulence. There is a door upstage, R., leading into a small room used as a study by* SIR JOHN FLETCHER, *and double doors down L., leading into the hall. There are large curtained windows upstage.*

TIME: *About 7 p.m.*

On the rise of the curtain, OLIVIA BROWN *is lying on the sofa, telephoning. She is wearing a negligée. The telephone is resting on her stomach, and her engagement book is on her lap. She looks comfortable and happy. On the floor in front of her are a pile of magazines in some disorder. As the curtain goes up she is dialling a number and Big Ben is heard striking the half-hour.*

OLIVIA. Treasury? Extension 35987 please . . . Hullo, Dicky? Olivia. Is there a chance of a word with the Chancellor? . . . Don't give me that. If I know him he's in the middle of a nice game of battleships with you at this moment. . . . Well, I won't keep him a second. Are you afraid I'll make him drop a stitch in his budget or something? . . . Go on, Dicky. . . . All right, you can take me out on Friday week. . . . Right. (*After a pause.*) Sir Thomas? This is Olivia Brown. I'm so sorry to disturb you when I know you must be so busy. It's about Thursday night. You can come, can't you? . . . Oh, that is a shame, I'm so disappointed. Celia Wentworth, the novelist, is simply aching to meet you. She's simply mad about your memoirs. She says she thinks you're wasting your talents as a politician. You ought to have been a writer. . . . Oh, that's sweet of you. Thank you so much. She would have been heartbroken. . . . Yes, eight-thirty. I'm very grateful. Goodbye.

OLIVIA *rings off. At once the telephone rings.*

Hullo? . . . Miss Wentworth? I've been trying to get you all day. This is Olivia Brown speaking; could you dine on

Thursday night? Do come . . . come after the ballet, then
. . . half-past eight. I can't leave it any later because John
may have to get back to the Ministry. . . . Well, you'll just
have to cut the last ballet that's all. What is it? . . . Oh, my
dear, you don't want to see that again . . . all those great
swans chasing that absurd young man. . . . I've got the
Chancellor of the Exchequer coming and he's such an
admirer of yours. . . . Yes, he absolutely worships your
Resplendent Valley. . . . You will? Splendid. . . . Yes, eight-
thirty. You know the address, don't you? You'll find it in
the book under Fletcher . . . John Fletcher. . . . That's right.
*She rings off again and begins to write in her notebook. After a short
pause the telephone rings again.*
Hullo. . . . Who wants her? . . . Oh, hullo, Joan darling, I
didn't recognize your voice. . . . No, really? . . . Oh, John
never tells me a thing. I rely on you for all my information.
. . . Well, who'll be the new Under-Secretary for War? . . .
No! Not poor old Freddy? . . . Oh, I *am* glad. Off the dust-
heap at last! Laura will be delighted. I'll give her a ring.
. . . It just shows how right he's been to have sat there all
those years looking stern and saying nothing. . . . Oh, no,
darling, he wasn't thinking anything, either. I'm sure
you're wrong. He was never a Liberal. He was super'd from
Eton. . . . Super'd? . . . Removed for not being in a high
enough form. . . . Never even got a prize. No Cabinet
Minister ever does. I always feel so sorry for the little boys
who get prizes—marked for failure before they start. . . .
POLTON, *a middle-aged, highly respectable-looking parlour-maid,
comes in with a telegram on a salver.* OLIVIA *nods to her to open it.*
Oh well, of course, John's different. He went to one of those
Canadian co-educational establishments and he graduated,
or whatever they call it, wonderfully high: but then he did
play ice hockey very well and, of course, he doesn't count,
being only a wartime Cabinet Minister. . . . (*She has read
the telegram and now gives a shriek.*)
POLTON *hesitates in the doorway.*
Oh! . . . Sorry, darling, it's the most wonderful news. It's a
wire from Michael . . . my little son, he's arrived in England.

POLTON *goes out.*

(*Reading.*) 'Arrived safely. See you late tonight.' I knew he was on his way from Canada, but I didn't know he'd sailed. They never tell you a thing. . . . No, I haven't seen him for five years. I sent him over in '39. . . . Polton! Polton!— Darling, I must ring off, do you mind? I feel too excited. . . . I'll ring you tomorrow morning.

POLTON *comes in again.*

OLIVIA. Polton, my son has arrived in England.

POLTON. (*Smiling benignly.*) Yes, Madam, I heard you saying so on the telephone. I'm so glad.

She takes the telephone from OLIVIA *and puts it on the table.*

OLIVIA. Thank you, Polton. It really is wonderful news. (*She re-reads the telegram.*) Silly boy! Why didn't he say which station he was arriving at, and I could have gone to meet him——

POLTON. I suppose there'll be someone with the little chap to look after him, won't there, Madam?

OLIVIA. Oh no, I don't think so.

POLTON. (*Appalled.*) You don't mean he's come all that way from Canada all by his little self?

OLIVIA. He's not quite such a little self as all that, you know. He's—well, let me see—he was over twelve when he went away, so now he must be—anyway, quite old enough to look after himself.

POLTON. (*Gazing at* OLIVIA.) Mercy! I'd never have believed it, I will say.

OLIVIA. Thank you, Polton. (*She crosses to mirror.*) Tell cook to have something cold left out and have the little room next to mine got ready.

MISS DELL *comes in.*

MISS DELL. (*To* POLTON.) I've finished in the study. Good night, Polton.

OLIVIA. Oh, Miss Dell——

MISS DELL. (*To* OLIVIA.) Would you tell Sir John that if he wishes to work late tonight I shall be free from eight-thirty onwards, and that I've also left some papers on his desk to sign.

OLIVIA. I do hope he won't have to work late again. Don't you think he's looking tired, Miss Dell?

MISS DELL. I was going on to say, Mrs. Brown, that I hope you'll be able to exert your influence on him and try to get him to let up just a little. After all, we don't want him cracking up on us, do we?

OLIVIA. I'll try to exert my influence. My little son Michael has just arrived in England.

MISS DELL. Oh, I am glad. That will be nice for you. (*She moves to the door.*) And would you tell him, too, that R.M.B.3 have been through twice, and want him to ring them most urgently?

OLIVIA. (*Absently.*) Yes. Where do you think he'll come in; Glasgow, Liverpool?

MISS DELL. I really couldn't say, but I'll certainly find out. And his wife's solicitors want an answer by tomorrow.

OLIVIA. Oh yes. What about?

MISS DELL. The Barton and Burgess affair.

OLIVIA. What's that?

MISS DELL. Sir John will know.

OLIVIA. Come on, tell me.

MISS DELL. It's not at all important. You won't forget R.M.B.3, will you? It's vital he rings them as soon as he comes in.

OLIVIA. I'll see he does.

MISS DELL. I'm off to collect a report he particularly wants to-night. In case I don't see you again, good night, Mrs. Brown.

OLIVIA. Good night, Miss Dell.

Exit MISS DELL.

POLTON *comes in from study.*

Polton, I'm afraid Sir John will have to stay at his club to-night, so you'd better have his bag packed. I did ask you to tell cook to have something to eat left out for my son, didn't I?

POLTON. Yes, madam, I was going to get cook to make him a nice milk pudding.

OLIVIA. Oh. Don't you think something a little more substantial?

POLTON. Well, madam, if he's very late we don't want anything to sit too heavily on his little tummy, do we?

OLIVIA. (*Delighted.*) No, I suppose we don't—except that as I've told you, Polton, it really isn't such a little tummy as all that. It may even be quite a big tummy by now.

POLTON. Oh, no, madam.

OLIVIA. Well, I don't know, Polton. Isn't it funny not to know what one's own son looks like? I think we'd better make it cold meat and salad.

POLTON. Very good, madam, if you think so.

The telephone rings.

OLIVIA. (*Picking up the receiver.*) Hullo. . . . No, he's out at the moment. Who wants him? Well, have you tried him at the Ministry? . . . Oh, I see. Well, I'm expecting him at any minute. He usually comes in about this time. . . . No, I'm afraid his secretary has just gone out. . . . Can't I give him a message? . . . No, this isn't Lady Fletcher. . . . I see. If he comes in before six-thirty you want him to ring you. . . .

SIR JOHN *has come in in time to hear* OLIVIA's *last words. He is a man about forty-five, dressed in formal clothes. He takes the receiver from* OLIVIA.

JOHN. Fletcher here——

OLIVIA. Oh, hullo, darling.

She gives him an affectionate peck on the cheek and then wanders over to a tray on which is a decanter of whisky and some glasses. She is pouring out a drink while JOHN *continues to telephone.*

JOHN. I see. . . . Yes, well, I'm afraid I can't give the specifications until I see the report. . . .

OLIVIA. Whisky? (*He nods.*)

JOHN. . . . I should have had it this afternoon. . . . No, but one of my secretaries is fetching it now. I'll read it tonight and get in touch with you first thing tomorrow. Thank you. . . . Goodbye.

He rings off.

OLIVIA. (*From the drink table.*) Darling, you mustn't work late again tonight.

JOHN. Why not?

OLIVIA. Miss Dell thinks you're looking very tired and I agree with her.

JOHN. By the way, did Miss Dell leave any messages for me?

OLIVIA. Oh, yes, and one very important one. You're to call up your wife's solicitors.

JOHN. Oh, yes? (*He begins to take off his shoes.*)

OLIVIA. You're to give them an answer tomorrow morning on the Barton and Burgess affair.

JOHN. I see.

OLIVIA. Darling, what is the Barton and Burgess affair?

JOHN. Barton and Burgess are my wife's bookmakers. She incurred a very large debt with them, mostly after we were separated. Her solicitors think I should pay. I don't. That is the Barton and Burgess affair. Any other messages?

OLIVIA. No, I don't think so. Darling, I think you ought to pay that debt, don't you?

JOHN. Frankly, no. She receives a very handsome settlement, and can well afford to pay her own racing debts. Are you sure there weren't any other messages?

OLIVIA. Wait a minute, now. There was a thing you had to ring up. Three letters and a figure. R something. Darling, don't you think if you paid that bill it would avoid a lot of unpleasantness? (*She sits on sofa and gives him his glass.*)

JOHN. That's not the way I see it. Do you think you can possibly remember what the other two letters and the figure are of the thing that I have to ring up?

OLIVIA. Now let me see. There was an R and a B, I think.

JOHN. R.B.Y.4?

OLIVIA. That's right. You're to ring them up at once.

JOHN *reaches a hand for the telephone.*

Or was it R.M.B.3?

JOHN. (*Patiently.*) Or possibly B.R.F.6?

OLIVIA. Yes. No. It's no good. I can't remember.

JOHN. Well, it doesn't matter. They'll call again. I shall be sitting up all night working, anyway.

OLIVIA. (*Disturbed.*) Oh, oh——

JOHN. What's the matter?

OLIVIA. I'm afraid, if you really insist on sitting up all night, it won't be here, but at your Club.

JOHN. Why?

OLIVIA. Michael's arrived.

JOHN. Michael?

OLIVIA. He'll be home in a few hours.

JOHN. Oh. Your son?

OLIVIA *nods*.

I'm very glad.

OLIVIA. You don't look very glad.

JOHN. For your sake, I mean.

OLIVIA. Oh, darling, you'll find him most companionable. He's mad about politics. He's the head speaker of his little organization. Terribly amusing. You'll love him, you know.

JOHN. Do you think he'll love me?

OLIVIA. Of course he will.

JOHN. What makes you so certain?

OLIVIA. I do, so he will.

JOHN. So I'm to stay at my Club as long as Michael is in the neighbourhood?

OLIVIA. Oh, no. Of course not. Just for tonight.

JOHN. I can come back tomorrow?

OLIVIA. Yes, of course.

JOHN. Tell me, how old is he, by the way?

OLIVIA. Over sixteen.

JOHN. I thought he'd come back to join up.

OLIVIA. Yes, he has.

JOHN. Then he must be over seventeen.

OLIVIA. Perhaps he is.

JOHN. Don't you know the age of your own son?

OLIVIA. No, darling, not exactly. Let me see, now—He was twelve when we sent him away at the beginning of the war——

JOHN. When's his birthday?

OLIVIA. You have a horrible statistical mind. May the fourteenth.

JOHN. Then he's exactly seventeen and eight months.

OLIVIA. Oh—is that all? Oh, then he's still quite a baby.

JOHN. I doubt if he'll think so.

OLIVIA. You know what Polton said when I told her how old he was? She said she simply didn't believe it.

JOHN. I don't believe it, either. But, as the papers say, we must face facts, and the facts are these: You have a grown-up son——

OLIVIA. Oh! (*Opens her mouth to speak.*)

JOHN. Or nearly a grown-up son, about to descend on you at any moment to face a situation which I gather you have not yet had the courage to tell him in any of your letters.

OLIVIA. (*Protestingly.*) Darling, it's not the kind of thing you can write about in a letter. The censor wouldn't have passed it——

JOHN. There seems to be some confusion in your mind between the Department of War Censorship and the Lord Chamberlain. Anyway, whatever your excuse is, it is true, isn't it—you've told him nothing whatever about me?

OLIVIA. Oh, yes, I *have* told him something.

JOHN. What?

OLIVIA. That I'd met you, and that you were very nice.

JOHN. Thank you. When did you tell him that?

OLIVIA. Well—when I did meet you—about two years ago.

JOHN. Three years ago. Anything since?

OLIVIA. Well, I occasionally told him I'd been to a theatre with you, or something—or that I'd had dinner with you— or something.

JOHN. I see. In this case 'or something' appears to cover quite a wide field.

OLIVIA. Darling—he's only a little boy. How could I tell him things he wouldn't understand?

JOHN. Olivia, darling, he is *not* a little boy——

OLIVIA. Yes, he is. Just because he's seventeen doesn't mean he's grown up. I'll show you his letters—they're absolutely crammed with corking and tophole and—white mice and catapults. He's just a little boy and he wouldn't understand.

JOHN. Well, then—what are you going to tell him?

OLIVIA. The truth, I suppose.

JOHN. But you've just said he's too occupied with white mice and catapults to understand the truth.

OLIVIA. Then I'll tell him as much of the truth as he can understand.

JOHN. And how much is that?

OLIVIA. Oh, you are maddening! You know perfectly well what I mean.

JOHN. I'm sorry to catechize you like this, Olivia, but this is a crisis in your life that's arisen—in my life, too, come to that —and I haven't lived with you for three years without realizing that, if left to deal with it yourself, the chances are a hundred to one on your making an awful muck of it. Darling, be fair now. Isn't that true?

OLIVIA. No, it isn't. Not this time. After all, he *is* my own son and I know exactly how to deal with him.

JOHN. Well, all I'm asking is that you give me some indication of how you intend to deal with him. Come on, now—have a little rehearsal. What are you going to tell him?

OLIVIA. (*At length.*) Well—I'll say: 'Three years ago your father died, and I went to live in St. John's Wood.'

JOHN. Four years ago, and Swiss Cottage.

OLIVIA. Don't interrupt.

JOHN. I was being Michael. We can assume that, unlike his mother, he has some slight idea of space and time. By the way, was he very fond of his father?

OLIVIA. No, I don't think he was awfully. Anyway, he was always much fonder of me——

JOHN. Oh, well, that's better. Go on, go on.

OLIVIA. Well, don't be so cross!

JOHN. I'm not cross. I always sound cross when I'm worried.

OLIVIA. Put your feet up and be comfortable.

JOHN. Go on, now!

OLIVIA. (*Pushes him back, picks up his legs.*) Well, then, I'll say: 'One day I went to a cocktail party given by your Aunt Ethel who married the Gas Light and Coke Company, and lives in Park Lane, and there I met a man called John Fletcher whom I didn't know was *the* John Fletcher, in spite of his Canadian accent, because he seemed too amusing and

young to be a Captain of Industry and a Cabinet Minister
and all the rest of it, and who seemed to like me.'

JOHN. You understate. However, go on.

OLIVIA. 'Well—I went to lunch with him a couple of times and
then one night I had dinner with him——'

JOHN. Or something.

OLIVIA. Shut up. 'And he told me he was in love with me.'

JOHN. He said nothing of the kind. He was much too cautious
for that.

OLIVIA. 'Well—in a sort of underhand, roundabout politician's
way he gave me to understand that he didn't find me
altogether repulsive, but that he was unable to proceed
any further in the matter because he already had a wife
from whom he was separated and who anyway was a bit of
a bitch——'

JOHN. Tell me, darling, what's that?

OLIVIA. 'He already had a wife who didn't understand him,
but whom he couldn't divorce until after the war, on account
of Dr. Goebbels. So——'

JOHN. Wait a minute, wait a minute. You're skating over the
crux of the whole thing. I think Michael would want you
to expand this Goebbels theme——

OLIVIA. 'Well—he couldn't divorce his wife—who, God knows,
had given him every reason for it, because meanwhile he'd
been called into the Government to make tanks—and a nice
juicy divorce case involving a British Cabinet Minister
wouldn't look too well on the front pages of the Berlin
newspapers and might lead to tales of Babylonian orgies in
the Cabinet Room at 10 Downing Street.' How's that?

JOHN. Better. Go on.

OLIVIA. 'Well, then he asked me—very *comme il faut*—whether I
would wait until after the war when he would be free to
ask for my hand in marriage and I said no, that's silly.
After all, we're neither of us getting any younger and the
war might go on for years and years and years'—and it
certainly looked as if it would then, do you remember.

JOHN. (*Drowsily.*) I do. I do. I do. I do.

OLIVIA. 'So then he said—*again very comme il faut*—in that case he would resign from the Cabinet and go ahead with his divorce and I said, oh, no, you're far too useful making tanks, and anyway that would make me a sort of *femme fatale*, and I'm far too much in love with you to want to be that——'

JOHN. Did you say that? (*Takes her cheeks in his hands.*)

OLIVIA. Of course I said it, and it made you more—(*Together*) *comme il faut* than ever. (*Proceeding.*) You said you would exert every endeavour to find a formula to suit everyone, so I just packed my things and moved in that night. Since when not a ripple has stirred the calm surface of our domestic bliss—as Celia Wentworth would say.

JOHN. Who's Celia Wentworth?

OLIVIA. The novelist. She's dining here on Thursday. So's Tom Markham. (*Hands him list from table.*) There's the list. I've got the Randalls, too.

JOHN. Oh, who are the Randalls?

OLIVIA. John, really! They're only the most famous theatrical couple in the world, that's all. They never, never, never dine out.

JOHN. They're dining here on Thursday.

OLIVIA. (*Proudly.*) I know.

JOHN. How do you do it?

OLIVIA. It's a gift.

JOHN. And what would you say if I ask you—why do you do it?

OLIVIA. Oh, fun, I suppose. Or is it, perhaps, because I'm a bit of a snob?

JOHN. No. I don't think it's that.

OLIVIA. No. I don't think it's that, either. Or perhaps it is because subconsciously I resent a little not being Lady Fletcher, so perhaps I'm a bit too eager to anticipate my wifely privileges. Do you understand what I mean?

JOHN. I understand perfectly. I'm sorry I asked. (*He kisses the top of her head.*) It was stupid of me to ask, I'm sorry.

OLIVIA. That's all right. I know it must seem awfully silly— this ambition of mine to 'found a salon'. I laugh at myself sometimes.

JOHN. Nothing to laugh at in this list. Pretty damn good.

OLIVIA. It's not bad, is it? Darling, do you forgive me for being a snob?

JOHN. I'll forgive you for anything.

OLIVIA. No, no, seriously—I mean it.

JOHN. Darling, seriously—anything in the world that gives you pleasure gives me as much for just that same reason. If that sounds pompous and sentimental, I'm sorry, but I mean it.

OLIVIA. I'm quite fond of you, Sir John, do you know that?

JOHN. I'm quite fond of you, Mrs. Brown.

OLIVIA. Another whisky?

JOHN. No, thanks. I'd love a little more water in this, if you don't mind.

OLIVIA *rises and takes glass to drink table.*

OLIVIA. Just your slave girl, that's all I am.

JOHN. (*Drowsily.*) Slave girl, Slave girl——

OLIVIA. Well—what do you think about my story for Michael? Do you think it will do?

JOHN. It'll have to do. It's the truth.

OLIVIA. Of course, I shan't tell him anything like that at all.

JOHN. Oh, dear God above! (*Opens his eyes, starts up with jerk.*)

OLIVIA. All right, John dear, go to sleep if you want to.

JOHN. How can I go to sleep when you say things calculated to give me heart failure?

OLIVIA. What would be the use of going through all that rigmarole?

JOHN. Well, then, what, might I ask, was the idea of that rehearsal just now?

OLIVIA. Oh, because you asked me to. I shall just say that you're a very old friend, and that we're going to be married after the war.

JOHN. That's true. But what about (*he sweeps his hand round the room*) all this?

OLIVIA. Oh, I shall say that you've made me a present of one of your houses. (*Crosses to sofa with drink.*)

JOHN. Well, that's very generous of me.

OLIVIA. Oh, yes. For an old friend you're very generous.

JOHN. Thank you. Don't you think it's rather odd my giving you a house and then coming and sleeping in it myself?

OLIVIA. Not odd at all. You'll be here as my guest.

JOHN. Thank you.

OLIVIA. Not at all. Stay as long as you like.

JOHN. Very kind of you.

OLIVIA. (*Thoughtfully.*) Or on second thoughts, how would it be if I were your confidential secretary? What do you think of that, John?

JOHN. You know perfectly well what I think. I think that anything less than the full unvarnished truth is likely to prove fatal.

OLIVIA. I see. Confidential secretary no good?

JOHN. (*Rising.*) Confidential secretary no good.

OLIVIA. And the generous friend?

JOHN. And the generous friend.

OLIVIA. Then I don't see what's left.

JOHN. The truth, woman. The truth.

OLIVIA. But surely the truth is not the kind of thing one should tell one's sixteen-year-old boy?

JOHN. Madam, your son is nearly eighteen, and I think it better that he hear the truth from his mother's lips than from one of his bar cronies.

OLIVIA. Oh, John, I feel quite embarrassed. I've never been embarrassed by the situation before, and now I find myself blushing whenever I think of it. I feel like a bad, bad woman. (*She stands in a corner in an attitude suggesting intense shame.*)

JOHN. Well, in the eyes of many people, that's just what you are.

OLIVIA. Oh, surely not, in this day and age——

JOHN. In this day and age.

OLIVIA. In that case you must be a bad, bad man.

JOHN. A vile seducer.

OLIVIA. You—a vile seducer! (*Laughing.*)

JOHN. What's so funny about that?

OLIVIA. You couldn't seduce a fly.

JOHN. Is that so? I was a devil when I was a young man.

OLIVIA. I know you were a devil. The madcap of the Toronto Elks.

JOHN. Never mind. You'd be surprised. I've seduced hundreds of women in my time.

OLIVIA. Just name me one. That's all I ask. Just one.

JOHN. Well, anyway, I seduced you.

OLIVIA. Oh, no, you didn't. If there was any seducing to be done, I was the one that did it.

JOHN. (*Thoughtfully.*) Yes, I think that's true.

OLIVIA. You bet it's true. Go on, go to sleep.

JOHN. (*Defiantly.*) Not until you've promised to tell Michael the truth, the whole truth, and nothing but the truth.

OLIVIA. (*Embracing him.*) I promise, you vile seducer.

JOHN. But can I trust you?

OLIVIA. Not an inch.

POLTON *comes in. Neither* OLIVIA *nor* JOHN *relaxes their very intimate position.*

POLTON. I've packed your bag, sir.

JOHN. What? Oh, yes. Thank you, Polton. (*To* OLIVIA.) Damn!

OLIVIA. I know, darling, and I'm very sorry, but it's only for tonight.

POLTON. Did you want me to put in any papers, sir?

JOHN. No, they won't be here until later. I'll put them in myself. All right, Polton; thank you.

OLIVIA. Oh, Polton. I was too excited just now to tell you. I've managed to make up the table for Thursday. There's the plan . . . you see I've put—oh well, you can read it yourself.

POLTON. There'll be twelve, madam?

OLIVIA. Yes. We'd better start saving up rations. . . . So Sir John and I will be dining out tonight.

JOHN. Are we dining out?

OLIVIA. Yes, dear. Only tonight. Saving up for Thursday.

POLTON. Shall I ring up the Savoy and book a table, madam?

OLIVIA. Yes, do. Ask for our usual table, will you, Polton?

POLTON. Very good, madam.

She goes out.

JOHN *yawns.*

OLIVIA. (*Turning out the lights.*) Did you have a very tiring day?

JOHN. Pretty tiring. I was bullied at question-time.

OLIVIA. Badly?

JOHN. Very badly. All about the new tank. At least ten of them were screaming for my blood.

OLIVIA. I'll have them here and bully them.

JOHN. I wish you would.

OLIVIA. Don't they know what a terrific job you've done?

JOHN is lying on the sofa; OLIVIA is standing behind him—both dimly seen in the firelight.

JOHN. I don't know that I've done such a terrific job, Olivia. Certainly you wouldn't have thought so if you could have heard them this afternoon. At the end of it I knew that if one more of them got up and was unkind, I'd have burst into tears there and then on the Speaker's lap.

OLIVIA. (*Angrily.*) Joan says the new tank is a miracle.

JOHN. Joan, for once, is right. At the moment, I can't say so.

OLIVIA. I don't care. I'd have told them straight out.

JOHN. I'm sure you would. Still, the curse is, some details are still on the secret list.

OLIVIA. Well, if you can keep a secret, why can't they?

JOHN. I don't know. Olivia, if you love me, don't mention the words 'new tank' again.

OLIVIA. No, no, I promise. (*She looks down at him.*) Go on, sleep away, you great baby! I'll write some letters.

JOHN. Don't go too far away.

OLIVIA. Why not?

JOHN. (*Sleepily.*) Because I adore you.

OLIVIA goes to a chair and sits. At the same time Big Ben is heard chiming three-quarters of the hour. In the middle of the chimes POLTON enters in some agitation.

POLTON. (*Entering.*) Madam!

MICHAEL comes in.

MICHAEL. Hullo, Mum.

OLIVIA. (*With a shriek.*) Michael, darling! (*She runs across and embraces him.*) Your telegram said late tonight. I wasn't expecting you for hours.

JOHN sits up abruptly.

MICHAEL. I didn't see why I should wait all day for a train. I got a lift from a pilot chap I know. He was taking an Anson down to Reading and I came on from there.

OLIVIA. (*She embraces him again.*) You don't look so much older, but you're much thinner. Didn't they give you enough to eat over there?

MICHAEL. Of course they did.

OLIVIA. Oh, it's wonderful to see you, Michael——

OLIVIA *puts on the lights.* MICHAEL *has become conscious of* JOHN, *who is now unobtrusively trying to change from his slippers back to his shoes. He has just succeeded in putting on one shoe, as* MICHAEL *turns towards him and waits to be introduced.*

(*Without embarrassment.*) Oh, I'm sorry. This is Sir John Fletcher —my son Michael.

JOHN. How do you do?

MICHAEL. How do you do, sir?

OLIVIA. (*Quickly.*) Poor man, his shoes were hurting him.

MICHAEL. Oh, really?

OLIVIA. (*With a gay laugh.*) So I told him to take them off if they were hurting him.

MICHAEL. Yes, I see.

JOHN. (*With another gay laugh.*) Well, they've stopped hurting me now, so, if you don't mind, I'll put them on again.

OLIVIA. Oh, yes, do. (*Crossing with* MICHAEL.) You remember? I told you all about him in my letters. I want you to be particularly nice to him, Michael—because he's a very old friend of mine—that's to say, anyway, I want you to get on—— (*She tails off.*)

MICHAEL. (*Stiffly.*) Oh, yes.

JOHN. Did you have a good trip?

MICHAEL. Yes, thank you, sir.

OLIVIA. Oh, don't call him sir, Michael. Call him—I know— call him Uncle John.

MICHAEL. Why?

OLIVIA. Well—because it would—well—be nice.

JOHN. (*Quickly.*) I agree with Michael. I don't see why he should call me Uncle John when I'm not his Uncle John.

OLIVIA. (*Unhappily.*) Yes—but you're such a very old friend.

JOHN. Quite so, but that's hardly the point. (*He glares at her.*)
    MICHAEL *is looking round the room, taking it in for the first time.*

OLIVIA. How do you like it here, Michael? (*Crosses to* MICHAEL.)

MICHAEL. It's not bad. Did you get it furnished?

OLIVIA. Well—yes—in a sort of way.

MICHAEL. (*Noticing a picture over the mantelpiece.*) Hullo—you've
    still got the Sickert, I see.

OLIVIA. Yes, darling. It looks well there, don't you think?

MICHAEL. (*Doubtfully.*) Ye-es. I think it looked better in Baron's
    Court, somehow.

OLIVIA. Oh.

MICHAEL. I know what it is, you've changed the frame, haven't
    you?

OLIVIA. That's right. The old one was so heavy. How do you
    like the rest of the room?

MICHAEL. Swell. The landlady seems a decent old girl.

OLIVIA. Landlady?

MICHAEL. The old girl that let me in, isn't she the landlady?

OLIVIA. Well—no, darling. She's more of a sort of—parlour-
    maid.

MICHAEL. She's a funny old thing. (*Pointing to sofa.*) I suppose
    that becomes a bed, does it?

They both move down to the back of the sofa. JOHN *rises.*

OLIVIA. Er—no, darling.

MICHAEL. Where do you sleep, then? (*He looks round the room.*)

OLIVIA. (*Faintly.*) Upstairs.

MICHAEL. You've got another room upstairs?

OLIVIA. Yes, darling——

MICHAEL. I'll sleep here tonight, then. I thought I'd probably
    have to sleep out.

OLIVIA. Well—as a matter of fact, darling, there's quite a nice
    little room for you upstairs.

MICHAEL. Another room?

OLIVIA. Yes, dear.

MICHAEL. Gosh! How much are you paying for all this?

OLIVIA. (*Kissing him.*) Oh—not an awful lot.

MICHAEL. Are you sure you can afford it?

OLIVIA. (*Taking him by the arm.*) Darling—don't let's talk about such things at the moment. Remember, there's someone else in the room.

MICHAEL. Oh, yes. Sorry. (*To* JOHN.) Can I get you a drink, sir?

JOHN. What? Oh, no, thanks. I don't think I'll have another. (*To* OLIVIA.) Olivia—I know you and Michael want to be alone. But I can't very well leave until these papers arrive. Would you mind if I went into—our—this room here— (*he points to the study door*) and did a little work meanwhile?

OLIVIA. No, of course not, John.

JOHN. I'll make myself scarce as soon as these papers arrive.

OLIVIA. Oh no, there's no need to do that. Remember, we're having dinner together.

JOHN. Yes, I know, but wouldn't you rather——?

OLIVIA. Oh no. That's all right. We'll all three have dinner together. That'll be fun, won't it, Michael?

MICHAEL (*Without enthusiasm.*) Yes, corking.

OLIVIA. (*With a triumphant look at* JOHN.) There you are, you see, John. Corking.

JOHN. (*Meaningly.*) But are you sure you have time to say all you have to say to each other before dinner?

OLIVIA. Don't you worry about that, John.

JOHN. Oh, well, that's splendid. (*To* MICHAEL.) I'll see you later, then.

MICHAEL. Yes, sir.

JOHN. By the way, how old are you, Michael?

MICHAEL. Seventeen and eight months.

JOHN. Really? As old as that? Well, one can hardly call you a little boy then, can one?

MICHAEL. (*Explosively.*) I should bloody well hope not!

OLIVIA. (*Sharply and reprovingly.*) Michael!

Delighted, JOHN *goes into the study.*

MICHAEL. (*Furiously.*) Now what was all that about my being a little boy?

OLIVIA. Darling——

MICHAEL. What did the silly old poop mean?

OLIVIA. (*Gently reproving.*) He said you weren't a little boy. Besides, he's not a silly old poop.

MICHAEL. That's what you say.

OLIVIA. You know who he is, don't you?

MICHAEL. He's the Minister for Tank Production.

OLIVIA. That's right. He's in the Cabinet.

MICHAEL. That doesn't make him any the less of an old poop.

OLIVIA. Michael!

MICHAEL. You should hear what my organization in Canada says about him.

OLIVIA. But, surely, your organization in Canada speaks very highly of him?

MICHAEL. Oh no, they don't. Not my friends, anyway. They say he's a menace to world industrial reorganization.

OLIVIA. (*Sinking on to sofa.*) Oh. Do they say that?

MICHAEL. Have you read his book?

OLIVIA. No, I haven't had time yet——

MICHAEL. *A Defence of Private Enterprise?*

OLIVIA.—what with the Red Cross——

MICHAEL. Well, I have, and it nearly made me sick.

OLIVIA. Oh, dear!

MICHAEL. We had a debate on his policy the other day, and do you know what the vote was?

OLIVIA. No.

MICHAEL. That he was nothing but a rank monopolistic reactionary.

OLIVIA. Oh.

MICHAEL. Disgusting!

OLIVIA. Oh.

MICHAEL. (*Sitting.*) Anyway, don't let's talk any more about him. Tell me about yourself. How have you been?

OLIVIA. Oh, all right.

MICHAEL. You don't look awfully well.

OLIVIA. Don't I?

MICHAEL. No. A bit—sort of—haggard, somehow.

OLIVIA. Haggard?

MICHAEL. Well—I expect it's just your being older.

OLIVIA. Well, darling—I am older.

MICHAEL. (*Cheerfully.*) Oh, well—not as old as all that. You've still got plenty of time ahead of you.

OLIVIA. Thank you, Michael.

MICHAEL. Poor old Mum! I bet you've had a pretty rotten time of it. Are you glad to have someone to take care of you at last?

OLIVIA. (*Tearfully.*) Oh, Michael!

MICHAEL. (*Puts his arm around her.*) What's the matter?

OLIVIA. (*Recovering herself.*) It's nothing. I'm sorry. It's just that you're not quite how I expected you, somehow.

MICHAEL. I'm older, you know.

OLIVIA. Oh, darling, you don't look any older——

MICHAEL. Oh, Mum, I must——

OLIVIA. No, you don't. (*She puts her arms around him.*) You still look my little Michael. How was Canada?

MICHAEL. Corking.

OLIVIA. You haven't got a Canadian accent.

MICHAEL. Haven't I? Well, you see, there were quite a lot of us English boys in the school, and we rather kept together.

OLIVIA. (*Smiling.*) They took good care of you, anyway?

MICHAEL. Take care of us? They were wonderful to us—they really were. I told you all about the house and everything, didn't I? Wasn't I good about writing?

OLIVIA. You were marvellous.

MICHAEL. I bet you didn't read any of them.

OLIVIA. Oh, Michael, I have all your letters in a drawer upstairs, and I read them over and over. I can tell you all about the house, and the Wilkinsons, and the neighbours, and Professor Mason who stammers and caught you imitating him one day—that was naughty of you, darling—and the Wilburs who live in the big house on the lake, and let you go fishing. There!

MICHAEL. Not bad. I take it all back.

OLIVIA. They do seem to have been most terribly kind to you, anyway.

MICHAEL. You don't know the half of it. Do you know that when Dad died, old Mrs. Wilkinson, who didn't know anything about him at all, except through me—of course, I had talked about both of you quite a bit—well, she cried. She really cried. I don't think I'll ever forget that, somehow——

OLIVIA. She wrote me an awfully nice letter.

MICHAEL. Can you tell me anything more about it, or would you rather not?

OLIVIA. Well, darling, there really isn't much to tell. You know how ill he was before you went away—overwork, of course, and then because of the war there was even more work. I tried to get him to let up, but you know him, he wouldn't. I suppose I should have tried more—I don't know.

MICHAEL. I bet you did everything you could.

OLIVIA. I hope so, Michael. I do hope so.

MICHAEL. Poor old Mum. I'm most terribly sorry.

OLIVIA. Thank you, darling.

He pats her sleeve, then strokes the material admiringly.

MICHAEL. By jove! That's a jolly nice bit of stuff!

OLIVIA. Do you like it?

MICHAEL. I bet you didn't get that at Pontings.

OLIVIA. No, darling, I didn't.

MICHAEL. I bet it was Derry and Toms——

OLIVIA. No, it wasn't Derry and Toms, either.

MICHAEL. Where was it, then?

OLIVIA. Oh, a little shop—you wouldn't know it——

MICHAEL. What's it called?

OLIVIA. Molyneux.

MICHAEL. Never heard of it.

OLIVIA. Really?

MICHAEL. What's the matter with Derry and Toms?

OLIVIA. Nothing's the matter with Derry and Toms. Derry and Toms is very nice, too—only Molyneux is a bit—er—nearer.

The telephone rings. She gets up to answer it.

Oh, dear, that telephone never stops ringing. You'll have to be my secretary, Michael. (*Lifting receiver.*) Hullo—oh, hullo, Freddy. . . . Oh, I haven't for-forgotten lunch. . . . He's charming. . . . Yes, I met him at Bobby's party. . . .

MICHAEL *rises and watches* OLIVIA.

. . . Yes, do bring him. . . . I'd love to meet him again. . . . Right. One-fifteen at the Dorchester. . . . No, no, I won't forget this time. Goodbye. (*She rings off, and picks up her engagement book.*)

MICHAEL *is still staring at her.*

Penny for your thoughts.

MICHAEL. I was just thinking how much you'd changed.

OLIVIA. Changed? For the better or the worse?

MICHAEL. I don't know. Just changed.

OLIVIA. (*Sitting.*) Oh!

MICHAEL. Even your voice has changed. When you were speaking to that chap on the 'phone, it might have been Aunt Ethel talking——

OLIVIA. Aunt Ethel has a nice voice.

MICHAEL. A bit Park Lane, isn't it?

OLIVIA. (*Testily.*) She lives in Park Lane.

MICHAEL. I know. Tell me—what made you leave Baron's Court?

OLIVIA. Well—it was rather a gloomy flat, didn't you think? And then the blitz was on, so I took a basement bed-sit. in —er—Swiss Cottage.

MICHAEL. Then you came on here?

OLIVIA. Yes. (*She fans herself with the engagement book.*)

MICHAEL. Did you ever manage to let the old flat?

OLIVIA. It's in the hands of the agents, and I haven't heard from them for ages——

MICHAEL. But you must find out. After all, an extra two or three pounds a week would be very useful, wouldn't it?

OLIVIA. Well, yes.

MICHAEL. Did Dad leave very much?

OLIVIA. No, not much.

MICHAEL. I can see I shall have to make some money for you pretty quickly.

OLIVIA. Michael—that reminds me—you know all those letters you wrote me about wanting to get a job between now and the time you're called up——?

MICHAEL. (*Eagerly.*) Yes. Have you found me anything?

OLIVIA. Well, I think I have found you something—and rather nice, too.

MICHAEL. How much money?

OLIVIA. About seven or eight pounds a week.

MICHAEL. Oh, gosh! Oh, gosh! What is it?

OLIVIA. Well, you're to go tomorrow morning and see a Mr. Symonds. He hasn't promised anything, but if you make a good impression, he may give you something in the Ministry of Tank Production.

Pause.

MICHAEL. Has *he* got anything to do with it? (*Rises.*)

OLIVIA. Yes, he has, darling, he's gone to a great deal of trouble, and I want you to thank him, very nicely.

MICHAEL. Gosh, seven or eight pounds! Well, I suppose one can't afford to be too choosey, if the job's worth all that money. Still, I can't say I care for the thought of having him as my boss, all the same.

OLIVIA. Oh, darling, he *is* the Minister. I don't suppose you're likely to bump into him very much in *your* work.

MICHAEL. (*Squarely defiant.*) I shall take jolly good care I don't.

Pause.

OLIVIA. (*Kneeling beside him.*) Oh, Michael, I wish you'd forget all these tiresome prejudices of yours and try and like him just a little. Believe me, it's terribly important for me that you do.

MICHAEL. Why?

OLIVIA. Well—he's such a very old friend.

MICHAEL. Let's talk about that some other time.

OLIVIA. Darling, there's something I have to say to you.

MICHAEL. Yes, Mum, what is it?

OLIVIA. (*Getting up.*) Oh, dear, this is so difficult. (*Bending down to kiss him.*) It's so wonderful to have you back——

MICHAEL. It's nice to be back.

She wanders away from him.

OLIVIA. Michael, do you think of me as being terribly old?

MICHAEL. (*Reassuringly.*) Oh, no, Mum. Not old at all. Sort of middle-aged, really——

OLIVIA. Yes, I see. Well, now, you know how fond I was of your father, don't you?

MICHAEL. Yes, Mum, of course I know

OLIVIA. Well, after all, that's really no reason why I should think of spending the rest of my life entirely alone——

MICHAEL. Of course you won't be alone. You're going to have me from now on.

OLIVIA. I know, dear, and I'm more grateful than I can say to have you with me. But, darling, you'll get married yourself one day, and then I shall have no one——

MICHAEL. Don't worry about that. We'll have you to live with us.

OLIVIA. Oh, I see——

MICHAEL. Besides, I don't think I'm going to get married.

OLIVIA. Why not?

MICHAEL. It's a bit frustrating, I think.

OLIVIA. Oh, is it?

MICHAEL. Yes. Go on, Mum. What were you going to tell me?

OLIVIA. (*With a sudden access of courage.*) Michael, what would you say if I told you that I was thinking of getting married again?

MICHAEL. What? (*He begins to laugh.*)

OLIVIA. (*Bewildered.*) What are you laughing at?

MICHAEL. Oh, Mum; oh, Mum! Poor old Mum!

OLIVIA. Why poor old Mum?

MICHAEL. (*Contrite.*) I'm awfully sorry. Most rude of me—only—— (*He chokes with laughter again.*)

OLIVIA. Only what?

MICHAEL. Nothing. Yes, of course, go ahead and get married. We'll just have to find the right man for you, that's all. Poor old Mum!

OLIVIA. (*With sudden fury.*) Don't call me poor old Mum!

POLTON *comes in with a Ministry dispatch box.*

Oh, Polton?

POLTON. Oh, pardon me, madam, but I thought Sir John was here. Miss Dell has left these papers from the Ministry of Information.

She gives the box to OLIVIA *and goes out.*

OLIVIA. Oh, yes, thank you, Polton. (*Calling.*) John, your papers have come.

JOHN. (*Off stage.*) Thank you, I'll be right out.

MICHAEL. Is that all you've got to say to me?

OLIVIA. Yes—that's all I've got to say to you.

MICHAEL. (*Taking cigarette from box.*) Do you mind if I have a cigarette?

OLIVIA. Oh, Michael, you don't smoke?

MICHAEL. Oh, yes. Four or five a day.

OLIVIA. Oh, Michael! Four or five a day? That's an awful lot.

He lights his cigarette and blows a couple of nonchalant smoke rings.
Oh, darling!

MICHAEL. What's the matter?

OLIVIA. Nothing. It's just that I can't bear to see you smoke. It does something to me here.

JOHN comes in from the study.

JOHN. (*Delighted.*) Smoking? Whisky and soda? (*Crosses to drink table.*)

OLIVIA. Don't be absurd, John.

MICHAEL. I'll have a whisky. I quite like it.

OLIVIA. No, indeed, you'll do nothing of the kind. If you have anything at all, you'll have a glass of sherry.

MICHAEL. Oh, all right. I thought sherry was very difficult to get in England.

JOHN. Difficult, but not impossible.

MICHAEL. Thank you. (*Takes drink from JOHN.*)

JOHN. I think I'll have a drink myself if you don't mind.

MICHAEL. ⎫
　　　　 ⎬ (*Together.*) Go ahead.
OLIVIA. ⎭

　　MICHAEL has wandered up to the window, and for a moment he has his back to the other two. JOHN, in soundless speech and pantomime, asks OLIVIA if she has told him. OLIVIA shakes her head. JOHN, still soundlessly, asks why not. OLIVIA shrugs her shoulders despairingly. JOHN, by gesticulation and pantomime, implies that she must do it now, or he'll be very angry, and that he is going into the study again. OLIVIA shakes her head violently. JOHN continues his gesticulations, stopping abruptly as MICHAEL turns round.

MICHAEL. You know, Mum, it's funny how small London looks after Montreal.

JOHN. Well——

OLIVIA. Darling—It's much bigger.

MICHAEL. But the houses are so mean-looking. You ought to see the Mount Royal Hotel, Montreal. There's a building for you. (*To* JOHN.) Of course, you must know it—I was forgetting.

JOHN. It's some time since I've seen it, though. (*Crossing to pick up the Ministry box.*) Well—I think I'd better go and read this report.

OLIVIA. (*Getting up very quickly from her chair and going up to the door.*) No. You stay here and talk to Michael. I have to go and change for dinner.

JOHN. Oh, but surely—haven't you got a lot more to say to Michael—a *lot* more.

OLIVIA. Yes, after dinner. He has something to say to *you.* He wants to thank you, very nicely. I'm sure you two are going to get on—quite corkingly.

She goes out.

JOHN *takes* MICHAEL's *glass.*

JOHN. Another?

MICHAEL. No, thank you.

JOHN. No, of course not.

MICHAEL. You know, I'm very interested to meet you, Sir John.

JOHN. Oh, well, I'm very interested to meet you.

MICHAEL. You see, our organization discussed you the other day.

JOHN. Oh, really? How nice.

MICHAEL. Yes.

JOHN. Come to any conclusions?

MICHAEL. Oh, yes. Lots. I won't tell you what they were, though.

JOHN. Oh? Why not?

MICHAEL. Isn't that obvious?

JOHN. Is it?

MICHAEL. I told Mum, as a matter of fact.

JOHN. What did she say?

MICHAEL. She said 'Oh'.

JOHN. You have a very remarkable mother, Michael.

MICHAEL. Do you think so?

JOHN. Very remarkable indeed.

MICHAEL. Oh, I don't know.

JOHN. (*Extending his case.*) Will you have a cigarette?

MICHAEL. No, thanks. I've just finished one.

JOHN. Oh, yes, of course. Mustn't encourage you to smoke too much, must I?

MICHAEL. No.

JOHN. Well, Michael, did your mother tell you that there was a possibility of your coming to work for me?

MICHAEL. Yes, thank you.

JOHN. Not at all.

MICHAEL. What *is* the job?

JOHN. (*Motioning* MICHAEL *to sit.*) You'll be in Symonds' department, that is, if he likes you. He's one of my under-secretaries. I don't imagine he'll try you too heavily at first. You'll probably spend the first couple of weeks making tea for the office.

MICHAEL. Tea for the office?

JOHN. (*Apologetically.*) I was just joking.

MICHAEL. Oh, I see.

JOHN. You mustn't expect too much responsibility at first. We've all got to start somewhere, you know.

MICHAEL. Naturally.

JOHN. Anyway, you'll be getting a lot of money for a boy of your age. Do you know how much I got when I first started?

MICHAEL. No. How much?

JOHN. About seventeen bob a week. I started as an office boy.

MICHAEL. (*Coldly.*) Really? According to my organization you inherited Fletcher-Pratt from your father—Black Fletcher —who fought the Canadian Trades Unions.

Pause.

JOHN. Black Fletcher was not the name I knew my father by. However, it's quite true that my father, James Fletcher, was chairman of the board of the Canadian branch at the time, but I had to work my way up like anyone else.

MICHAEL. Yes—but surely from slightly nearer the top than anyone else——

JOHN. No—no nearer the top than anyone else. Tell me, are you terribly left-wing?

MICHAEL. No, not more than most people. I'm just an anti-fascist.

JOHN. Aren't we all, these days?

MICHAEL. I don't know. Are we?

JOHN. I thought that was what we're all fighting against.

MICHAEL. That's what some of us are fighting against, all right.

JOHN. Oh. Only some of us?

MICHAEL. Well, what James P. Whitstable says is that, whereas the last war was fought on vertical lines of nationalistic imperialism, the present war is being fought on horizontal lines of proletarian realism.

JOHN. Tell me, who said this?

MICHAEL. James P. Whitstable. He's the treasurer of our organization.

JOHN. Oh. Only the treasurer?

MICHAEL. And another thing he says is that our real enemy is not so much the enemy as some of those who pretend to be the enemy's enemy.

JOHN. A very sound man, this Mr. Whitstable.

MICHAEL. He's over nineteen.

JOHN. I see. Just tottering into his twenties.

MICHAEL. And again, he says that fascism doesn't only wear a brown shirt. It *can* wear a black coat and a stiff white collar.
Pause.

JOHN. (*Covering his collar with his hand.*) If James P. Whitstable were only here, Michael, I might, who knows, be able to answer him. But as a matter of fact, I'm a little out of practice at this sort of argument. You see, for the past three years I have been working on an average of fourteen hours a day trying to produce certain engines of war, designed to kill, with a maximum efficiency——

MICHAEL. Maximum efficiency?

JOHN.——as many of my country's enemies as possible. So you see, Michael, I'm just a little tired——

MICHAEL. Gosh, Sir John, I should think that you would be. I hear that the new tank——

JOHN. (*Pleadingly.*) No, Michael, not the new tank, if you don't mind.

MICHAEL. (*Remorselessly.*) Yes, I was reading about it only this morning.

JOHN. Michael, did you do much skating in Canada?

MICHAEL. A fair amount. I say it looks as if there is going to be a pretty good stink over the new tank, judging by the *Evening Standard*.

JOHN. (*Desperately.*) Did you play any ice hockey while you were there?

MICHAEL. Yes, I did. (*Whispering in* JOHN's *ear.*) Tell me, is it true that you can put your hand through the armour plating?

JOHN. No.

MICHAEL. A chap on the boat said you could.

JOHN. (*Hoarsely.*) Olivia!

MICHAEL. She's just gone to dress. And then I met another chap who said the turret was an absolute disgrace. Is it?

JOHN. No.

MICHAEL. And another thing I heard was that the only way it could go up hill was backwards. Is that true, too?

JOHN. No. Who told you this? That chap on the boat?

MICHAEL. No. Another chap who'd heard from his brother who knew a chap in a tank regiment. I must say it seems pretty odd to me if after three years of preparation, that's the best sort of tank you can produce. (*Laughing.*) And I'm jolly sure it isn't inefficiency. Whatever else can be said about you big business men, no one can say you're inefficient.

JOHN. (*Through his hands, faintly.*) Thank you very much, Michael.

MICHAEL. It's the folly of the whole system. Big business men running a public service. What happens? They cut each other's throats, they line their own pockets, and then people are surprised when after three years they get a tank that can't even go up hill in the ordinary way.

Something suspiciously like a sob comes from JOHN.

I see you have no answer. I can't say I'm surprised.

OLIVIA *comes in and looks with alarm at* JOHN.

OLIVIA. Well, I'm all ready. John, John, dear, what *is* the matter?

JOHN. (*Raising his head.*) Nothing, Olivia, nothing at all.

MICHAEL. (*Offhandedly.*) I think a few things I said may have upset him a little bit.

OLIVIA. What were the things about?

JOHN. (*Weakly.*) We were discussing the new tank, ice hockey——

OLIVIA. Oh! (*To* MICHAEL.) I thought I told you I wanted you to make friends with him.

MICHAEL. I know, Mum. But I get a bit worked up about politics.

OLIVIA. I don't care. Now say you're sorry to Sir John for upsetting him.

MICHAEL. (*Taking a step towards* JOHN.) I'm sorry, Sir John, for upsetting you.

JOHN. Quite all right.

MICHAEL. Truce for dinner?

JOHN. Yes, truce for dinner.

OLIVIA. That's better. (*Taking him towards the door.*) Now go upstairs and get ready for dinner. Polton will show you your room.

MICHAEL. Polton?

OLIVIA. The parlourmaid.

MICHAEL. Oh, the parlourmaid.

He goes out.

OLIVIA. Well, John? You didn't get on?

JOHN. I'm afraid we didn't get on.

OLIVIA. Politics?

JOHN. Politics. He also accused me of nepotism, fraud, incompetence, peculation, and treachery.

OLIVIA. Did he really? Isn't he naughty?

JOHN. At times, my darling, you have a positive genius for understatement.

OLIVIA. He *is* a problem, isn't he?

JOHN. He's a problem all right.

OLIVIA. You do understand now why I found it so terribly difficult to tell him?

JOHN. Darling, I understand perfectly.

OLIVIA. You see, you thought he'd be a grown young man and

I thought he'd be a little boy, and he really isn't either, is he?

JOHN. No, he's too old to spank and too young to punch on the nose.

OLIVIA. No, I think it's his being away from England for so long.

JOHN. Olivia, I was away from England for years and years and years.

OLIVIA. Yes, but you're very different. No, I mean, his being away from his home and from me. He's just got a lot of funny notions in his head that I shall have to get out, that's all.

JOHN. If you should run out of ideas on that score, I'll be delighted to co-operate.

OLIVIA. No, no, John. You mustn't interfere.

JOHN. I was only going to suggest——

OLIVIA. Wait a minute, John, I'm trying to find the right approach.

JOHN. I beg your pardon.

OLIVIA. I know how to handle him.

JOHN. A couple of minutes ago, you said——

OLIVIA. I know, I know, something's coming. I'll wait until he's in bed, then I'll take him up a cup of nice hot Ovaltine.

JOHN. With a dash of something in it?

OLIVIA. No. I'll sit on the side of his bed and talk to him as if he were about forty years old—you know, a real man of the world. He'll love that. I'll even ask his advice—just as one would an elder brother, and in a few minutes the whole problem will be settled, for good and all. What do you think of that, John?

JOHN. (*Despondently.*) It's a very pretty picture. You'll probably spill the Ovaltine on his bed and spoil the whole thing.

OLIVIA. (*Leaning over the back of sofa and kissing him.*) You're a gloomy old thing, aren't you, but you're very sweet.

JOHN. Well, I don't feel very sweet.

OLIVIA. Oh, John, you've always wanted a son.

JOHN. Not like that.

OLIVIA. He's a darling, he always was.

JOHN. You mean he was born that way?

OLIVIA. Don't worry, in a few weeks I shall be quite jealous of the way you two are getting on—I know it. (*Crosses and looks in mirror.*) He looks very young, don't you think, John? Joan's going to be at the Savoy tonight.

JOHN. (*Busy with his box and papers.*) I fail to see the connection. (*Suddenly.*) Oh, God! Am I to be spared nothing?

OLIVIA. What's the matter?

JOHN. They've sent the wrong report.

OLIVIA. Oh, darling! I *am* sorry.

JOHN. (*Gets up from sofa and goes to the telephone.*) This is the last straw. The camel's back is broken. (*As he dials.*) Idiots! Fools! Incompetent half-wits! They'd be sacked in a week from any decently-run business. I don't care if they're all Field-Marshals. I'll tell them so myself.

OLIVIA. Yes, darling. Do.

JOHN. (*Into receiver.*) Hullo. R.M.B.3? Who's that? . . . Oh, General Parker. This is John Fletcher. You remember a certain report I asked for from your office? . . . Yes, quite safely, thank you, only you see it happens to be the wrong report. . . . Oh, the wrong envelope? Yes, of course. That would explain it. . . . Not at all. . . . Well, I'd be very grateful if you could have the right one sent to the Savoy in half an hour's time. . . . That's right. Thank you. Goodbye. (*He rings off.*)

OLIVIA. That's certainly one way of telling them.

JOHN. He got it from the tone of my voice.

Enter MICHAEL.

MICHAEL. Mum, do you mind leaving me alone with Sir John Fletcher a moment?

JOHN. (*Retreating hastily.*) Oh, God!

OLIVIA. (*Rising from sofa.*) But why, darling—and if it's anything about the new tank——

MICHAEL. It isn't about the new tank.

OLIVIA. Oh, God—— (*Joining* JOHN *by the fire, and catching hold of his hand.*)

MICHAEL. I want him to give me an explanation of something jolly fishy that's going on in this house——

OLIVIA. Surely there isn't anything you can't say in front of me?

MICHAEL. All right, then. I've just been having a talk with whatsername—Polton, and she told me that this house belongs to him, and every darned thing in it. Is that true?

JOHN. Yes, that is true.

MICHAEL. So then I went into Mum's room, and, by gosh! In the wardrobe there, I found about fifty dresses which I'd never seen before——

OLIVIA. (*Quickly.*) Michael, with clothes rationing, there couldn't possibly be as many as that.

JOHN. Nothing like as many.

MICHAEL. (*Furiously.*) Did you or did you not pay for them?

JOHN. Yes, I paid for them.

MICHAEL. And all those jewels and things on the dressing table?

JOHN. Yes, I paid for those, too.

MICHAEL. And the weighing machine in the bathroom?

OLIVIA. (*Quickly.*) Oh, no, Michael, I paid for that.

MICHAEL. With your money, or with the money he gave you?

OLIVIA. Well—— (*She looks at John in doubt.*)

JOHN. With the money I gave her.

MICHAEL. I don't need to hear any more. I understand the situation perfectly.

He goes out quickly.

OLIVIA. (*Following him.*) No, darling, you don't understand, and I beg you to reserve judgment until you've heard the whole story.

MICHAEL. (*Off stage.*) I don't need to hear it. You've been weak, he's been vile.

OLIVIA. (*Off stage.*) Michael, really! Stop it at once. You're not to talk to us like that—do you hear?

MICHAEL. (*Off stage.*) Very well. I shan't say another word until I've thought out what I'm going to do.

OLIVIA *comes back.*

OLIVIA. (*She looks despairingly at* JOHN, *then motions to him that she has decided what to do. Calling sharply.*) Michael!

They both lean forward to see whether he is coming.

M

She calls again, but this time in a gentle, loving voice.

Michael—Michael—darling——

MICHAEL *comes back, and walks slowly to the chair, C.*

Michael, darling, come here and sit down. I'll tell you what we're going to do. (*She sits on sofa.*) We'll all three go out, and over dinner John and I will tell you the whole story from beginning to end. How's that?

MICHAEL. Very well. But on one condition. This dinner's on me.

OLIVIA. Oh, but darling, wouldn't it be better if——

MICHAEL. I'm not going to let *him* pay for dinner.

OLIVIA. But, darling, you can't afford to take us to the Savoy.

MICHAEL. No, that's quite true. We'll have to go somewhere else. I know, the Tuck Inn.

OLIVIA. ⎱
JOHN. ⎰ (*Together.*) The Tuck Inn?

MICHAEL. You remember it—in Puffin's Corner, off Belvedere Road, Baron's Court.

OLIVIA. Oh, yes. But, darling, are you sure that's quite the best place——

MICHAEL. It's a corking place.

JOHN *rises and goes to the telephone.*

We used to get a jolly good three-course meal there for one and fourpence. Don't you remember—you used to take me there on Annie's afternoon out? Besides, they'll know me there and we'll get service.

OLIVIA. Yes, but, darling, wouldn't it be better to go somewhere around here——

JOHN. (*Who had been dialling.*) R.M.B.3? Hullo, General Parker? This is John Fletcher. About that report. Instead of the Savoy, will you have it sent to Tuck Inn, Puffin's Corner, off Belvedere Road, Baron's Court. . . . No, no, no, off Belvedere Road. . . . *Baron's* Court. . . . *Puffin's* Corner. . . . *Tuck* Inn.

OLIVIA. (*To* MICHAEL.) It's such an awfully long way.

MICHAEL. Not by Underground. We'll be there inside half an hour.

OLIVIA. (*Faintly.*) John's car is outside——

MICHAEL. I'm sorry—I'm afraid we can't use his car. (*Firmly.*) We'll go by Underground.

JOHN. (*With sudden defiance.*) Oh, no we won't. We'll go by 'bus.

MICHAEL. (*Sullenly.*) I don't think I know how to get there by 'bus.

JOHN. But I do. We'll queue up and get a number 24 to Trafalgar Square. Then we'll change and queue up for a number 96. At South Kensington we'll change and queue up for a number 49. That'll take us to the top of Belvedere Road. We can walk the rest.

Long pause.

OLIVIA. (*Rising and crossing to the door.*) Well—if we're going to walk, I'd better change my shoes.

JOHN. (*Calling after her.*) And get a mackintosh. It looks like rain

OLIVIA *nods, sadly, and goes out.* MICHAEL *and* JOHN *are sitting, with arms folded, glaring belligerently at each other.*

CURTAIN

END OF ACT ONE

ACT II

SCENE: *The same, a few days later.*

TIME: *About 7 p.m.*

OLIVIA *is sitting at her desk, doing her accounts.* JOHN *is walking up and down, dictating a speech to* MISS DELL.

JOHN. (*Dictating.*) And now, in conclusion, let me turn for a few moments to a subject that is uppermost in all our minds these days—a vexed subject and one on which I am little qualified to speak—but a subject, nevertheless——(*Breaking off.*) Is that too many subjects, Miss Dell?

MISS DELL. I don't think so, Sir John. We've often had more.

JOHN. Very well. (*Dictating.*)—but a subject, nevertheless, on which I have at least as much right to hold and express an opinion as any other subject——

MISS DELL. Subject.

JOHN. Quite so. (*Dictating.*) —as any other citizen of this empire. I refer, of course, to the question of the future of British industry in the years immediately following the peace.

The telephone rings.

Now, before I begin, I would like to make it quite clear——

The telephone rings again.

OLIVIA *rises from her desk and crosses to answer it.*

—that if that telephone rings again I shall go mad.

OLIVIA. Sorry, dear.

JOHN. Why can't Polton answer it in the hall?

OLIVIA. It still wouldn't stop it ringing in here, would it? Besides, it might be something important—you never know. (*Into the receiver.*) Hullo. . . . Oh, hullo, Joan, darling. . . .

JOHN. (*With a gesture of despair.*) That means half an hour at least, Miss Dell.

OLIVIA. Darling, I mustn't talk for long, because John is in here working. . . . Yes, I'm having his study redecorated,

300

poor pet, and he's got nowhere else to go. . . . No, apple-
green—it's so much more restful for a study, don't you
think? . . . Sybil thinks it's per——

She is about to sit on the sofa, but she catches JOHN's *eye, and rises
abruptly.*

—fect. . . . Oh, she did, did she? . . . Darling, I really must
stop or John'll throw something at me.

JOHN *gets up.*

Was there anything important? . . . Michael? . . . Yes, he
is rather a lamb, isn't he? . . . Well, just over sixteen. . . .
No, it's all right now. I'm glad to say he's settling down
very nicely. . . . Of course, I had to talk to him for hours—
you know how young he is. . . .

JOHN *coughs warningly to indicate that* MISS DELL *is in the room.*
MISS DELL *is reading her notes, apparently oblivious of the conversation.*

(*Out of the corner of her mouth.*) Darling, do you mind if I don't
talk at the moment. Il y a une personne ici . . . oui, c'est ça.
. . . Yes. Goodbye. (*She rings off.*) Sorry, John dear, only you
know how that woman talks.

JOHN. (*Meaningly.*) Quite so.

OLIVIA. Well, short of banging the receiver down in her face,
I don't see what I could have done. She thinks Michael's
adorable.

JOHN. Really?

OLIVIA. She said he was the most fetching thing she'd seen for
months.

JOHN. Indeed?

OLIVIA. (*Going back to her desk.*) All right, dear, go on with
your speech. It sounds awfully good. Where are you
making it?

JOHN. At Dumfries.

OLIVIA. (*Busy with her accounts again.*) Oh. How nice.

JOHN. Why do you consider it nice for me to make a speech at
Dumfries?

There is a pause. OLIVIA, *deep in her work, does not reply.*

(*Repeating louder.*) I said, why do you consider it nice for me to
make a speech at Dumfries?

OLIVIA. What? Oh, I don't know. Don't interrupt me, do you mind, dear? I'm in the middle of my accounts.

JOHN. I'm most terribly sorry, Miss Dell.

MISS DELL. Not at all, Sir John.

JOHN. Where did I get to?

MICHAEL *comes in.*

MISS DELL. (*Reading from her notes.*) Before I begin I would like to make it quite clear——

JOHN. Oh, yes. Before I begin I would like to make it quite clear——

MICHAEL. (*Going to his mother and kissing her.*) Hullo, Mum.

OLIVIA. Oh, hullo, Michael. Had a nice day at the office?

MICHAEL. Not bad, thanks.

JOHN. (*Who has risen when* MICHAEL *came in.*) Good evening, Michael.

MICHAEL. (*With a stiff little bow.*) Good evening.

OLIVIA. I hope they're not working you too hard at the office, darling. Nine to seven seems awfully long for a boy of your age——

MICHAEL. (*Sitting down.*) Well, of course, it's jolly silly their keeping us there till seven. There's never any work to do after six. We just sit about doing nothing.

OLIVIA. Yes, that does seem silly. John, darling, couldn't you do something about that?

JOHN. (*Controlling himself with difficulty.*) Olivia, my dear, roughly five thousand people work in my Ministry. I'm afraid I can't see my way to ordering the loss of some thirty thousand man-hours per week in order that Michael may get home a little sooner.

OLIVIA. Oh, well, of course, if you put it like that——

JOHN. I'm afraid I must put it like that.

MICHAEL. Mark you, not everyone seems to have to stay there till seven—not by a long chalk. I notice quite a few people seem to be able to manage to sneak off home early.

He shoots a meaning glance at JOHN, *as he says this,* JOHN'S *patience, as we can see from his twitching fingers, is on the point of exhaustion.*

JOHN. If you are referring to me, Michael, it may interest you to know that I'm in the middle of some rather trying and responsible work, and I'd be grateful for a few brief moments of peace and bloody quiet. (*To* MISS DELL.) Now where did I get to?

MISS DELL. —before I begin I would like to make it quite clear——

JOHN. Oh, yes. Haven't I got beyond that?

MICHAEL *is tiptoeing up to the desk.* JOHN *notices this.*

(*To* MISS DELL.) What in the world is going on?

OLIVIA. All right, dear. He only wanted his book. He left it in a drawer. Here you are, darling. (*She gives him the book from a drawer in the desk, and then by accident bangs the drawer as she shuts it.*) Ssh! Be quiet, Michael.

MICHAEL *tiptoes back to the chair. When he has sat down again,* JOHN *looks at* MISS DELL.

MISS DELL. (*Whispering.*) Before I begin I would like to make it quite clear—— (*She then realizes she is whispering, and repeats the sentence in a normal voice.*)

JOHN. I would like to make it quite clear that I am no politician. It was as a business man that I was brought into this government, and it is as a business man, pure and simple, that I address you now.

He exchanges a glance with MICHAEL, *who has stopped reading and is glaring at him.*

(*Abruptly.*) Cut out 'pure and simple', Miss Dell.

It is as a plain business man that I address you now.

MICHAEL *nods.* JOHN *pretends not to see him.*

As many of you know, I am a Canadian by birth. All my life I have stood for a policy of closer industrial union and co-ordination within the Empire. Our left-wing friends have dubbed this policy as reactionary and imperialistic. Very well, then. If it is reaction, if it is imperialism, then I *am* a reactionary, and I *am* an imperialist. Am I ashamed of being so? Far from it. Very far from it, indeed. I glory in my unrepentance.

MICHAEL, *with no change of expression, remains staring fixedly at* JOHN.

So let our young intellectuals scoff and sneer, let them hurl their odium at my head. I still stand where yet I stood.

OLIVIA. } (*Together.*) Stand still——
MISS DELL. }

JOHN. I do not stand still. I still stand. Sticks and stones may break my bones, but words will never hurt me.

MICHAEL. Harm me.

MISS DELL. Hurt me. I think Sir John was right, it's hurt me.

MICHAEL. (*Rising.*) I'm pretty sure it's harm me.

MISS DELL. Oh, no, Mr. Brown, it's hurt me.

MICHAEL. I ought to know, it's harm me.

OLIVIA. (*Coming down to the sofa.*) I learnt it as injure me.

MICHAEL. Oh, no, Mum. Injure me wouldn't scan. It's harm me, I know.

MISS DELL. (*Firmly.*) Hurt me. Words can never hurt me.

JOHN. (*With controlled fury.*) It is quite possible that the dictum may hold true of yourself, Miss Dell, but I can assure you that the words that Mrs. Brown and her son are muttering are hurting and harming and injuring me like blue hell. (*He gets up.*) Now, may I please, please have ten minutes of quiet. That's all I ask, and it is not very much—and I shall have finished my speech.

MISS DELL. I'm so sorry, Sir John.

JOHN. It's quite all right, Miss Dell. We can continue now.
    MICHAEL *goes back to the chair.* JOHN *sits on the couch. He then catches sight of* OLIVIA, *who is doing a five-finger exercise on her cheek.*

OLIVIA. (*Murmuring.*) But words—can—nev—er—inj—ure me.
She shakes her head, and is about to repeat all this when she meets JOHN'*s glare and hurriedly turns back to her desk.*

JOHN. (*Continuing.*) So let me turn to a brief outline of the economic policy for which I stand. The Empire is a family—a family which—a family whose—no—a family from which— (*To* MICHAEL, *suddenly.*) Do you mind not staring at me like that?

MICHAEL. I was thinking.

JOHN. You know, if you turned the other way round, the light would be much better for you.

MICHAEL. I can see all right, thanks.
    OLIVIA, *from her desk, signals to* MICHAEL, *by elaborate and*

smiling pantomime, to humour JOHN *by changing his position.*
MICHAEL, *with a patient shrug, agrees, and twists himself around
acrobatically so that his back is to* JOHN. JOHN *is startled by all
this, and rises.*

JOHN. The Empire is a family whose branches reach out over
a quarter of the known earth. As a child is bound to his
mother by eternal yet invisible ties of blood and affection,
and woe betide any interloper who tries to break them, so
too, in the larger sphere of world economics, the sanctity of
family life——

MICHAEL *emits a short, sharp laugh.* JOHN *turns to* OLIVIA.

May we go into the dining-room, Olivia?

OLIVIA. (*Rising and crossing to him.*) Oh, darling, I'm afraid the
servants are in there, laying the table for the party tonight——

JOHN. Very well. Thank you, Miss Dell. That'll be all for
today.

MISS DELL. (*Rising.*) Very good, Sir John.

JOHN. I'll do the whole thing over tomorrow morning.

MICHAEL. (*Crossing to the door.*) If I'm disturbing you, don't
worry. I was going upstairs, anyway.

MICHAEL *goes out.*

MISS DELL *looks inquiringly at* JOHN.

MISS DELL. In that case, shall we continue?

JOHN. No, thank you, Miss Dell. It's hardly worth going on
now. I'm rather out of the mood. It wasn't very good,
anyway.

MISS DELL. Very well, Sir John. Good night, Mrs. Brown.
Good night.

JOHN. Good night, Miss Dell.

MISS DELL *goes out.*

OLIVIA. (*Embracing him.*) Poor John! Don't worry, darling;
your study will be ready for you tomorrow.

JOHN. It's all right. I never should try to do a thing like that
when I'm so dead tired. That's the trouble, really.

OLIVIA. Poor lamb!

JOHN. (*Nuzzling her cheek.*) Is that a new scent you have on?

OLIVIA. Yes, darling. Do you like it?

JOHN. I like it very much indeed, indeed I do.

MICHAEL *comes in and goes up to the desk at the back.*
JOHN *and* OLIVIA *do not notice him at once.*

OLIVIA. Well, darling, I got it—— (*She turns and sees* MICHAEL.) Hullo, Michael.

MICHAEL. Can I borrow this? (*He holds a pad and pencil which he has taken from the desk.*)

OLIVIA. Yes, darling. Going to write a letter?

MICHAEL. No, some notes.

OLIVIA. What on?

MICHAEL. This book I'm reading.

OLIVIA. What *is* the book? (*She takes it from under his arm and glances at the title.*) Diagnosis and Treatment of Poisoning. Darling—what are you reading this for?

MICHAEL. (*With a glance at* JOHN.) Because I'm interested in the subject.

He goes out.

OLIVIA. Is he going to poison you, do you think?

JOHN. I shouldn't be surprised. The only thing is, he'd better watch out I don't get in first.

OLIVIA. (*Worried.*) Do you think he's still terribly unhappy about it all.

JOHN. Unhappy? I should say not. He's having the time of his life.

OLIVIA. (*Doubtfully.*) I'm not so sure.

JOHN. He's enjoying every minute of it.

OLIVIA. I don't know, darling. I thought at first he'd got over it, but the last day or so he's been so—sort of moody.

JOHN. Moody—exactly. He's playing Hamlet.

OLIVIA. Hamlet? What do you mean?

JOHN. Haven't you noticed? You watch him.

OLIVIA. I *have* noticed an odd look about him at moments. Do you think that's what it is?

JOHN. Certainly. That's his 'antic disposition'. He does it at the office, too, so Symonds tells me. He's always coming in, giving the typists a demoniac glare. It scares them out of their wits. And then what about that black tie?

OLIVIA. Isn't there an office rule about that?

JOHN. Darling, he can wear any damn tie he likes. That's his 'inky cloak'.

OLIVIA. Oh, John! Then he must be upset about it.

JOHN. Nonsense. You told me yourself he never cared for his father. Besides, it's well over three years since he died. It's just sheer play-acting—for our benefit.

OLIVIA. Come to think of it, I believe his school did do Hamlet once.

JOHN. (*Triumphantly.*) There you are! And I bet he played the Prince.

OLIVIA. No, I don't think so. I think he played a lady-in-waiting.

JOHN. Well, it doesn't matter. He knows the play, anyway. You'd better watch out for a closet scene, Olivia. He'll be telling you to throw away the worser part of your heart and live the purer with the other half.

OLIVIA. I'll smack his bottom for him, if he does. (*She laughs.*) Oh, it really *is* rather sweet, isn't it?

JOHN. It isn't so sweet if you remember how the play ends. (*He laughs as a thought strikes him.*) That book! Don't you see?

OLIVIA. No, what?

JOHN. Well, you remember how he tried to get me to admit I'd known his father?

OLIVIA. Yes, that's true. I had to deny it, too, you know. Then he suggested that Jack had probably been your doctor without my knowing it—as if I wouldn't have known it.

JOHN. Don't you see? In default of a ghost he's trying to find out how I poisoned him.

OLIVIA. Oh, darling! Really!

JOHN. Your son has a very lively imagination. He's having a lovely time. He's up to tricks. Still, at least, he means to absolve you from complicity in the crime. . . . (*Chuckling.*) 'Nor let thy soul contrive against thy mother aught.' *I'm* the villain—the 'bloody, bawdy villain. Remorseless, lecherous, treacherous, kindless villain! Oh, vengeance!' (*He shudders.*) By Jove! I've scared myself now.

OLIVIA. Oh, but it's too absurd! I'm sure he couldn't really believe——

JOHN. You don't know your own son, my dear.

OLIVIA. I'll just have to give him a good talking to, that's all.

JOHN. (*Derisively.*) Ha, ha!

OLIVIA. What's so funny about that?

JOHN. Nothing. Darling, if you're going past the whisky decanter, I think I'd love a little whisky in that.

OLIVIA. (*Rising.*) Did your wife wait on you hand and foot as I do?

JOHN. No. I had to wait on her.

OLIVIA. Is that why you left her?

JOHN. Partly. And partly because she preferred the embraces of a certain young Guards' officer to my own. (*He lies down full length on the couch.*)

OLIVIA. How long were you in love with her?

JOHN. About ten days.

OLIVIA. How long was she in love with you?

JOHN. You're very inquisitive, this evening, aren't you?

OLIVIA. Am I? Not specially. Why? Have I asked you that question before?

JOHN. You certainly have.

OLIVIA. Well, then—I forget the answer.

JOHN. You don't forget it. You just like to hear me say it. She was never in love with me. She married me for my money.

She gives him the glass.

OLIVIA. Oh—that reminds me. Have you done anything about that racing debt of hers?

JOHN. No.

OLIVIA. Are you going to?

JOHN. No.

OLIVIA. What'll happen, then?

JOHN. Barton and Burgess will just have to write off eight hundred pounds. Or else post her at Tattersall's.

OLIVIA. You're a hard man, aren't you? Has it ever occurred to you that I might be living with you for your money?

JOHN. That thought is never absent from my mind.

OLIVIA. Seriously, I mean it. Have you ever thought that?

JOHN. I refuse to answer such a lunatic question seriously.

OLIVIA. It's not such a lunatic question, really. Michael thinks I am.

JOHN. Michael thinks I poisoned his father.

OLIVIA. Yes, but he may be right about me.

JOHN. You're not putting on an antic disposition, too, are you?

OLIVIA. No, Michael's put the idea into my head.

JOHN. (*Rising and crossing to her.*) Just put it out of your head, will you.

OLIVIA. It's not that I don't love you. I know I love you. But— I love all this, too.

JOHN. Well, who wouldn't?

OLIVIA. Lots of people. Michael for one.

Pause.

JOHN. Oh, damn Michael! (*He takes her hand.*)

OLIVIA. He thinks I'm a useless parasite.

JOHN. Does it really matter what a crazy adolescent thinks of you?

OLIVIA. (*Unhappily.*) He's my son.

MICHAEL *comes in and walks slowly to the desk.*

JOHN. Hullo, Michael.

OLIVIA. Hullo, darling.

They watch him for a moment.

JOHN. Made some nice notes?

MICHAEL. (*Leaning on the desk, his back to them.*) Thank you.

JOHN *sits down in the traditional Hamlet pose.*

JOHN. (*Whispering.*) 'To be or not to be.'

OLIVIA *motions to him angrily to stop.*

OLIVIA. (*Cheerfully.*) Well, Michael, how about a nice glass of sherry?

MICHAEL. (*Moving slowly from the desk towards the door.*) No, thank you, Mum. Not at the moment.

OLIVIA. Where are you going, darling?

MICHAEL. Upstairs.

OLIVIA. But you've only just come downstairs.

MICHAEL. Yes, I know.

OLIVIA. Well, before you disappear altogether, darling, don't forget to put on a dark suit for the party tonight.

MICHAEL. Party? What party?

OLIVIA. Don't be so vague and tiresome. I told you we were having a dinner-party tonight.

MICHAEL. Do you mind if I don't come?

OLIVIA. Oh, darling. I wanted to show you off.

MICHAEL. I'd rather be alone.

OLIVIA. Oh, all right.

He has arrived at the door when JOHN *rises.*

JOHN. (*In lugubrious tones.*) Michael, you needn't go upstairs again, I'm going out.

OLIVIA. Have you got to go, dear?

JOHN. Yes, I've a few things to do at the office.

OLIVIA. Well, don't be late for dinner.

JOHN. No.

OLIVIA. That reminds me—I'd better be getting a move on myself.

MICHAEL. (*Sharply.*) You're not going out, are you.

OLIVIA. No, darling. Just upstairs, to dress for dinner. Why?

MICHAEL. Nothing. By the way, are either of you doing anything tomorrow night?

OLIVIA. I'm not. Are you, John?

JOHN. I don't think so. Why?

MICHAEL. How would you both like to come and see a show with me?

OLIVIA *and* JOHN *exchange a glance.* OLIVIA *is patently delighted.*

OLIVIA. Darling, what a charming thought! We'd both love it. (*Suddenly cautious.*) Oh, you don't expect John to queue up for the gallery——

MICHAEL. Oh, no, that's all right. I've already got the seats. Good ones, too—in the front row of the stalls.

JOHN. What is the show, Michael?

MICHAEL. Well—it's a sort of thriller, I think. It's called *Murder in the Family.*

JOHN *guffaws, with evident enjoyment. He goes out without replying.* (*Furiously.*) Oh, crumbs!

OLIVIA. (*Sharply.*) Michael, you're to stop this ridiculous nonsense at once, do you hear?

MICHAEL. (*Sulkily.*) What nonsense?

OLIVIA. This Hamlet nonsense.

MICHAEL. I don't know what you mean.

OLIVIA. Yes, you do, and I'm warning you, Michael. It's getting beyond a joke. (*Pointing to his tie.*) And take that ridiculous thing off.

MICHAEL. What ridiculous thing?

OLIVIA. That ridiculous black tie. (*As to a small child.*) Go on, take it off this minute.

He pulls off his tie quickly and gives it to her.

That's better. And in future I want you to behave less like a moonstruck little half-wit and more like a human being. Is that understood?

MICHAEL. Yes, Mum.

OLIVIA. Good.

OLIVIA *has achieved the door in a stern and dignified exit, when she suddenly relents and goes back to him.*

Darling, I didn't mean to be unkind. Here—take it back.

She holds out the tie, but MICHAEL *makes no move to take it.*

MICHAEL. I don't want it, thanks.

OLIVIA. Go on, take it.

MICHAEL. No, you keep it.

OLIVIA. Darling—Michael, Michael——

MICHAEL. Yes?

OLIVIA. Smile at me. Go on, smile at me.

MICHAEL *gives her a very quick, mirthless smile. She laughs.*

That's better. There, take it back. (*She puts the tie on his lap.*) You can dress in black silk tights for all I care. (*She goes towards the door.*) Only you'd better not—it might annoy John.

She goes out.

POLTON. (*In the hall.*) Shall I do the napkins, ma'am, or will you?

OLIVIA. (*Also in the hall.*) You do them, would you mind? You do them so much better than I do. I'm going up to dress.

MICHAEL *goes up to the window, as* POLTON *comes in with a tray with a cocktail shaker, an ice bucket, and a napkin on it, which she puts on the drink table.* MICHAEL *moves towards her.*

MICHAEL. Polton, do you mind if I ask you a question?

POLTON. Well, no, sir—if it isn't too awkward——

MICHAEL. Well, it may be a bit awkward. I just wanted to know what *you* felt about what's going on in this house?

POLTON. (*Cautiously.*) You mean—Sir John and Mrs. Brown, sir?

MICHAEL. Yes.

POLTON. Well, sir, I look at it like this. Mind you, I wouldn't have no truck, in the normal way, with two people who carried on without being married. Living in sin, you might call it—begging your pardon, sir, if I'm taking a liberty——

MICHAEL. No. After all, that's what it is——

POLTON. Oh, no, sir, it's not. Not with Sir John and Mrs. Brown. It's different with them. They behave just like two people who've been lawfully married for years and years, and to see them together you wouldn't know they hadn't been, bless 'em.

MICHAEL. (*Puzzled.*) But don't you find that wrong?

POLTON. Wrong? I wouldn't be staying in this house if I did, I can tell you that straight. I don't hold with no immorality, no unlicensed carryings-on in any shape nor form, and I don't hold with those who do, neither. (*Collecting her tray and preparing to go out.*) Would that be all, sir?

MICHAEL. Yes, thank you, Polton, that's all.

POLTON. Thank *you*, sir.

She goes out.

MICHAEL. Oh, crumbs! (*He goes quickly to the window. There is a ring at the door.*) It's all right, Polton. Don't bother, it's for me. I'll answer the door.

He throws his tie on the ice bucket and goes out. Presently he is heard talking to DIANA FLETCHER, *as they approach.*

(*Off.*) Would you come this way, please?

DIANA. (*Off.*) Thank you.

MICHAEL. (*Off.*) Shall I lead the way?

DIANA. (*Off.*) Hullo, I'm sure I've seen that picture before somewhere.

MICHAEL. (*Off.*) Yes. Do you mind hurrying. I don't want anyone to see us.

They come in. She is about twenty-five, and very decorative.

DIANA. Are you the mysterious Mr. Brown?

MICHAEL. Yes, that's right.

DIANA. You sounded older on the telephone.

MICHAEL. Did I? I'm much older than I look. Just in case of accidents, you *are* Lady Fletcher, aren't you?

DIANA. Yes.

MICHAEL. The wife of Sir John Fletcher?

DIANA. (*She has something in her eye.*) Yes, in a manner of speaking.

MICHAEL. Won't you sit down?

DIANA. Thank you.

MICHAEL. Dry them with this.

DIANA. Dry what?

MICHAEL. Tears.

DIANA. I have some mascara in my eye.

She crosses to the couch.

MICHAEL. Oh, well, won't you have a cigarette?

DIANA. No, thank you. (*She has sat down.*) Look, would you mind awfully telling me what all this is about? I have rather an important engagement——

MICHAEL. Yes. Right-ho. By the way, it's jolly good of you to come.

DIANA. Well, you said it was a matter of life or death, and that I was to learn something to my particular advantage.

MICHAEL. Well, that's true. I'll tell you—— (*He realizes suddenly that he has no tie.*) Oh, excuse me a second. (*He crosses to get it.*) I'm frightfully sorry. I don't know what you must have thought of me—without a tie.

DIANA. Do you usually keep your ties on ice?

MICHAEL. No. My mother took it away from me—so I threw it there.

DIANA. Oh, I see.

MICHAEL. As a matter of fact, it's jolly lucky everyone's out at the moment. I thought I'd probably have to smuggle you up to my bedroom——

DIANA. Oh?

MICHAEL. Oh!

DIANA. Well, really——

MICHAEL. I mean—that's to say—just to talk, you know—I didn't mean—you know——

DIANA. Look, Mr. Brown, it's been most awfully nice meeting you, but I think, if you don't mind, I'd better be going——

MICHAEL. Oh, no. Please, Lady Fletcher. There's no danger. You'll regret it for ever afterwards if you do.

DIANA. Well, then, will you kindly say what you have to say to me.

MICHAEL. Yes. O.K. Lady Fletcher, I hate to distress you unnecessarily, but I feel it my duty.

DIANA. Oh!

MICHAEL. Lady Fletcher, do you know whose house this is?

DIANA. No—I don't think so—whose?

MICHAEL. Your husband's.

DIANA. John's? (*She rises hurriedly.*) Now I've got to go. I'm definitely not going to run into him, if I can avoid it.

MICHAEL. No, it's all right. He's at his office—he'll be there for hours. I do understand how you must feel about seeing him again, after the way he's treated you.

DIANA. What?

She drops her powder-puff. MICHAEL *retrieves it.*

Oh, yes. Stupid of me. Thank you. (*Looking around.*) It doesn't look like his taste.

MICHAEL. You're quite right. Do you know whose taste it is?

DIANA. No. Whose? Yours?

MICHAEL. No.

DIANA. Whose, then?

MICHAEL. I'm afraid what I have to say to you may come as a great shock—do you mind?

DIANA. No.

MICHAEL. (*Sibilantly.*) It's his mistress's taste.

DIANA. Mistress's? In the plural?

MICHAEL. (*Shocked.*) No, in the singular.

DIANA. Oh, I see. You mean this is where he lives with—oh, I've heard such a lot about her—Olivia Brown?

MICHAEL. Exactly.

DIANA. And you're her brother?

MICHAEL. No.

DIANA. Oh, her son?

MICHAEL. (*Excitedly.*) Now, perhaps you see why I asked you to come round——

DIANA. No, I don't, I'm afraid.

MICHAEL. I want you to meet her and talk to her.

DIANA. Good Lord, no!

MICHAEL. Please, Lady Fletcher. Swallow your pride and confront her.

DIANA. Confront her?

MICHAEL. Yes, reason with her. I'm sure you could get her to see how wrong it all is.

DIANA. How wrong all what is?

MICHAEL. What she's doing, of course.

DIANA. Oh, do make sense! What *is* she doing—for heaven's sake?

MICHAEL. Living in sin with your husband.

DIANA *begins to see daylight. She laughs softly.*

DIANA. Oh, that's really rather charming.

MICHAEL. How do you mean—charming?

DIANA. You want me to confront your mother and reason with her?

MICHAEL. Yes.

DIANA. Get her to see the error of her ways?

MICHAEL. Well—yes.

DIANA. Tell her to stop being a wicked woman?

MICHAEL. (*Hurt.*) Don't make a joke of it.

DIANA. (*Contrite.*) I'm sorry, Mr. Brown. I didn't mean to make a joke of it. Forgive me.

MICHAEL. That's all right. I understand your being hard and bitter. Anyone would be, after all you've been through.

DIANA. Yes—but—I'm afraid I can't very well confront Mrs. Brown and reason with her, because, you see, it really isn't any business of mine——

MICHAEL. But, of course it's your business. You don't seem to understand. After all, it's your husband who's her paramour.

DIANA *laughs.*

What are you laughing at?

DIANA. Nothing. It just seemed a funny word to use in connection with John, that's all.

MICHAEL. Well, it's true, anyway, isn't it?

DIANA. Oh, yes, it's true. Delightfully true. You're not shocked, Mr. Brown?

MICHAEL. (*Shocked only at the suggestion.*) Me, shocked? It'd take more than that to shock me. I know all about life. Nelson and Lady Hamilton. Louis XV and Madame Pompadour—all that's all right. But this is different.

DIANA. Why?

MICHAEL. Well, she can't be in love with him.

DIANA. Why not?

MICHAEL. But she can't be. She's too old.

DIANA. Really? How old? As old as John?

MICHAEL. Good Lord, no, not nearly as old as that. I can't understand what any woman can see in *him*, unless it's his money.

DIANA. That *was* one of John's good points.

MICHAEL. (*Violently.*) I hate her being the parasite of a rich old voluptuary!

DIANA *bursts out laughing again.*

(*Contrite.*) I'm awfully sorry, I didn't mean to speak about your husband like that.

DIANA. That's all right. Thank you, Mr. Brown.

MICHAEL. You're not in love with him any more?

DIANA. No, it's a moot point whether I ever was.

MICHAEL. Are you sure you don't want him back?

DIANA. Quite, quite sure.

MICHAEL. Oh, crumbs!

DIANA. What, Mr. Brown?

MICHAEL. I thought you could have appealed to my mother to give him back to you.

DIANA. Poor Mr. Brown! Are you very unhappy about it all?

MICHAEL. Oh, no, not really. Thanks very much.

DIANA. Well, that's a relief. (*She begins to laugh again.*)

MICHAEL. How old are you?

DIANA. (*Her laughter stopping rather abruptly.*) Is that awfully important?

MICHAEL. No. I suppose I shouldn't ask. Only you're so much

younger than I thought you were going to be—I suppose
I shouldn't say that, either.

DIANA. (*Radiant again.*) Oh, yes, you should. Thank you,
Mr. Brown.

OLIVIA *comes in.*

OLIVIA. Oh, darling, I didn't know you had someone here.

MICHAEL. This is my mother—Lady Fletcher.

OLIVIA. (*With barely a flicker of surprise.*) Oh, how do you
do?

DIANA. (*Greatly relieved at this reception.*) How do you do? (*Perhaps
she over-does it just a fraction.*)

MICHAEL. (*Annoyed at his mother's composure.*) Lady Fletcher is
Sir John's wife, Mum.

OLIVIA. (*With a gay smile.*) Yes, dear, of course. (*To* DIANA.)
How nice of you to drop in on us like this!

DIANA. Well, the truth is, Mrs. Brown, I didn't really drop in
on you. I was invited, by your son——

OLIVIA. Oh, really? Where did you two run into each
other?

MICHAEL. We didn't——

DIANA. (*Quickly, drowning his voice.*) In Hyde Park. Wasn't it
funny?

OLIVIA. Amazing. Quite amazing.

DIANA. Of course, I had simply no idea—when he said his
name was Brown—that he——

OLIVIA. Yes, of course, I do understand. So many Browns.
Won't you sit down, and have a drink——

DIANA. It's very kind of you, but I don't think I will, if you
don't mind——

OLIVIA. (*Crossing to the drink table.*) It's no trouble, really. I'm
making one, anyway. We're having a party tonight. Such
a strain on the rations, but John does love to entertain his
friends, so, of course, I have to try and cope——

DIANA. I know. Such a bore, isn't it, in wartime, trying to do
anything in the way of entertaining? Still, if you'll forgive
me, I think I really must begin to wend my way home. I
have a few friends coming in to see me.

OLIVIA. Oh, well, in that case, it would be wrong of me to

keep you. (*Extending her hand, gaily.*) Well, it's been so nice to have met you at last.

They shake hands again.

DIANA. It's been charming. Perhaps you'll drop in on me, one day.

OLIVIA. I'd love to—where do you live now?

DIANA. Grosvenor House. The number's in the book. Your son knows it, as a matter of fact.

OLIVIA. Oh, really? That's fine. My dear—may I say it? I *do so* admire that hat.

DIANA. (*More than pleased.*) Oh, do you? Aage Thaarup made it for me. He's so clever, don't you think?

OLIVIA. Brilliant, positively brilliant! I must start going to him again.

DIANA. (*Turning and shaking hands again.*) Goodbye.

OLIVIA. Well, goodbye.

They are beaming at each other when JOHN *walks in.*

JOHN. Diana!

DIANA. Hullo, John!

JOHN. What is the meaning of this?

OLIVIA. (*Quickly.*) The most amazing coincidence, dear. She ran into Michael in the park and came back with him without the least idea in the world——

MICHAEL. (*Defiantly.*) That's not true. She only said that to shield me. I rang her up and asked her to come round.

OLIVIA. (*Quickly.*) Silly boy! What does it matter whether you rang her up or ran into her in the park? (*To* DIANA.) I have a lunatic son, Lady Fletcher. You really must forgive him. (*She has her arm on* MICHAEL'S *shoulder.*)

DIANA. But, of course I forgive him. I'm really very grateful to him for giving me the chance of meeting you.

OLIVIA. Most kind.

DIANA. I really must fly.

OLIVIA. Lady Fletcher has some friends waiting for her, John.

JOHN. Oh. Well—remember me to him, will you?

DIANA. Yes, I will. How are you, John?

JOHN. Very well, thank you, Diana. How are you?

DIANA. Bearing up.

JOHN. I want to apologize if this incident has caused you any embarrassment.

DIANA. Oh, but not at all. I've enjoyed it, really. I must go now.

OLIVIA. Show Lady Fletcher out, Michael.

MICHAEL *goes out.*

DIANA. (*Shaking hands yet again.*) Goodbye, John. Nice seeing you again. Goodbye once more, Mrs. Brown. Don't be too angry with your son, will you? He means awfully well, you know.

She goes.

OLIVIA. (*In a dead voice.*) Why *did* you say that about embarrassment, John?

JOHN. Well—what *is* the point of trying to pass off a situation like that with small talk?

OLIVIA. There isn't a situation in the world that can't be passed off with small talk. (*She sits.*) Gosh, I've never had a worse five minutes in all my life.

JOHN. (*Taking her hand.*) It must have been awful for you. I'm most terribly sorry.

OLIVIA. Whatever possessed him to do a thing like that?

JOHN. Play-acting again, I suppose.

OLIVIA. Oh, John, you may be wrong about that.

JOHN. Don't worry about it.

OLIVIA. (*Desperately.*) I must, I must worry.

MICHAEL *comes back.*

MICHAEL. (*Sullenly.*) Well, it didn't work, did it?

JOHN. No, Michael, it didn't work. Now look here, young man, you and I are going upstairs to have a little talk——

MICHAEL. (*Pathetically insolent.*) Really? That *will* be interesting. (*He turns away and puts his hands in his pockets.*)

JOHN. (*Crossing to him.*) It's going to be a good deal more— Michael, when I speak to you—don't turn your back on me—take your hands——

OLIVIA *rises and crosses to* JOHN.

OLIVIA. Darling, will you go upstairs and get ready for dinner. Michael, come and sit down.

JOHN *goes out.*

I wish I knew what was in your mind.

MICHAEL. (*Murmuring.*) I don't think you'd like it if you did.

OLIVIA. I might and I might not. Sometimes you seem to be playing a game with John and me and yourself—and that's when I'm angry with you. At other times—well—I'm not so sure. I don't want you to be unhappy, you know.

MICHAEL. I'm not. Don't worry.

OLIVIA. John says you're not, too. He says you're enjoying every moment of it.

MICHAEL. Did he say that?

OLIVIA. Yes, he did. He said you were play-acting, and I must say I agreed with him.

MICHAEL. I may have been play-acting sometimes—I don't know.

OLIVIA. Darling—there you are, you see——

MICHAEL. But if I have, it's because I've had to. What chance have I got fighting a man like that on level terms?

OLIVIA. Why do you feel you have to fight him?

MICHAEL. Because I hate him.

OLIVIA. Oh, no, Michael, you don't hate him. You've just worked yourself up into thinking a lot of ridiculous things about him, but you don't hate him. Nobody could hate John.

MICHAEL. I hate him more than anything on earth. I hate him for what he's done to you.

OLIVIA. What do you mean?

MICHAEL. (*Passionately.*) Don't you know what he's done to you? He's changed you—so that you're no more like my mother than—than any of a hundred society women I could pick out for you any day of the week at the Dorchester. You're not *you* any more. That's why I hate him.

OLIVIA. Darling, that's a bad thing to say. Are you sure, it's true?

MICHAEL. Don't you know it's true? *Think* back to Sandringham Crescent, when Dad was alive, and there were just the three of us. You were happy then, weren't you?

OLIVIA. I wasn't unhappy, Michael.

MICHAEL. But you were in love with Dad, weren't you?

OLIVIA. Darling, it's a long, long time ago. It's hard to remember what one felt like at the beginning——

MICHAEL. You mean you didn't stay in love?

OLIVIA. No, darling, I'm afraid we didn't.

MICHAEL. Oh, Mum, but why?

OLIVIA. There isn't any why about these things, Michael. They happen, and that's all. Perhaps we married too young, or perhaps it was the difficult, struggling life we led that made it so hard to stay in love.

MICHAEL. But surely Dad made an awful lot of money out of his practice, didn't he?

OLIVIA. Not an awful lot, Michael. And less and less as the years went on.

MICHAEL. You mean he wasn't a success.

OLIVIA. He was unlucky.

MICHAEL. But, Mum, I thought—that he——

OLIVIA. Of course you did, you were only a little boy. Thank God we managed to keep it from you. Don't think I ever resented his not being a success. I never asked for nor expected another sort of life. With you and him—I suppose it was you who turned the scales—(*She kisses him.*) I would have been quite content to have lived the rest of my life as the wife of an unsuccessful doctor in Baron's Court.

MICHAEL. (*Sullenly.*) It's not fair to talk of him like that, after he's dead.

OLIVIA. Are you play-acting now, Michael?

MICHAEL. (*Miserably.*) Yes, I suppose so. It's only because I know what's coming.

OLIVIA. If you know, tell me.

MICHAEL. You're going on to say that when you met Sir John Fletcher, you fell in love for the first time in your life.

OLIVIA. (*Quietly.*) Yes, I was going to say that, because it's true.

MICHAEL. You're going to say that all this—grandeur—doesn't really mean anything to you, because you'd be just as happy with him in a slum as you are here.

OLIVIA. No. I wasn't going to say that. All this grandeur—as you call it, is very important to me. I sometimes think I only began to live when I moved into this house. It's hard to separate that feeling from my love for John; and if, in falling in love with John, I've become a Dorchester society woman and therefore you no longer recognize me, I'm sorry, but there's nothing I can do about it.

MICHAEL. Nothing?

OLIVIA. Nothing at all.

MICHAEL. I see. (*He rises and goes towards the drink table.*) Can I have a glass of sherry?

OLIVIA. Go ahead.

MICHAEL. Well, that settles that, doesn't it?

OLIVIA. (*Firmly.*) Yes, Michael. That settles that.

MICHAEL. And what's going to happen to me, meanwhile?

OLIVIA. You'll go on living here with us, of course.

MICHAEL. (*Quietly.*) No, I won't.

OLIVIA. (*Sharply.*) Michael—are you trying a little blackmail?

MICHAEL. Oh, no, I'm not play-acting now—if that's what you think.

OLIVIA. You realize what it would mean to me if you went away?

MICHAEL. I don't think you realize what it would mean to me if I stayed.

OLIVIA. Where do you think you'll go to?

MICHAEL. I can get digs. I won't go far away. We'll still see each other.

OLIVIA. That *will* be nice for both of us, won't it?

MICHAEL. (*Miserably.*) I'm sorry, Mum. I can't think of anything else to do.

OLIVIA. (*In a hard voice.*) Oh, well—after all, you're nearly eighteen. There's no reason why you shouldn't go off on your own, if you feel you must.

MICHAEL. None at all.

He is standing by the drink table, but has not taken a drink. He is facing OLIVIA. Now he takes out his pipe.

OLIVIA. All right, then, I'll go out with you tomorrow and we'll look for digs.

MICHAEL. Yes, tomorrow's a good chance. It's my day off.

There is a pause.

OLIVIA. (*Violently.*) Stop smoking that ridiculous pipe. (*Recovering herself.*) You'd better go now, Michael. My friends will be arriving in a minute.

MICHAEL. All right—Mum.

He moves towards the door.

OLIVIA. Michael—you don't think you might grow to dislike him a little less?

MICHAEL. I'm sorry, Mum, but I can't help what I feel.

OLIVIA. I see. Well, *we're* still friends, aren't we?

Pause. MICHAEL *suddenly collapses on to her lap and sobs like a small child.*

MICHAEL. Don't go on with it, Mum! Please don't! Please! I can't bear it.

OLIVIA, *bewildered, strokes his head.*

JOHN. (*In the hall.*) No, he's not in his room, Polton.

POLTON. (*Also outside.*) Then he must be in the drawing-room, sir.

MICHAEL *gets up quickly, and moves to the fire as* JOHN *comes in.*

JOHN. It's nearly half-past eight, you know.

There is a pause.

Michael, it occurred to me that if you really have nothing to do this evening, I'm fairly sure that Symonds——

MICHAEL. (*His back to* JOHN.) Are you worrying about me?

JOHN. No, Michael. I thought I might save you from a dull evening, that's all. However, you can please yourself.

MICHAEL. Thanks, I shall.

He goes out.

After he has gone there is a pause.

JOHN. Will you make the cocktails or shall I?

OLIVIA. (*Crossing to the drink table.*) I will.

She begins absently to mix the ingredients. JOHN, *from the opposite side of the room, by the fire, watches her, puzzled and anxious.*

JOHN. Am I dressed smartly enough for your party?

OLIVIA. What, darling?

JOHN. (*Lighting a cigarette.*) Am I dressed smartly enough for your party?

OLIVIA. Yes. (*With an effort at recovery.*) That's a new suit, isn't it?

JOHN. Oh, no. It's an old one. I've had it for years. In fact, I'm not sure I wasn't wearing it at your sister Ethel's that night we first met——

OLIVIA. (*Quietly.*) No. That was a grey one.

JOHN. Yes, of course. I should have remembered that.

There is another pause, while OLIVIA *continues to mix the cocktails.*

OLIVIA. John, dear?

JOHN. Yes?

OLIVIA. He's won, you know.

JOHN. Michael?

OLIVIA. Yes. It's either you or him.

JOHN. And you're choosing him?

OLIVIA. Yes.

There is another pause.

JOHN. I've been expecting this.

OLIVIA. I know you have.

JOHN. Does it mean you're going to leave me?

OLIVIA. Yes.

Pause.

JOHN. I don't know what to say, Olivia. If I told you that your love for me is the one good thing that ever happened to me, and that if you left me it will be the hardest blow I've ever had to bear, would that make any difference?

OLIVIA. It would be very nice to hear, darling, but it wouldn't make any difference——

JOHN. If I resigned tomorrow, got my divorce, and asked you to marry me?

OLIVIA. It would still be you or Michael——

JOHN. I just can't see life ahead without you—I'm not threatening suicide or trying to get your sympathy, but it's a plain and simple fact that, if you leave me, life will not be worth living——

OLIVIA. Don't go on, darling. No matter however much I cry, it won't make any difference.

POLTON *comes in.*

POLTON. (*Announcing.*) Miss Wentworth.

POLTON *goes out.*

OLIVIA. (*Going up to greet her guest.*) Oh, Miss Wentworth. How charming of you to come.

MISS WENTWORTH. I'm delighted to be here.

OLIVIA. You do know Sir John Fletcher?

The telephone rings and JOHN *picks up the receiver.*

MISS WENTWORTH. Of course I do.

OLIVIA. Of course, you met him at Bobbie's party.

MISS WENTWORTH. It's a long time since we met.

JOHN. (*Answering the telephone.*) Yes, that's quite all right. I'm so looking forward to seeing you.

OLIVIA. (*To* MISS WENTWORTH.) May I say before the others come how much I enjoyed your last book?

MISS WENTWORTH. I'm so glad.

OLIVIA. (*With a 'Society' laugh.*) I cry even now when I think of it. Most moving! Most moving!

JOHN. (*Putting the receiver down.*) The Randalls have been delayed at the theatre; they'll be late.

MISS WENTWORTH. Oh, are the Randalls coming? Delightful.

OLIVIA. I hear they're rehearsing a new comedy.

POLTON *comes in.*

POLTON. (*Announcing.*) Sir Thomas and Lady Markham.

OLIVIA. (*Over her shoulder to* MISS WENTWORTH.) I do think that in times like these it's far better to make people laugh than to make them cry.

The CURTAIN *begins to fall as* OLIVIA *goes forward to greet* SIR THOMAS *and* LADY MARKHAM.

Darling, you haven't been for ages——

CURTAIN

END OF ACT TWO

ACT III

SCENE: *The sitting-room of a flat in Baron's Court, about three months later.*

The late Mr. Brown's taste is more in evidence than Olivia's, and Mr. Brown's taste was not good. The flat comprises the top floor of a tall Victorian mansion, and consists of the large living-room, a kitchen, part of which is visible when the door is open (back centre), and Olivia's and Michael's bedrooms, the two doors of which are Left, Olivia's above the fireplace and Michael's below it. The door leading to the hall is up R. A Gothic window R. shows a line of Gothic roofs across the street.

The stage is empty when the curtain rises. The radio, which is up L., is playing. MICHAEL *comes in, throws his hat, gloves, a copy of* The Labour Monthly *and a copy of* The Tatler *in a wrapper on the couch, and sits down. He rises to turn off the radio and sits down again to read* The Labour Monthly.

OLIVIA. (*Coming out of the kitchen and kissing him.*) Hullo, darling. Had a nice day?

MICHAEL. Hullo, Mum. All right, thanks. What about you?

OLIVIA. Not so bad. You want your food at once, don't you?

MICHAEL. If you don't mind awfully. I've got a date at a quarter to.

OLIVIA. (*Going into the kitchen.*) All right, darling. I won't be a second.

MICHAEL *rises and goes to sit at the table, still reading his* Labour Monthly. OLIVIA *comes back from the kitchen with an omelette and a tureen of vegetables. Now that we get a better view of her we see that her appearance has undergone a transformation. She is wearing a plain grey skirt and a gay apron.*

OLIVIA. It's a dried egg omelette again, I'm afraid.

MICHAEL. It looks jolly good. Aren't *you* going to eat?

OLIVIA. It's too early for me, darling. I'll make myself something later.

MICHAEL. That means bread and cheese and a cup of tea—if I know you.

OLIVIA. I never feel hungry at night.

MICHAEL. I wish you'd eat more. I'm getting quite worried about you.

OLIVIA. (*Going to the kitchen.*) I can't stand my own cooking, that's the trouble. Even so, I eat like a horse. I've put on five pounds since we came here.

MICHAEL. That's not from eating.

OLIVIA. (*Coming down again from the kitchen with another tureen and the bread.*) What is it from, then? A good conscience? You may be right, darling. Eat your nice omelette. (MICHAEL *begins to eat.*) What's your date?

MICHAEL. I'm going to a film at the Forum.

OLIVIA. Who with?

MICHAEL. (*Gloomily.*) Sylvia.

OLIVIA. Sylvia Hart? I thought that was all over.

MICHAEL. (*Forlornly.*) So did I—only she went and rang up and apologized, and now it's all on again. (*He sighs deeply.*)

OLIVIA. You don't look very pleased about it, darling.

MICHAEL. Well—the thing is—she only rang up because Sparky Stevens has gone back from his leave, and with Bill Evans being away she had no one else to take her out.

OLIVIA. (*Going back to the kitchen with the tea-cloth.*) I see. Why don't you take out one of the nice girls from the office?

MICHAEL. Good Lord, no, Mum! They're ninety in the office. The youngest is twenty-eight.

OLIVIA. (*As she comes down again from the kitchen.*) The poor old things! It's a wonder they can work.

MICHAEL. (*Who is still reading his* Labour Monthly.) Smashing! Here's another article by Laski. I love him, don't you?

OLIVIA. (*Vaguely.*) I don't think I know him, darling.

MICHAEL. Oh, yes, you do, Mum. Don't you remember I gave you that article of his to read in the last *Labour Monthly*? It was on 'Exchange Equalization and the Export Problem'.

OLIVIA. (*Not listening.*) Oh, yes, of course. Charming.

MICHAEL. This one's on 'Inflation and the Standardization of Wages'. I'll let you read it later. Oh, by the way, your

Tatler's come. (*He gives her the wrapped periodical from the sofa.*)

OLIVIA. Oh, my *Tatler*. Good old Joan, she never forgets.

MICHAEL. (*After a pause, during which* OLIVIA *unwraps her* Tatler.) Gosh! Did you know that in 1926 the average wage of the non-skilled industrial worker in England was only twenty-eight and threepence?

OLIVIA. Good Lord! What *has* Laura Ryde-Davis done to her hair?

MICHAEL. (*Chuckling.*) Oh, corking! He's certainly letting the Government have it this month—Old Laski.

OLIVIA. I didn't know Ciro's had opened again, did you?

MICHAEL. What? No, I didn't.

OLIVIA. Darling—eat your omelette, it'll get cold.

MICHAEL. I've finished, thanks.

OLIVIA. Was it as bad as that?

MICHAEL. No, it was delicious. I'm just not hungry, that's all.

OLIVIA. (*Going to the table for the plate.*) I do it exactly the way the man says on the wireless, but it never seems to come out right. (*She goes up to the kitchen.*) I made you an austerity gateau, but it sat down. So I had to open a tin. One day I'll use a real egg and see what happens. (*She comes back with a plate of fruit.*)

MICHAEL. Thanks awfully. (*He begins to eat again, while still reading.*) Gosh, this is interesting.

OLIVIA *goes back to her* Tatler.

(*Reading.*) 'The budget deficit which led to the artificially created crisis of 1931 could have been totally liquidated by wartime counter-inflationary methods in less than a month.'

OLIVIA. (*Sharply.*) My God!

MICHAEL. What's the matter?

OLIVIA. Nothing, darling. Just something in the *Tatler*——

MICHAEL. What?

OLIVIA. It's not important.

MICHAEL. Let's have a look. (*Crossing to* OLIVIA *and reading over her shoulder.*) 'Sir John Fletcher and his beautiful wife enjoying a joke at Ciro's.' Gosh, it *is* her, too.

OLIVIA. Well—why not? They were still quite friends—I hope

he *has* gone back to her. It would settle everything very nicely. Go on with your dinner, darling, or you'll be late.

MICHAEL *goes back to the table.* OLIVIA *studies the photograph again.* My God, she's still wearing that same idiotic hat she had on the day you brought her round!

MICHAEL. It was a jolly nice hat. You admired it yourself.

OLIVIA. I admired it because when a woman sticks a thing like that on her head you've got to say something or burst. Poor darling, what does she look like—a sort of agitated peahen. (*Examining the picture more closely.*) John never did photograph very well.

MICHAEL. I thought it was rather good of him.

OLIVIA. Oh, no, it's awful. He's much better-looking than that. What's it say? Enjoying a joke! Hm. I should think he was, laughing at that hat.

MICHAEL. Oh, Mum, don't worry about it.

OLIVIA. I don't. It's nothing to do with me, anyway—if he does go and make an idiot of himself again.

MICHAEL. You still mind about it, don't you?

OLIVIA. (*Collecting the tureens and taking them to the kitchen.*) I've far too much on my hands trying to feed you and keeping this flat clean to worry about whether I'm happy or not. (*Defiantly.*) As a matter of fact, I've been perfectly happy these last three months.

MICHAEL. (*Wistfully.*) Gosh! Is that true?

OLIVIA. (*Coming back from the kitchen.*) Of course it is. It's a clear conscience. I know my omelettes are uneatable and my gateaux sit down, but at least I try and cope—which is more than some people do. Enjoying a joke at Ciro's! In a happy mood at the Dorchester! I wonder if that crowd realizes how ridiculous they all are. What does your paper say about them?

MICHAEL. (*Delighted.*) Oh, Laski says that in the New World everyone will have to work his passage or be pushed overboard.

OLIVIA. He's right.

MICHAEL. He says that crowd's absolutely finished, even though they don't know it yet.

N

OLIVIA. (*Vehemently.*) He's absolutely right. Pushed overboard—every one of them! I must read that article. Where is it?

MICHAEL. (*Eagerly.*) It comes in the one on 'Inflation and the Standardization of Wages'. Here we are.

OLIVIA. (*Less eagerly.*) Oh. Yes, yes. Well, I'll take it to bed with me. (*She picks up her handkerchief from the chair, and then goes back to the kitchen.*)

MICHAEL. Mum—don't you ever feel bored here sometimes, all by yourself?

OLIVIA. (*From the kitchen.*) *No.* Not often. Why?

MICHAEL. I just wondered. Tell me—has that man who lives downstairs, Mr. Dangerfield, been up to see you lately? (*Taking his dirty plate to the kitchen.*)

OLIVIA. Mr. Dangerfield is constantly up to see me, especially when you leave the front door unlocked, as you nearly always do, darling.

MICHAEL. Don't you like Mr. Dangerfield?

OLIVIA. (*Coming out of the kitchen.*) I detest Mr. Dangerfield.

MICHAEL. Oh! Pity!

OLIVIA. Why pity?

MICHAEL. I have just thought—well—he's rather a nice chap in many ways—and now he's retired from his job, with quite a nice pension——

OLIVIA. (*As she folds the cloth and puts it in the drawer of the chest.*) Darling, I know quite well that you are doing your best to marry me off to Mr. Dangerfield, but I must warn you that your efforts, which I'm sure are very well meant, are doomed to bitter disappointment. I find Mr. Dangerfield a cracking old bore. (*She bangs the drawer.*)

MICHAEL. Oh.

OLIVIA. Aren't you going to be late for Sylvia?

MICHAEL. (*Putting his hand on his stomach as though Sylvia's name gave him a pain.*) Ah, yes. I'd better tidy up.

OLIVIA. You like her?

MICHAEL. A bit more than that.

OLIVIA. (*Crossing to him.*) Darling! Are you in love?

MICHAEL. Sometimes I am and sometimes I'm not.

OLIVIA. Which are you at the moment?

MICHAEL. I am.

OLIVIA. Oh, you poor little lamb! (*Taking his face in her hands.*) Is she in love with you?

MICHAEL. Gosh, no! She's not in love with anyone. I'm only about fifth or sixth on her list. I can't afford to take her to the Savoy.

OLIVIA. I must say she really doesn't sound awfully nice. Why do you love her so much?

MICHAEL. (*Sadly.*) We men can't help our feelings.

He goes out.

OLIVIA. No, of course not.

MICHAEL. (*Off.*) I'd ask you to come along—only——

OLIVIA. (*Crossing to the desk.*) Yes, darling, I quite understand.

MICHAEL. (*Off.*) I hate leaving you alone all the time.

OLIVIA. That's all right, darling. As a matter of fact, I've found myself a lovely new hobby. I'm teaching myself to type on your typewriter.

She begins to type, with great concentration.

MICHAEL. (*Off.*) Oh, Mum, you're not? But that's wonderful.

OLIVIA. Mr. Laski would approve?

MICHAEL. (*Off.*) You bet he would. So do I.

OLIVIA. 'The time has come for all good men to——' I'm getting very good at it, you'd be surprised. Except that I can never find the Y. I love to hear the bell. How much does a typist earn, Michael?

MICHAEL. (*Coming back.*) Not much, I'm afraid, Mum.

OLIVIA. Oh, well. Enough to keep me in my old age, I expect. Michael, darling, why have you got your hair slicked down in that horrid way?

MICHAEL. Don't you like it?

OLIVIA. No. Does Sylvia?

MICHAEL. I don't know.

OLIVIA. I think it's revolting. (*She kisses him, then starts back.*) Michael, what have you got on?

MICHAEL. What do you mean?

OLIVIA. You're smelling of something. What is it?

MICHAEL. Well, as a matter of fact, I bought some eau de

Cologne stuff in a shop. Of course, it's not eau de Cologne, but it smells like it.

OLIVIA. I'm glad you think so, darling. My, you *are* cutting a dash this evening, aren't you? I hope she'll be impressed.

MICHAEL. So do I. I think the time has come for me to take a firm line with her.

OLIVIA. That's right.

MICHAEL. I'll do that tonight.

OLIVIA. That's right, darling. You asphyxiate her with your eau de Cologne, and then give her a good sound talking to.

MICHAEL. (*Worried.*) Is it too much?

OLIVIA. No, darling, I'm only joking. It's lovely. Run along, now. Have a good time.

MICHAEL. Thanks, Mum. Good night.

OLIVIA. Good night, dear.

He goes out.

OLIVIA *goes to the desk, picks up* The Tatler, *and looks at it. She makes a face in imitation of Diana Fletcher and throws the magazine in the waste-paper basket. She goes to the kitchen and puts one or two of the things in the cupboard, and after looking at the washing-up decides to leave it. She then enters as though she were a typist coming into her office. At the door she says 'Good morning, Mr. Jones', to an imaginary gentleman on the left, and 'Good morning, Mr. Peters', to a similar gentleman down left, then from down centre, in answer to an imaginary question, she replies, 'Am I late? No? Yes? Oh!' She then sits at the desk and with care and concentration begins to type, mostly with one finger, though at certain bolder moments, with two.*

JOHN *appears noiselessly in the doorway. He is breathing heavily, but soundlessly, and leans for a second against the wall to recover his breath, gazing meanwhile at the back of* OLIVIA's *head. Finally, he takes out his glasses, tiptoes up to* OLIVIA, *and looks over her shoulder.*

JOHN. (*Reading.*) 'Now is the time for all good men—'

OLIVIA. (*Appalled.*) John!

JOHN. '—to say that Diana Fletcher is a silly bitch.' Really, Olivia!

OLIVIA. John! Go away! Go away at once.

JOHN. Please let me recover my breath first. You ought to warn your visitors to bring their alpenstocks with them.

OLIVIA. How did you get in?

JOHN. Through what I gathered was the front-door.

OLIVIA. (*Rising.*) That little idiot left it unlocked again. Go away, John! I'll get Mr. Dangerfield to throw you out.

JOHN. Who's Mr. Dangerfield?

OLIVIA. He lives in the flat below, and he's as strong as a bull.

JOHN. Go and get him. I need exercise.

OLIVIA. (*Imploringly.*) Oh, John, please go. Please. You gave me your sacred solemn word of honour not to try and see me again.

JOHN. Yes, I did, didn't I?

OLIVIA. Well, then, aren't you ashamed of yourself?

JOHN. Yes, I am.

OLIVIA. Then why don't you go? Don't you see, every second you stay makes it worse.

JOHN. Yes, it does, doesn't it? Much worse.

OLIVIA. I warn you—Michael's in that room there——

JOHN. Oh, no, he isn't. It's not for nothing I've been sitting in my car at Puffin's Corner for the last half-hour waiting for him to come out. It was rather exciting. Like a gangster film. My driver was most intrigued. I told her I was watching a hot-bed of international spies——

OLIVIA. Anyway, he's just gone round the corner for a packet of cigarettes. He'll be back in a minute.

JOHN. Oh, no, he won't. He's gone to the cinema with his girl friend—Miss Sylvia Hart—and he'll be away for hours.

OLIVIA. How do you know?

JOHN. You forget he works in my Ministry.

OLIVIA. Really, John! You, the Minister, spying on a little boy to find out when his mother's going to be alone. That's pretty, I must say.

JOHN. I can only repeat—Olivia—I'm bitterly, bitterly ashamed of myself.

OLIVIA. Well, you don't look it.

JOHN. It would never do for a Cabinet Minister to look ashamed of himself. Oh, darling, I'm so glad to see you again. Have you—or is it my imagination, have you put on a little weight?

OLIVIA. Certainly not. As a matter of fact, I've taken it off.

JOHN. Well, whatever you've done, it certainly suits you. (*Looking round.*) What a charming place you have here!

OLIVIA. You needn't be patronizing. I know it isn't looking its best at the moment.

JOHN *is gazing at a pair of oars over the kitchen door.*

JOHN. No, I think it's delightful. (*Reading the inscription.*) 'J. F. Brown, Guy's Hospital, Rowing Club—Stroke, 1922 to 1923.' Charming!

OLIVIA. (*Furiously.*) Well, where the hell else can I put them?

JOHN. Nowhere else. I think they look delightful there. (*Pointing to sofa.*) I suppose that becomes a bed. (*He notices the Sickert above the fireplace.*) Ah, so that's where the Sickert got to, is it?

OLIVIA. It's mine, you know. Only the frame was yours, and I left you that.

JOHN. (*Quietly.*) Yes, you left me the frame. (*He begins to laugh.*)

OLIVIA. What are you laughing at?

JOHN. That apron.

OLIVIA. What's the matter with it?

JOHN. Nothing, nothing. I've never seen you in an apron before, that's all. It looks charming.

OLIVIA. Thank you. I don't wear it for that reason, you know.

JOHN. I know you don't.

OLIVIA. (*Enraged.*) Have you come here to taunt me?

JOHN. No, no, Olivia. I don't mean to taunt you.

OLIVIA. Oh, yes, you do. You mock at the flat, you jeer at those—(*Pointing at the oars.*)—you accuse me of pinching the Sickert, you tell me I'm looking as fat as a barrel, and finally you sneer at my apron. I want you to know, John, that this apron is an article of clothing that I'm very proud to wear.

JOHN. But, of course you are. I understand that perfectly.

OLIVIA. Oh, no you don't. You don't understand at all—how could you—you and your crowd—understand what a wonderful feeling it gives me to know that I'm working my passage at last? As for your crowd, John, they're finished—

absolutely finished! In the New World they're all going to
be—what's the phrase?

JOHN. Swept aside like so much chaff?

OLIVIA. No, no . . . not swept. . . .

JOHN. Pushed overboard?

OLIVIA. (*Triumphantly.*) That's it, pushed overboard—they're
all going to be pushed overboard. You should read what the
Labour Monthly has to say about them. You should read that
article by—er—by——

JOHN. Ivor Montagu?

OLIVIA. No, no.

JOHN. Palme Dutt?

OLIVIA. No, no, no—Professor something——

JOHN. Laski?

OLIVIA. That's right. Professor Laski. You should read what
Professor Laski says about the New World——

JOHN. I do.

OLIVIA. You do?

JOHN. Yes. Very forceful stuff, I think. I agree with a lot of it.
I admit I'm not absolutely sure of his views on the exchange
and monetary problems. Now what do you think about those?

OLIVIA. (*A shade tearfully.*) What do I think about them? I
think they're all absolutely wonderful——

JOHN. Really? Then how do you reconcile them with his views
on the retroactive nature of the inflationary tendency——

OLIVIA. (*Tearfully.*) I don't know what the retroactive whatnot
of the inflationary thingummy is, John, and you know it—
anyway, it's got nothing to do with my apron. Now will
you please, please go back to Westminster and to your wife
—who I'm sure is waiting for you with open arms—— (*She
backs away from him.*)

JOHN. (*Moving after her.*) What are you talking about?

OLIVIA. You're not the only one who has ways and means of
finding out things.

JOHN. You don't really think I've gone back to Diana, do you?

OLIVIA. I don't care whether you have or you haven't, John.
I've finished with you, can't you understand that? I've
finished with you for good and all.

JOHN. Do you mean that?

OLIVIA. Of course I mean it. I've made my decision, and I'm not going back on it, and I'd be grateful if in future you don't come slumming.

There is a pause. JOHN *seems at a loss to know what to do. He crosses to the mantelpiece for a cigarette.*

No, there are none there. Unlike some people, we can't afford to have cigarettes lying about all over the place. Here. (*She takes a battered carton from the pocket of her apron and gives him one cigarette from it.*)

JOHN. Thank you.

OLIVIA. But once that's smoked, out you go, for good and all. Is that understood?

JOHN. Yes.

She looks keenly at his hair.

What's the matter?

OLIVIA. You've gone awfully grey these last three months.

JOHN. Yes, I know.

OLIVIA. Have you been working terribly hard?

JOHN. Pretty hard. That's not the reason for the grey hair, though.

OLIVIA. (*Snapping.*) What, then? Too many late nights at Ciro's?

JOHN. Since you left me, Olivia, I've been out one night, and one night only. I took Diana to Ciro's to discuss a matter of business.

OLIVIA. Funny business?

JOHN. Serious business. The Barton and Burgess affair.

OLIVIA. I thought she was suing you for that.

JOHN. She was.

OLIVIA. You don't mean to say you've given way and paid her?

JOHN. Isn't that what you wanted me to do? You said it would avoid unpleasantness—don't you remember?

OLIVIA. It's nothing to do with me, John, anyway, what you do. It's your life, and you can wreck it as you please.

Pause.

JOHN. Olivia, will you marry me?

OLIVIA. What?

JOHN. I said, will you marry me?

OLIVIA. How—why—what do you mean?

JOHN. I've left the Ministry.

OLIVIA. John! Not because of me?

JOHN. No, Olivia. I promise you that. I've been turned out.

OLIVIA. Oh, no! That's dreadful. No, John!

JOHN. No. Don't give me your sympathy—much as I like to have it. My job's finished, and with it, the Ministry. I left Number Ten only half an hour ago.

OLIVIA. Oh, was he—nice about it?

JOHN. Very.

From his breast pocket he takes out a large cigar.

OLIVIA. I see. The new tank was a success, wasn't it?

JOHN. Yes, it was.

OLIVIA. I always knew it would be. I always knew all those wicked things they said about it weren't true. What else did he say to you?

JOHN. I would like to tell you some time, only just now I've too much on my mind. I'm asking you to marry me.

OLIVIA. John, you have a wife.

JOHN. She's agreed to a divorce.

OLIVIA. How do you know?

JOHN. I've seen to that.

OLIVIA. The Barton and Burgess affair? You *are* a wily old fox, really. You never do anything without a motive. You're ruthless.

JOHN. Will you marry me?

OLIVIA. You know I can't.

JOHN. Why not?

OLIVIA. You know why not.

JOHN. Still Michael?

OLIVIA. Still Michael.

JOHN. He has no right to object——

OLIVIA. Right doesn't enter into it. It's still a question of you or him, and unfortunately he hates you.

JOHN. Well, I hate him.

OLIVIA. Don't say that!

JOHN. (*Rising.*) Well, it's true. Our lives have been split and blasted apart by a little moral gangster with an Œdipus complex and a passion for self-dramatization.

OLIVIA. Calling him names won't help.

JOHN. It helps me. What's he acting now? Young Woodley, or the Mad Casanova of Fulham?

OLIVIA. So that's why you came round to see me, is it?

JOHN. Yes, that's why I trekked from 10 Downing Street to Puffin's Corner.

OLIVIA. Why didn't you say so straight away?

JOHN. I needed a little time to gain courage.

OLIVIA. What made you think I'd say yes?

JOHN. I had hoped against hope that three months of Baron's Court would have weakened that iron resolution a little——

OLIVIA. It's not an iron resolution, John. It's an instinct. And three months of Baron's Court hasn't weakened it. It's confirmed it. I'm happy here.

JOHN. Weren't you happy with me?

OLIVIA. What's that got to do with it?

JOHN. I wanted to know, that's all.

OLIVIA. Of course I was happy with you, John—gloriously happy, and you know it. But Michael was right about me, all the same. It was a silly, idle life to live. If I'd gone on like that, what sort of place would I have had in the New World?

JOHN. Look, Olivia. I'll resign from Fletcher Prat tomorrow, I'll give all my money—to *The Labour Monthly*, I'll take a tenth-floor flat in Bethnal Green—with no lift, no sofa, no telephone—I'll conform in any way you like to this New World of yours and Michael's.

OLIVIA. (*Pathetically.*) It's no good, John. You don't want a New World.

JOHN. I want you, Olivia, and if I can get you I'll take a New World, an Old World, a Middle-aged World, or any damn world at all. Don't I stand the faintest glimmer of a chance?

OLIVIA. As long as Michael is with me, none at all.

JOHN. Suppose he marries this girl of his?

OLIVIA. Don't be absurd. He's much too young. Besides, she's an unparalleled hussy.

JOHN. Is he very much in love with her?

OLIVIA. He thinks he is.

JOHN. She's giving him a bad time?

OLIVIA. Horrible, poor lamb.

JOHN. (*With relish.*) Good!

OLIVIA. It's very unbecoming in you to be unkind, John.

There is a pause.

JOHN. I think I'd better go. (*He has picked up his hat from the sofa.*)

OLIVIA. I think you had. I wish I could offer you a drink, only——

JOHN. Only you can't afford to keep it. I quite understand.

OLIVIA. I believe I *have* got some whisky in a medicine bottle somewhere——

JOHN. I really don't want a drink. I'm leaving for Canada to-morrow, Olivia.

OLIVIA. Canada?

JOHN. Yes.

OLIVIA. Oh? For long?

JOHN. Quite some time.

OLIVIA. I see. Permanently. I suppose you'll be settling down there one day and getting married.

JOHN. I don't think I'll marry again.

OLIVIA. Oh, yes, you will. Only don't let it be another Diana.

JOHN. I thought you didn't care what happened to me.

OLIVIA. Well, perhaps I do, a little.

JOHN. Have you any plans for the future?

OLIVIA. Don't worry about me, John. I'll be all right.

JOHN. I'm sure I wish you every happiness.

OLIVIA. I wish you exactly the same.

They make a move towards each other.

JOHN. Goodbye. (*He turns abruptly away.*)

OLIVIA. Where are you going now, back home to Westminster?

JOHN. Yes, I've a few things to do.

OLIVIA. (*Going up to the door.*) You shouldn't work late at night, John? Aren't you even going to have any dinner?

JOHN. No, why should I?

He goes out.

OLIVIA *comes back to the sofa, and begins to cry. After a pause* JOHN *comes back.*

You know, Olivia, I might have some if you'll dine with me.

OLIVIA. No—that would be highly immoral.

JOHN. Well, I didn't say 'or something', you know.

OLIVIA. There are other kinds of immorality.

JOHN. Oh, do come, Olivia. It will be our last dinner together. (*Pause.*) I promise not to mention marriage.

OLIVIA. Or Michael?

JOHN. Or Michael.

OLIVIA. Well, what would we talk about, then?

JOHN. (*Eagerly.*) We could talk about the new tank, and what the Prime Minister said to me.

OLIVIA. Oh, yes. I do want to hear about that. Where would we go—supposing we did go?

JOHN. The Savoy?

OLIVIA. Oh, no, John. Not the Savoy. If we went anywhere, we could go to a little place I know, next to Baron's Court Station—Antoine's. It's French, you know.

JOHN. Sounds French.

OLIVIA. It's very quiet there—very good value for money.

JOHN. It sounds delightful.

OLIVIA. It is.

JOHN. Delightful.

She rises and moves towards the door. He follows her.

OLIVIA. Oh, I've forgotten the washing-up. Oh, well, I could leave that until later. This is our last dinner together. You must stick to your bargain. The new tank, what the Prime Minister said. No marriage, no Michael.

He crosses his heart.

All right, I'll go and slip on a dress. I won't be a second.

She goes out. JOHN *glances round the room, and then turns on the radio. He takes off his jacket and, going into the kitchen, puts on an apron which is hanging on the cupboard and begins to wash up.*

MICHAEL *comes in, looking very sour and sullen. He throws his hat, gloves, and* Labour Monthly *on the couch, and is just going into his own room when he realizes that the radio is on, and returns to*

turn it off. He has got to the door of his own room again when JOHN
puts his head round the kitchen door.

JOHN. You're back early, Michael?

MICHAEL. (*After a second's speechless astonishment.*) What the dickens
do you think you're doing?

JOHN. Washing-up.

MICHAEL. So I see, but what the dickens are you doing in this
flat, anyway. (*He moves towards the kitchen.*)

JOHN. I came round to ask your mother to marry me,
Michael.

MICHAEL. Oh, you did, did you?

JOHN. Yes.

MICHAEL. Have you seen her yet?

JOHN. Yes.

MICHAEL. What did she say?

JOHN. She said 'No'.

MICHAEL. Good for her!

JOHN. Yes. Well, your mother's refusal of me, Michael, at least
has one compensation. It has relieved me of the bitter
obligation of having to be polite to you. So from now on,
young man, one more crack out of you will end in tears, and
the tears, this time, will not be mine——

MICHAEL. So—you'd assault a chap in his own flat, would you?

JOHN. No. I'd take the chap by the seat of his pants, down six
flights of stairs, and assault him on the pavement in front
of his own flat.

MICHAEL. (*Nervously.*) You could get six months for that.

JOHN. (*Gently.*) You underestimate my feeling towards you,
Michael. I could hang for it.

MICHAEL. Gosh! Oh, well, I'm not surprised you feel like that
—all things considered.

JOHN. I'm glad you realize that.

MICHAEL. Still, it seems to me there's no reason why we should
be uncivilized about things. You dislike me, I dislike you.
Well, that's too bad, but we needn't behave like primeval
apes about it.

JOHN. Possibly not. Nevertheless, I reserve the right to behave
like one the minute I feel myself sufficiently provoked.

MICHAEL. Don't worry. If you can be a good loser, I can be a good winner. Won't you sit down?

JOHN. What did you say?

MICHAEL. Won't you sit down?

JOHN. (*Moving towards the chair above the table.*) Thank you.

MICHAEL. Sit on the sofa. It's more comfortable.

JOHN. (*Sitting.*) I'll be quite comfortable here, thank you.

MICHAEL. (*Looking round.*) I'm afraid the flat isn't quite looking its best at the moment.

JOHN. What did you say?

MICHAEL. The flat isn't looking its best at the moment.

JOHN. I thought that's what you said. It's funny, you sounded so much like your mother.

MICHAEL. Oh, really? Tell me—what do you think of it?

JOHN. The flat? I think it's charming.

MICHAEL. Oh, no, it isn't. You're just being polite. I'm afraid it's pretty ghastly—really.

JOHN. What's the matter with it?

MICHAEL: (*Sitting.*) It's so inconvenient, having no lift. I'm thinking seriously of moving, as a matter of fact.

JOHN. Oh, really, where to?

MICHAEL. I've seen quite a nice little flat in Montpelier Square —ground floor—Adamses' house.

JOHN. Adamses'?

MICHAEL. That's what Mum says. She doesn't think we can afford it.

JOHN. And you think you can?

MICHAEL. Oh, yes. I don't see why not. Can I get you a drink?

JOHN. Your mother said there wasn't anything in the house.

MICHAEL. (*Rising, taking a bottle out of his hip pocket and going into the kitchen.*) What mothers don't know would fill a book. It's only gin, I'm afraid. Awful muck, I think, but I was hoping to entertain a girl friend here tonight, and this is the only thing she'll drink.

JOHN. I see. What happened to your girl friend, Michael? Why aren't you still at the cinema?

MICHAEL. (*Off.*) Oh—we had a row. When she got to the cinema and saw what the film was, she said she didn't want to see it.

MICHAEL *comes back with two glasses of gin which he has filled in the kitchen.*

JOHN. I see. What was the film?

MICHAEL. The Life of Maxim Gorky—Part VI.

JOHN. Oh, I see.

MICHAEL. Jolly good film. I've seen it twice. Of course, you'd hate it.

JOHN. Why should I hate it?

MICHAEL. It's very anti-fascist. (*There is an awkward pause. MICHAEL backs slightly. He raises his glass.*) Well—bung-ho!

JOHN. Bung-ho!

They both take a sip. MICHAEL, evidently unused to the taste, splutters slightly and makes a wry face. It is plain from JOHN's expression that the gin is very strong, and perhaps not as authentic as it might be.

MICHAEL. (*Scornfully.*) Woman's drink!

JOHN. I quite agree.

MICHAEL. Is it all right?

JOHN. Oh, yes, very good gin.

MICHAEL. It had better be. I paid sixteen and fourpence for it, in the black market.

JOHN. (*Astounded.*) The—black market?

MICHAEL. Yes. I don't approve of it, of course, but—well—she likes gin, you see.

JOHN. Tell me a little more about this girl friend of yours, Michael.

MICHAEL. Sylvia Hart?

JOHN. Yes. Is she pretty?

MICHAEL. (*Mournfully.*) She's the most beautiful girl in the whole world. She's an actress, too.

JOHN. Oh? What's she playing?

MICHAEL. She doesn't actually act, if you see what I mean—not on the stage, anyway——

JOHN. But like the dickens off it?

MICHAEL. She's just left dramatic school——

JOHN. Hasn't got a job, yet?

MICHAEL. No, but she nearly saw Korda last week, and now she treats me like a little boy. The only time she was even human to me was one night when I took her to Oddenino's.

JOHN. Why didn't you go on taking her to Oddenino's?

MICHAEL. I couldn't afford it.

JOHN. Ah, I see.

MICHAEL. Besides, Sparky Stevens takes her to the Savoy.

JOHN. Do you think he's taken her there tonight?

MICHAEL. I'm sure of it. Of course, tomorrow she'll lie like blazes, and I'll never know one way or the other.

JOHN. Would you like me to find out?

MICHAEL. I certainly would.

JOHN *goes to the telephone.*

JOHN. This Sparky Stevens, I take it, has substance?

MICHAEL. Oh, yes. He's a Flight-Lieutenant. He's a chap in the R.A.F. she's rather keen on, who's suddenly come up to town.

JOHN. Tell me, what's this fine feathered friend of yours wearing? (*He is dialling a number.*)

MICHAEL. A green dress with a red thingummy on the collar.

JOHN. (*Into receiver.*) Restaurant please, Mr. Gondolfo? (*To* MICHAEL.) Anything on her head.

MICHAEL. A sort of veil pinned on top.

JOHN. (*Into receiver.*) Hullo, Mr. Gondolfo? This is John Fletcher. I wonder, could you tell me, has a Flight-Lieutenant Sparky Stevens a reservation for tonight? . . . Coming in now? . . . With a young lady?

JOHN.   ⎫ (*Simultaneously.*) In a green dress with a red
MICHAEL. ⎭   thingummy on the collar?

JOHN. I see. Thank you very much, Mr. Gondolfo. No, not tonight. I'm dining elsewhere. . . . Good night. (*He rings off.*) I'm afraid, Michael, your suspicions are only too correct.

MICHAEL. (*Gloomily.*) Isn't that just typical of her?

JOHN. From what you've told me of Miss Sylvia Hart, I should say it was.

MICHAEL. What's the answer to it—that's what I want to know?

JOHN. I'm not sure if there is one, Michael. I know from my own experience that if one is unlucky enough to fall in love with one of the Sylvia Harts of this world there's nothing to do but sit back, take what comes, and pray for a quick release. (*He takes a sip of the gin, which proves to be as potent as it was before.*)

There is a pause.

MICHAEL. You're speaking of your wife, I suppose. Did she have a Sparky Stevens?

JOHN. (*With a sadly reminiscent nod.*) Only his name was Loopy Buckeridge.

MICHAEL. (*Interested.*) Tell me, did he have a moustache?

JOHN. Oh, yes, sported a vast, silky affair—Guards type.

MICHAEL. Sparky has one, too. An enormous one, R.A.F. type.

JOHN. What an extraordinary coincidence! Tell me, does Sparky make hunting noises?

MICHAEL. Aeroplane noises.

JOHN. Equally irritating. Is he inclined to stand on his head in public places?

MICHAEL. He once did a thing he called a victory roll in the Regent Palace.

JOHN. I suppose that made Sylvia laugh?

MICHAEL. (*Bitterly.*) Laugh? She screamed and screamed. She's talked about it ever since.

JOHN. (*Moved.*) I know, old boy, I know. I feel for you very deeply.

MICHAEL. How did you get away from Diana?

JOHN. I was lucky. She got away from me.

MICHAEL. Even then, how did you stop being in love with her?

JOHN. Again I was lucky. I fell in love with someone else—someone far, far nicer.

There is a pause.

MICHAEL. (*Rising.*) Have another drink? (*He goes into the kitchen with the two glasses.*)

JOHN. No, I don't think I will, thank you, Michael.

MICHAEL. (*Off.*) I think I will.

JOHN. I wouldn't, if I were you.

MICHAEL. (*Off.*) Perhaps I'd better not. I want to keep my head.

JOHN. You're welcome to it, I'm sure.

MICHAEL *either does not hear this or chooses to ignore it.*

MICHAEL. I don't believe you ever *were* in love with Mum.

JOHN. I know you don't.

MICHAEL. After all, she's nothing like Diana.

JOHN. Perhaps that's one of the reasons I'm so much in love with her.

MICHAEL. Even then, it doesn't make sense. After all, Mum's getting on.

JOHN. So am I.

MICHAEL. (*Coming into the room.*) But—but—well, I just don't believe you're in love with her, that's all.

JOHN. (*Urgently.*) Michael—when you walk into a room and you find Sylvia in there, do you suddenly feel as though someone has hit you very hard, right here? (*He thumps his stomach.*)

MICHAEL. Well—yes—I do.

JOHN. Do you say the wrong things when you talk to her?

MICHAEL. Oh, yes, often.

JOHN. Do you find yourself stammering and blushing?

MICHAEL. Yes.

JOHN. And, at night, when you try to remember what she looks like, and then when you finally do, do you feel as if someone had hit you very hard here again, then there's a flutter of doves——?

MICHAEL. Gosh, yes! I do.

JOHN. Those are your symptoms, Michael. I'm more than twice your age. Double their intensity and you'll know what I feel for your mother.

MICHAEL. (*Disturbed, but recovering himself.*) Oh, well, she couldn't feel anything like that about you.

JOHN. Why do you say that, Michael?

MICHAEL. I know it; that's all.

JOHN. (*Rising and taking off his apron.*) All right, Michael, we won't say any more. I'm sorry I raised the subject. As you said a minute ago, you've won and I've lost. Let it rest at that. But you will admit that your mother is a very beautiful and charming woman.

MICHAEL. Well, yes. I suppose so.

JOHN. Well—thanks to you—she's decided to work her passage through the New World. Very right, very proper.

Only—tell me this—is there no better use to be made of beauty and charm—austerity age though this may be—than to consign them to a hermit's life in a kitchen? I'm only asking for information, Michael. It's going to be your world—you and your generation are going to administer it.

MICHAEL. (*Hotly.*) And we're jolly well going to administer it, too—without the help of any reactionary old fogies——

JOHN. All right, all right. Only remember this. Ten years from now, when you're a successful commissar, living in an enormous mansion in Park Lane, with huge Adam's ceilings, and Sylvia Hart as your paramour, drinking bottle after bottle of black-market gin, I shall have a very good chuckle, as I pass by, selling my State-owned matches in the street.

MICHAEL. (*Scornfully.*) That's mere deviationism——

JOHN. Now what the hell is that?

MICHAEL. (*A little surprised by this question.*) Deviationism?

JOHN. Yes, deviationism?

MICHAEL. Well, it's—er—well——

JOHN. Well?

MICHAEL. (*With surprising candour.*) It's a word I usually say in an argument when I can't think of anything else.

JOHN. Even to Sylvia?

MICHAEL. (*Rising at the name like a rocketing pheasant.*) Sylvia!

JOHN. (*Mimicking him.*) Sylvia!

MICHAEL. (*In agony.*) Oh, gosh! Just think of her at the Savoy with that great baboon, Sparky Stevens!

JOHN. (*Sadistically.*) He's probably sending her into hysterics with vocal imitations of a Spitfire.

MICHAEL. You know—I've a jolly good mind to go along there and surprise them.

JOHN. Well, why don't you?

MICHAEL. Oh, the usual.

JOHN. Well, here——

JOHN *deliberately takes out his wallet and removes from it a five-pound note.*

MICHAEL. Oh, no—I couldn't.

JOHN. Why not?

MICHAEL. I wouldn't be able to pay you back for ages——

JOHN. That's all right. I don't mind.

MICHAEL. It mightn't be for months.

JOHN. Years if you like.

MICHAEL. I couldn't, really—thanks all the same——

JOHN. Just as you please.

MICHAEL. (*Taking the note.*) Well, perhaps I will. Thanks awfully. Do you think they'll give me a table?

JOHN. (*Rising.*) Do you want me to use my influence? (*He crosses to the telephone.*)

MICHAEL. Oh, yes, do. Try and get me one dead opposite theirs, where I can sit and glare——

JOHN. (*Picking up the receiver.*) You know—I'm beginning to feel quite sorry for this Miss Sylvia Hart——

MICHAEL. Just a minute. I've got an even better idea.

JOHN. What?

MICHAEL. (*Awkwardly.*) Are you doing anything for dinner?

JOHN. Well—er—why, exactly?

MICHAEL. Would you dine with me?

JOHN. At the Savoy?

MICHAEL. Of course, at the Savoy.

JOHN. Well, that's very kind of you, Michael. The only thing is——

MICHAEL. (*Excitedly.*) Oh, please, do. Please. It'd make all the difference. Gosh! Just think of her face when I walk in with you. Oh, boy! She'll have a fit.

JOHN. Why should she have a fit?

MICHAEL. Me—with a Cabinet Minister! She'd never forget it as long as she lives. She's the most terrible snob.

JOHN. (*Practical as ever.*) Do you think she'd know who I am?

MICHAEL. Gosh, I hadn't thought of that.

JOHN. (*Replacing the receiver.*) Well, wait a minute. I tell you what we can do. We'll have the head waiter walk in front of us and just as we go past their table he can say in a very loud voice, 'Table for the Right Honourable Sir John Fletcher, Bart., and his friend, Mr. Michael Brown'.

MICHAEL. (*Gleefully.*) Don't you think just plain 'Mr. Michael Brown'?

JOHN. No, no, I think 'his friend' is nicer, don't you? Less formal, somehow.

MICHAEL. Maybe you're right.

JOHN. (*With his arm round* MICHAEL's *shoulder.*) Then we might dally for a moment just within earshot of them, and I can be heard saying to you in a fairly loud voice just what the Prime Minister said to me about the new tank.

MICHAEL. That's a good idea!

JOHN. Then you might pretend to recognize Sylvia suddenly, give her a polite but frigid bow, and another to Sparky, and then we'll pass on to our table—with me still talking about the Prime Minister in a fairly loud voice.

MICHAEL. That's a wonderful idea!

JOHN. Do you think you can do it? I know from experience that you're a very facile actor, but do you think you can do it?

MICHAEL. Yes. Just let me try.

JOHN. All right, all right. Let's pretend (*Spreading out his arms.*) this is the Savoy. See if you can get some music on the radio. (MICHAEL *goes to the radio.*) Little Carrol Gibbons is usually playing his head off. Sparky and Sylvia will be sitting over there—and our table will be there. There's a flight of stairs at the Savoy, now don't fall down them. (*They are now ready to make their entrance into the Savoy.* MICHAEL *is in front of* JOHN, *and just a little nervous.*) Let yourself go. Pretend you know everybody. Are you ready? (*They begin to walk.*) The Prime Minister, blah, blah, blah——

MICHAEL *gives a start and pretends to see* SYLVIA *and* SPARKY. *He bows stiffly and very formally twice, with his arms sticking out from his sides.* JOHN *begins to laugh.* MICHAEL *looks uncomfortable.* Yes. I was afraid of that. You know, if you don't mind my saying so, you have rather a quaint and florid style. Perhaps you'd better watch me. Now I'll be you and you be me. Start again.

They return to their starting-point, and prepare to come in again, JOHN *leading the way this time, which he does with a great deal of assurance and swagger.* MICHAEL *follows close on his heels, with more concentration than assurance. They walk right round the sofa, as before, but this time round the table as well and sit at it.*

(*As he walks.*) You said that to the Prime Minister, Sir John? Well, fancy . . .

This line takes them round the table and to their seats at it. JOHN *leans forward the better to see the supposed table at which* SYLVIA *and* SPARKY *are sitting.*)

That young lady hasn't fainted over there, by any chance? Gosh, corking!

MICHAEL. Corking!

OLIVIA *comes in.*

JOHN. (*To* OLIVIA, *in a 'Society' voice.*) Oh, hullo, won't you join us? Let me give you the idea. This is the Savoy. That young lady you see being carried out unconscious is Miss Sylvia Hart——

OLIVIA. (*In acute alarm.*) John, John, don't you think it would be an even nicer idea if you were to put your feet up on this lovely sofa just for a few minutes?

MICHAEL. (*Going to door.*) Don't worry, Mum——

OLIVIA. It's overwork, you know. . . .

MICHAEL. (*As he goes out.*) Sir John's all right. I'll be back in a minute. I'll just brush up a bit.

He goes out.

JOHN. Won't you join us?

OLIVIA. Is this still the Savoy?

JOHN. Still the Savoy.

OLIVIA. Would you care to tell me, what the hell is going on here?

They sit at the table.

JOHN. Well, a little gleam of hope has appeared on the horizon —hope not only for you and me, but for the world as well.

OLIVIA. Make sense, John. Do make sense.

JOHN. Your son, madam, is growing up.

OLIVIA. Where's the hope for the world in that?

JOHN. On the horizon. A little speck of light that may one day become a sunrise.

OLIVIA. John, have you been drinking?

JOHN. Yes, I've been drinking gin. With your son.

OLIVIA. I didn't know there was any gin in the flat.

JOHN. What mothers don't know would fill a book.

OLIVIA. John! Really!

JOHN. Would you care to dance?

OLIVIA. John!

Nevertheless, she rises and they begin to dance.

JOHN. I'd forgotten how well you dance.

OLIVIA. I'm a little out of practice.

JOHN. Even practice can't improve perfection.

They have each done an isolated turn and are back in each other's arms when MICHAEL *comes back. He glares at them for a moment while they continue to dance. He then turns off the radio and is going back to his own room, when he changes his mind, stopping at the door.*

MICHAEL. (*At length.*) I suppose we can get a table for three, can't we, Sir John?

OLIVIA. (*Joyously.*) Michael, darling! Why, are you coming, too?

MICHAEL. Gosh, I'm giving the dinner.

JOHN *goes to the telephone.*

OLIVIA. You are? How wonderful. John, you don't have to telephone Antoine's. There's always plenty of room there.

MICHAEL. We're going to the Savoy.

OLIVIA. (*Shocked.*) The Savoy—oh, no—certainly not the Savoy! Antoine's is much nicer.

MICHAEL. No, Antoine's is no good.

OLIVIA. Antoine's is charming.

JOHN. I'd love to go to Antoine's, but I'm afraid Michael is right, it's got to be the Savoy.

OLIVIA. No, no, not the Savoy.

MICHAEL. Oh, Mum, do come. Sir John's car is outside.

JOHN. Yes, in Puffin's Corner.

MICHAEL. We can go in style.

OLIVIA. His car? (*Firmly.*) If we must go to the Savoy, I shall certainly not go in a car. We'll walk.

JOHN.　　⎱
　　　　　⎰What!
MICHAEL.

MICHAEL. But why, when we've got a car?

OLIVIA. We'll walk, or take a bus.

JOHN. Are you sure you know how to get there by 'bus?

OLIVIA. Of course I do. We'll take a number 72—or is it a 73?

JOHN. Or number 74?

OLIVIA. No. You go to Notting Hill Gate, and then you change. Or does a number 72 go to Notting Hill Gate?

JOHN. Perhaps it would if we asked it nicely.

OLIVIA. Well, wherever it does go to you change and take a number—anyway, we'll get to the Savoy, somehow.

JOHN. Some day.

OLIVIA. Michael, darling, go and put the cover on my typewriter.

MICHAEL crosses from where he has been sitting on the sofa, and JOHN *crosses to get his hat and gloves from the sofa.* OLIVIA *rises and moves up stage, catching sight of the unwashed dishes as she does so.*

Oh, I've forgotten the washing-up. (*There is a moment's awful silence.*) Well, we could all do that later, couldn't we? You are a fine pair, you two. You'll have a lot to answer for, over dinner. Michael, dear, go and put the light on the stairs.

MICHAEL. (*Kissing her.*) All right, Mum.

OLIVIA. Get my mackintosh, John.

MICHAEL. Only do hurry.

He goes out.

OLIVIA. It might rain, you never can tell.

JOHN *takes her mackintosh from where it is hanging on the wall outside the kitchen and puts it round her. He takes her in his arms.*

JOHN. Oh, darling, I do love you so much. (*Taking the mackintosh off and throwing it on the sofa.*) I don't think you'll need this. It's going to be a lovely evening.

MICHAEL. (*Off stage.*) Come on, you two, for heaven's sake, get cracking!

JOHN. (*Calling after him.*) All right, in a minute. You must remember, Michael, your mother and I are getting on.

He kisses her.

CURTAIN

THE WINSLOW BOY

FOR

MASTER PAUL CHANNON

In the hope that he will live to see a world
in which this play
will point no
moral

ACT I   A SUNDAY MORNING IN JULY

ACT II   AN EVENING IN APRIL
                    (NINE MONTHS LATER)

ACT III AN EVENING IN JANUARY
                    (NINE MONTHS LATER)

ACT IV   AN AFTERNOON IN JUNE
                    (FIVE MONTHS LATER)

The action of the play takes place in Arthur Winslow's house in Kensington, London, and extends over two years of a period preceding the war of 1914–1918.

The Winslow Boy was first produced at the Lyric Theatre, London, on May 23rd, 1946, with the following cast:

RONNIE WINSLOW	*Michael Newell*
VIOLET	*Kathleen Harrison*
ARTHUR WINSLOW	*Frank Cellier*
GRACE WINSLOW	*Madge Compton*
DICKIE WINSLOW	*Jack Watling*
CATHERINE WINSLOW	*Angela Baddeley*
JOHN WATHERSTONE	*Alastair Bannerman*
DESMOND CURRY	*Clive Morton*
MISS BARNES	*Mona Washbourne*
FRED	*Brian Harding*
SIR ROBERT MORTON	*Emlyn Williams*

The play directed by GLEN BYAM SHAW

ACT I

SCENE: *The drawing-room of a house in Courtfield Gardens, South Kensington, on a morning in July, at some period not long before the war of* 1914–1918.

The furnishings betoken solid but not undecorative upper middle-class comfort.

On the rise of the curtain A BOY *of about fourteen, dressed in the uniform of an Osborne naval cadet, is discovered. There is something rigid and tense in his attitude, and his face is blank and without expression.*

There is the sound of someone in the hall. As the sound comes nearer, he looks despairingly round, as if contemplating flight. An elderly maid (VIOLET) *comes in, and stops in astonishment at sight of him.*

VIOLET. Master Ronnie!

RONNIE. (*With ill-managed sang-froid.*) Hello, Violet.

VIOLET. Why, good gracious! We weren't expecting you back till Tuesday.

RONNIE. Yes, I know.

VIOLET. Why ever didn't you let us know you were coming, you silly boy? Your mother should have been at the station to meet you. The idea of a child like you wandering all over London by yourself. I never did. However did you get in? By the garden, I suppose.

RONNIE. No. The front-door. I rang and cook opened it.

VIOLET. And where's your trunk and your tuck box?

RONNIE. Upstairs. The taximan carried them up——

VIOLET. Taximan? You took a taxi?

RONNIE *nods.*

All by yourself? Well, I don't know what little boys are coming to, I'm sure. What your father and mother will say, I don't know——

RONNIE. Where are they, Violet?

VIOLET. Church, of course.

RONNIE. (*Vacantly.*) Oh, yes. It's Sunday, isn't it?

VIOLET. What's the matter with you? What have they been doing to you at Osborne?

RONNIE. (*Sharply.*) What do you mean?

VIOLET. They seem to have made you a bit soft in the head, or something. Well—I suppose I'd better get your unpacking done—Mr. Dickie's been using your chest of drawers for all his dress clothes and things. I'll just clear 'em out and put 'em on his bed—that's what I'll do. He can find room for 'em somewhere else.

RONNIE. Shall I help you?

VIOLET. (*Scornfully.*) I know *your* help. With *your* help I'll be at it all day. No, you just wait down here for your mother and father. They'll be back in a minute.

RONNIE *nods and turns hopelessly away.* VIOLET *looks at his retreating back, puzzled.*

Well?

RONNIE. (*Turning.*) Yes?

VIOLET. Don't I get a kiss or are you too grown up for that now?

RONNIE. Sorry, Violet.

He goes up to her and is enveloped in her ample bosom.

VIOLET. That's better. My, what a big boy you're getting!

She holds him at arm's length and inspects him.

Quite the little naval officer, aren't you?

RONNIE. (*Smiling forlornly.*) Yes. That's right.

VIOLET. Well, well—I must be getting on——

She goes out. RONNIE, *left alone, resumes his attitude of utter dejection. He takes out of his pocket a letter in a sealed envelope. After a second's hesitation, he opens it, and reads the contents. The perusal appears to increase his misery.*

He makes for a moment as if to tear it up; then changes his mind again, and puts it back in his pocket. He gets up and takes two or three quick steps towards the hall door. Then he stops, uncertainly.

There is the sound of voices in the hall. RONNIE *jumps to his feet; then, with a strangled sob runs to the garden door, and down the iron steps into the garden.*

*The hall door opens and the rest of the Winslow family file in. They
are* ARTHUR *and* GRACE—*Ronnie's father and mother—and* DICKIE
and CATHERINE—*his brother and sister. All are carrying prayer-
books, and wear that faintly unctuous after-church air.*

ARTHUR *leans heavily on a stick. He is a man of about sixty, with
a rather deliberately cultured patriarchal air.* GRACE *is about ten
years younger, with the faded remnants of prettiness.* DICKIE *is
an Oxford undergraduate, large, noisy, and cheerful.* CATHERINE,
*approaching thirty, has an air of masculinity about her which is at
odd variance with her mother's intense femininity.*

GRACE. (*As she enters.*) —But he's so old, dear. From the back
of the church you really can't hear a word he says——

ARTHUR. He's a good man, Grace.

GRACE. But what's the use of being good, if you're inaudible?

CATHERINE. A problem in ethics for you, Father.

ARTHUR *is standing with his back to fireplace. He looks round at
the open garden door.*

ARTHUR. There's a draught, Grace.

GRACE *goes to the door and closes it.*

GRACE. Oh, dear—it's coming on to rain.

DICKIE. I'm on Mother's side. The old boy's so doddery now
he can hardly finish the course at all. I timed him today.
It took him seventy-five seconds dead from a flying start to
reach the pulpit, and then he needed the whip coming
round the bend. I call that pretty bad going.

ARTHUR. I don't think that's very funny, Richard.

DICKIE. Oh, don't you, Father?

ARTHUR. Doddery though Mr. Jackson may seem now, I very
much doubt if he failed in his pass mods. when he was at
Oxford.

DICKIE. (*Aggrieved.*) Dash it—Father—you promised not to
mention that again this vac——

GRACE. You did, you know, Arthur.

ARTHUR. There was a condition to my promise—if you remember—that Dickie should provide me with reasonable evidence of his intentions to work.

DICKIE. Well, haven't I, Father? Didn't I stay in all last night
—a Saturday night—and work?

ARTHUR. You stayed in, Dickie. I would be the last to deny that.

GRACE. You *were* making rather a noise, dear, with that old gramophone of yours. I really can't believe you could have been doing much work with that going on all the time——

DICKIE. Funnily enough, Mother, it helps me to concentrate——

ARTHUR. Concentrate on what?

DICKIE. Work, of course.

ARTHUR. That was not what you appeared to be concentrating on when I came down to fetch a book—sleep, may I say, having been rendered out of the question by the hideous sounds emanating from this room.

DICKIE. Edwina and her father had just looked in on their way to the Graham's dance—they only stayed a minute——

GRACE. What an idiotic girl that is! Oh, sorry, Dickie—I was forgetting. You're rather keen on her, aren't you?

ARTHUR. You would have had ample proof of that fact, Grace, if you had seen them in the attitude I caught them in last night.

DICKIE. We were practising the Bunny Hug.

GRACE. The what, dear?

DICKIE. The Bunny Hug. It's the new dance.

CATHERINE. (*Helpfully.*) It's like the Turkey Trot—only more dignified.

GRACE. I thought that was the tango.

DICKIE. No. More like a Fox Trot, really. Something between a Boston Glide and a Kangaroo Hop.

ARTHUR. We appear to be straying from the point. Whatever animal was responsible for the posture I found you in does not alter the fact that you have not done one single stroke of work this vacation.

DICKIE. Oh. Well, I do work awfully fast, you know—once I get down to it.

ARTHUR. That assumption can hardly be based on experience, I take it.

DICKIE. Dash it, Father! You are laying in to me this morning.

ARTHUR. It's time you found out, Dickie, that I'm not spending two hundred pounds a year keeping you at Oxford, merely to learn to dance the Bunny Hop.

DICKIE. Hug, Father.

ARTHUR. The exact description of the obscenity is immaterial.

GRACE. Father's quite right, you know, dear. You really have been going the pace a bit, this vac.

DICKIE. Yes, I know, Mother—but the season's nearly over now——

GRACE. (*With a sigh.*) I wish you were as good about work as Ronnie.

DICKIE. (*Hotly.*) I like that. That's a bit thick, I must say. All Ronnie ever has to do with his footling little homework is to add two and two.

ARTHUR. Ronnie is at least proving a good deal more success-ful in adding two and two than you were at his age.

DICKIE. (*Now furious.*) Oh, yes. *I* know. *I* know. *He* got into Osborne and *I* failed. That's going to be brought up again——

GRACE. Nobody's bringing it up, dear——

DICKIE. Oh, yes they are. It's going to be brought up against me all my life. Ronnie's the good little boy, I'm the bad little boy. You've just stuck a couple of labels on us that nothing on earth is ever going to change.

GRACE. Don't be so absurd, dear——

DICKIE. It's not absurd. It's quite true. Isn't it, Kate?

CATHERINE *looks up from a book she has been reading in the corner.*

CATHERINE. I'm sorry, Dickie. I haven't been listening. Isn't what quite true?

DICKIE. That in the eyes of Mother and Father nothing that Ronnie does is ever wrong, and nothing I do is ever right?

CATHERINE. (*After a pause.*) If I were you, Dickie dear, I'd go and have a nice lie down before lunch.

DICKIE. (*After a further pause.*) Perhaps you're right.

He goes towards the hall door.

ARTHUR. If you're going to your room I suggest you take that object with you.

*He points to a gramophone—*1912 *model, with horn—lying on a table.* It's out of place in a drawing-room.

O

DICKIE, *with an air of hauteur, picks up the gramophone and carries it to the door.*

It might help you to concentrate on the work you're going to do this afternoon.

DICKIE *stops at the door, and then turns slowly.*

DICKIE. (*With dignity.*) That is out of the question, I'm afraid.

ARTHUR. Indeed? Why?

DICKIE. I have an engagement with Miss Gunn.

ARTHUR. On a Sunday afternoon? Escorting her to the National Gallery, no doubt?

DICKIE. No. The Victoria and Albert Museum.

He goes out with as much dignity as is consistent with the carrying of a very bulky gramophone.

GRACE. How stupid of him to say that about labels. There's no truth in it at all—is there, Kate?

CATHERINE. (*Deep in her book.*) No, Mother.

GRACE. Oh, dear, it's simply pelting. What are you reading, Kate?

CATHERINE. Len Rogers's Memoirs.

GRACE. Who's Len Rogers?

CATHERINE. A Trades Union Leader.

GRACE. Does John know you're a Radical?

CATHERINE. Oh, yes.

GRACE. And a Suffragette?

CATHERINE. Certainly.

GRACE. (*With a smile.*) And he still wants to marry you?

CATHERINE. He seems to.

GRACE. Oh, by the way, I've asked him to come early for lunch—so that he can have a few words with Father first.

CATHERINE. Good idea. I hope you've been primed, have you Father?

ARTHUR. (*Who has been nearly asleep.*) What's that?

CATHERINE. You know what you're going to say to John, don't you? You're not going to let me down and forbid the match, or anything, are you? Because I warn you, if you do, I shall elope——

ARTHUR. (*Taking her hand.*) Never fear, my dear. I'm far too delighted at the prospect of getting you off our hands at last.

CATHERINE. (*Smiling.*) I'm not sure I like that 'at last'.

GRACE. Do you love him, dear?

CATHERINE. John? Yes, I do.

GRACE. You're such a funny girl. You never show your feelings much, do you? You don't behave as if you were in love.

CATHERINE. How does one behave as if one is in love?

ARTHUR. One doesn't read Len Rogers. One reads Byron.

CATHERINE. I do both.

ARTHUR. An odd combination.

CATHERINE. A satisfying one.

GRACE. I meant—you don't talk about him much, do you?

CATHERINE. No. I suppose I don't.

GRACE. (*Sighing.*) I don't think you modern girls have the feelings our generation did. It's this New Woman attitude.

CATHERINE. Very well, Mother. I love John in every way that a woman can love a man, and far, far more than he loves me. Does that satisfy you?

GRACE. (*Embarrassed.*) Well, really, Kate darling—I didn't ask for anything quite like that—— (*To* ARTHUR.) What are you laughing at, Arthur?

ARTHUR. (*Chuckling.*) One up to the New Woman.

GRACE. Nonsense. She misunderstood me, that's all. (*At the window.*) Just look at the rain! (*Turning to* CATHERINE.) Kate, darling, does Desmond know about you and John?

CATHERINE. I haven't told him. On the other hand, if he hasn't guessed, he must be very dense.

ARTHUR. He *is* very dense.

GRACE. Oh, no. He's quite clever, if you really get under his skin.

ARTHUR. Oddly enough, I've never had that inclination.

GRACE. I think he's a dear. Kate darling, you *will* be kind to him, won't you?

CATHERINE. (*Patiently.*) Yes, Mother. Of course I will.

GRACE. He's really a very good sort——

She breaks off suddenly and stares out of the window.

Hullo! There's someone in our garden.

CATHERINE. (*Coming to look.*) Where?

GRACE. (*Pointing.*) Over there, do you see?

CATHERINE. No.

GRACE. He's just gone behind that bush. It was a boy, I think. Probably Mrs. Williamson's awful little Dennis.

CATHERINE. (*Leaving the window.*) Well, whoever it is must be getting terribly wet.

GRACE. Why can't he stick to his own garden?

There is a sound of voices outside in the hall.

GRACE. Was that John?

CATHERINE. It sounded like it.

GRACE. (*After listening.*) Yes. It's John. (*To* CATHERINE.) Quick! In the dining-room!

CATHERINE. All right.

She dashes across to the dining-room door.

GRACE. Here! You've forgotten your bag.

She darts to the table and picks it up.

ARTHUR. (*Startled.*) What on earth is going on?

GRACE. (*In a stage whisper.*) We're leaving you alone with John. When you've finished cough or something.

ARTHUR. (*Testily.*) What do you mean, or something?

GRACE. I know. Knock on the floor with your stick—three times. Then we'll come in.

ARTHUR. You don't think that might look a trifle coincidental?

GRACE. Sh!

She disappears from view as the hall door opens and VIOLET *comes in.*

VIOLET. (*Announcing.*) Mr. Watherstone.

JOHN WATHERSTONE *comes in. He is a man of about thirty, dressed in an extremely well-cut morning coat and striped trousers, an attire which, though excused by church parade, we may well feel has been donned for this occasion.*

ARTHUR. How are you, John? I'm very glad to see you.

JOHN. How do you do, sir?

ARTHUR. Will you forgive me not getting up? My arthritis has been troubling me rather a lot, lately.

JOHN. I'm very sorry to hear that, sir. Catherine told me it was better.

ARTHUR. It was, for a time. Now it's worse again. Do you smoke? (*He indicates a cigarette-box.*)

JOHN. Yes, sir. I do. Thank you. (*He takes a cigarette, adding hastily.*) In moderation, of course.

ARTHUR. (*With a faint smile.*) Of course.

Pause, while JOHN *lights his cigarette and* ARTHUR *watches him.*

Well, now. I understand you wish to marry my daughter.

JOHN. Yes, sir. That's to say, I've proposed to her and she's done me the honour of accepting me.

ARTHUR. I see. I trust when you corrected yourself, your second statement wasn't a denial of your first? (JOHN *looks puzzled.*) I mean, you do *really* wish to marry her?

JOHN. Of course, sir.

ARTHUR. Why, of course? There are plenty of people about who don't wish to marry her.

JOHN. I mean, of course, because I proposed to her.

ARTHUR. That, too, doesn't necessarily follow. However, we don't need to quibble. We'll take the sentimental side of the project for granted. As regards the more practical aspect, perhaps you won't mind if I ask you a few rather personal questions?

JOHN. Naturally not, sir. It's your duty.

ARTHUR. Quite so. Now, your income. Are you able to live on it?

JOHN. No, sir. I'm in the regular army.

ARTHUR. Yes, of course.

JOHN. But my army pay is supplemented by an allowance from my father.

ARTHUR. So I understand. Now, your father's would be, I take it, about twenty-four pounds a month.

JOHN. Yes, sir, that's exactly right.

ARTHUR. So that your total income—with your subaltern's pay and allowances plus the allowance from your father, would be, I take it, about four hundred and twenty pounds a year?

JOHN. Again, exactly the figure.

ARTHUR. Well, well. It all seems perfectly satisfactory. I really don't think I need delay my congratulations any longer. (*He extends his hand, which* JOHN, *gratefully, takes.*)

JOHN. Thank you, sir, very much.

ARTHUR. I must say, it was very good of you to be so frank and informative.

JOHN. Not at all.

ARTHUR. Your answers to my questions deserve an equal frankness from me about Catherine's own affairs. I'm afraid she's not—just in case you thought otherwise—the daughter of a rich man.

JOHN. I didn't think otherwise, sir.

ARTHUR. Good. Well, now——

He suddenly cocks his head on one side and listens. There is the sound of a gramophone playing 'Hitchy-koo' from somewhere upstairs.
Would you be so good as to touch the bell?

JOHN *does so.*

Thank you. Well, now, continuing about my own financial affairs. The Westminster Bank pay me a small pension— three hundred and fifty to be precise—and my wife has about two hundred a year of her own. Apart from that we have nothing, except such savings as I've been able to make during my career at the bank. The interest from which raises my total income to approximately eight hundred pounds per annum.

VIOLET *comes in.*

VIOLET. You rang, sir?

ARTHUR. Yes, Violet. My compliments to Mr. Dickie and if he doesn't stop that cacophonous hullaballoo at once, I'll throw him and his infernal machine into the street.

VIOLET. Yes, sir. What was that word again? Cac—something——

ARTHUR. Never mind. Say anything you like, only stop him.

VIOLET. Well, sir, I'll do my best, but you know what Master Dickie's like with his blessed old ragtime.

ARTHUR. Yes, Violet, I do.

VIOLET. I could say you don't think it's quite right on a Sunday.

ARTHUR. (*Roaring.*) You can say I don't think it's quite right on any day. Just stop him making that confounded din, that's all.

VIOLET. Yes, sir.

She goes out.

ARTHUR. (*Apologetically.*) Our Violet has no doubt already been explained to you?

JOHN. I don't think so, sir. Is any explanation necessary?

ARTHUR. I fear it is. She came to us direct from an orphanage when she was fourteen, as a sort of under-between-maid on probation, and in that capacity she was quite satisfactory; but I am afraid, as parlourmaid, she has developed certain marked eccentricities in the performance of her duties, due, no doubt, to the fact that she has never fully known what those duties were. Well, now, where were we? Ah, yes. I was telling you about my sources of income, was I not?

JOHN. Yes, sir.

ARTHUR. Now, in addition to the ordinary expenses of life, I have to maintain two sons—one at Osborne, and the other at Oxford—neither of whom, I'm afraid, will be in a position to support themselves for some time to come—one because of his extreme youth and the other because of—er —other reasons.

The gramophone stops suddenly.

So, you see, I am not in a position to be very lavish as regards Catherine's dowry.

JOHN. No, sir. I quite see that.

ARTHUR. I propose to settle on her one-sixth of my total capital, which, worked out to the final fraction, is exactly eight hundred and thirty-three pounds six shillings and eight pence. But let us deal in round figures and say eight hundred and fifty pounds.

JOHN. I call that very generous, sir.

ARTHUR. Not as generous as I would have liked, I'm afraid. However—as my wife would say—beggars can't be choosers.

JOHN. Exactly, sir.

ARTHUR. Well, then, if you're agreeable to that arrangement, I don't think there's anything more we need discuss.

JOHN. No, sir.

ARTHUR. Splendid.

Pause. ARTHUR *takes his stick, and raps it, with an air of studied unconcern, three times on the floor. Nothing happens.*

JOHN. Pretty rotten weather, isn't it?

ARTHUR. Yes. Vile.

He raps again. Again nothing happens.

Would you care for another cigarette?

JOHN. No, thank you, sir. I'm still smoking.

ARTHUR *takes up his stick to rap again, and then thinks better of it. He goes slowly but firmly to the dining-room door, which he throws open.*

ARTHUR. (*In apparent surprise.*) Well, imagine that! My wife and daughter are in here of all places. Come in, Grace. Come in, Catherine. John's here.

GRACE *comes in, with* CATHERINE *behind.*

GRACE. Why, John—how nice! (*She shakes hands.*) My, you do look a swell! Doesn't he, Kate, darling?

CATHERINE. Quite one of the Knuts.

Pause. GRACE *is unable to repress herself*

GRACE. (*Coyly.*) Well?

ARTHUR. Well, what?

GRACE. How did your little talk go?

ARTHUR. (*Testily.*) I understood you weren't supposed to know we were having a little talk.

GRACE. Oh, you are infuriating! Is everything all right, John?

JOHN *nods, smiling.*

Oh, I'm so glad. I really am.

JOHN. Thank you, Mrs. Winslow.

GRACE. May I kiss you? After all, I'm practically your mother, now.

JOHN. Yes. Of course.

He allows himself to be kissed.

ARTHUR. While I, by the same token, am practically your father, but if you will forgive me——

JOHN. (*Smiling.*) Certainly, sir.

ARTHUR. Grace, I think we might allow ourselves a little modest celebration at luncheon. Will you find me the key of the cellars?

He goes out through the hall door.

GRACE. Yes, dear. (*She turns at the door. Coyly.*) I don't suppose you two will mind being left alone for a few minutes, will you?

She follows her husband out. JOHN *goes to* CATHERINE *and kisses her.*

CATHERINE. Was it an ordeal.

JOHN. I was scared to death.

CATHERINE. My poor darling——

JOHN. The annoying thing was that I had a whole lot of neatly turned phrases ready for him and he wouldn't let me use them.

CATHERINE. Such as?

JOHN. Oh—how proud and honoured I was by your acceptance of me, and how determined I was to make you a loyal and devoted husband—and to maintain you in the state to which you were accustomed—all that sort of thing. All very sincerely meant.

CATHERINE. Anything about loving me a little?

JOHN. (*Lightly.*) That I thought we could take for granted. So did your father, incidentally.

CATHERINE. I see. (*She gazes at him.*) Goodness, you do look smart!

JOHN. Not bad, is it? Poole's.

CATHERINE. What about *your* father? How did he take it?

JOHN. All right.

CATHERINE. I bet he didn't.

JOHN. Oh, yes. He's been wanting me to get married for years. Getting worried about grandchildren, I suppose.

CATHERINE. He disapproves of me, doesn't he?

JOHN. Oh, no. Whatever makes you think that?

CATHERINE. He has a way of looking at me through his monocle that shrivels me up.

JOHN. He's just being a colonel, darling, that's all. All colonels look at you like that. Anyway, what about the way your father looks at me! Tell me, are all your family as scared of him as I am?

CATHERINE. Dickie is, of course; and Ronnie, though he doesn't need to be. Father worships him. I don't know about Mother being scared of him. Sometimes, perhaps. I'm not—ever.

JOHN. You're not scared of anything, are you?

CATHERINE. Oh, yes. Heaps of things.

JOHN. Such as?

CATHERINE. (*With a smile.*) Oh—they're nearly all concerned with you.

RONNIE *looks cautiously in at the window door. He now presents a very bedraggled and woebegone appearance, with his uniform wringing wet, and his damp hair over his eyes.*

JOHN. You might be a little more explicit——

RONNIE. (*In a low voice.*) Kate!

CATHERINE *turns and sees him.*

CATHERINE. (*Amazed.*) Ronnie! What on earth——

RONNIE. Where's Father?

CATHERINE. I'll go and tell him——

RONNIE. (*Urgently.*) No, don't. Please, Kate, don't!

CATHERINE, *halfway to the door, stops, puzzled.*

CATHERINE. What's the trouble, Ronnie?

RONNIE, *trembling on the edge of tears, does not answer her. She approaches him.*

You're wet through. You'd better go and change.

RONNIE. No.

CATHERINE. (*Gently.*) What's the trouble, darling? You can tell me.

RONNIE *looks at* JOHN.

You know John Watherstone, Ronnie. You met him last holidays, don't you remember?

RONNIE *remains silent, obviously reluctant to talk in front of a comparative stranger.*

JOHN. (*Tactfully.*) I'll disappear.

CATHERINE. (*Pointing to dining-room.*) In there, do you mind?

JOHN *goes out quietly.* CATHERINE *gently leads* RONNIE *further into the room.*

Now, darling, tell me. What is it? Have you run away?

RONNIE *shakes his head, evidently not trusting himself to speak.*

What is it, then?

RONNIE *pulls out the document from his pocket which we have seen him reading in an earlier scene, and slowly hands it to her.* CATHERINE *reads it quietly.*

Oh, God!

RONNIE. I didn't do it.

CATHERINE *re-reads the letter in silence.*

RONNIE. Kate, I didn't. Really, I didn't.

CATHERINE. (*Abstractedly.*) No, darling. (*She seems uncertain what to do.*) This letter is addressed to Father. Did you open it?

RONNIE. Yes.

CATHERINE. You shouldn't have done that——

RONNIE. I was going to tear it up. Then I heard you come in from church and ran into the garden—I didn't know what to do——

CATHERINE. (*Still distracted.*) Did they send you up to London all by yourself?

RONNIE. They sent a petty officer up with me. He was supposed to wait and see Father, but I sent him away. (*Indicating letter.*) Kate—shall we tear it up, now?

CATHERINE. No, darling.

RONNIE. We could tell Father term had ended two days sooner——

CATHERINE. No, darling.

RONNIE. I didn't do it—really I didn't——

DICKIE *comes in from the hall. He does not seem surprised to see* RONNIE.

DICKIE. (*Cheerfully.*) Hullo, Ronnie, old lad. How's everything?
RONNIE *turns away from him.*

CATHERINE. You knew he was here?

DICKIE. Oh, yes. His trunks and things are all over our room. Trouble?

CATHERINE. Yes.

DICKIE. I'm sorry.

CATHERINE. You stay here with him. I'll find Mother.

DICKIE. All right.
CATHERINE *goes out by the hall door. There is a pause.*

DICKIE. What's up, old chap?

RONNIE. Nothing.

DICKIE. Come on—tell me.

RONNIE. It's all right.

DICKIE. Have you been sacked.
RONNIE *nods.*
Bad luck. What for?

RONNIE. I didn't do it!

DICKIE. (*Reassuringly.*) No, of course you didn't.

RONNIE. Honestly, I didn't.

DICKIE. That's all right, old chap. No need to go on about it. I believe you.

RONNIE. You don't.

DICKIE. Well, I don't know what it is they've sacked you for, yet——

RONNIE. (*In a low voice.*) Stealing.

DICKIE. (*Evidently relieved.*) Oh, is that all? Good Lord! I didn't know they sacked chaps for *that*, these days.

RONNIE. I didn't do it.

DICKIE. Why, good heavens, at school we used to pinch everything we could jolly well lay our hands on. All of us. I remember there was one chap—Carstairs his name was—captain of cricket, believe it or not—absolutely nothing was safe with him—nothing at all. Pinched a squash racket of mine once, I remember——

He has quietly approached RONNIE, *and now puts his arm on his shoulder.*
Believe me, old chap, pinching's nothing. Nothing at all. I say—you're a bit damp, aren't you?

RONNIE. I've been out in the rain——

DICKIE. You're shivering a bit, too, aren't you? Oughtn't you to go and change? I mean, we don't want you catching pneumonia——

RONNIE. I'm all right.

GRACE comes in, with CATHERINE following. GRACE comes quickly to RONNIE, who, as he sees her, turns away from DICKIE and runs into her arms.

GRACE. There, darling! It's all right, now.

RONNIE begins to cry quietly, his head buried in her dress.

RONNIE. (*His voice muffled.*) I didn't do it, Mother.

GRACE. No, darling. Of course you didn't. We'll go upstairs now, shall we, and get out of these nasty wet clothes.

RONNIE. Don't tell Father.

GRACE. No, darling. Not yet. I promise. Come along now.

She leads him towards the door held open by CATHERINE.

Your new uniform, too, What a shame!

She goes out with him.

DICKIE. I'd better go and keep 'cave' for them. Ward off the old man if he looks like going upstairs.

CATHERINE *nods.*

(*At door.*) I say—who's going to break the news to him eventually? I mean, someone'll have to.

CATHERINE. Don't let's worry about that now.

DICKIE. Well, you can count me out. In fact, I don't want to be within a thousand miles of that explosion.

He goes out. CATHERINE *comes to the dining-room door, which she opens, and calls 'John!'* JOHN *comes in.*

JOHN. Bad news?

CATHERINE *nods. She is plainly upset, and dabs her eyes with her handkerchief.*

That's rotten for you. I'm awfully sorry.

CATHERINE. (*Violently.*) How can people be so cruel!

JOHN. (*Uncomfortably.*) Expelled, I suppose?

He gets his answer from her silence, while she recovers herself.

CATHERINE. God, how little imagination some people have! Why should they torture a child of that age, John, darling? What's the point of it?

JOHN. What's he supposed to have done?

CATHERINE. Stolen some money.

JOHN. Oh.

CATHERINE. Ten days ago, it said in the letter. Why on earth didn't they let us know? Just think what that poor little creature has been going through these last ten days down there, entirely alone, without anyone to look after him, knowing what he had to face at the end of it! And then, finally, they send him up to London with a petty officer—is it any wonder he's nearly out of his mind?

JOHN. It does seem pretty heartless, I admit.

CATHERINE. Heartless? It's cold, calculated inhumanity. God, how I'd love to have that Commanding Officer here for just two minutes! I'd—I'd——

JOHN. (*Gently.*) Darling, it's quite natural you should feel angry about it, but you must remember, he's not really at school. He's in the Service.

CATHERINE. What difference does that make?

JOHN. Well, they have ways of doing things in the Service which may seem to an outsider horribly brutal—but at least they're always scrupulously fair. You can take it from me, that there must have been a very full inquiry before they'd take a step of this sort. What's more, if there's been a delay of ten days, it would only have been in order to give the boy a better chance to clear himself——

Pause. CATHERINE *is silent.*

I'm sorry, Catherine, darling. I'd have done better to keep my mouth shut.

CATHERINE. No. What you said was perfectly true——

JOHN. It was tactless of me to say it, though. I'm sorry.

CATHERINE. (*Lightly.*) That's all right.

JOHN. Forgive me?

He lays his arm on her shoulder.

CATHERINE. (*Taking his hand.*) Nothing to forgive.

JOHN. Believe me, I'm awfully sorry. (*After a pause.*) How will your father take it?

CATHERINE. (*Simply.*) It might kill him——

There is the sound of voices in the hall.

Oh, heavens! We've got Desmond to lunch. I'd forgotten——

JOHN. Who?

CATHERINE. Desmond Curry—our family solicitor. Oh, Lord! (*In a hasty whisper.*) Darling—be polite to him, won't you?

JOHN. Why? Am I usually so rude to your guests?

CATHERINE. No, but he doesn't know about us yet——

JOHN. Who does?

CATHERINE. (*Still in a whisper.*) Yes, but he's been in love with me for years—it's a family joke——

VIOLET *comes in.*

VIOLET. (*Announcing.*) Mr. Curry.

DESMOND CURRY *comes in. He is a man of about forty-five, with the figure of an athlete gone to seed. He has a mildly furtive manner, rather as if he had just absconded with his firm's petty cash, but hopes no one is going to be too angry about it.* JOHN, *when he sees him, cannot repress a faint smile at the thought of his loving* CATHERINE. VIOLET *has made her exit.*

CATHERINE. Hullo, Desmond. I don't think you know John
    Watherstone——

DESMOND. No—but, of course, I've heard a lot about him——

JOHN. How do you do?

He wipes the smile off his face, as he meets CATHERINE'S *glance.*
    There is a pause.

DESMOND. Well, well, well. I trust I'm not early.

CATHERINE. No. Dead on time, Desmond—as always.

DESMOND. Capital. Capital.

There is another pause, broken by CATHERINE *and* JOHN *both sud-*
    denly speaking at once.

CATHERINE. ⎱ (*Simultaneously.*)   ⎰ Tell me, Desmond——
JOHN.   ⎰   ⎱ Pretty ghastly this rain——

JOHN. I'm so sorry——

CATHERINE. It's quite all right. I was only going to ask how
    you did in your cricket match yesterday, Desmond.

DESMOND. Not too well, I'm afraid. My shoulder's still giving
    me trouble——

There is another pause.

(*At length.*) Well, well. I hear I'm to congratulate you both——

CATHERINE. Desmond—you know?

DESMOND. Violet told me, just now—in the hall. Yes—I must
    congratulate you both.

CATHERINE. Thank you so much, Desmond.

JOHN. Thank you.

DESMOND. Of course, it's quite expected, I know. Quite
    expected. Still it was rather a surprise, hearing it like that
    —from Violet in the hall——

CATHERINE. We were going to tell you, Desmond dear. It was
    only official this morning, you know. In fact, you're the first
    person to hear it.

DESMOND. Am I? Am I, indeed? Well, I'm sure you'll both be
    very happy.

CATHERINE. ⎱ (*Murmuring* ⎰ Thank you, Desmond.
JOHN.   ⎰ *together.*) ⎱ Thank you.

DESMOND. Only this morning? Fancy.

    GRACE *comes in.*

GRACE. Hullo, Desmond, dear.

DESMOND. Hullo, Mrs. Winslow.

GRACE. (*To* CATHERINE.) I've got him to bed——

CATHERINE. Good.

DESMOND. Nobody ill, I hope?

GRACE. No, no. Nothing wrong at all——

ARTHUR *comes in, with a bottle under his arm. He rings the bell.*

ARTHUR. Grace, when did we last have the cellars seen to?

GRACE. I can't remember, dear.

ARTHUR. Well, they're in a shocking condition. Hullo, Desmond. How are you? You're not looking well.

DESMOND. Am I not? I've strained my shoulder, you know——

ARTHUR. Well, why do you play these ridiculous games of yours? Resign yourself to the onrush of middle age, and abandon them, my dear Desmond.

DESMOND. Oh, I could never do that. Not give up cricket. Not altogether.

JOHN. (*Making conversation.*) Are you any relation of D. W. H. Curry who used to play for Middlesex?

DESMOND. (*Whose moment has come.*) I am D. W. H. Curry.

GRACE. Didn't you know we had a great man in the room?

JOHN. Gosh! Curry of Curry's match?

DESMOND. That's right.

JOHN. Hat trick against the Players in—what year was it?

DESMOND. 1895. At Lord's. Twenty-six overs, nine maidens, thirty-seven runs, eight wickets.

JOHN. Gosh! Do you know you used to be a schoolboy hero of mine?

DESMOND. Did I? Did I, indeed?

JOHN. Yes. I had a signed photograph of you.

DESMOND. Yes. I used to sign a lot once, for schoolboys, I remember.

ARTHUR. Only for schoolboys, Desmond?

DESMOND. I fear so—yes. Girls took no interest in cricket in those days.

JOHN. Gosh! D. W. H. Curry—in person. Well, I'd never have thought it.

DESMOND. (*Sadly.*) I know. Very few people would nowadays——

CATHERINE. (*Quickly.*) Oh, John didn't mean that, Desmond——

DESMOND. I fear he did. (*He moves his arm.*) This is the main trouble. Too much office work and too little exercise, I fear.

ARTHUR. Nonsense. Too much exercise and too little office work.

VIOLET comes in, in response to a bell rung by ARTHUR some moments before.

VIOLET. You rang, sir?

ARTHUR. Yes, Violet. Bring some glasses, would you?

VIOLET. Very good, sir.

She goes out.

ARTHUR. I thought we'd try a little of the Madeira before luncheon—we're celebrating, you know, Desmond——

GRACE jogs his arm furtively, indicating DESMOND.

(*Adding hastily.*) —my wife's fifty-fourth birthday——

GRACE. Arthur! Really!

CATHERINE. It's all right, Father. Desmond knows——

DESMOND. Yes, indeed. It's wonderful news, isn't it? I'll most gladly drink a toast to the—er—to the——

ARTHUR. (*Politely.*) Happy pair, I think, is the phrase that is eluding you——

DESMOND. Well, as a matter of fact, I was looking for something new to say——

ARTHUR. (*Murmuring.*) A forlorn quest, my dear Desmond.

GRACE. (*Protestingly.*) Arthur, really! You mustn't be so rude.

ARTHUR. I meant, naturally, that no one—with the possible exception of Voltaire—could find anything new to say about an engaged couple——

DICKIE comes in.

Ah, my dear Dickie—just in time for a glass of Madeira in celebration of Kate's engagement to John——

VIOLET comes in with a tray of glasses. ARTHUR begins to pour out the wine.

DICKIE. Oh, is that all finally spliced up now? Kate definitely being entered for the marriage stakes. Good egg!

ARTHUR. Quite so. I should have added just now—with the

possible exception of Voltaire and Dickie Winslow. (*To* VIOLET.) Take these round, will you, Violet?

VIOLET goes first to GRACE, *then to* CATHERINE, *then to* JOHN, DESMOND, DICKIE, *and finally* ARTHUR.

CATHERINE. Are we allowed to drink our own healths?

ARTHUR. I think it's permissible.

GRACE. No. It's bad luck.

JOHN. We defy augury. Don't we, Kate?

GRACE. You mustn't say that, John dear. I know. You can drink each other's healths. That's all right.

ARTHUR. Are my wife's superstitious terrors finally allayed? Good.

The drinks have now been handed round.

ARTHUR. (*Toasting.*) Catherine and John!

*All drink—*CATHERINE *and* JOHN *to each other.* VIOLET *lingers, smiling, in the doorway.*

(*Seeing* VIOLET.) Ah, Violet. We mustn't leave you out. You must join this toast.

VIOLET. Well—thank you, sir.

He pours her out a glass.

Not too much, sir, please. Just a sip.

ARTHUR. Quite so. Your reluctance would be more convincing if I hadn't noticed you'd brought an extra glass——

VIOLET. (*Taking glass from* ARTHUR.) Oh, I didn't bring it for myself, sir. I brought it for Master Ronnie—— (*She extends her glass.*) Miss Kate and Mr. John.

She takes a sip, makes a wry face, and hands the glass back to ARTHUR.

ARTHUR. You brought an extra glass for Master Ronnie, Violet?

VIOLET. (*Mistaking his bewilderment.*) Well—I thought you might allow him just a sip, sir. Just to drink the toast. He's that grown up these days.

She turns to go. The others, with the exception of DESMOND, *who is staring gloomily into his glass, are frozen with apprehension.*

ARTHUR. Master Ronnie isn't due back from Osborne until Tuesday, Violet.

VIOLET. (*Turning.*) Oh, no, sir. He's back already. Came back unexpected this morning, all by himself.

ARTHUR. No, Violet. That isn't true. Someone has been playing a joke——

VIOLET. Well, I saw him with my own two eyes, sir, as large as life, just before you come in from church—and then I heard Mrs. Winslow talking to him in his room——

ARTHUR. Grace—what does this mean?

CATHERINE. (*Instinctively taking charge.*) All right, Violet. You can go——

VIOLET. Yes, miss.

She goes out.

ARTHUR. (*To* CATHERINE.) Did *you* know Ronnie was back?

CATHERINE. Yes——

ARTHUR. And you, Dickie?

DICKIE. Yes, Father.

ARTHUR. Grace?

GRACE. (*Helplessly.*) We thought it best you shouldn't know— for the time being. Only for the time being, Arthur.

ARTHUR. (*Slowly.*) Is the boy very ill?

No one answers. ARTHUR *looks from one face to another in bewilderment.*

Answer me, someone! Is the boy very ill? Why must I be kept in the dark like this? Surely I have the right to know. If he's ill I must be with him——

CATHERINE. (*Steadily.*) No, Father. He's not ill.

ARTHUR *suddenly realizes the truth from her tone of voice.*

ARTHUR. Will someone tell me what has happened, please?

GRACE *looks at* CATHERINE *with helpless inquiry.*

CATHERINE *nods.* GRACE *takes a letter from her dress.*

GRACE. (*Timidly.*) He brought this letter for you—Arthur.

ARTHUR. Read it to me, please——

GRACE. Arthur—not in front of——

ARTHUR. Read it to me, please.

GRACE *again looks at* CATHERINE *for advice, and again receives a nod.* GRACE *begins to read.*

GRACE. (*Reading.*) 'Confidential. I am commanded by My Lords Commissioners of the Admiralty to inform you that they have received a communication from the Commanding Officer of the Royal Naval College at Osborne, reporting the theft of a five-shilling postal order at the College on the 7th instant, which was afterwards cashed at the Post Office. Investigation of the circumstances of the case leaves no other conclusion possible than that the postal order was taken by your son, Cadet Ronald Arthur Winslow. My Lords deeply regret that they must therefore request you to withdraw your son from the College.' It's signed by someone—I can't quite read his name——

She turns away quickly to hide her tears. CATHERINE *puts a comforting arm on her shoulder.* ARTHUR *has not changed his attitude. There is a pause, during which we can hear the sound of a gong in the hall outside.*

ARTHUR. (*At length.*) Desmond—be so good as to call Violet.

DESMOND *does so. There is another pause, until* VIOLET *comes in.*

VIOLET. Yes, sir.

ARTHUR. Violet, will you ask Master Ronnie to come down and see me, please?

GRACE. Arthur—he's in bed.

ARTHUR. You told me he wasn't ill.

GRACE. He's not at all well.

ARTHUR. Do as I say, please, Violet.

VIOLET. Very good, sir.

She goes out.

ARTHUR. Perhaps the rest of you would go in to luncheon? Grace, would you take them in?

GRACE. (*Hovering.*) Arthur—don't you think——

ARTHUR. (*Ignoring her.*) Dickie, will you decant that bottle of claret I brought up from the cellar? I put it on the sideboard in the dining-room.

DICKIE. Yes, Father.

He goes out.

ARTHUR. Will you go in, Desmond? And John?

The two men go out into the dining-room, in silence. GRACE *still hovers.*

GRACE. Arthur?

ARTHUR. Yes, Grace?

GRACE. Please don't—please don't—— (*She stops, uncertainly.*)

ARTHUR. What mustn't I do?

GRACE. Please don't forget he's only a child——

> ARTHUR *does not answer her.*

> CATHERINE *takes her mother's arm.*

CATHERINE. Come on, Mother.

She leads her mother to the dining-room door. At the door GRACE *looks back at* ARTHUR. *He has still not altered his position and is ignoring her. She goes into the dining-room, followed by* CATHERINE. ARTHUR *does not move after they are gone. After an appreciable pause there comes a timid knock on the door.*

ARTHUR. Come in.

> RONNIE *appears in the doorway. He is in a dressing-gown. He stands on the threshold.*

Come in and shut the door.

> RONNIE *closes the door behind him.*

Come over here.

> RONNIE *walks slowly up to his father.* ARTHUR *gazes at him steadily for some time, without speaking.*

(*At length.*) Why aren't you in your uniform?

RONNIE. (*Murmuring.*) It got wet.

ARTHUR. How did it get wet?

RONNIE. I was out in the garden in the rain.

ARTHUR. Why?

RONNIE. (*Reluctantly.*) I was hiding.

ARTHUR. From me?

> RONNIE *nods.*

Do you remember once, you promised me that if ever you were in trouble of any sort you would come to me first?

RONNIE. Yes, Father.

ARTHUR. Why didn't you come to me now? Why did you have to go and hide in the garden?

RONNIE. I don't know, Father.

ARTHUR. Are you so frightened of me?

> RONNIE *does not reply.* ARTHUR *gazes at him for a moment, then picks up the letter.*

In this letter it says you stole a postal order.

> RONNIE *opens his mouth to speak.*

> ARTHUR *stops him.*

Now, I don't want you to say a word until you've heard

what *I've* got to say. If you did it, you must tell me. I shan't be angry with you, Ronnie—provided you tell me the truth. But if you tell me a lie, I shall know it, because a lie between you and me can't be hidden. I shall know it, Ronnie —so remember that before you speak. (*Pause.*) Did you steal this postal order?

RONNIE. (*Without hesitation.*) No, Father. I didn't.

ARTHUR. (*Staring into his eyes.*) Did you steal this postal order?

RONNIE. No, Father. I didn't.

ARTHUR *continues to stare into his eyes for a second, then relaxes and pushes him gently away.*

ARTHUR. Go on back to bed.

RONNIE *goes gratefully to the door.*

And in future I trust that a son of mine will at least show enough sense to come in out of the rain.

RONNIE. Yes, Father.

He disappears. ARTHUR *gets up quite briskly and goes to the telephone in the corner of the room.*

ARTHUR. (*At telephone.*) Hullo. Are you there? (*Speaking very distinctly.*) I want to put a trunk call through, please. A trunk call . . . Yes . . . The Royal Naval College, Osborne . . . That's right . . . Replace receiver? Certainly.

He replaces receiver and then, after a moment's meditation, turns and walks briskly into the dining-room.

CURTAIN

ACT II

SCENE: *The same, nine months later. It is about six o'clock, of a spring evening.*

DICKIE *is winding up his gramophone which, somehow or other, appears to have found its way back into the drawing-room. A pile of books and an opened notebook on the table provide evidence of interrupted labours.*

The gramophone, once started, emits a scratchy and muffled rendering of an early ragtime. DICKIE *listens for a few seconds with evident appreciation, then essays a little* pas seul.

CATHERINE *comes in. She is in evening dress.* DICKIE *switches off gramophone.*

DICKIE. Hullo. Do you think the old man can hear this upstairs?

CATHERINE. I shouldn't think so. I couldn't.

DICKIE. Soft needle and an old sweater down the horn. Is the doctor still with him?

CATHERINE *nods.*

What's the verdict, do you know?

CATHERINE. I heard him say Father needed a complete rest.

DICKIE. Don't we all.

CATHERINE. (*Indicating books.*) It doesn't look as if *you* did. He said he ought to go to the country and forget all his worries——

DICKIE. Fat chance there is of that, I'd say.

CATHERINE. I know.

DICKIE. I say, you look a treat. New dress?

CATHERINE. Is it likely? No, it's an old one I've had done up.

DICKIE. Where are you going to?

CATHERINE. Daly's. Dinner first—at the Cri.

DICKIE. Nice. You wouldn't care to take me along with you, I suppose?

CATHERINE. You suppose quite correctly.

DICKIE. John wouldn't mind.

383

CATHERINE. I dare say not. I would.

DICKIE. I wish I had someone to take me out. In your new feminist world do you suppose women will be allowed to do some of the paying?

CATHERINE. Certainly.

DICKIE. Really? Then the next time you're looking for someone to chain themselves to Mr. Asquith you can jolly well call on me——

CATHERINE. (*Laughing.*) Edwina might take you out if you gave her the hint. She's very rich——

DICKIE. If I gave Edwina a hint of that sort I wouldn't see her this side of doomsday.

CATHERINE. You sound a little bitter, Dickie dear.

DICKIE. Oh, no. Not bitter. Just realistic.

VIOLET *comes in with an evening paper on a salver.*

DICKIE. Good egg! The *Star*!

CATHERINE *makes a grab for it and gets it before* DICKIE.

VIOLET. You won't throw it away, will you, miss? If there's anything in it again, cook and I would like to read it, after you.

CATHERINE *is hastily turning over the pages, with* DICKIE *craning his head over her shoulder.*

CATHERINE. No. That's all right, Violet.

VIOLET *goes out.*

Here it is. (*Reading.*) 'The Osborne cadet.' There are two more letters. (*Reading.*) 'Sir. I am entirely in agreement with your correspondent, Democrat, concerning the scandalously high-handed treatment by the Admiralty of the case of the Osborne Cadet. The efforts of Mr. Arthur Winslow to secure a fair trial for his son have evidently been thwarted at every turn by a soulless oligarchy——'

DICKIE. Soulless oligarchy. That's rather good——

CATHERINE. —'it is high time private and peaceful citizens of this country awoke to the increasing encroachment of their ancient freedom by the new despotism of Whitehall. The Englishman's home was once said to be his castle. It seems it is rapidly becoming his prison. Your obedient servant, *Libertatis Amator*.'

DICKIE. Good for old Amator!

CATHERINE. The other's from Perplexed. (*Reading.*) 'Dear Sir. I cannot understand what all the fuss is about in the case of the Osborne Cadet. Surely we have more important matters to get ourselves worked up about than a fourteen-year-old boy and a five-shilling postal order.' Silly old fool!

DICKIE. How do you know he's old?

CATHERINE. Isn't it obvious? (*Reading.*) 'With the present troubles in the Balkans and a certain major European Power rapidly outbuilding our navy, the Admiralty might be forgiven if it stated that it had rather more urgent affairs to deal with than Master Ronnie Winslow's little troubles. A further inquiry before the Judge Advocate of the Fleet has now fully confirmed the original findings that the boy was guilty. I sincerely trust that this will finally end this ridiculous and sordid little storm in a teacup. I am, sir, etc., Perplexed.'

Pause.

DICKIE. (*Reading over her shoulder.*) 'This correspondence must now cease.—Editor.' Damn!

CATHERINE. Oh, dear! How hopeless it seems, sometimes.

DICKIE. Yes, it does, doesn't it? (*Thoughtfully, after a pause.*) You know, Kate—don't give me away to the old man, will you—but the awful thing is, if it hadn't been my own brother, I think I might quite likely have seen Perplexed's point.

CATHERINE. Might you?

DICKIE. Well, I mean—looking at it from every angle and all that—it does seem rather a much ado about damn all. I mean to say—a mere matter of pinching. (*Bitterly.*) And it's all so beastly expensive. Let's cheer ourselves up with some music. (*He sets machine going.*)

CATHERINE. (*Listening to the record.*) Is that what it's called?

DICKIE. Come and practise a few steps.

CATHERINE *joins him and they dance, in the manner of the period, with arms fully outstretched and working up and down, pump-handle style.*

(*Surprised.*) I say! Jolly good!

CATHERINE. Thank you, Dickie.

DICKIE. Who taught you? John, I suppose.

CATHERINE. No. I taught John, as it happens——

DICKIE. Feminism—even in love?

CATHERINE *nods, smiling. Pause, while they continue to dance.*
When's the happy date now?

CATHERINE. Postponed again.

DICKIE. Oh, no. Why?

CATHERINE. His father's gone abroad for six months.

DICKIE. Why pay any attention to that old—(*He substitutes the word.*)—gentleman?

CATHERINE. I wouldn't—but John does—so I have to.

Something in her tone makes DICKIE *stop dancing and gaze at her seriously.*

DICKIE. I say—nothing wrong, is there?

CATHERINE *shakes her head, smiling, but not too emphatically.*
I mean—you're not going to be left on the altar rails or anything, are you?

CATHERINE. Oh, no. I'll get him past the altar rails, if I have to drag him there.

DICKIE. (*As they resume their dance.*) Do you think you might have to?

CATHERINE. Quite frankly, yes.

DICKIE. Competition?

CATHERINE. Not yet. Only—differences of opinion.

DICKIE. I see. Well, take some advice from an old hand, will you?

CATHERINE. Yes, Dickie.

DICKIE. Suppress your opinions. Men don't like 'em in their lady friends, even if they agree with 'em. And if they don't —it's fatal. Pretend to be half-witted, like Edwina, then he'll adore you.

CATHERINE. I know. I do, sometimes, and then I forget. Still, you needn't worry. If there's ever a clash between what I believe and what I feel, there's not much doubt about which will win.

DICKIE. That's the girl. Of course, I don't know why you didn't fall in love with Ramsay MacDonald——

ARTHUR *comes in. He is walking with more difficulty than when we last saw him.* DICKIE *and* CATHERINE *hastily stop dancing, and* DICKIE *turns off the gramophone.*

CATHERINE. (*Quickly.*) It was entirely my fault, Father. I enticed Dickie from his work to show me a few dance steps.

ARTHUR. Oh? I must admit I am surprised you succeeded.

DICKIE. (*Getting off the subject.*) What did the doctor say, Father?

ARTHUR. He said, if I remember his exact words, that we weren't quite as well as when we last saw each other. That information seems expensive at a guinea. (*Seeing the evening paper.*) Oh, is that the *Star*? Let me see it, please.

CATHERINE *brings it over to him.*

John will be calling for you here, I take it?

CATHERINE. Yes, Father.

ARTHUR. It might be better, perhaps, if you didn't ask him in. This room will shortly be a clutter of journalists, solicitors, barristers, and other impedimenta.

CATHERINE. Is Sir Robert Morton coming to see you here?

ARTHUR. (*Deep in the* Star.) I could hardly go and see him, could I?

DICKIE, *in deference to his father's presence, has returned to his books.* ARTHUR *reads the* Star. CATHERINE *glances at herself in the mirror, and then wanders to the door.*

CATHERINE. I must go and do something about my hair.

DICKIE. What's the matter with your hair?

CATHERINE. Nothing, except I don't like it very much.

She goes out. DICKIE *opens two more books with a busy air and chews his pencil.* ARTHUR *finishes reading the* Star *and stares moodily into space.*

ARTHUR. (*At length.*) I wonder if I could sue "Perplexed".

DICKIE. It might be a way of getting the case into court.

ARTHUR. On the other hand, he has not been libellous. Merely base.

He throws the paper away and regards DICKIE *thoughtfully.*

DICKIE, *feeling his father's eye on him, is elaborately industrious.*

ARTHUR. (*At length, politely.*) Do you mind if I disturb you for a moment?

DICKIE. (*Pushing books away.*) No, Father.

ARTHUR. I want to ask you a question. But before I do I must impress on you the urgent necessity for an absolutely truthful answer.

DICKIE. Naturally.

ARTHUR. Naturally means by nature, and I'm afraid I have not yet noticed that it has invariably been your nature to answer my questions truthfully.

DICKIE. Oh. Well, I will, this one, Father, I promise.

ARTHUR. Very well. (*He stares at him for a moment.*) What do you suppose one of your bookmaker friends would lay in the way of odds against your getting a degree?

Pause.

DICKIE. Oh. Well, let's think. Say—about evens.

ARTHUR. Hm. I rather doubt if at that price your friend would find many takers.

DICKIE. Well—perhaps seven to four against.

ARTHUR. I see. And what about the odds against your eventually becoming a Civil Servant?

DICKIE. Well—a bit steeper, I suppose.

ARTHUR. Exactly. Quite a bit steeper.

Pause.

DICKIE. You don't want to have a bet, do you?

ARTHUR. No, Dickie. I'm not a gambler. And that's exactly the trouble. Unhappily I'm no longer in a position to gamble two hundred pounds a year on what you yourself admit is an outside chance.

DICKIE. Not an outside chance, Father. A good chance.

ARTHUR. Not good enough, Dickie, I'm afraid—with things as they are at the moment. Definitely not good enough. I fear my mind is finally made up.

There is a long pause.

DICKIE. You want me to leave Oxford—is that it?

ARTHUR. I'm very much afraid so, Dickie.

DICKIE. Oh. Straight away?

ARTHUR. No. You can finish your second year

DICKIE. And what then?

ARTHUR. I can get you a job in the bank.

DICKIE. (*Quietly.*) Oh, Lord!

Pause.

ARTHUR. (*Rather apologetically.*) It'll be quite a good job, you
know. Luckily my influence in the bank still counts for
something.

DICKIE *gets up and wanders about, slightly in a daze.*

DICKIE. Father—if I promised you—I mean, *really* promised
you—that from now on I'll work like a black——

ARTHUR *shakes his head slowly.*

It's the case, I suppose?

ARTHUR. It's costing me a lot of money.

DICKIE. I know. It must be. Still, couldn't you—I mean, isn't
there any way——

ARTHUR *again shakes his head.*

Oh, Lord!

ARTHUR. I'm afraid this is rather a shock for you. I'm sorry.

DICKIE. What? No. No, it isn't, really. I've been rather expecting it, as a matter of fact—especially since I've heard you
are hoping to brief Sir Robert Morton. Still, I can't say
but what it isn't a bit of a slap in the face.

There is a ring at the front door.

ARTHUR. There is a journalist coming to see me. Do you mind
if we talk about this some other time?

DICKIE. No. Of course not, Father.

DICKIE *begins forlornly to gather his books.*

ARTHUR. (*With a half-smile.*) I should leave those there, if I
were you.

DICKIE. Yes. I will. Good idea.

He goes to the door.

ARTHUR. (*Politely.*) Tell me—how is your nice friend, Miss
Edwina Gunn, these days?

DICKIE. Very well, thanks awfully.

ARTHUR. You don't suppose she'd mind if you took her to the
theatre—or gave her a little present perhaps?

DICKIE. Oh, I'm sure she wouldn't.

ARTHUR. I'm afraid I can only make it a couple of sovereigns.

ARTHUR *has taken out his sovereign case and now extracts two
sovereigns.* DICKIE *comes and takes them.*

DICKIE. Thanks awfully, Father.

ARTHUR. With what's left over you can always buy something for yourself.

DICKIE. Oh. Well, as a matter of fact, I don't suppose there will be an awful lot left over. Still, it's jolly decent of you— I say, Father—I think I could do with a little spot of something. Would you mind?

ARTHUR. Of course not. You'll find the decanter in the dining-room.

DICKIE. Thanks awfully.

He goes to dining-room door.

ARTHUR. I must thank you, Dickie, for bearing what must have been a very unpleasant blow with some fortitude.

DICKIE. (*Uncomfortably.*) Oh. Rot, Father.

He goes out. ARTHUR *sighs deeply.*

VIOLET *comes in at the hall door.*

VIOLET. (*Announcing proudly.*) The *Daily News*!

MISS BARNES *comes in. She is a rather untidily dressed woman of about forty with a gushing manner.*

MISS BARNES. Mr. Winslow? So good of you to see me.

ARTHUR. How do you do?

MISS BARNES. (*Simpering.*) You're surprised to see a lady reporter? I know. Everyone is. And yet why not? What could be more natural?

ARTHUR. What indeed? Pray sit down——

MISS BARNES. My paper usually sends me out on stories which have a special appeal to women—stories with a little heart, you know, like this one—a father's fight for his little boy's honour——

ARTHUR *visibly winces.*

ARTHUR. I venture to think this case has rather wider implications than that——

MISS BARNES. Oh, yes. The political angle. I know. Very interesting but not *quite* my line of country. Now, what I'd really like to do—is to get a nice picture of you and your little boy together. I've brought my assistant and camera. They're in the hall. Where is your little boy?

ARTHUR. My son is arriving from school in a few minutes. His mother has gone to the station to meet him.

MISS BARNES. (*Making a note.*) From school? How interesting. So you got a school to take him? I mean, they didn't mind the unpleasantness?

ARTHUR. No.

MISS BARNES. And why is he coming back this time?

ARTHUR. He hasn't been expelled again, if that is what you're implying. He is coming to London to be examined by Sir Robert Morton, whom we are hoping to brief——

MISS BARNES. Sir Robert Morton! (*She whistles appreciatively.*) Well!

ARTHUR. Exactly.

MISS BARNES. (*Doubtingly.*) But do you *really* think he'll take a little case like this?

ARTHUR. (*Explosively.*) It is *not* a little case, madam——

MISS BARNES. No, no. Of course not. But still—Sir Robert Morton!

ARTHUR. I understand that he is the best advocate in the country. He is certainly the most expensive——

MISS BARNES. Oh, yes. I suppose if one is prepared to pay his fee one can get him for almost *any* case.

ARTHUR. Once more, madam—this is *not* almost any case——

MISS BARNES. No, no. Of course not. Well, now, perhaps you wouldn't mind giving me a few details. When did it all start?

ARTHUR. Nine months ago. The first I knew of the charge was when my son arrived home with a letter from the Admiralty informing me of his expulsion. I telephoned Osborne to protest and was referred by them to the Lords of the Admiralty. My solicitors then took the matter up, and demanded from the Admiralty the fullest possible inquiry. For weeks we were ignored, then met with a blank refusal, and only finally got reluctant permission to view the evidence.

MISS BARNES. (*Indifferently.*) Really?

ARTHUR. My solicitors decided that the evidence was highly unsatisfactory, and fully justified the re-opening of proceedings. We applied to the Admiralty for a Court Martial. They ignored us. We applied for a civil trial. They ignored us again.

MISS BARNES. They ignored you?

ARTHUR. Yes. But after tremendous pressure had been brought to bear—letters to the papers, questions in the House, and other means open to private citizens of this country—the Admiralty eventually agreed to what they called an independent inquiry.

MISS BARNES. (*Vaguely.*) Oh, good!

ARTHUR. It was not good, madam. At that independent inquiry, conducted by the Judge Advocate of the Fleet—against whom I am saying nothing, mind you—my son,—a child of fourteen, was not represented by counsel, solicitors, or friends. What do you think of that?

MISS BARNES. Fancy!

ARTHUR. You may well say fancy.

MISS BARNES. And what happened at the inquiry?

ARTHUR. What do you think happened? Inevitably he was found guilty again, and thus branded for the second time before the world as a thief and a forger——

MISS BARNES. (*Her attention wandering.*) What a shame!

ARTHUR. I need hardly tell you, madam, that I am not prepared to let the matter rest there. I shall continue to fight this monstrous injustice with every weapon and every means at my disposal. Now, it happens I have a plan——

MISS BARNES. Oh, what charming curtains! What are they made of? (*She rises and goes to window.*)

ARTHUR *sits for a moment in paralysed silence.*

ARTHUR (*At last.*) Madam—I fear I have no idea.

There is the sound of voices in the hall.

MISS BARNES. Ah. Do I hear the poor little chap himself?

The hall door opens and RONNIE *comes in boisterously, followed by* GRACE. *He is evidently in the highest of spirits.*

RONNIE. Hullo, Father! (*He runs to him.*)

ARTHUR. Hullo. Ronnie.

RONNIE. I say, Father! Mr. Moore says I'm to tell you I needn't come back until Monday if you like. So that gives me three whole days.

ARTHUR. Mind my leg!

RONNIE. Sorry, Father.

ARTHUR. How are you, my boy?

RONNIE. Oh, I'm absolutely tophole, Father. Mother says I've grown an inch——

MISS BARNES. Ah! Now that's exactly the way I'd like to take my picture. Would you hold it, Mr. Winslow? (*She goes to hall door and calls.*) Fred! Come in now, will you?

RONNIE. (*In a sibilant whisper.*) Who's she?

FRED *appears. He is a listless photographer, complete with apparatus.*

FRED. (*Gloomily.*) Afternoon, all.

MISS BARNES. That's the pose I suggest.

FRED. Yes. It'll do.

He begins to set up his apparatus. ARTHUR, *holding* RONNIE *close against him in the pose suggested, turns his head to* GRACE.

ARTHUR. Grace, dear, this lady is from the *Daily News*. She is extremely interested in your curtains.

GRACE. (*Delighted.*) Oh, really! How nice!

MISS BARNES. Yes, indeed. I was wondering what they were made of.

GRACE. Well, it's an entirely new material, you know. I'm afraid I don't know what it's called, but I got them at Barkers last year. Apparently it's a sort of mixture of wild silk and——

MISS BARNES. (*Now genuinely busy with her pencil and pad.*) Just a second, Mrs. Winslow. I'm afraid my shorthand isn't very good. I must just get that down——

RONNIE. (*To* ARTHUR.) Father, are we going to be in the *Daily News*?

ARTHUR. It appears so——

RONNIE. Oh, good! They get the *Daily News* in the school library and everyone's bound to see it——

FRED. Quite still, please——

He takes his photograph.

All right, Miss Barnes. (*He goes out.*)

MISS BARNES. (*Engrossed with* GRACE.) Thank you, Fred. (*To* ARTHUR.) Goodbye, Mr. Winslow, and the very best of good fortune in your inspiring fight. (*Turning to* RONNIE.) Goodbye, little chap. Remember, the darkest hour is just before the dawn. Well, it was very good of you to tell me

P

all that, Mrs. Winslow. I'm sure our readers will be most interested.

GRACE *shows her out.*

RONNIE. What's she talking about?

ARTHUR. The case, I imagine.

RONNIE. Oh, the case. Father, do you know the train had fourteen coaches?

ARTHUR. Did it indeed?

RONNIE. Yes. All corridor.

ARTHUR. Remarkable.

RONNIE. Of course, it was one of the very biggest expresses. I walked all the way down it from one end to the other.

ARTHUR. I had your half-term report, Ronnie.

RONNIE. (*Suddenly silenced by perturbation.*) Oh, yes?

ARTHUR. On the whole it was pretty fair.

RONNIE. Oh, good.

ARTHUR. I'm glad you seem to be settling down so well. Very glad indeed.

GRACE *comes in.*

GRACE. What a charming woman, Arthur!

ARTHUR. Charming. I trust you gave her full details about our curtains?

GRACE. Oh, yes. I told her everything.

ARTHUR. (*Wearily.*) I'm so glad.

GRACE. I do think women reporters are a good idea——

RONNIE. (*Excitedly.*) I say, Father, will it be all right for me to stay still Monday? I mean, I won't be missing any work—only Divinity—— (*He jogs his father's leg again.*)

ARTHUR. Mind my leg!

RONNIE. Oh, sorry, Father. Is it bad?

ARTHUR. Yes, it is. (*To* GRACE.) Grace, take him upstairs and get him washed. Sir Robert will be here in a few minutes.

GRACE. (*To* RONNIE.) Come on, darling.

RONNIE. All right. (*On his way to the door with his mother.*) I say, do you know how long the train took? 123 miles in two hours and fifty-two minutes. That's an average of 46.73 recurring miles an hour—I worked it out. Violet! Violet! I'm back.

He disappears, still chattering shrilly.

GRACE *stops at the door.*

GRACE. Did the doctor say anything, dear?

ARTHUR. A great deal; but very little to the purpose.

GRACE. Violet says he left an ointment for your back. Four massages a day. Is that right?

ARTHUR. Something of the kind.

GRACE. I think you had better have one now, hadn't you, Arthur?

ARTHUR. No.

GRACE. But, dear, you've got plenty of time before Sir Robert comes, and if you don't have one now, you won't be able to have another before you go to bed.

ARTHUR. Precisely.

GRACE. But really, Arthur, it does seem awfully silly to spend all this money on doctors if you're not even going to do what they say.

ARTHUR. *(Impatiently.)* All right, Grace. All right. All right.

GRACE. Thank you, dear.

CATHERINE *comes in.*

CATHERINE. Ronnie's back, judging by the noise——

GRACE. *(Examining her.)* I must say that old frock has come out very well. John'll never know it isn't brand new——

CATHERINE. He's late, curse him.

ARTHUR. Grace, go on up and attend to Ronnie, and prepare the witch's brew for me. I'll come up when you are ready.

GRACE. Very well, dear. *(To CATHERINE.)* Yes, that does look good. I must say Mme Dupont's a treasure.

She goes out.

ARTHUR. *(Wearily.)* Oh, Kate, Kate! Are we both mad, you and I?

CATHERINE. What's the matter, Father?

ARTHUR. I don't know. I suddenly feel suicidally inclined. *(Bitterly.)* A father's fight for his little boy's honour. Special appeal to all women. Photo inset of Mrs. Winslow's curtains! Is there any hope for the world?

CATHERINE. *(Smiling.)* I think so, Father.

ARTHUR. Shall we drop the whole thing, Kate?

CATHERINE. I don't consider that a serious question, Father.

ARTHUR. (*Slowly.*) You realize that, if we go on, your marriage settlement must go?

CATHERINE. (*Lightly.*) Oh, yes. I gave that up for lost weeks ago.

ARTHUR. Things are all right between you and John, aren't they?

CATHERINE. Oh, yes, Father, of course. Everything's perfect.

ARTHUR. I mean—it won't make any difference between you, will it?

CATHERINE. Good heavens, no!

ARTHUR. Very well, then. Let us pin our faith to Sir Robert Morton.

CATHERINE *is silent.* ARTHUR *looks at her as if he had expected an answer, then nods.*

I see I'm speaking only for myself in saying that.

CATHERINE. (*Lightly.*) You know what I think of Sir Robert Morton, Father. Don't let's go into it again, now. It's too late, anyway.

ARTHUR. It's not too late. He hasn't accepted the brief yet.

CATHERINE. (*Shortly.*) Then I'm rather afraid I hope he never does. And that has nothing to do with my marriage settlement either.

Pause. ARTHUR *looks angry for a second, then subsides.*

ARTHUR. (*Mildly.*) I made inquiries about that fellow you suggested—I am told he is not nearly as good an advocate as Morton——

CATHERINE. He's not nearly so fashionable.

ARTHUR. (*Doubtfully.*) I want the best——

CATHERINE. The best in this case certainly isn't Morton.

ARTHUR. Then why does everyone say he is?

CATHERINE. (*Roused.*) Because if one happens to be a large monopoly attacking a Trade Union or a Tory paper libelling a Labour Leader, he *is* the best. But it utterly defeats me how you or anyone else could expect a man of his record to have even a tenth of his heart in a case where the boot is entirely on the other foot——

ARTHUR. Well, I imagine, if his heart isn't in it, he won't accept the brief.

CATHERINE. He might still. It depends what there is in it for him. Luckily there isn't much——

ARTHUR. (*Bitterly.*) There is a fairly substantial cheque——

CATHERINE. He doesn't want money. He must be a very rich man.

ARTHUR. What does he want, then?

CATHERINE. Anything that advances his interests.

ARTHUR *shrugs his shoulders. Pause.*

ARTHUR. I believe you are prejudiced because he spoke against woman's suffrage.

CATHERINE. I am. I'm prejudiced because he is always speaking against what is right and just. Did you read his speech in the House on the Trades Disputes Bill?

GRACE. (*Calling off.*) Arthur! Arthur!

ARTHUR. (*Smiling.*) Oh, well—in the words of the Prime Minister—let us wait and see.

He turns at the door. You're my only ally, Kate. Without you I believe I should have given up long ago.

CATHERINE. Rubbish.

ARTHUR. It's true. Still, you must sometimes allow me to make my own decisions. I have an instinct about Morton.

CATHERINE *does not reply.*

(*Doubtfully.*) We'll see which is right—my instinct or your reason, eh?

He goes out.

CATHERINE. (*Half to herself.*) I'm afraid we will.

DICKIE *comes out of the dining-room door.*

DICKIE. (*Bitterly.*) Hullo, Kate.

CATHERINE. Hullo, Dickie.

DICKIE *crosses mournfully to the other door.*

What's the matter? Edwina jilted you or something?

DICKIE. Haven't you heard?

CATHERINE *shakes her head.*

I'm being scratched from the Oxford Stakes at the end of the year——

CATHERINE. Oh, Dickie! I'm awfully sorry——

DICKIE. Did you know it was in the wind?

CATHERINE. I knew there was a risk——

DICKIE. You might have warned a fellow. I fell plumb into the old man's trap. My gosh, I could just about murder that little brother of mine. (*Bitterly.*) What's he have to go about pinching postal orders for? And why the hell does he have to get himself nabbed doing it? Silly little blighter!

He goes out gloomily. There is a ring at the front-door. CATHERINE, *obviously believing it is* JOHN, *picks up her cloak and goes to the hall door.*

CATHERINE. (*Calling.*) All right, Violet. It's only Mr. Watherstone. I'll answer it.

She goes out. There is the sound of voices in the hall, and then CATHERINE *reappears, leading in* DESMOND *and* SIR ROBERT MORTON. SIR ROBERT *is a man in the early forties, cadaverous and immensely elegant. He wears a long overcoat, and carries his hat and stick. He looks rather a fop, and his supercilious expression bears out this view.*

(*As she re-enters.*) I'm so sorry. I was expecting a friend. Won't you sit down, Sir Robert! My father won't be long.

SIR ROBERT *bows slightly, and sits down on a hard chair, still in his overcoat.*

Won't you sit here? It's far more comfortable.

SIR ROBERT. No, thank you.

DESMOND. (*Fussing.*) Sir Robert has a most important dinner engagement, so we came a little early.

CATHERINE. I see.

DESMOND. I'm afraid he can only spare us a very few minutes of his most valuable time this evening. Of course, it's a long way for him to come—so far from his chambers—and very good of him to do it, too, if I may say so——

He bows to SIR ROBERT, *who bows slightly back.*

CATHERINE. I know. I can assure you we're very conscious of it.

SIR ROBERT *gives her a quick look, and a faint smile.*

DESMOND. Perhaps I had better advise your father of our presence——

CATHERINE. Yes, do, Desmond. You'll find him in his bedroom —having his back rubbed.

DESMOND. Oh. I see.

He goes out. There is a pause.

CATHERINE. Is there anything I can get you, Sir Robert? A whisky and soda or a brandy?

SIR ROBERT. No, thank you.

CATHERINE. Will you smoke?

SIR ROBERT. No, thank you.

CATHERINE. (*Holding her cigarette.*) I hope you don't mind me smoking?

SIR ROBERT. Why should I?

CATHERINE. Some people find it shocking.

SIR ROBERT. (*Indifferently.*) A lady in her own home is surely entitled to behave as she wishes.

Pause.

CATHERINE. Won't you take your coat off, Sir Robert?

SIR ROBERT. No, thank you.

CATHERINE. You find it cold in here? I'm sorry.

SIR ROBERT. It's perfectly all right.

Conversation languishes again. SIR ROBERT *looks at his watch.*

CATHERINE. What time are you dining?

SIR ROBERT. Eight o'clock.

CATHERINE. Far from here?

SIR ROBERT. Devonshire House.

CATHERINE. Oh. Then of course you mustn't on any account be late.

SIR ROBERT. No.

There is another pause.

CATHERINE. I suppose you know the history of this case, do you, Sir Robert?

SIR ROBERT. (*Examining his nails.*) I believe I have seen most of the relevant documents.

CATHERINE. Do you think we can bring the case into Court by a collusive action?

SIR ROBERT. I really have no idea——

CATHERINE. Curry and Curry seem to think that might hold——

SIR ROBERT. Do they? They are a very reliable firm.

Pause. CATHERINE *is on the verge of losing her temper.*

CATHERINE. I'm rather surprised that a case of this sort should interest you, Sir Robert.

SIR ROBERT. Are you?

CATHERINE. It seems such a very trivial affair, compared to most of your great forensic triumphs.

SIR ROBERT, *staring languidly at the ceiling, does not reply.*

I was in Court during your cross-examination of Len Rogers, in the Trades Union embezzlement case.

SIR ROBERT. Really?

CATHERINE. It was masterly.

SIR ROBERT. Thank you.

CATHERINE. I suppose you heard that he committed suicide a few months ago?

SIR ROBERT. Yes. I had heard.

CATHERINE. Many people believed him innocent, you know.

SIR ROBERT. So I understand. (*After a faint pause.*) As it happens, however, he was guilty.

GRACE *comes in hastily.*

GRACE. Sir Robert? My husband's so sorry to have kept you, but he's just coming.

SIR ROBERT. It's perfectly all right. How do you do?

CATHERINE. Sir Robert is dining at Devonshire House, Mother.

GRACE. Oh, really? Oh, then you have to be punctual, of course, I do see that. It's the politeness of princes, isn't it?

SIR ROBERT. So they say.

GRACE. In this case the other way round, of course. Ah, I think I hear my husband on the stairs. I hope Catherine entertained you all right?

SIR ROBERT. (*With a faint bow to* CATHERINE.) Very well, thank you.

ARTHUR *comes in, followed by* DESMOND.

ARTHUR. Sir Robert? I am Arthur Winslow.

SIR ROBERT. How do you do?

ARTHUR. I understand you are rather pressed for time.

GRACE. Yes. He's dining at Devonshire House——

ARTHUR. Are you indeed? My son should be down in a minute. I expect you will wish to examine him.

SIR ROBERT. (*Indifferently.*) Just a few questions. I fear that is all I will have time for this evening——

ARTHUR. I am rather sorry to hear that. He has made the journey especially from school for this interview and I was hoping that by the end of it I should know definitely yes or no if you would accept the brief.

DESMOND. (*Pacifically.*) Well, perhaps Sir Robert would consent to finish his examination some other time?

SIR ROBERT. It might be arranged.

ARTHUR. Tomorrow?

SIR ROBERT. Tomorrow is impossible. I am in Court all the morning and in the House of Commons for the rest of the day. (*Carelessly.*) If a further examination should prove necessary it will have to be some time next week.

ARTHUR. I see. Will you forgive me if I sit down. (*He sits in his usual chair.*) Curry has been telling me you think it might be possible to proceed by Petition of Right.

CATHERINE. What's a Petition of Right?

DESMOND. Well—granting the assumption that the Admiralty, as the Crown, can do no wrong——

CATHERINE. (*Murmuring.*) I thought that was exactly the assumption we refused to grant.

DESMOND. In law, I mean. Now, a subject can sue the Crown, nevertheless, by Petition of Right, redress being granted as a matter of grace—and the custom is for the Attorney-General—on behalf of the King—to endorse the Petition, and allow the case to come to Court.

SIR ROBERT. It is interesting to note that the exact words he uses on such occasions are: Let Right be done.

ARTHUR. Let Right be done? I like that phrase, sir.

SIR ROBERT. It has a certain ring about it—has it not? (*Languidly.*) Let Right be done.

RONNIE *comes in. He is in an Eton suit, looking very spick and span.*

ARTHUR. This is my son Ronald. Ronnie, this is Sir Robert Morton.

RONNIE. How do you do, sir?

ARTHUR. He is going to ask you a few questions. You must answer them all truthfully—as you always have. (*He begins to struggle out of his chair.*) I expect you would like us to leave——

SIR ROBERT. No. Provided, of course, that you don't interrupt.

(*To* CATHERINE.) Miss Winslow, will you sit down, please?
CATHERINE *takes a seat abruptly.*

SIR ROBERT. (*To* RONNIE.) Will you stand at the table, facing
me? (RONNIE *does so.*) That's right.

SIR ROBERT *and* RONNIE *now face each other across the table.* SIR
ROBERT *begins his examination very quietly.*

Now, Ronald, how old are you?

RONNIE. Fourteen and seven months.

SIR ROBERT. You were, then, thirteen and ten months old
when you left Osborne: is that right?

RONNIE. Yes, sir.

SIR ROBERT. Now I would like you to cast your mind back to
July 7th of last year. Will you tell me in your own words
exactly what happened to you on that day?

RONNIE. All right. Well, it was a half-holiday, so we didn't
have any work after dinner——

SIR ROBERT. Dinner? At one o'clock?

RONNIE. Yes. At least, until prep at seven.

SIR ROBERT. Prep at seven?

RONNIE. Just before dinner I went to the Chief Petty Officer
and asked him to let me have fifteen and six out of what I
had in the school bank——

SIR ROBERT. Why did you do that?

RONNIE. I wanted to buy an air pistol.

SIR ROBERT. Which cost fifteen and six?

RONNIE. Yes, sir.

SIR ROBERT. And how much money did you have in the school
bank at the time?

RONNIE. Two pounds three shillings.

ARTHUR. So you see, sir, what incentive could there possibly
be for him to steal five shillings?

SIR ROBERT. (*Coldly.*) I must ask you to be good enough not to
interrupt me, sir. (*To* RONNIE.) After you had withdrawn
the fifteen and six what did you do?

RONNIE. I had dinner.

SIR ROBERT. Then what?

RONNIE. I went to the locker-room and put the fifteen and six
in my locker.

SIR ROBERT. Yes. Then?

RONNIE. I went to get permission to go down to the Post Office. Then I went to the locker-room again, got out my money, and went down to the Post Office.

SIR ROBERT. I see. Go on.

RONNIE. I bought my postal order——

SIR ROBERT. For fifteen and six?

RONNIE. Yes. Then I went back to college. Then I met Elliot minor, and he said: 'I say, isn't it rot? Someone's broken into my locker and pinched a postal order. I've reported it to the P.O.'

SIR ROBERT. Those were Elliot minor's exact words?

RONNIE. He might have used another word for rot——

SIR ROBERT. I see. Continue——

RONNIE. Well, then just before prep I was told to go along and see Commander Flower. The woman from the Post Office was there, and the Commander said: 'Is this the boy?' and she said: 'It might be. I can't be sure. They all look so much alike.'

ARTHUR. You see? She couldn't identify him.

SIR ROBERT *glares at him.*

SIR ROBERT. (*To* RONNIE.) Go on.

RONNIE. Then she said: 'I only know that the boy who bought a postal order for fifteen and six was the same boy that cashed one for five shillings.' So the Commander said: 'Did you buy a postal order for fifteen and six?' And I said: 'Yes', and then they made me write Elliot minor's name on an envelope, and compared it to the signature on the postal order—then they sent me to the sanatorium and ten days later I was sacked—I mean—expelled.

SIR ROBERT. I see. (*Quietly.*) Did you cash a postal order belonging to Elliot minor for five shillings?

RONNIE. No, sir.

SIR ROBERT. Did you break into his locker and steal it?

RONNIE. No, sir.

SIR ROBERT. And that is the truth, the whole truth, and nothing but the truth?

RONNIE. Yes, sir.

DICKIE *has come in during this, and is standing furtively in the doorway, not knowing whether to come in or go out.* ARTHUR *waves him impatiently to a seat.*

SIR ROBERT. Right. When the Commander asked you to write Elliot's name on an envelope, how did you write it? With Christian name or initials?

RONNIE. I wrote Charles K. Elliot.

SIR ROBERT. Charles K. Elliot. Did you by any chance happen to see the forged postal order in the Commander's office?

RONNIE. Oh, yes. The Commander showed it to me.

SIR ROBERT. Before or after you had written Elliot's name on the envelope?

RONNIE. After.

SIR ROBERT. After. And did you happen to see how Elliot's name was written on the postal order?

RONNIE. Yes, sir. The same.

SIR ROBERT. The same? Charles K. Elliot?

RONNIE. Yes, sir.

SIR ROBERT. When you wrote on the envelope, what made you choose that particular form?

RONNIE. That was the way he usually signed his name——

SIR ROBERT. How did you know?

RONNIE. Well—he was a great friend of mine——

SIR ROBERT. That is no answer. How did you know?

RONNIE. I'd seen him sign things.

SIR ROBERT. What things?

RONNIE. Oh—ordinary things.

SIR ROBERT. I repeat: what things?

RONNIE. (*Reluctantly.*) Bits of paper.

SIR ROBERT. Bits of paper? And why did he sign his name on bits of paper?

RONNIE. I don't know.

SIR ROBERT. You do know. Why did he sign his name on bits of paper?

RONNIE. He was practising his signature.

SIR ROBERT. And you saw him?

RONNIE. Yes.

SIR ROBERT. Did he know you saw him?

RONNIE. Well—yes——

SIR ROBERT. In other words he showed you exactly how he wrote his signature?

RONNIE. Yes. I suppose he did.

SIR ROBERT. Did you practise writing it yourself?

RONNIE. I might have done.

SIR ROBERT. What do you mean you might have done? Did you or did you not?

RONNIE. Yes——

ARTHUR. (*Sharply.*) Ronnie! You never told me that.

RONNIE. It was only for a joke——

SIR ROBERT. Never mind whether it was for a joke or not. The fact is you practised forging Elliot's signature——

RONNIE. It wasn't forging——

SIR ROBERT. What do you call it then?

RONNIE. Writing.

SIR ROBERT. Very well. Writing. Whoever stole the postal order and cashed it also *wrote* Elliot's signature, didn't he?

RONNIE. Yes.

SIR ROBERT. And, oddly enough, in the exact form in which you had earlier been practising *writing* his signature——

RONNIE. (*Indignantly.*) I say. Which side are you on?

SIR ROBERT. (*Snarling.*) Don't be impertinent! Are you aware that the Admiralty sent up the forged postal order to Mr. Ridgely-Pearce—the greatest handwriting expert in England?

RONNIE. Yes.

SIR ROBERT. And you know that Mr. Ridgeley-Pearce affirmed that there was no doubt that the signature on the postal order and the signature you wrote on the envelope were by one and the same hand?

RONNIE. Yes.

SIR ROBERT. And you still say that you didn't forge that signature?

RONNIE. Yes, I do.

SIR ROBERT. In other words, Mr. Ridgeley-Pearce doesn't know his job?

RONNIE. Well, he's wrong anyway.

SIR ROBERT. When you went into the locker-room after dinner, were you alone?

RONNIE. I don't remember.

SIR ROBERT. I think you do. Were you alone in the locker-room?

RONNIE. Yes.

SIR ROBERT. And you knew which was Elliot's locker?

RONNIE. Yes. Of course.

SIR ROBERT. Why did you go in there at all?

RONNIE. I've told you. To put my fifteen and six away.

SIR ROBERT. Why?

RONNIE. I thought it would be safer.

SIR ROBERT. Why safer than your pocket?

RONNIE. I don't know.

SIR ROBERT. You had it in your pocket at dinner-time. Why this sudden fear for its safety?

RONNIE. (*Plainly rattled.*) I tell you, I don't know——

SIR ROBERT. It was rather an odd thing to do, wasn't it? The money was perfectly safe in your pocket. Why did you suddenly feel yourself impelled to put it away in your locker?

RONNIE. (*Almost shouting.*) I don't know.

SIR ROBERT. Was it because you knew you would be alone in the locker-room at that time?

RONNIE. No.

SIR ROBERT. Where was Elliot's locker in relation to yours?

RONNIE. Next to it, but one.

SIR ROBERT. Next, but one. What time did Elliot put his postal order in his locker?

RONNIE. I don't know. I didn't even know he had a postal order in his locker. I didn't know he had a postal order at all——

SIR ROBERT. Yet you say he was a great friend of yours——

RONNIE. He didn't tell me he had one.

SIR ROBERT. How very secretive of him! What time did you go to the locker-room?

RONNIE. I don't remember.

SIR ROBERT. Was it directly after dinner?

RONNIE. Yes. I think so.

SIR ROBERT. What did you do after leaving the locker-room?

RONNIE. I've told you. I went for permission to go to the Post Office.

SIR ROBERT. What time was that?

RONNIE. About a quarter past two.

SIR ROBERT. Dinner is over at a quarter to two. Which means that you were in the locker-room for half an hour?

RONNIE. I wasn't there all that time——

SIR ROBERT. How long were you there?

RONNIE. About five minutes.

SIR ROBERT. What were you doing for the other twenty-five?

RONNIE. I don't remember.

SIR ROBERT. It's odd that your memory is so good about some things and so bad about others——

RONNIE. Perhaps I waited outside the C.O.'s office.

SIR ROBERT. (*With searing sarcasm.*) Perhaps you waited outside the C.O.'s office! And perhaps no one saw you there either?

RONNIE. No. I don't think they did.

SIR ROBERT. What were you thinking about outside the C.O.'s office for twenty-five minutes?

RONNIE. (*Wildly.*) I don't even know if I was there. I can't remember. Perhaps I wasn't there at all.

SIR ROBERT. No. Perhaps you were still in the locker-room rifling Elliot's locker——

ARTHUR. (*Indignantly.*) Sir Robert, I must ask you——

SIR ROBERT. Quiet!

RONNIE. I remember now. I remember. Someone did see me outside the C.O.'s office. A chap called Casey. I remember I spoke to him.

SIR ROBERT. What did you say?

RONNIE. I said: 'Come down to the Post Office with me. I'm going to cash a postal order.'

SIR ROBERT. (*Triumphantly.*) *Cash* a postal order.

RONNIE. I mean get.

SIR ROBERT. You said cash. Why did you say cash if you meant get.

RONNIE. I don't know.

SIR ROBERT. I suggest cash was the truth.

RONNIE. No, no. It wasn't. It wasn't really. You're muddling me.

SIR ROBERT. You seem easily muddled. How many other lies have you told?

RONNIE. None. Really I haven't——

SIR ROBERT. (*Bending forward malevolently.*) I suggest your whole testimony is a lie——

RONNIE. No! It's the truth——

SIR ROBERT. I suggest there is barely one single word of truth in anything you have said either to me, or to the Judge Advocate, or to the Commander, I suggest that you broke into Elliot's locker, that you stole the postal order for five shillings belonging to Elliot, that you cashed it by means of forging his name——

RONNIE. (*Wailing.*) I didn't. I didn't.

SIR ROBERT. I suggest that you did it for a joke, meaning to give Elliot the five shillings back, but that when you met him and he said he had reported the matter you got frightened and decided to keep quiet——

RONNIE. No, no, no. It isn't true——

SIR ROBERT. I suggest that by continuing to deny your guilt you are causing great hardship to your own family, and considerable annoyance to high and important persons in this country——

CATHERINE. (*On her feet.*) That's a disgraceful thing to say!

ARTHUR. I agree.

SIR ROBERT. (*Leaning forward and glaring at* RONNIE *with the utmost venom.*) I suggest, that the time has at last come for you to undo some of the misery you have caused by confessing to us all now that you are a forger, a liar, and a thief!

RONNIE. (*In tears.*) I'm not! I'm not! I'm not! I didn't do it——

GRACE *has flown to his side and now envelops him.*

ARTHUR. This is outrageous, sir——

JOHN *appears at the door, dressed in evening clothes.*

JOHN. Kate, dear, I'm late. I'm most terribly sorry——

He stops short as he takes in the scene, with RONNIE *sobbing hysteri-cally on his mother's breast, and* ARTHUR *and* CATHERINE *glaring indignantly at* SIR ROBERT, *who is engaged in putting his papers together.*

SIR ROBERT. (*To* DESMOND.) Can I drop you anywhere? My car is at the door.

DESMOND. Er—no—I thank you——

SIR ROBERT. (*Carelessly.*) Well, send all this stuff round to my chambers tomorrow morning, will you?

DESMOND. But—but will you need it now?

SIR ROBERT. Oh, yes. The boy is plainly innocent. I accept the brief.

He bows to ARTHUR *and* CATHERINE *and walks languidly to the door, past the bewildered* JOHN, *to whom he gives a polite nod as he goes out.* RONNIE *continues to sob hysterically.*

CURTAIN

ACT III

SCENE: *The same, nine months later. The time is about ten-thirty p.m.*

ARTHUR *is sitting in his favourite armchair, reading aloud from an evening paper, whose wide headline:* 'WINSLOW DEBATE: FIRST LORD REPLIES' *we can read on the front page. Listening to him are* RONNIE *and* GRACE, *though neither of them seems to be doing so with much concentration.* RONNIE *is finding it hard to keep his eyes open, and* GRACE, *darning socks in the other armchair, has evidently other and, to her, more important matters on her mind.*

ARTHUR. (*Reading.*) —'The Admiralty, during the whole of this long-drawn-out dispute, have at no time acted hastily or ill-advisedly, and it is a matter of mere histrionic hyperbole for the right honourable and learned gentleman opposite to characterize the conduct of my department as that of callousness so inhuman as to amount to deliberate malice towards the boy Winslow. Such unfounded accusations I can well choose to ignore. (An honourable Member: "You can't.") Honourable Members opposite may interrupt as much as they please, but I repeat—there is nothing whatever that the Admiralty has done, or failed to do, in the case of this cadet for which I, as First Lord, need to apologize. (Further Opposition interruptions.)' (*He stops reading and looks up.*) I must say it looks as if the First Lord's having rather a rough passage—— (*He breaks off, noticing* RONNIE'S *head has fallen back on the cushions and he is asleep.*) I trust my reading isn't keeping you awake. (*There is no answer.*) I say I trust my reading isn't keeping you awake! (*Again there is no answer. Helplessly.*) Grace!

GRACE. My poor sleepy little lamb! It's long past his bedtime, Arthur.

ARTHUR. Grace, dear—at this very moment your poor sleepy little lamb is the subject of a very violent and heated debate

410

in the House of Commons. I should have thought, in the circumstances, it might have been possible for him to contrive to stay awake for a few minutes past his bedtime——

GRACE. I expect he's over-excited.

ARTHUR *and* GRACE *both look at the tranquilly oblivious form on the sofa.*

ARTHUR. A picture of over-excitement. (*Sharply.*) Ronnie! (*No answer.*) Ronnie!

RONNIE. (*Opening his eyes.*) Yes, Father?

ARTHUR. I am reading the account of the debate. Would you like to listen, or would you rather go to bed?

RONNIE. Oh, I'd like to listen, of course, Father. I was listening, too, only I had my eyes shut——

ARTHUR. Very well. (*Reading.*) 'The First Lord continued amid further interruptions: The chief point of criticism against the Admiralty appears to centre in the purely legal question of the Petition of Right brought by Mr. Arthur Winslow and the Admiralty's demurrer thereto. Sir Robert Morton has made great play with his eloquent reference to the liberty of the individual menaced, as he puts it, by the new despotism of bureaucracy—and I was as moved as any honourable Member opposite by his resonant use of the words: Let Right be done—the time-honoured phrase with which in his opinion the Attorney-General should without question have endorsed Mr. Winslow's Petition of Right. Nevertheless, the matter is not nearly as simple as he appears to imagine. Cadet Ronald Winslow is a servant of the Crown, and has therefore no more right than any other member of His Majesty's forces to sue the Crown in open court. To allow him to do so would undoubtedly raise the most dangerous precedents. There is no doubt whatever in my mind that in certain cases private rights may have to be sacrificed for the public good——' (*He looks up.*) And what other excuse, pray, did Charles the First make for ship money and——'

RONNIE, *after a manful attempt to keep his eyes open by self-pinchings and other devices, has once more succumbed to oblivion.*

(*Sharply.*) Ronnie! Ronnie!

RONNIE *stirs, turns over, and slides more comfortably into the cushions.* Would you believe it!

GRACE. He's dead tired. I'd better take him up to his bed——

ARTHUR. No. If he must sleep, let him sleep there.

GRACE. Oh, but he'd be much more comfy in his little bed——

ARTHUR. I dare say: but the debate continues and until it's ended the cause of it all will certainly not make himself comfy in his little bed.

VIOLET *comes in.*

VIOLET. There are three more reporters in the hall, sir. Want to see you very urgently. Shall I let them in?

ARTHUR. No. Certainly not. I issued a statement yesterday. Until the debate is over I have nothing more to say. .

VIOLET. Yes, sir. That's what I told them, but they wouldn't go.

ARTHUR. Well, make them. Use force, if necessary.

VIOLET. Yes, sir. And shall I cut some sandwiches for Miss Catherine, as she missed her dinner?

GRACE. Yes, Violet. Good idea.

VIOLET *goes out.*

VIOLET. (*Off.*) It's no good. No more statements.

Voices answer her, fading at length into silence. GRACE *puts a rug over* RONNIE, *now sleeping very soundly.*

ARTHUR. Grace, dear——

GRACE. Yes?

ARTHUR. I fancy this might be a good opportunity of talking to Violet.

GRACE. (*Quite firmly.*) No, dear.

ARTHUR. Meaning that it isn't a good opportunity? Or meaning that you have no intention at all of ever talking to Violet?

GRACE. I'll do it one day, Arthur. Tomorrow, perhaps. Not now.

ARTHUR. I believe you'd do better to grasp the nettle. Delay only adds to your worries——

GRACE. (*Bitterly.*) My worries? What do you know about my worries?

ARTHUR. A good deal, Grace. But I feel they would be a lot lessened if you faced the situation squarely.

GRACE. It's easy for you to talk, Arthur. You don't have to do it.

ARTHUR. I will, if you like.

GRACE. No, dear.

ARTHUR. If you explain the dilemma to her carefully—if you even show her the figures I jotted down for you yesterday —I venture to think you won't find her unreasonable.

GRACE. It won't be easy for her to find another place.

ARTHUR. We'll give her an excellent reference.

GRACE. That won't alter the fact that she's never been properly trained as a parlourmaid and—well—you know yourself how we're always having to explain her to people. No, Arthur, I don't mind how many figures she's shown, it's a brutal thing to do.

ARTHUR. Facts are brutal things.

GRACE. (*A shade hysterically.*) Facts? I don't think I know what facts are any more——

ARTHUR. The facts, at this moment, are that we have a half of the income we had a year ago and we're living at nearly the same rate. However you look at it that's bad economics——

GRACE. I'm not talking about economics, Arthur. I'm talking about ordinary, common or garden facts—things we took for granted a year ago and which now don't seem to matter any more.

ARTHUR. Such as?

GRACE. (*With rising voice.*) Such as a happy home and peace and quiet and an ordinary respectable life, and some sort of future for us and our children. In the last year you've thrown all that overboard, Arthur. There's your return for it, I suppose. (*She indicates the headline in the paper.*) And it's all very exciting and important, I'm sure, but it doesn't bring back any of the things that we've lost. I can only pray to God that you know what you're doing.

RONNIE *stirs in his sleep.* GRACE *lowers her voice at the end of her speech. There is a pause.*

ARTHUR. I know exactly what I'm doing, Grace. I'm going to publish my son's innocence before the world, and for that end I am not prepared to weigh the cost.

GRACE. But the cost may be out of all proportion——

ARTHUR. It may be. That doesn't concern me. I hate heroics, Grace, but you force me to say this. An injustice has been done. I am going to set it right, and there is no sacrifice in the world I am not prepared to make in order to do so.

GRACE. (*With sudden violence.*) Oh, I wish I could see the sense of it all! (*Pointing to* RONNIE.) He's perfectly happy, at a good school, doing very well. No one need ever have known about Osborne, if you hadn't gone and shouted it out to the whole world. As it is, whatever happens now, he'll go through the rest of his life as the boy in that Winslow case —the boy who stole that postal order——

ARTHUR. (*Grimly.*) The boy who didn't steal that postal order.

GRACE. (*Wearily.*) What's the difference? When millions are talking and gossiping about him, a did or a didn't hardly matters. The Winslow boy is enough. You talk about sacrificing everything for him: but when he's grown up he won't thank you for it, Arthur—even though you've given your life to—publish his innocence as you call it.

ARTHUR *makes an impatient gesture.*

Yes, Arthur—your life. You talk gaily about arthritis and a touch of gout and old age and the rest of it, but you know as well as any of the doctors what really is the matter with you. (*Nearly in tears.*) You're destroying yourself, Arthur, and me and your family besides. For what, I'd like to know? I've asked you and Kate to tell me a hundred times but you never will. For what, Arthur?

ARTHUR *has struggled painfully out of his seat and now approaches her.*

ARTHUR. (*Quietly.*) For Justice, Grace.

GRACE. That sounds very noble. Are you sure it's true? Are you sure it isn't just plain pride and self-importance and sheer brute stubbornness?

ARTHUR. (*Putting a hand out.*) No, Grace. I don't think it is. I really don't think it is——

GRACE. (*Shaking off his hand.*) No. This time I'm not going to cry and say I'm sorry, and make it all up again. I can stand anything if there is a reason for it. But for no reason at all, it's unfair to ask so much of me. It's unfair——

She breaks down. As ARTHUR *puts a comforting arm around her she pushes him off and goes out of the door.* RONNIE *has, meanwhile, opened his eyes.*

RONNIE. What's the matter, Father?

ARTHUR. (*Turning from the door.*) Your mother is a little upset——

RONNIE. (*Drowsily.*) Why? Aren't things going well?

ARTHUR. Oh, yes. (*Murmuring.*) Very well. (*He sits with more than his usual difficulty, as if he were utterly exhausted.*) Very well indeed.

RONNIE *contentedly closes his eyes again.*

(*Gently.*) You'd better go to bed now, Ronnie. You'll be more comfortable——

He sees RONNIE *is asleep again. He makes as if to wake him, then shrugs his shoulders and turns away.* VIOLET *comes in with sandwiches on a plate and a letter on a salver.*

Thank you, Violet.

VIOLET *puts the sandwiches on the table and hands* ARTHUR *the letter.* ARTHUR *puts it down on the table beside him without opening it.* VIOLET *turns to go out.*

ARTHUR. Oh, Violet——

VIOLET. (*Turning placidly.*) Yes, sir?

ARTHUR. How long have you been with us?

VIOLET. Twenty-four years come April, sir.

ARTHUR. As long as that?

VIOLET. Yes, sir. Miss Kate was that high when I first came. (*She indicates a small child.*) and Mr. Dickie hadn't even been thought of——

ARTHUR. I remember you coming to us now. I remember it well. What do you think of this case, Violet?

VIOLET. A fine old rumpus that is, and no mistake.

ARTHUR. It is, isn't it? A fine old rumpus.

VIOLET. There was a bit in the *Evening News.* Did you read it, sir.

ARTHUR. No. What did it say?

VIOLET. Oh, about how it was a fuss about nothing and a shocking waste of the Government's time, but how it was a good thing all the same because it could only happen in England——

ARTHUR. There seems to be a certain lack of logic in that argument——

VIOLET. Well, perhaps they put it a bit different, sir. Still, that's what it said all right. And when you think it's all because of our Master Ronnie—I have to laugh about it sometimes. I really do. Wasting the Government's time at his age! I never did. Well, wonders will never cease.

ARTHUR. I know. Wonders will never cease.

VIOLET. Well—would that be all, sir?

ARTHUR. Yes, Violet. That'll be all.

CATHERINE *comes in.*

CATHERINE. Good evening, Violet.

VIOLET. Good evening, miss.

She goes out.

CATHERINE. Hullo, Father. (*She kisses him. Indicating* RONNIE.) An honourable Member described that this evening as a piteous little figure, crying aloud to humanity for justice and redress. I wish he could see him now.

ARTHUR. (*Testily.*) It's long past his bedtime. What's happened? Is the debate over?

CATHERINE. As good as. The First Lord gave an assurance that in future there would be no inquiry at Osborne or Dartmouth without informing the parents first. That seemed to satisfy most Members——

ARTHUR. But what about *our* case? Is he going to allow us a fair trial?

CATHERINE. Apparently not.

ARTHUR. But that's iniquitous. I thought he would be forced to——

CATHERINE. I thought so, too. The House evidently thought otherwise.

ARTHUR. Will there be a division?

CATHERINE. There may be. If there is the Government will win.

ARTHUR. What is the motion?

CATHERINE. To reduce the First Lord's salary by a hundred pounds. (*With a faint smile.*) Naturally no one really wants to do that. (*Indicating sandwiches.*) Are these for me?

ARTHUR. Yes.

CATHERINE *starts to eat the sandwiches.*

So we're back where we started, then?

CATHERINE. It looks like it.

ARTHUR. The debate has done us no good at all?

CATHERINE. It's aired the case a little, perhaps. A few more thousand people will say to each other at breakfast to-morrow: 'That boy ought to be allowed a fair trial.'

ARTHUR. What's the good of that, if they can't make themselves heard?

CATHERINE. I think they can—given time.

ARTHUR. Given time?

Pause.

But didn't Sir Robert make any protest when the First Lord refused a trial?

CATHERINE. Not a verbal protest. Something far more spectacular and dramatic. He'd had his feet on the Treasury table and his hat over his eyes during most of the First Lord's speech—and he suddenly got up very deliberately, glared at the First Lord, threw a whole bundle of notes on the floor, and stalked out of the House. It made a magnificent effect. If I hadn't known I could have sworn he was genuinely indignant——

ARTHUR. Of course he was genuinely indignant. So would any man of feeling be——

CATHERINE. Sir Robert, Father dear, is not a man of feeling. I don't think any emotion at all can stir that fishy heart——

ARTHUR. Except perhaps a single-minded love of justice.

CATHERINE. Nonsense. A single-minded love of Sir Robert Morton.

ARTHUR. You're very ungrateful to him considering all he's done for us these last months——

CATHERINE. I'm not ungrateful, Father. He's been wonderful —I admit it freely. No one could have fought a harder fight.

ARTHUR. Well, then——

CATHERINE. It's only his motives I question. At least I *don't* question them at all. I know them.

ARTHUR. What are they?

CATHERINE. First—publicity—you know—look at me, the

staunch defender of the little man—and then second—a nice popular stick to beat the Government with. Both very useful to an ambitious man. Luckily for him we've provided them.

ARTHUR. Luckily for us too, Kate.

CATHERINE. Oh, I agree. But don't fool yourself about him, Father, for all that. The man is a fish, a hard, cold-blooded, supercilious, sneering fish.

VIOLET *enters.*

VIOLET. (*Announcing.*) Sir Robert Morton.

CATHERINE *chokes over her sandwich.*

SIR ROBERT *comes in.*

SIR ROBERT. Good evening.

CATHERINE. (*Still choking.*) Good evening.

SIR ROBERT. Something gone down the wrong way?

CATHERINE. Yes.

SIR ROBERT. May I assist? (*He pats her on the back.*)

CATHERINE. Thank you.

SIR ROBERT. (*To* ARTHUR.) Good evening sir. I thought I would call and give you an account of the day's proceedings, but I see your daughter has forestalled me.

CATHERINE. Did you know I was in the gallery?

SIR ROBERT. (*Gallantly.*) With such a charming hat, how could I have missed you?

ARTHUR. It was very good of you to call, sir, nevertheless——

SIR ROBERT. (*Seeing* RONNIE.) Ah. The *casus belli*—dormant——

ARTHUR *goes to wake him.*

SIR ROBERT. No, no. I beg of you. Please do not disturb his innocent slumbers.

CATHERINE. *Innocent* slumbers?

SIR ROBERT. Exactly. Besides, I fear since our first encounter he is, rather pardonably, a trifle nervous of me.

CATHERINE. Will you betray a technical secret, Sir Robert? What happened in that first examination to make you so sure of his innocence?

SIR ROBERT. Three things. First of all, he made far too many damaging admissions. A guilty person would have been much more careful and on his guard. Secondly, I laid him a trap; and thirdly, left him a loophole. Anyone who was guilty would have fallen into the one and darted through the other. He did neither.

CATHERINE. The trap was to ask him suddenly what time Elliot put the postal order in his locker, wasn't it?

SIR ROBERT. Yes.

ARTHUR. And the loophole?

SIR ROBERT. I then suggested to him that he had stolen the postal order for a joke—which, had he been guilty, he would surely have admitted to as being the lesser of two evils.

CATHERINE. I see. It was very cleverly thought out.

SIR ROBERT. (*With a little bow.*) Thank you.

ARTHUR. May we offer you some refreshment, Sir Robert? A whisky and soda?

SIR ROBERT. No thank you. Nothing at all.

ARTHUR. My daughter has told me of your demonstration during the First Lord's speech. She described it as—magnificent.

SIR ROBERT. (*With a glance at* CATHERINE.) Did she? That was good of her. It's a very old trick, you know. I've done it many times in the Courts. It's nearly always surprisingly effective——

CATHERINE *catches her father's eye and nods triumphantly.*

(*To* CATHERINE.) Was the First Lord at all put out by it—did you notice?

CATHERINE. How could he have failed to be? (*To* ARTHUR, *approaching his chair.*) I wish you could have seen it, Father—it was—— (*She notices the letter on the table beside* ARTHUR *and snatches it up with a sudden gesture. She examines the envelope.*) When did this come?

ARTHUR. A few minutes ago. Do you know the writing?

CATHERINE. Yes. (*She puts the letter back on the table.*)

ARTHUR. Whose is it?

CATHERINE. I shouldn't bother to read it, if I were you.

ARTHUR *looks at her, puzzled, then takes up the letter.*

ARTHUR. (*To* SIR ROBERT.) Will you forgive me?

SIR ROBERT. Of course.

ARTHUR *opens the letter and begins to read.* CATHERINE *watches him for a moment, and then turns with a certain forced liveliness to* SIR ROBERT.

CATHERINE. Well, what do you think the next step should be?

SIR ROBERT. I have already been considering that, Miss Winslow. I believe that perhaps the best plan would be to renew our efforts to get the Director of Public Prosecutions to act.

CATHERINE. (*With one eye on her father.*) But do you think there's any chance of that?

SIR ROBERT. Oh, yes. In the main it will chiefly be a question of making ourselves a confounded nuisance——

CATHERINE. We've certainly done that quite successfully so far—thanks to you——

SIR ROBERT. (*Suavely.*) Ah. That is perhaps the only quality I was born with—the ability to make myself a confounded nuisance.

He, too, has his eye on ARTHUR, *sensing something amiss.*

ARTHUR *finishes reading the letter.*

CATHERINE. (*With false vivacity.*) Father—Sir Robert thinks we might get the Director of Public Prosecutions to act——

ARTHUR. What?

SIR ROBERT. We were discussing how to proceed with the case——

ARTHUR. The case? (*He stares, a little blankly, from one to the other.*) Yes. We must think of that, mustn't we? (*Pause.*) How to proceed with the case? (*To* SIR ROBERT, *abruptly.*) I'm afraid I don't think, all things considered, that much purpose would be served by going on——

SIR ROBERT *and* CATHERINE *stare at him blankly.*

CATHERINE *goes quickly to him and snatches the letter from his lap. She begins to read.*

SIR ROBERT. (*With a sudden change of tone.*) Of course we must go on.

ARTHUR. (*In a low voice.*) It is not for you to choose, sir. The choice is mine.

SIR ROBERT. (*Harshly.*) Then you must reconsider it. To give up now would be insane.

ARTHUR. Insane? My sanity has already been called in question tonight—for carrying the case as far as I have.

SIR ROBERT. Whatever the contents of that letter, or whatever has happened to make you lose heart, I insist that we continue the fight——

ARTHUR. Insist? We? It is my fight—my fight alone—and it is for me alone to judge when the time has come to give up.

SIR ROBERT. (*Violently.*) But why give up? Why? In heaven's name, man, why?

ARTHUR. (*Slowly.*) I have made many sacrifices for this case. Some of them I had no right to make, but I made them none the less. But there is a limit and I have reached it. I am sorry, Sir Robert. More sorry, perhaps, than you are, but the Winslow case is now closed.

SIR ROBERT. Balderdash!

ARTHUR *looks surprised at this unparliamentary expression.* CATHERINE *has read and re-read the letter, and now breaks the silence in a calm, methodical voice.*

CATHERINE. My father doesn't mean what he says, Sir Robert.

SIR ROBERT. I am glad to hear it.

CATHERINE. Perhaps I should explain this letter——

ARTHUR. No, Kate.

CATHERINE. Sir Robert knows so much about our family affairs, Father, I don't see it will matter much if he learns a little more. (*To* SIR ROBERT.) This letter is from a certain Colonel Watherstone who is the father of the man I'm engaged to. We've always known he was opposed to the case, so it really comes as no surprise. In it he says that our efforts to discredit the Admiralty in the House of Commons today have resulted merely in our making the name of Winslow a nation-wide laughing-stock. I think that's his phrase. (*She consults the letter.*) Yes. That's right. A nation-wide laughing-stock.

SIR ROBERT. I don't care for his English.

CATHERINE. It's not very good, is it? He goes on to say that unless my father will give him a firm undertaking to drop this whining and reckless agitation—I suppose he means the case—he will exert every bit of influence he has over his son to prevent him marrying me.

SIR ROBERT. I see. An ultimatum.

CATHERINE. Yes—but a pointless one.

SIR ROBERT. He has no influence over his son?

CATHERINE. Oh, yes. A little, naturally. But his son is of age, and his own master——

SIR ROBERT. Is he dependent on his father for money?

CATHERINE. He gets an allowance. But he can live perfectly well—we both can live perfectly well without it.

Pause. SIR ROBERT *stares hard at her, then turns abruptly to* ARTHUR.

SIR ROBERT. Well, sir?

ARTHUR. I'm afraid I can't go back on what I have already said. I will give you a decision in a few days——

SIR ROBERT. Your daughter seems prepared to take the risk——

ARTHUR. I am not. Not, at least, until I know how great a risk it is——

SIR ROBERT. How do you estimate the risk, Miss Winslow?

Pause. CATHERINE, *for all her bravado, is plainly scared. She is engaged in lighting a cigarette as* SIR ROBERT *asks his question.*

CATHERINE. (*At length.*) Negligible.

SIR ROBERT *stares at her again. Feeling his eyes on her, she returns his glance defiantly. Pause.*

SIR ROBERT. (*Returning abruptly to his languid manner.*) I see. May I take a cigarette, too?

CATHERINE. Yes, of course. I thought you didn't smoke.

SIR ROBERT. Only occasionally. (*To* ARTHUR.) I really must apologize to you, sir, for speaking to you as I did just now. It was unforgivable.

ARTHUR. Not at all, sir. You were upset at giving up the case —and, to be frank, I liked you for it——

SIR ROBERT. (*With a deprecating gesture.*) It has been rather a tiring day. The House of Commons is a peculiarly exhausting place, you know. Too little ventilation, and far too much hot air—I really am most truly sorry.

ARTHUR. Please.

SIR ROBERT. (*Carelessly.*) Of course, you must decide about the case as you wish. That really is a most charming hat, Miss Winslow——

CATHERINE. I'm glad you like it.

SIR ROBERT. It seems decidedly wrong to me that a lady of your political persuasion should be allowed to adorn herself with such a very feminine allurement. It really looks so awfully like trying to have the best of both worlds——

CATHERINE. I'm not a militant, you know, Sir Robert. I don't go about breaking shop windows with a hammer or pouring acid down pillar boxes.

SIR ROBERT. (*Languidly.*) I am truly glad to hear it. Both those activities would be highly unsuitable in that hat——

CATHERINE *glares at him but suppresses an angry retort.*

I have never yet fully grasped what active steps you take to propagate your cause, Miss Winslow.

CATHERINE. (*Shortly.*) I'm an organizing secretary at the West London Branch of the Woman's Suffrage Association.

SIR ROBERT. Indeed? Is the work hard?

CATHERINE. Very.

SIR ROBERT. But not, I should imagine, particularly lucrative.

CATHERINE. The work is voluntary and unpaid.

SIR ROBERT. (*Murmuring.*) Dear me! What sacrifices you young ladies seem prepared to make for your convictions——

VIOLET *enters.*

VIOLET. (*To Catherine.*) Mr. Watherstone is in the hall, miss. Says he would like to have a word with you in private—most particular——

Pause.

CATHERINE. Oh. I'll come out to him——

ARTHUR. No. See him in here.

He begins to struggle out of his chair. SIR ROBERT *assists him.*

You wouldn't mind coming to the dining-room, would you, Sir Robert, for a moment?

SIR ROBERT. Not in the least.

CATHERINE. All right, Violet.

VIOLET. Will you come in, sir.

JOHN *comes in. He is looking depressed and anxious.* CATHERINE *greets him with a smile, which he returns only half-heartedly. This exchange is lost on* ARTHUR, *who has his back to them, but not on* SIR ROBERT.

CATHERINE. Hello, John.

JOHN. Hullo. (*To* ARTHUR.) Good evening, sir.

ARTHUR. Good evening, John. (*He goes on towards dining-room.*)

CATHERINE. I don't think you've met Sir Robert Morton.

JOHN. No, I haven't. How do you do, sir?

SIR ROBERT. I think you promised me a whisky and soda. (*Turning to* JOHN.) May I offer my very belated congratulations?

JOHN. Congratulations? Oh, yes. Thank you.

ARTHUR *and* SIR ROBERT *go into dining-room. There is a pause.* CATHERINE *is watching* JOHN *with an anxious expression.*

JOHN. (*Indicating* RONNIE.) Is he asleep?

CATHERINE. Yes.

JOHN. Sure he's not shamming?

CATHERINE. Yes.

JOHN. (*After a pause.*) My father's written your father a letter.

CATHERINE. I know. I've read it.

JOHN. Oh.

CATHERINE. Did you?

JOHN. Yes. He showed it to me.

Pause. JOHN *is carefully not looking at her.*

(*At length.*) Well, what's his answer?

CATHERINE. My father? I don't suppose he'll send one.

JOHN. You think he'll ignore it?

CATHERINE. Isn't that the best answer to blackmail?

JOHN. (*Muttering.*) It was damned high-handed of the old man, I admit.

CATHERINE. High-handed?

JOHN. I tried to get him not to send it——

CATHERINE. I'm glad.

JOHN. The trouble is—he's perfectly serious.

CATHERINE. I never thought he wasn't.

JOHN. If your father does decide to go on with the case, I'm very much afraid he'll do everything he threatens.

CATHERINE. Forbid the match?

JOHN. Yes.

CATHERINE. (*Almost pleadingly.*) Isn't that rather an empty threat, John?

JOHN. (*Slowly.*) Well, there's always the allowance——

CATHERINE. (*Dully.*) Yes, I see. There's always the allowance.

JOHN. I tell you, Kate darling, this is going to need damned careful handling; otherwise we'll find ourselves in the soup.

CATHERINE. Without your allowance would we be in the soup?

JOHN. And without your settlement. My dear girl, of course we would. Dash it all, I can't even live on my pay as it is, but with two of us——

CATHERINE. I've heard it said that two can live as cheaply as one.

JOHN. Don't you believe it. Two can live as cheaply as two, and that's all there is to it.

CATHERINE. Yes, I see. I didn't know.

JOHN. Unlike you I have a practical mind, Kate. I'm sorry, but it's no good dashing blindly ahead without thinking of these things first. The problem has got to be faced.

CATHERINE. I'm ready to face it, John. What do you suggest?

JOHN. (*Cautiously.*) Well—I think you should consider very carefully before you take the next step——

CATHERINE. I can assure you we will, John. The question is— what *is* the next step?

JOHN. Well—this is the way I see it. I'm going to be honest now. I hope you don't mind——

CATHERINE. No. I should welcome it.

JOHN. Your young brother over there pinches or doesn't pinch a five-bob postal order. For over a year you and your father fight a magnificent fight on his behalf, and I'm sure everyone admires you for it——

CATHERINE. Your father hardly seems to——

JOHN. Well, he's a diehard. Like these old Admirals you've been up against. I meant ordinary reasonable people, like myself. But now look—you've had two inquiries, the Petition of Right case which the Admiralty had thrown out of Court, and the Appeal. And now, good heavens, you've had the whole damned House of Commons getting themselves worked up into a frenzy about it. Surely, darling, that's

Q

enough for you? My God! Surely the case can end there?

CATHERINE. (*Slowly.*) Yes. I suppose the case can end there.

JOHN. (*Pointing to* RONNIE.) *He* won't mind.

CATHERINE. No. I know he won't.

JOHN. Look at him! Perfectly happy and content. Not a care in the world. How do you know what's going on in his mind? How can you be so sure he didn't do it?

CATHERINE. (*Also gazing down at* RONNIE.) I'm not so sure he didn't do it.

JOHN. (*Appalled.*) Good Lord! Then why in heaven's name have you and your father spent all this time and money trying to prove his innocence?

CATHERINE. (*Quietly.*) His innocence or guilt aren't important to me. They are to my father. Not to me. I believe he didn't do it; but I may be wrong. To prove that he didn't do it is of hardly more interest to me than the identity of the college servant, or whoever it was, who did it. All that I care about is that people should know that a Government Department has ignored a fundamental human right and that it should be forced to acknowledge it. That's all that's important to me.

JOHN. But, darling, after all those long noble words, it does really resolve itself to a question of a fourteen-year-old kid and a five-bob postal order, doesn't it?

CATHERINE. Yes, it does.

JOHN. (*Reasonably.*) Well now, look. There's a European war blowing up, there's a coal strike on, there's a fair chance of civil war in Ireland, and there's a hundred and one other things on the horizon at the moment that I think you genuinely could call *important*. And yet, with all that on its mind, the House of Commons takes a whole day to discuss him (*pointing to* RONNIE) and his bally postal order. Surely you must see that's a little out of proportion——

Pause. CATHERINE *raises her head slowly.*

CATHERINE. (*With some spirit.*) All I know is, John, that if ever the time comes that the House of Commons has so much on its mind that it can't find time to discuss a Ronnie Winslow and his bally postal order, this country will be a far poorer place than it is now. (*Wearily.*) But you needn't go on, John dear. You've said quite enough. I entirely see your point of view.

JOHN. I don't know whether you realize that all this publicity you're getting is making the name of Winslow a bit of a— well——

CATHERINE. (*Steadily.*) A nation-wide laughing-stock, your father said.

JOHN. Well, that's putting it a bit steep. But people do find the case a bit ridiculous, you know. I mean, I get chaps coming up to me in the mess all the time and saying: 'I say, is it true you're going to marry the Winslow girl? You'd better be careful. You'll find yourself up in front of the House of Lords for pinching the Adjutant's bath.' Things like that. They're not awfully funny—

CATHERINE. That's nothing. They're singing a verse about us at the Alhambra—

> Winslow one day went to heaven
> And found a poor fellow in quod.
> The fellow said I didn't do it,
> So naturally Winslow sued God.

JOHN. Well, darling—you see——

CATHERINE. Yes. I see. (*Quietly.*) Do you want to marry me, John?

JOHN. What?

CATHERINE. I said: Do you want to marry me?

JOHN. Well, of course I do. You know I do. We've been engaged for over a year now. Have I ever wavered before?

CATHERINE. No. Never before.

JOHN. (*Correcting himself.*) I'm not wavering now. Not a bit— I'm only telling you what I think is the best course for us to take.

CATHERINE. But isn't it already too late? Even if we gave up the case, would you still want to marry—the Winslow girl?

JOHN. All that would blow over in no time.

CATHERINE. (*Slowly.*) And we'd have the allowance——

JOHN. Yes. We would.

CATHERINE. And that's so important——

JOHN. (*Quietly.*) It is, darling. I'm sorry, but you can't shame me into saying it isn't.

CATHERINE. I didn't mean to shame you——

JOHN. Oh, yes you did. I know that tone of voice.

CATHERINE. (*Humbly.*) I'm sorry.

JOHN. (*Confidently.*) Well, now—what's the answer?

CATHERINE. (*Slowly.*) I love you, John, and I want to be your wife.

JOHN. Well, then, that's all I want to know. Darling! I was sure nothing so stupid and trivial could possibly come between us.

He kisses her. She responds wearily. The telephone rings. After a pause she releases herself and picks up the receiver.

CATHERINE. Hullo . . . Yes . . . Will you wait a minute? (*She goes to the dining-room door and calls.*) Sir Robert! Someone wants you on the telephone——

SIR ROBERT comes out of the dining-room.

SIR ROBERT. Thank you. I'm so sorry to interrupt.

CATHERINE. You didn't. We'd finished our talk.

SIR ROBERT looks at her inquiringly. She gives him no sign. He walks to the telephone.

SIR ROBERT. (*Noticing sandwiches.*) How delicious. May I help myself?

CATHERINE. Do.

SIR ROBERT. (*Into receiver.*) Hello . . . Yes, Michael . . . F.E.? I didn't know he was going to speak . . . I see . . . Go on . . .

SIR ROBERT listens, with closed eyelids, munching a sandwich, meanwhile.

(*At length.*) Thank you, Michael.

He rings off. ARTHUR *has appeared in the dining-room doorway.*

SIR ROBERT. (*To* ARTHUR.) There has been a most interesting development in the House, sir.

ARTHUR. What?

SIR ROBERT. My secretary tells me that a barrister friend of mine who, quite unknown to me, was interested in the case, got on his feet shortly after nine-thirty and delivered one of the most scathing denunciations of a Government Department ever heard in the House. (*To* CATHERINE.) What a shame we missed it—his style is quite superb——

ARTHUR. What happened?

SIR ROBERT. The debate revived, of course, and the First Lord, who must have felt himself fairly safe, suddenly found himself under attack from all parts of the House. It appears that rather than risk a division he has this moment given an undertaking that he will instruct the Attorney-General to endorse our Petition of Right. The case of Winslow versus Rex can now therefore come to Court.

There is a pause. ARTHUR *and* CATHERINE *stare at him unbelievingly.* (*At length.*) Well, sir. What are my instructions?

ARTHUR. (*Slowly.*) The decision is no longer mine, sir. You must ask my daughter.

SIR ROBERT. What are my instructions, Miss Winslow?

CATHERINE *looks down at the sleeping* RONNIE. ARTHUR *is watching her intently.* SIR ROBERT, *munching sandwiches, is also looking at her.*

CATHERINE. (*In a flat voice.*) Do you need my instructions, Sir Robert? Aren't they already on the Petition? Doesn't it say: Let Right be done?

JOHN *makes a move of protest towards her. She does not look at him. He turns abruptly to the door.*

JOHN. (*Furiously.*) Kate! Good night.

He goes out. SIR ROBERT, *with languid speculation, watches him go.*

SIR ROBERT. (*His mouth full.*) Well, then—we must endeavour to see that it is.

CURTAIN

ACT IV

SCENE: *The same, about five months later. It is a stiflingly hot June day—nearly two years less one month since* RONNIE'S *dismissal from Osborne. The glass door to the garden stands open, and a bath chair, unoccupied, has been placed near by.* ON THE RISE OF THE CURTAIN *the stage is empty and the telephone is ringing insistently.*

DICKIE *comes in from the hall carrying a suitcase, evidently very hot, his straw hat pushed on to the back of his head and panting from his exertions. He is wearing a neat, dark blue suit, a sober tie, and a stiff collar. He puts the suitcase down and mops his face with his handkerchief. Then he goes to the hall door and calls:*

DICKIE. Mother! (*There is no reply.*) Violet! (*Again no reply.*) Anyone about?

He goes to the telephone—taking off the receiver.

Hullo . . . No, not senior—junior . . . I don't know where he is . . . *Daily Mail?* . . . No, I'm the brother . . . Elder brother —that's right . . . Well—I'm in the banking business . . . That's right. Following in father's footsteps . . . My views on the case? Well—I—er—I don't know I have any, except, I mean, I hope we win and all that . . . No, I haven't been in Court. I've only just arrived from Reading . . . Reading . . . Yes. That's where I work . . . Yes, I've come up for the last two days of the trial. Verdict's expected tomorrow, isn't it? . . . Twenty-two, last March . . . *Seven* years older . . . No. He was thirteen when it happened, but now he's fifteen . . . Well, I suppose, if I'm anything I'm a sort of Liberal-Conservative . . . Single . . . No. No immediate prospects. I say, is this at all interesting to you? . . . Well, a perfectly ordinary kid, just like any other—makes a noise, does fretwork, doesn't wash and all that . . . Doesn't wash . . . (*Alarmed.*) I say, don't take that too literally. I mean he does, sometimes . . . Yes. All right. Goodbye . . .

He rings off and exits through centre door. Telephone rings again. He

430

comes back to answer it, when GRACE *dressed for going out, comes out of the dining-room.*

GRACE. Oh, hullo, darling. When did you get here?

She picks up the telephone receiver.

(*Into receiver.*) Everyone out.

She rings off and embraces DICKIE.

You're thinner. I like your new suit.

DICKIE. Straight from Reading's Savile Row. Off the peg at three and a half guineas. (*Pointing to telephone.*) I say—does that go on all the time?

GRACE. All blessed day. The last four days it simply hasn't stopped.

DICKIE. I had to fight my way in through an army of reporters and people——

GRACE. Yes, I know. You didn't say anything, I hope, Dickie dear. It's better not to say a word——

DICKIE. I don't think I said anything much . . . (*Carelessly.*) Oh, yes. I did say that I personally thought he did it——

GRACE. (*Horrified.*) Dickie! You didn't! (*He is smiling at her.*) Oh, I see. It's a joke. You mustn't say things like that, even in fun, Dickie dear——

DICKIE. How's it all going?

GRACE. I don't know. I've been there all four days now and I've hardly understood a word that's going on. Kate says the judge is against us, but he seems a charming old gentleman to me. (*Faintly shocked.*) Sir Robert's so rude to him——

Telephone rings. GRACE *answers it automatically.*

Nobody in.

She rings off and turns to garden door.

(*Calling.*) Arthur! Lunch! I'll come straight down. Dickie's here. (*To* DICKIE.) Kate takes the morning session, then she comes home and relieves me with Arthur, and I go to the Court in the afternoons, so you can come with me as soon as she's in.

DICKIE. Will there be room for me?

GRACE. Oh, yes. They reserve places for the family. You never saw such crowds in all your life. And such excitement! Cheers and applause and people being turned out. It's thrilling—you'll love it, Dickie.

DICKIE. Well—if I don't understand a word——

GRACE. Oh, that doesn't matter. They all get so terribly worked up you find yourself getting worked up, too. Sir Robert and the Attorney-General go at each other hammer and tongs —you wait and hear them—all about Petitions and demurrers and prerogatives and things. Nothing to do with Ronnie at all—seems to me——

DICKIE. How did Ronnie get on in the witness box?

GRACE. Two days he was cross-examined. Two whole days. Imagine it, the poor little pet! I must say he didn't seem to mind much. He said two days with the Attorney-General wasn't nearly as bad as two minutes with Sir Robert. Kate says he made a very good impression with the jury——

DICKIE. How is Kate, Mother?

GRACE. Oh, all right. You heard about John, I suppose——

DICKIE. Yes. That's what I meant. How has she taken it?

GRACE. You can never tell with Kate. She never lets you know what she's feeling. We all think he's behaved very badly——

ARTHUR *appears at the garden door, walking very groggily.*

Arthur! You shouldn't have come up the stairs by yourself.

ARTHUR. I had little alternative.

GRACE. I'm sorry, dear. I was talking to Dickie.

GRACE *helps* ARTHUR *into the bath chair.*

ARTHUR. How are you, Dickie?

DICKIE. (*Shaking hands.*) Very well, thank you, Father.

ARTHUR. I've been forced to adopt this ludicrous form of propulsion. I apologize.

He wheels himself into the room and examines DICKIE.

You look very well. A trifle thinner, perhaps——

DICKIE. Hard work, Father.

ARTHUR. Or late hours?

DICKIE. You can't keep late hours in Reading.

ARTHUR. You could keep late hours anywhere. I've had quite a good report about you from Mr. Lamb.

DICKIE. Good egg! He's a decent old stick, the old baa-lamb. I took him racing last Saturday. Had the time of his life and lost his shirt.

ARTHUR. Did he? I have no doubt that, given the chance,

you'll succeed in converting the entire Reading branch of
the Westminster Bank into a bookmaking establishment.
Mr. Lamb says you've joined the Territorials.

DICKIE. Yes, Father.

ARTHUR. Why have you done that?

DICKIE. Well, from all accounts there's a fair chance of a bit
of a scrap quite soon. If there is I don't want it to be all
over before I can get in on it——

ARTHUR. If there is what you call a scrap you'll do far better
to stay in the bank——

DICKIE. Oh, no, Father. I mean, the bank's all right—but still
—a chap can't help looking forward to a bit of a change—I
can always go back to the bank afterwards——

The telephone rings. ARTHUR *takes receiver off and puts it down on
table.*

GRACE. Oh, no, dear. You can't do that.

ARTHUR. Why not?

GRACE. It annoys the exchange.

ARTHUR. I prefer to annoy the exchange rather than have the
exchange annoy me. (*To* GRACE.) Catherine's late. She was
in at half-past yesterday.

GRACE. Perhaps they're taking the lunch interval later today.

ARTHUR. Lunch interval? This isn't a cricket match. (*Looking
at her.*) Nor, may I say, is it a matinée at the Gaiety. Why
are you wearing that highly unsuitable get-up?

GRACE. Don't you like it, dear? I think it's Mme Dupont's
best.

ARTHUR. Grace—your son is facing a charge of theft and
forgery——

GRACE. Oh, dear! It's so difficult! I simply can't be seen in
the same old dress, day after day. (*A thought strikes her.*) I
tell you what, Arthur. I'll wear my black coat and skirt
tomorrow—for the verdict.

ARTHUR *glares at her, helplessly, then turns his chair to the
dining-room.*

ARTHUR. Did you say my lunch was ready?

GRACE. Yes, dear. It's only cold. I did the salad myself. Violet
and cook are at the trial.

DICKIE. Is Violet still with you? She was under sentence last time I saw you——

GRACE. She's been under sentence for the last six months, poor thing—only she doesn't know it. Neither your father nor I have the courage to tell her——

ARTHUR. (*Stopping at door.*) I have the courage to tell her.

GRACE. It's funny that you don't, then, dear.

ARTHUR. I will.

GRACE. (*Hastily.*) No, no, you mustn't. When it's to be done, I'll do it.

ARTHUR. You see, Dickie? These taunts of cowardice are daily flung at my head; but should I take them up I'm forbidden to move in the matter. Such is the logic of women.

He goes into the dining-room. DICKIE, *who has been holding the door open, closes it after him.*

DICKIE. (*Seriously.*) How *is* he?

GRACE *shakes her head quietly.*

Will you take him away after the trial?

GRACE. He's promised to go into a nursing home.

DICKIE. Do you think he will?

GRACE. How do I know? He'll probably find some new excuse——

DICKIE. But surely, if he loses this time, he's lost for good, hasn't he?

GRACE. (*Slowly.*) So they say, Dickie dear—I can only hope it's true.

DICKIE. How did you keep him away from the trial?

GRACE. Kate and Sir Robert together. He wouldn't listen to me or the doctor.

DICKIE. Poor old Mother! You must have been having a pretty rotten time of it, one way and another——

GRACE. I've said my say, Dickie. He knows what I think. Not that he cares. He never has—all his life. Anyway, I've given up worrying. He's always said he knew what he was doing. It's my job to try and pick up the pieces, I suppose.

CATHERINE *comes in.*

CATHERINE. Lord! The heat! Mother, can't you get rid of those reporters—Hullo, Dickie.

DICKIE. (*Embracing her.*) Hullo, Kate.

CATHERINE. Come to be in at the death.

DICKIE. Is that what it's going to be?

CATHERINE. Looks like it. I could cheerfully strangle that old brute of a judge, Mother. He's dead against us.

GRACE. (*Fixing her hat in the mirror.*) Oh, dear!

CATHERINE. Sir Robert's very worried. He said the Attorney-General's speech made a great impression on the jury. I must say it was very clever. To listen to him yesterday you would have thought that a verdict for Ronnie would simultaneously cause a mutiny in the Royal Navy and triumphant jubilation in Berlin.

ARTHUR *appears in his chair, at the dining-room door.*

ARTHUR. You're late, Catherine.

CATHERINE. I know, Father. I'm sorry. There was such a huge crowd outside as well as inside the Court that I couldn't get a cab. And I stayed to talk to Sir Robert.

GRACE. (*Pleased.*) Is there a bigger crowd even than yesterday, Kate?

CATHERINE. Yes, Mother. Far bigger.

ARTHUR. How did it go this morning?

CATHERINE. Sir Robert finished his cross-examination of the postmistress. I thought he'd demolished her completely. She admitted she couldn't identify Ronnie in the Commander's office. She admitted she couldn't be sure of the time he came in. She admitted that she was called away to the telephone while he was buying his fifteen-and-six postal order, and that all Osborne cadets looked alike to her in their uniforms, so that it might quite easily have been another cadet who cashed the five shillings. It was a brilliant cross-examination. So gentle and quiet. He didn't bully her, or frighten her—he just coaxed her into tying herself into knots. Then, when he'd finished the Attorney-General asked her again whether she was absolutely positive that the same boy that bought the fifteen-and-six postal order also cashed the five-shilling one. She said yes. She was quite, quite sure because Ronnie was such a good-looking little boy that she had specially noticed him. She hadn't said that in her examination-in-chief. I could see those twelve good men and true nodding away to each other. I believe it undid the whole of that magnificent cross-examination.

ARTHUR. If she thought him so especially good-looking, why couldn't she identify him the same evening?

CATHERINE. Don't ask me, Father. Ask the Attorney-General. I'm sure he has a beautifully reasonable answer.

DICKIE. Ronnie good-looking! What utter rot! She must be lying, that woman.

GRACE. Nonsense, Dickie! I thought he looked very well in the box yesterday, didn't you, Kate?

CATHERINE. Yes, Mother.

ARTHUR. Who else gave evidence for the other side?

CATHERINE. The Commander, the Chief Petty Officer, and one of the boys at the College.

ARTHUR. Anything very damaging?

CATHERINE. Nothing that we didn't expect. The boy showed obviously he hated Ronnie and was torn to shreds by Sir Robert. The Commander scored, though. He's an honest man and genuinely believes Ronnie did it.

GRACE. Did you see anybody interesting in Court, dear?

CATHERINE. Yes, Mother. John Watherstone.

GRACE. John? I hope you didn't speak to him, Kate.

CATHERINE. Of course I did.

GRACE. Kate, how could you! What did he say?

CATHERINE. He wished us luck.

GRACE. What impertinence! The idea of John Watherstone coming calmly up in Court to wish you luck—I think it's the most disgraceful, cold-blooded——

ARTHUR. Grace—you will be late for the resumption.

GRACE. Oh, will I? Are you ready, Dickie?

DICKIE. Yes, Mother.

GRACE. You don't think that nice, grey suit of yours you paid so much money for——

ARTHUR. What time are they resuming, Kate?

CATHERINE. Two o'clock.

ARTHUR. It's twenty past two now.

GRACE. Oh, dear! We'll be terribly late. Kate—that's your fault. Arthur, you must finish your lunch——

ARTHUR. Yes, Grace.

GRACE. Promise now.

ARTHUR. I promise.

GRACE. (*To herself.*) I wonder if Violet will remember to pick up those onions. Perhaps I'd better do it on the way back from the Court. (*As she passes* CATHERINE.) Kate, dear, I'm so sorry——

CATHERINE. What for, Mother?

GRACE. John proving such a bad hat. I never did like him very much, you know.

CATHERINE. No, I know.

GRACE. Now, Dickie, when you get to the front-door put your head down, like me, and just charge through them all.

ARTHUR. Why don't you go out by the garden?

GRACE. I wouldn't like to risk this dress getting through that hedge. Come on, Dickie. I always shout: 'I'm the maid and don't know nothing', so don't be surprised.

DICKIE. Right-oh, Mother.

GRACE *goes out.* DICKIE *follows her.*

There is a pause.

ARTHUR. Are we going to lose this case, Kate?

CATHERINE *quietly shrugs her shoulders.*

It's our last chance.

CATHERINE. I know.

ARTHUR. (*With sudden violence.*) We've got to win it.

CATHERINE *does not reply.*

What does Sir Robert think?

CATHERINE. He seems very worried.

ARTHUR. (*Thoughtfully.*) I wonder if you were right, Kate. I wonder if we could have had a better man.

CATHERINE. No, Father. We couldn't have had a better man.

ARTHUR. You admit that now, do you?

CATHERINE. Only that he's the best advocate in England and for some reason—prestige, I suppose—he seems genuinely anxious to win this case. I don't go back on anything else I've ever said about him.

ARTHUR. The papers said that he began today by telling the judge he felt ill and might have to ask for an adjournment. I trust he won't collapse——

CATHERINE. He won't. It was just another of those brilliant tricks of his that he's always boasting about. It got him the sympathy of the Court and possibly—no, I won't say that——

ARTHUR. Say it.

CATHERINE. (*Slowly.*) Possibly provided him with an excuse if he's beaten.

ARTHUR. You don't like him, do you?

CATHERINE. (*Indifferently.*) There's nothing in him to like or dislike, Father. I admire him.

DESMOND *appears at the garden door. Standing inside the room, he knocks diffidently.* CATHERINE *and* ARTHUR *turn and see him.*

DESMOND. I trust you do not object to me employing this rather furtive entry. The crowds at the front-door are most alarming——

ARTHUR. Come in, Desmond. Why have you left the Court?

DESMOND. My partner will be holding the fort. He is perfectly competent, I promise you.

ARTHUR. I'm glad to hear it.

DESMOND. I wonder if I might see Catherine alone. I have a matter of some urgency to communicate to her——

ARTHUR. Oh. Do you wish to hear this urgent matter, Kate?

CATHERINE. Yes, Father.

ARTHUR. Very well. I shall go and finish my lunch.

He wheels his chair to the dining-room door. DESMOND *flies to help.*

DESMOND. Allow me.

ARTHUR. Thank you. I can manage this vehicle without assistance.

He goes out.

DESMOND. I fear I should have warned you of my visit. Perhaps I have interrupted——

CATHERINE. No, Desmond. Please sit down.

DESMOND. Thank you. I'm afraid I have only a very short time. I must get back to Court for the cross-examination of the judge-advocate.

CATHERINE. Yes, Desmond. Well?

DESMOND. I have a taxicab waiting at the end of the street.

CATHERINE. (*Smiling.*) How very extravagant of you, Desmond.

DESMOND. (*Also smiling.*) Yes. But it shows you how rushed this visit must necessarily be. The fact of the matter is—it suddenly occurred to me during the lunch recess that I had far better see you today.

CATHERINE. (*Her thoughts far distant.*) Why?

DESMOND. I have a question to put to you, Kate, which, if I had postponed putting until after the verdict, you might— who knows—have thought had been prompted by pity—if we had lost. Or—if we had won, your reply might—again who knows—have been influenced by gratitude. Do you follow me, Kate?

CATHERINE. Yes, Desmond. I think I do.

DESMOND. Ah. Then possibly you have some inkling of what the question is I have to put to you?

CATHERINE. Yes. I think I have.

DESMOND. (*A trifle disconcerted.*) Oh.

CATHERINE. I'm sorry, Desmond. I ought, I know, to have followed the usual practice in such cases, and told you I had no inkling whatever.

DESMOND. No, no. Your directness and honesty are two of the qualities I so much admire in you. I am glad you have guessed. It makes my task the easier——

CATHERINE. (*In a matter-of-fact voice.*) Will you give me a few days to think it over?

DESMOND. Of course. Of course.

CATHERINE. I need hardly tell you how grateful I am, Desmond.

DESMOND. (*A trifle bewildered.*) There is no need, Kate. No need at all——

CATHERINE *has risen brusquely.*

CATHERINE. You mustn't keep your taxi waiting——

DESMOND. Oh, bother my taxi! (*Recovering himself.*) Forgive me, Kate, but you see I know very well what your feelings for me really are.

CATHERINE. (*Gently.*) You do, Desmond?

DESMOND. Yes, Kate. I know quite well they have never

amounted to much more than a sort of—well—shall we say, friendliness? As warm friendliness, I hope. Yes, I think perhaps we can definitely say, warm. But no more than that. That's true, isn't it?

CATHERINE. (*Quietly.*) Yes, Desmond.

DESMOND. I know, I know. Of course, the thing is that even if I proved the most devoted and adoring husband that ever lived—which, I may say—if you give me the chance, I intend to be—your feelings for me would never—could never—amount to more than that. When I was young it might, perhaps, have been a different story. When I played cricket for England——

He notices the faintest expression of pity that has crossed CATHERINE'S *face.*

(*Apologetically.*) And, of course, perhaps even that would not have made so much difference. Perhaps you feel I cling too much to my past athletic prowess. I feel it myself, some-times—but the truth is I have not much else to cling to save that and my love for you. The athletic prowess is fading, I'm afraid, with the years and the stiffening of the muscles—but my love for you will never fade.

CATHERINE. (*Smiling.*) That's very charmingly said, Desmond.

DESMOND. Don't make fun of me, Kate, please. I meant it, every word. (*Clearing his throat.*) However, let's take a more mundane approach and examine the facts. Fact one: You don't love me, and never can. Fact two: I love you, always have, and always will. That is the situation—and it is a situation which, after most careful consideration, I am fully prepared to accept. I reached this decision some months ago, but thought at first it would be better to wait until this case, which is so much on all our minds, should be over. Then at lunch today I determined to anticipate the verdict tomorrow, and let you know what was in my mind at once. No matter what you feel or don't feel for me, no matter what you feel for anyone else, I want you to be my wife.

Pause.

CATHERINE. (*At length.*) I see. Thank you, Desmond. That makes everything much clearer.

DESMOND. There is much more that I had meant to say, but I shall put it in a letter.

CATHERINE. Yes, Desmond. Do.

DESMOND. Then I may expect your answer in a few days?

CATHERINE. Yes, Desmond.

DESMOND. (*Looking at his watch.*) I must get back to Court. (*He collects his hat, stick, and gloves.*) How did you think it went this morning?

CATHERINE. I thought the postmistress restored the Admiralty's case with that point about Ronnie's looks——

DESMOND. Oh, no, no. Not at all. There is still the overwhelming fact that she couldn't identify him. What a brilliant cross-examination, was it not?

CATHERINE. Brilliant.

DESMOND. He is a strange man, Sir Robert. At times, so cold and distant and—and——

CATHERINE. Fishlike.

DESMOND. Fishlike, exactly. And yet he has a real passion about this case. A real passion. I happen to know—of course this must on no account go any further—but I happen to know that he has made a very, very great personal sacrifice in order to bring it to court.

CATHERINE. Sacrifice? What? Of another brief?

DESMOND. No, no. That is no sacrifice to him. No—he was offered—you really promise to keep this to yourself?

CATHERINE. My dear Desmond, whatever the Government offered him can't be as startling as all that; he's in the Opposition.

DESMOND. As it happens it was quite startling, and a most graceful compliment, if I may say so, to his performance as Attorney-General under the last Government.

CATHERINE. What was he offered, Desmond?

DESMOND. The appointment of Lord Chief Justice. He turned it down simply in order to be able to carry on with the case of Winslow versus Rex. Strange are the ways of men are they not? Goodbye, my dear.

CATHERINE. Goodbye, Desmond.

Exit DESMOND.

CATHERINE *turns from the window deep in thought. She has a puzzled, strained expression. It does not look as though it were Desmond she was thinking of.* ARTHUR *opens dining-room door and peers round.*

ARTHUR. May I come in now?

CATHERINE. Yes, Father. He's gone.

ARTHUR. I'm rather tired of being gazed at from the street while eating my mutton, as though I were an animal at the Zoo.

CATHERINE. (*Slowly.*) I've been a fool, Father.

ARTHUR. Have you, my dear?

CATHERINE. An utter fool.

ARTHUR *waits for* CATHERINE *to make herself plain. She does not do so.*

ARTHUR. In default of further information, I can only repeat, have you, my dear?

CATHERINE. There can be no further information. I'm under a pledge of secrecy.

ARTHUR. Oh. What did Desmond want?

CATHERINE. To marry me.

ARTHUR. I trust the folly you were referring to wasn't your acceptance of him?

CATHERINE. (*Smiling.*) No, Father. (*She comes and sits on the arm of his chair.*) Would it be such folly, though?

ARTHUR. Lunacy.

CATHERINE. Oh, I don't know. He's nice, and he's doing very well as a solicitor.

ARTHUR. Neither very compelling reasons for marrying him.

CATHERINE. Seriously—I shall have to think it over.

ARTHUR. Think it over, by all means. But decide against it.

CATHERINE. I'm nearly thirty, you know.

ARTHUR. Thirty isn't the end of life.

CATHERINE. It might be—for an unmarried woman, with not much looks.

ARTHUR. Rubbish.

CATHERINE *shakes her head.*

Better far to live and die an old maid than to marry Desmond.

CATHERINE. Even an old maid must eat. (*Pause.*)

ARTHUR. I am leaving you and your mother everything, you know.

CATHERINE. (*Quietly.*) Everything?

ARTHUR. There is still a little left. (*Pause.*) Did you take my suggestion as regards your Suffrage Association?

CATHERINE. Yes, Father.

ARTHUR. You demanded a salary?

CATHERINE. I asked for one.

ARTHUR. And they're going to give it to you, I trust?

CATHERINE. Yes, Father. Two pounds a week.

ARTHUR. (*Angrily.*) That's insulting.

CATHERINE. No. It's generous. It's all they can afford. We're not a very rich organization—you know.

ARTHUR. You'll have to think of something else.

CATHERINE. What else? Darning socks? That's about my only other accomplishment.

ARTHUR. There must be something useful you can do.

CATHERINE. You don't think the work I am doing at the W.S.A. is useful?

ARTHUR *is silent.*

You may be right. But it's the only work I'm fitted for, all the same. (*Pause.*) No, Father. The choice is quite simple. Either I marry Desmond and settle down into quite a comfortable and not really useless existence—or I go on for the rest of my life earning two pounds a week in the service of a hopeless cause.

ARTHUR. A hopeless cause? I've never heard you say that before.

CATHERINE. I've never felt it before.

ARTHUR *is silent.* CATHERINE *leans her head against his chair.*

CATHERINE. John's going to get married next month.

ARTHUR. Did he tell you?

CATHERINE. Yes. He was very apologetic.

ARTHUR. Apologetic!

CATHERINE. He didn't need to be. It's a girl I know slightly. She'll make him a good wife.

ARTHUR. Is he in love with her?

CATHERINE. No more than he was with me. Perhaps, even, a little less.

ARTHUR. Why is he marrying her so soon after—after——

CATHERINE. After jilting me? Because he thinks there's going to be a war. If there is, his regiment will be among the first to go overseas. Besides, his father approves strongly. She's a general's daughter. Very, very suitable.

ARTHUR. Poor Kate!

Pause. He takes her hand slowly.

How I've messed up your life, haven't I?

CATHERINE. No, Father. Any messing-up that's been done has been done by me.

ARTHUR. I'm so sorry, Kate. I'm so sorry.

CATHERINE. Don't be, Father. We both knew what we were doing.

ARTHUR. Did we?

CATHERINE. I think we did.

ARTHUR. Yet our motives seem to have been different all along —yours and mine, Kate? Can we both have been right?

CATHERINE. I believe we can. I believe we have been.

ARTHUR. And yet they've always been so infernally logical, our opponents, haven't they?

CATHERINE. I'm afraid logic has never been on our side.

ARTHUR. Brute stubbornness—a selfish refusal to admit defeat. That's what your mother thinks have been our motives——

CATHERINE. Perhaps she's right. Perhaps that's all they've been.

ARTHUR. But perhaps brute stubbornness isn't such a bad quality in the face of injustice?

CATHERINE. Or in the face of tyranny. (*Pause.*) If you could go back, Father, and choose again—would your choice be different?

ARTHUR. Perhaps.

CATHERINE. I don't think so.

ARTHUR. I don't think so, either.

CATHERINE. I still say we both knew what we were doing. And we were right to do it.

ARTHUR *kisses the top of her head.*

ARTHUR. Dear Kate. Thank you.

There is a silence. A newsboy can be heard dimly, shouting from the street outside.

You aren't going to marry Desmond, are you?

CATHERINE. (*With a smile.*) In the words of the Prime Minister, Father—wait and see.

He squeezes her hand. The newsboy can still be heard—now a little louder.

ARTHUR. What's that boy shouting, Kate?

CATHERINE. Only—Winslow case—Latest.

ARTHUR. It didn't sound to me like 'Latest'.

CATHERINE *gets up to listen at the window. Suddenly we hear it quite plainly:* '*Winslow Case Result! Winslow Case Result!*' Result?

CATHERINE. There must be some mistake.

There is another sudden outburst of noise from the hall as the front-door is opened. It subsides again. VIOLET *comes in quickly with a broad smile.*

VIOLET. Oh, sir! Oh, sir!

ARTHUR. What's happened?

VIOLET. Oh, Miss Kate, what a shame you missed it! Just after they come back from lunch, and Mrs. Winslow she wasn't there neither, nor Master Ronnie. The cheering and the shouting and the carrying-on—you never heard anything like it in all your life—and Sir Robert standing there at the table with his wig on crooked and the tears running down his face—running down his face they were, and not able to speak because of the noise. Cook and me we did a bit of crying too, we just couldn't help it—you couldn't, you know. Oh, it was lovely! We did enjoy ourselves. And then cook had her hat knocked over her eyes by the man behind who was cheering and waving his arms about something chronic, and shouting about liberty—you would have laughed, miss, to see her, she was that cross—but she didn't mind really, she was only pretending, and we kept on cheering and the judge kept on shouting, but it wasn't any good, because even the jury joined in, and some of them climbed out of the box to shake hands with Sir Robert. And then outside in the street it was just the same—you couldn't move for the crowd, and you'd think they'd all gone mad the way they were carrying on. Some of them were shouting 'Good old Winslow!' and singing 'For he's a jolly good fellow', and cook had her hat knocked off again. Oh, it was lovely! (*To* ARTHUR.) Well, sir, you must be feeling nice and pleased, now it's all over?

ARTHUR. Yes, Violet. I am.

VIOLET. That's right. I always said it would come all right in the end, didn't I?

ARTHUR. Yes. You did.

VIOLET. Two years all but one month it's been, now, since Master Ronnie come back that day. Fancy.

ARTHUR. Yes.

VIOLET. I don't mind telling you, sir, I wondered sometimes whether you and Miss Kate weren't just wasting your time carrying on the way you have all the time. Still—you couldn't have felt that if you'd been in Court today——

She turns to go and stops.

Oh, sir, Mrs. Winslow asked me to remember most particular to pick up some onions from the greengrocer, but——

CATHERINE. That's all right, Violet. I think Mrs. Winslow is picking them up herself, on her way back——

VIOLET. I see, miss. Poor Madam! What a sell for her when she gets to the Court and finds it's all over. Well, sir—congratulations, I'm sure.

ARTHUR. Thank you, Violet.

Exit VIOLET.

ARTHUR. It would appear, then, that we've won.

CATHERINE. Yes, Father, it would appear that we've won.

She breaks down and cries, her head on her father's lap.

ARTHUR. (*Slowly.*) I would have liked to have been there.

Pause.

Enter VIOLET.

VIOLET. (*Announcing.*) Sir Robert Morton!

SIR ROBERT *walks calmly and methodically into the room. He looks as spruce and neat as ever, and* VIOLET'S *description of him in Court does not seem to tally with his composed features.*

CATHERINE *jumps up hastily and dabs her eyes.*

Exit VIOLET.

SIR ROBERT. I thought you might like to hear the actual terms of the Attorney-General's statement—— (*He pulls out a scrap of paper.*) So I jotted it down for you. (*Reading.*) 'I say now, on behalf of the Admiralty, that I accept the declaration of Ronald Arthur Winslow that he did not write the name on the postal order, that he did not take it and that he did not cash it, and that consequently he was innocent of the charge which was brought against him two years ago. I make that statement without any reservation of any description, intending it to be a complete acceptance of the boy's statements.'

He folds the paper up and hands it to ARTHUR.

ARTHUR. Thank you, sir. It is rather hard for me to find the words I should speak to you.

SIR ROBERT. Pray do not trouble yourself to search for them, sir. Let us take these rather tiresome and conventional expressions of gratitude for granted, shall we? Now, on the question of damages and costs. I fear we shall find the Admiralty rather niggardly. You are likely still to be left considerably out of pocket. However, doubtless we can apply a slight spur to the First Lord's posterior in the House of Commons——

ARTHUR. Please, sir—no more trouble—I beg. Let the matter rest here. (*He shows the piece of paper.*) This is all I have ever asked for.

SIR ROBERT. (*Turning to* CATHERINE.) A pity you were not in Court, Miss Winslow. The verdict appeared to cause quite a stir.

CATHERINE. So I heard. Why did the Admiralty throw up the case?

SIR ROBERT. It was a foregone conclusion. Once the handwriting expert had been discredited—not for the first time in legal history—I knew we had a sporting chance, and no jury in the world would have convicted on the postmistress's evidence.

CATHERINE. But this morning you seemed so depressed.

SIR ROBERT. Did I? The heat in the courtroom was very trying, you know. Perhaps I was a little fatigued——

Enter VIOLET.

VIOLET. (*To* ARTHUR.) Oh, sir, the gentlemen at the front door say please will you make a statement. They say they won't go away until you do.

ARTHUR. Very well, Violet. Thank you.

VIOLET. Yes, sir.

Exit VIOLET.

ARTHUR. What shall I say?

SIR ROBERT. (*Indifferently.*) I hardly think it matters. Whatever you say will have little bearing on what they write.

ARTHUR. What shall I say, Kate?

CATHERINE. You'll think of something, Father.

She begins to wheel his chair towards the door.

ARTHUR. (*Sharply.*) No! I refuse to meet the Press in this ridiculous chariot. (*To* CATHERINE.) Get me my stick!

CATHERINE. (*Protestingly.*) Father—you know what the doctor——

ARTHUR. Get me my stick!

CATHERINE, *without more ado, gets his stick for him. She and* SIR ROBERT *help him out of his chair.*

How is this? I am happy to have lived long enough to have seen justice done to my son——

CATHERINE. It's a little gloomy, Father. You're going to live for ages yet——

ARTHUR. Am I? Wait and see. I could say: This victory is not mine. It is the people who have triumphed—as they always will triumph—over despotism. How does that strike you, sir? A trifle pretentious, perhaps.

SIR ROBERT. Perhaps, sir. I should say it, none the less. It will be very popular.

ARTHUR. Hm! Perhaps I had better say what I really feel, which is merely: Thank God we beat 'em.

He goes out. SIR ROBERT *turns abruptly to* CATHERINE.

SIR ROBERT. Miss Winslow—might I be rude enough to ask you for a little of your excellent whisky?

CATHERINE. Of course.

She goes into the dining-room. SIR ROBERT, *left alone, droops his shoulders wearily. He subsides into a chair. When* CATHERINE *comes back with the whisky he straightens his shoulders instinctively, but does not rise.*

SIR ROBERT. That is very kind. Perhaps you would forgive me not getting up? The heat in that courtroom was really so infernal.

He takes the glass from her and drains it quickly. She notices his hand is trembling slightly.

CATHERINE. Are you feeling all right, Sir Robert?

SIR ROBERT. Just a slight nervous reaction—that's all. Besides, I have not been feeling myself all day. I told the Judge so, this morning, if you remember, but I doubt if he believed me. He thought it was a trick. What suspicious minds people have, have they not?

CATHERINE. Yes.

SIR ROBERT. (*Handing her back the glass.*) Thank you.

CATHERINE *puts the glass down, then turns slowly back to face him as if nerving herself for an ordeal.*

CATHERINE. Sir Robert—I'm afraid I have a confession and an apology to make to you.

SIR ROBERT. (*Sensing what is coming.*) Dear lady—I am sure the one is rash and the other superfluous. I would far rather hear neither——

CATHERINE. (*With a smile.*) I am afraid you must. This is probably the last time I shall see you and it is a better penance for me to say this than to write it. I have entirely misjudged your attitude to this case, and if in doing so I have ever seemed to you either rude or ungrateful, I am sincerely and humbly sorry.

SIR ROBERT. (*Indifferently.*) My dear Miss Winslow, you have never seemed to me either rude or ungrateful. And my attitude to this case has been the same as yours—a determination to win at all costs. Only—when you talk of gratitude—you must remember that those costs were not mine, but yours.

CATHERINE. Weren't they also yours, Sir Robert?

SIR ROBERT. I beg your pardon?

CATHERINE. Haven't you too made a certain sacrifice for the case?

Pause.

SIR ROBERT. The robes of that office would not have suited me.

CATHERINE. Wouldn't they?

SIR ROBERT. (*With venom.*) And what is more, I fully intend to have Curry expelled from the Law Society.

CATHERINE. Please don't. He did me a great service by telling me——

SIR ROBERT. I must ask you never to divulge it to another living soul, and even to forget it yourself.

CATHERINE. I shall never divulge it. I'm afraid I can't promise to forget it myself.

SIR ROBERT. Very well. If you choose to endow an unimportant incident with a romantic significance, you are perfectly at liberty to do so. I must go. (*He gets up.*)

CATHERINE. Why are you always at such pains to prevent people knowing the truth about you, Sir Robert?

SIR ROBERT. Am I, indeed?

CATHERINE. You know you are. Why?

SIR ROBERT. Perhaps because *I* do not know the truth about myself.

CATHERINE. That is no answer.

SIR ROBERT. My dear Miss Winslow, are you cross-examining me?

CATHERINE. On this point, yes. Why are you so ashamed of your emotions?

SIR ROBERT. Because, as a lawyer, I must necessarily distrust them.

CATHERINE. Why?

SIR ROBERT. To fight a case on emotional grounds, Miss Winslow, is the surest way of losing it. Emotions muddy the issue. Cold, clear logic—and buckets of it—should be the lawyer's only equipment.

CATHERINE. Was it cold, clear logic that made you weep today at the verdict?

Pause.

SIR ROBERT. Your maid, of course, told you that? It doesn't

matter. It will be in the papers tomorrow, anyway. (*Fiercely.*) Very well, then, if you must have it, here it is. I wept today because right had been done.

CATHERINE. Not justice?

SIR ROBERT. No. Not justice. Right. It is easy to do justice— very hard to do right. Unfortunately, while the appeal of justice is intellectual, the appeal of right appears for some odd reason to induce tears in court. That is my answer and my excuse. And now, may I leave the witness box?

CATHERINE. No. One last question. How can you reconcile your support of Winslow against the Crown with your political beliefs?

SIR ROBERT. Very easily. No one party has a monopoly of concern for individual liberty. On that issue all parties are united.

CATHERINE. I don't think so.

SIR ROBERT. You don't?

CATHERINE. No. Not all parties. Only some people from all parties.

SIR ROBERT. That is a wise remark. We can only hope, then, that those same people will always prove enough people. You would make a good advocate.

CATHERINE. Would I?

SIR ROBERT. Yes. (*Playfully.*) Why do you not canalize your feministic impulses towards the law courts, Miss Winslow, and abandon the lost cause of women's suffrage?

CATHERINE. Because I don't believe it *is* a lost cause.

SIR ROBERT. No? Are you going to continue to pursue it?

CATHERINE. Certainly.

SIR ROBERT. You will be wasting your time.

CATHERINE. I don't think so.

SIR ROBERT. A pity. In the House of Commons in days to come I shall make a point of looking up at the Gallery in the hope of catching a glimpse of you in that provocative hat.

RONNIE *comes in. He is fifteen now, and there are distinct signs of an incipient man-about-town. He is very smartly dressed in lounge suit and homburg hat.*

RONNIE. I say, Sir Robert, I'm most awfully sorry. I didn't know anything was going to happen.

SIR ROBERT. Where were you?

RONNIE. At the pictures.

SIR ROBERT. Pictures? What is that?

CATHERINE. Cinematograph show.

RONNIE. I'm most awfully sorry. I say—we won, didn't we?

SIR ROBERT. Yes. We won. Goodbye, Miss Winslow. Shall I see you in the House then, one day?

CATHERINE. (*With a smile.*) Yes, Sir Robert. One day. But not in the Gallery. Across the floor.

SIR ROBERT. (*With a faint smile.*) Perhaps. Goodbye. (*He turns to go.*)

CURTAIN